BROWSING COLLECTION
14-DAY CHECKOUT
No Holds • No Renewals

THE
WATCHMAKER'S
HAND

SHORT FICTION COLLECTIONS

Trouble in Mind
Triple Threat
More Twisted
Twisted

SHORT FICTION INDIVIDUAL STORIES

The Broken Doll,
  a Four-Story Cycle
Swiping Hearts,
  a Lincoln Rhyme Story
The Deadline Clock,
  a Colter Shaw Story
Scheme
A Perfect Plan,
  a Lincoln Rhyme Story
Cause of Death
Turning Point
Verona
The Debriefing
Ninth and Nowhere
The Second Hostage,
  a Colter Shaw Story
Captivated, a Colter Shaw Story
The Victims' Club
Surprise Ending
Double Cross
Vows, a Lincoln Rhyme Story
The Deliveryman,
  a Lincoln Rhyme Story
A Textbook Case

ORIGINAL AUDIO WORKS

The Muse
The Starling Project, a Radio Play
Stay Tuned
The Intruder
Date Night

EDITOR/CONTRIBUTOR

No Rest for the Dead (Contributor)
Watchlist (Creator/Contributor)
The Chopin Manuscript
  (Creator/Contributor)
The Copper Bracelet
  (Creator/Contributor)
Nothing Good Happens After
  Midnight (Editor/Contributor)
Ice Cold (Co-Editor/Contributor)
A Hot and Sultry Night for Crime
  (Editor/Contributor)
Books to Die For (Contributor)
The Best American Mystery
  Stories 2009 (Editor)

THE
WATCHMAKER'S
HAND

A LINCOLN RHYME NOVEL

JEFFERY
DEAVER

G. P. PUTNAM'S SONS

NEW YORK

PUTNAM

— EST. 1838 —

G. P. Putnam's Sons

Publishers Since 1838

An imprint of Penguin Random House LLC

penguinrandomhouse.com

Library of Congress Cataloging-in-Publication Data

Names: Deaver, Jeffery, author.
Title: The watchmaker's hand / Jeffery Deaver.
Description: New York: G. P. Putnam's Sons, 2023. |
Series: A Lincoln Rhyme novel
Identifiers: LCCN 2023038732 (print) | LCCN 2023038733 (ebook) |
ISBN 9780593422113 (hardcover) | ISBN 9780593422120 (e-book)
Subjects: LCGFT: Thrillers (Fiction). |
Detective and mystery fiction. | Novels.
Classification: LCC PS3554.E1755 W38 2023 (print) |
LCC PS3554.E1755 (ebook) | DDC 813/.54—dc23/eng/20230829
LC record available at https://lccn.loc.gov/2023038732
LC ebook record available at https://lccn.loc.gov/2023038733

Printed in the United States of America
1st Printing

Book design by Pauline Neuwirth
Title page image © Fernando Blanco Calzada / Shutterstock

For Jerry Sussman, patriot, family man and friend

e5ccebd2f80138b22ab8c840a6c5a9277d53bcff0c66b8033525dc8f6cbfd648

The computer algorithm hash translation of:
"Time is an illusion."
—ALBERT EINSTEIN

I

PERSON OF INTEREST

I.

HIS GAZE OVER the majestic panorama of Manhattan, 218 feet below, was interrupted by the alarm.

He had never before heard the urgent electronic pulsing on the job.

He was familiar with the sound from training, while getting his Fall Protection Certificate, but never on shift. His level of skill and the sophistication of the million-dollar contraption beneath him were such that there had never been a reason for the high-pitched sound to fill the cab in which he sat.

Scanning the ten-by-eight-inch monitors in front of him . . . yes, a red light was now flashing.

But at the same time, apart from the urgency of the electronics, Garry Helprin knew that this was a mistake. A sensor problem.

And, yes, seconds later the light went away. The sound went away.

He nudged the control to raise the eighteen-ton load aloft, and his thoughts returned to where they had been just a moment ago.

The baby's name. While his father hoped for William, and his wife's mother for Natalia, neither of those was going to happen. Perfectly fine names. But not for Peggy and him, not for their son or daughter. He'd suggested they have some fun with their parents. What they'd decided at last: Kierkegaard if a boy. Bashilda if a girl.

When she first told him these, Garry had said, "Bathsheba, you mean. From the Bible."

"No. Bashilda. My imaginary pony when I was ten."

Kierkegaard and Bashilda, they would tell the parents, and then move on to another topic—quickly. What a reaction they'd—

The alarm began to blare again, the light to flash. They were joined by another excited box on the monitor: the load moment indicator. The needle was tilting to the left above the words: *Moment Imbalance.*

Impossible.

The computer had calculated the weight of the jib in front of him—extending the length of a Boeing 777—and the weight on the jib behind. It then factored into the balance game the weight of the load in front and the weight of the concrete counterweights behind. Finally, it measured their distance from the center, where he sat in the cab of the crane.

"Come on, Big Blue. Really?"

Garry tended to talk to the machines he was operating. Some seemed to respond. This particular Baylor HT-4200 was the most talkative of them all.

Today, though, she was silent, other than the warning sound.

If the alarm was blaring for him, it was blaring in the supervisor's trailer too.

The radio clattered, and he heard in his headset: "Garry, what?"

He replied into the stalk mike, "Gotta be an LMI sensor problem. If there was moment five minutes ago, there's moment now. Nothing's changed."

"Wind?"

"None. Sensor, I'm . . ." He fell silent.

Feeling the tilt.

"Hell," he said quickly. "It *is* a moment fault. Forward jib is point three nine degrees down. Wait, now point four."

Was the load creeping toward the end of the blue latticed jib on its own? Had the trolley become detached from the drive cables?

Garry had never heard of that happening.

He looked forward. Saw nothing irregular.

Now: −.5

Nothing is more regulated and inspected on a construction site than the stability of a tower crane, especially one that soars this high into the sky and has within its perimeter a half-dozen structures—and hundreds, perhaps thousands, of human souls. Meticulous calculations are made of the load—in this case, 36,000 pounds of six-by-four-inch flange beams—and the counterweights, the rectangular blocks of cement, to make sure this particular crane can lift and swing the payload. Once that's signed off on, the info goes into the computer and the magic balance is maintained—moving the counterweights behind him back and forth ever so slightly to keep the needle at zero.

Moment . . .

−.51

He looked back at the counterweights. This was instinctive; he didn't know what he might see.

Nothing was visible.

−.52

The blaring continued.

−.54

He shut the alarm switch off. The accompanying indicator flashed *Warning* and the *Moment Imbalance* messages continued.

−.55

The super said, "We've hit diagnostics and don't see a sensor issue."

"Forget sensors," Garry said. "We're tilting."

−.58

"I'm going to manual." He shut off the controller. He'd been riding tower cranes for the past fifteen years, since he signed up with Moynahan Construction, after his stint as an engineer in the army. Digital controls made the job easier and safer, but he'd cut his teeth operating towers by hand, using charts and graphs and a pad attached to his thigh for calculations—and, of course, a needle balance indicator to get the moment just right. He now tugged on the joystick to draw the load trolley closer to center.

Then, switching to the counterweight control, he moved those away from the tower.

His eyes were fixed on the LMI, which still indicated moment imbalance forward.

He moved the weights, totaling a hundred tons, farther back.

This *had* to achieve moment.

It was impossible for it not to.

But it did not.

Back to the front jib.

He cranked the trolley closer to him. The flanges swung. He'd moved more quickly than he'd meant to.

He was looking at his coffee cup.

The chair—padded, comfortable—did not come factory-equipped with a cup holder. But Garry, an afficionado of any and all brews, had mounted one on the wall—far away from the electronics, of course.

The brown liquid was level; the cup was not.

Another glance at the LMI indicator.

A full −2 percent down in the front.

He worked the trolley control and brought the load of flanges closer yet.

Ah, yes, that did it.

The alarm light went out as the balance indicator now moved slowly back to −.5 and then 0, then 1, and kept rising. This was because the counterweights were so far back. Garry now reeled them in until they were as far forward as they could go.

It brought the LMI needle to 1.2.

This was normal. Cranes are made to lean backward slightly when there is no weight of a load on the front jib, which should, at rest, be about one degree. The main stability comes from the massive concrete base—that's what holds it upright when there's no balancing act going on.

"Got it, Danny," he radioed. "Stable. But I'll need maintenance. Got to be some counterweight issue."

"K. I think Will's off break."

Garry sat back and sipped his coffee, replaced the cup, listened to the wind. It would be some minutes before the mechanic arrived. To get to the cab from the ground, there was one way and one way only.

You climbed the mast.

But the cab was twenty-two stories above the ground. Which meant at least one, maybe two five-minute rest stops on the way up.

Guys on the site sometimes thought if you were a crane operator you were in lousy shape, sitting on your ass all day long. They forgot about the climb.

With no load to deliver, no hook block to steer carefully to the ground, he could sit back and enjoy the indescribable view. If Garry wanted, he could put a name to what he was looking at: the five boroughs of the city, a huge parcel of New Jersey, a thin band of Westchester, one of Long Island too.

But he wasn't interested in GPS information.

He was thrilled by the browns and grays and greens and white clouds and the endless blue—every shade far richer and bolder than when viewed by landlocked pedestrians below.

From a young age, Garry had known he wanted to build sky-scrapers. That's what he had made with his Legos. That's what he had begged his parents to take him to visit, even when his mother and father blanched at the idea of standing on observation decks. He only liked the open ones. "You know," his father had said, "sometimes people go crazy and throw themselves off the edge of high places. The fear takes them."

Naw, probably not. There was nothing to fear from heights. The higher he got, the calmer he became. Whether it was rock climbing, mountaineering, or building skyscrapers, heights comforted him.

He was, he told Peggy, "in heaven" when he was far, far aboveground.

Back to baby names.

Kierkegaard, Bashilda . . .

What would they really pick? Neither wanted a Junior. And they didn't want any names currently in vogue, which you could find easily in the tiny booklets on the Gristedes checkout lane.

He reached for his coffee cup.

No!

The level had changed again. The front jib was dipping once more.

−.4

A moment later, the duo of warning signs burst on again, and the alarm, which had defaulted back on, blared.

The balance indicator jumped to −1.2.

He hit Transmit. "Dan. She's moving again. Big-time."

"Shit. What's going on?"

"Can't reel the load any farther. I'm dropping it. Clear the zone. Tell me when."

"Yeah, okay."

He couldn't hear the command from here, but he had a view

through the Plexiglas straight down between his legs and saw the workers scatter quickly as the ground foreman told them to get out of the way.

Of course, "dropping" the load didn't mean that literally—yanking the release and letting the seventeen tons of steel free-fall to the ground. He eased the down lever and the bundle dropped fast. He could see, on his indicators and visually through the Plexiglas, exactly where it was on descent. At about thirty feet above the ground, he braked, and the bundle settled onto the concrete. Maybe some damage.

Too bad.

He adjusted the counterweights, hit the hook release and detached the load.

But this had no effect.

The word "impossible" came to his mind yet again.

He cranked the counterweights backward once more.

This *had* to arrest the forward tilt.

No load and the counterweights were at the far end of the back jib.

And still . . .

"Dan," he radioed, "we're five degrees down, forward jib. Counterweights're back."

−6.1

A crane is not meant to lean more than five degrees. Beyond that, the complicated skeletons of steel tubes and rods and plates begin to buckle and bend. The slewing plate—the huge turntable that swung the jib horizontally—was groaning.

He heard a distant but loud crack. Then another.

−7

Into the radio: "I'm losing it, Dan. Hit the siren."

Just moments later came the piercing emergency cry. This was not associated with a crane disaster specifically. It just meant some bad shit was going to happen. Instructions would be coming from the loudspeaker and on the radio.

"Garry, get out. Down the mast."

"In a minute . . ."

If Big Blue was going down, he was going to make sure she landed with as few injuries to those on the ground as possible.

He scanned the surroundings. There were buildings almost everywhere.

But fifty feet to the right of the jib was a gap between the office building in front of him and an apartment complex. Through the gap, he could see a street and a park. On this temperate day, there would be people outside, but they had most likely heard the siren and would be looking toward the akilter crane.

Cars and trucks, with windows rolled up?

"I'm aiming away from the buildings. Have somebody clear that park on Eighty-Ninth. And get a flagman into the street, stop traffic."

"Garry, get outta there while you can!"

"The park! Clear it!"

Creaking, groaning, the wind . . .

Another explosive snap.

He operated the swivel control and the slewing plate cried from binding against the bearings. The electric motor was laboring. Then, slowly, the jib responded.

"Come on, come on . . ."

Thirty feet from the gap.

Any minute now. He could feel it. Any minute she was going to drop.

Cars continued to stream past.

His decision was logical, but nonetheless stabbed his heart.

People were about to die because of him. Maybe fewer than if he didn't move the jib, but still . . .

The numbers rolled through his frantic mind.

Distance to the gap: twenty feet.

LMI: −8.2

"Come on," he whispered.

"Garry . . ."

"Clear the goddamn park! The street!" He tore the headset off as if the distraction of transmissions was gumming the mechanism further.

Twelve feet from the gap, nine degrees down.

The joystick was all the way to the right and the jib should have been swinging madly. But the binding metal of the slewing plate had slowed it to a crawl.

Slowed, but not stopped.

A sudden squeal. Nails on a chalkboard . . .

He jammed his teeth together at the sound.

Ten feet, ten degrees down.

Eight feet from the gap.

Please . . . A little farther . . .

Close. But if Big Blue failed now, the jib would slice through four or five floors of offices, all open design, hundreds of workers at desks and in cubicles, at coffee stations, in conference rooms. He could see them. A few were on their feet, staring at the tilting mast. No one was running. They were taking videos. Jesus . . .

Seven feet.

The motion stalled momentarily, then resumed, with the squeal and grinding even louder.

He nudged the stick to the left and it responded, swinging back a foot or two, then he shoved it to the right. The plate resumed its rotation in that direction, past the sticking point.

Six feet from the gap, down twelve degrees . . .

Crack . . .

The loud sound from behind made him jump.

What was it?

Ah, of course.

The exit door in the floor that led down to the mast, to the ladder, to safety, had buckled. He climbed from his seat briefly and tugged. Useless.

There was only one other exit—above him. But that gave no access to the mast.

Forget it now. Just get another five feet and she'll be clear.

The jib was still tilting down, but the LMI indicator had stopped at −13. The engineers, of course, had known that there was no point in going farther. A jib would never tilt that far forward.

Six feet away from the lifesaving gap, the mast suddenly pitched forward a few feet. Garry slipped from the seat and fell. He landed face-first on the bulb of the window. From here, he found himself looking straight downward, twenty-two stories, to the jobsite. He inhaled and exhaled deeply, leaving a design of condensation on the glass in front of him. It was, curiously, almost in the shape of a heart.

He thought of his wife.

And of their child, soon to be born.

Kierkegaard or Bashilda . . .

2.

AT SOME POINT, an open investigation slips over an unseen border and becomes a cold case.

Who knows what the time frame is? Some cops might say a year, some might say a decade.

Lincoln Rhyme didn't like the phrase. It suggested that the offense had been seized on by podcasters and documentary TV show producers to sell the ever-popular tale of an evildoer escaping justice.

The unsolved cases that drew the most attention were murders, of course. The spouse that went missing, the mafioso snitch, the abusive father who has "no idea" where his young son wandered off to. No one paid much attention to unsolved larcenies—other than the spectacular: the diamond heist, the armored truck stickup, the parachuting from a Boeing 727 with $200K in ransom (and where *are* you, D. B. Cooper?).

To Rhyme, an unsolved case was merely an unsolved case, whether twenty-four hours or one hundred years old, and it absolutely needed to be closed, larcenies included. Which was what was presently occupying much of his time.

This one was a few months old and the inability to solve it was giving Rhyme—and the NYPD and Homeland Security—more than a little concern.

A person they'd designated "Unknown Subject"—Unsub 212—had on February 12 (hence, the moniker) broken into the NYC Department of Structures and Engineering and downloaded a trove of infrastructure documents: blueprints, engineering diagrams, underground maps, plats, permit requests—all the bits and bytes of material involved in the gargantuan process of helping the organism of New York City grow and morph. To be safe, maybe, the unsub had also copped hundreds of hard copies of the same and other documents, maybe in case some of the digital files were encrypted.

At the time of the theft, everyone thought: *Terrorism.* Always a good default motive for a crime of this sort. Bombs would be planted, subways hijacked, buildings targeted with missiles or airplanes.

Rhyme and his wife and professional forensic partner, Amelia Sachs, had been brought in to try to identify the unsub via forensics. Despite the man's accidentally setting off an alarm and fleeing, leaving his burglar tools behind, they could come up with no leads. The city remained on high alert for a while, but no terrorist attacks ensued.

And so, Unsub 212's theft remained an active case, and his nickname was atop the evidence whiteboard in the corner of the parlor of Rhyme's nineteenth-century town house, the war room for the cases he and Sachs ran—she, as an NYPD detective, and he, a consulting forensic scientist. The boards were known throughout law enforcement as "murder boards," though this one offered details of a theft instead; there'd been no loss of life or injury in the incident. Rhyme and Sachs had turned their attention away from the case temporarily—to a couple of urgent organized crime prosecutions, but those were now finished. There was nothing more to do than wait to testify at trial as an expert witness—either at one or the other, of course, never together; defense lawyers would have a field day inquiring about the relationship status of the two. There was not, legally, any reason they could not testify jointly, but criminal trials are about four things: optics, optics, optics . . . and then the law.

So now it was back to the open—not "cold"—Unsub 212 case.

Rhyme aimed his motorized wheelchair toward the board. Injured on a crime scene years ago, rendered a quadriplegic, the former head of NYPD forensics was always searching out any medical treatments that might improve his condition. While there was no way, yet, to restore sensation below his neck, complicated procedures involving surgery and prosthetics had restored most movement to his right arm, which he exercised regularly. The chair, quite the "miracle of mobility," the literature declared, could also be deftly operated by his left ring finger, the one appendage that had escaped the consequences of the catastrophic accident.

The human body is nothing if not an assembly of marvels and flukes.

Sachs was reading out loud a report from the Major Cases detective in charge of the 212 case. "No persons of interest on the city payroll," she announced. She went on to explain that the officer had been interviewing employees of the DSE, thinking that it might be an inside job, as intangible property thefts often were when hackers were not involved. There was a video of the thief physically breaking into the server room, where he downloaded the files on a hard drive. It was clever: these days everyone protected against those sharp and bored Eastern European and Chinese hackers, but physically guarding data on-site lagged.

There was a video too of the unsub leaving the building. It

came to Rhyme and the investigators via the city's Domain Awareness System.

Aka, according to some civil libertarians, Big Brother.

The New York Police Department's DAS was a network of twenty thousand CCTV video cameras around the city. The system collected and stored video and data from a wealth of information: license plate readings, summonses, recordings of 911 calls, complaints, officers' reports, warrants and arrest notices. The entries numbered in the billions.

One of the DAS cameras had caught Unsub 212 walking out of the Engineering building, then disappearing around the corner. The alarm would be blaring, but he maintained a normal pace so as not to draw attention to himself.

How helpful was the vid? That was another matter. It recorded dark clothing, a hat. Head down, of course.

Rhyme's assessment: useless, other than offering the man's body build. Medium. A fact that was, he reflected, more or less useless too.

He glanced into the western portion of the parlor, where the lab was located behind a wall of floor-to-ceiling glass, sealed against contamination. Past the instruments and workstations— the envy of small- or even some medium-sized police labs—were brown shelves holding cataloged evidence. His eyes were on the small red plastic tool kit 212 had left behind when, after he'd gotten what he wanted, he'd had to flee.

They'd examined the box when the lead detective first brought it in and had done a thorough job. But, to Rhyme's irritation, it had yielded no fingerprints, DNA or other trace. This was also a surprise. Evidence that's abandoned quickly tends to be the most helpful—not, for instance, wiped clean of prints.

Sachs's hands went to her trim hips, in black jeans, and, head tilted, her long dark red hair fell straight down, plumb. "What was he after?"

The key question, of course.

Motive is irrelevant in a trial and Rhyme didn't particularly care for the topic during the investigation either, preferring evidence as the arrow that might point to the perp. Yet, ever skeptical Rhyme had to admit that, absent solid forensics, discovering a motive might lead you to a helpful location or even perps themselves. His metaphor in class: motive might give you the neighborhood, and forensic analysis was the door-knocking that might get you the bloody knife or recently fired, if not smoking, gun.

Clumsy, but he rather liked it.

In 212's case, though, no one involved in the investigation, nor anyone in city government, could figure out why the perp had committed the crime. Yes, he got plenty of details on infrastructure, tunnels, bridges, underground passages—of which there were enough beneath the five boroughs to form an entire shadow city. But how did that help the bad guys plan an attack? Even the dullest terrorists could find suitable targets in this target-rich city without having to resort to maps of tunnels or engineering diagrams.

The materials would also show which passages ran beneath banks or jewelry stores or fur warehouses. But digging upward into a vault for a heist is purely the stuff of 1970s TV movies, Amelia Sachs had pointed out. And stealing cash was pointless. The serial numbers of every twenty-, fifty- and hundred-dollar bill in circulation would fit on a single fifty-gigabyte thumb drive, and scanners to spot purloined bills were in use everywhere.

Gone were the good old days.

"Hm," Rhyme offered. It was a variation of a grunt. When he spoke, it was, more or less, to himself. "No obvious reason for the heist. And yet the data *were* stolen. And it was risky." He wheeled close to the board. "For. A. Purpose. And what might that be?"

Frustration sent his eyes to the bottle of Glenmorangie scotch sitting on a high shelf nearby. Rhyme's right arm and hand were largely functional, yes, and could easily grip a bottle, and open and pour it.

He could not, however, stand and snag it from the perch where his mother hen had set it. Coincidentally, that very individual—his caregiver, Thom Reston—happened to enter the parlor just then and notice Rhyme's gaze. He said, "It's morning."

"Aware of the time, thank you."

When Rhyme didn't look away from the colorful label, Thom said, "No."

The man was dressed impeccably, as always, today in tan slacks, a baby-blue shirt and a floral tie. He was slim yet strong, his muscles largely developed not from hunks of iron or machines but from moving Rhyme himself. It was Thom who got the man into and out of the chair and bed and bath.

Another grunt and dark glance toward the liquor.

It *was* early, no disputing, but the concept of "cocktail hour" had always been a moving target for Lincoln Rhyme.

He looked back at the whiteboard devoted to the DSE theft, but his going-nowhere meditation on the theft was interrupted by the hum of the door buzzer.

Rhyme looked up. It was Lon Sellitto, his former partner from the days before the accident. He was senior in Major Cases, Amelia Sachs's assignment, and was the detective who most often liaised with Rhyme when he was used by the NYPD as a consultant.

"He looks energized," Rhyme said, ordering the latch to open.

Inside, the big man, balding in an unenthusiastic way, sloughed off his brown raincoat and hung it. Not that Rhyme cared, but Sellitto seemed to buy the ugliest garments on the rack. And one *could* find colors that were not muddy-camel-brown, could one not? Sellitto's clothes were often wrinkled too, as today, a function of the man's round physique, Rhyme guessed. Most manufacturers presumably created garments out of textiles whose waiting state was smooth.

Then again, what did Rhyme know? Thom and Sachs bought his outfits—like today's taupe slacks, black polo shirt and forest-green cardigan. Someone once commented that what he was wearing looked comfortable. Thom had cut him a glance and Rhyme's planned response—"Wouldn't exactly know, now, would I?"—was replaced with an insincere smile.

Sellitto offered a brief nod to all in the room. Then a frown crossed his face as his eyes shot to an overlarge Sony TV screen mounted in the corner. "Why isn't the news on?"

"Lon."

"Is this the remote? No. Where's the remote?"

Thom picked it up from a shelf and powered the unit up.

Rhyme said, "Why don't you just tell us, instead of waiting for the anchor-bot?"

"A situation," Sellitto said, but didn't elaborate. He took the remote and clicked to one of the national stations. Depicted were a *Breaking News* bulletin, a crawl at the bottom that Rhyme was too far away to read, and video of damage at a construction site. Another message popped up. It reported *E. 89th Street, New York City.* This was replaced by: *One dead, six injured in crane collapse.*

Sellitto looked from Sachs to Rhyme. "It wasn't an accident. Somebody did it on purpose. They've sent the city a list of demands. And if they don't get what they want, they're going to do it again in twenty-four hours."

3.

THE MAYOR HAD received an email with a URL that took him to a private chat room on the anonymous message board 13Chan.

Rhyme read the words that Sellitto called up on the computer monitor in the center of the parlor.

> Nearly 50 million Americans live in housing they can't afford. 600,000 have no homes at all, and one third of those are families with children. Yet New York continues to encourage developers' building luxury high-rises, which it has done since the early twentieth century.
>
> The city is the largest landowner in the area. It holds 370 million square feet of property and its obsene how little of that is devouted to affordable housing. There are huge amounts of space in the city that are unused

and not being planned for development, which
we know because we have examined real estate
records.

Our demand is this: The city will create a
nonprofit corporation; to this corporation,
the city will transfer the properties that are
on the list below and convert them to
affordable housing.

We will be monitoring progress via
government records.

New York City will suffer one disaster every
twenty-four hours until the corporation is
created and the property is transferred.

The countdown has begun.

—The Kommunalka Project

The next page featured a list of properties throughout the five boroughs. Some seemed to be vacant land, but most were built-out structures, presumably abandoned: schools, a public housing tower, a former dock and helipad in Brooklyn that had been bought from the Defense Department, a research lab that had been owned by the National Institutes of Health and transferred to the City University of New York, warehouses that had been under lease to the state for storing census records, a former National Guard armory.

"The group's name?" Sachs asked.

No deep digging was necessary.

A brief search revealed that the word "Kommunalka" referred to a program used once upon a time in the Soviet Union—a frenzied building of communal apartments after World War II to address a housing shortage.

Sachs skimmed the articles. "Wonder if the perps did their

homework. Most of the Soviet buildings've been torn down and replaced by—you guessed it—expensive bourgeois apartments."

Rhyme was intrigued. Forensically, sabotage was no more interesting than his current stolen engineering document case. The deadline, however, and the risk of more death, now moved Unsub 212 to a lower priority.

Rhyme asked, "How did he do it? IED?"

Sellitto answered, "No explosives that anybody heard. Somehow, he got to the counterweights, tinkered with them. The foreman doesn't know. It changed the balance and the thing went down. Oh, you're going to be getting a—"

Rhyme's mobile whirred and he commanded, "Answer phone." He then said into the unit, "Yes?"

A woman's harried voice. "Captain Rhyme?"

"That's right."

"Please hold for Mayor Harrison."

A moment later the man's smooth voice came through the speaker. "Captain Rhyme."

"Mayor."

Knowing Rhyme wouldn't bother with such protocols, Sachs said, "You're on speaker with Detectives Sachs and Sellitto."

"Lon. You're there."

"Just briefing Lincoln and Amelia now."

"I wanted to let you know that we're not agreeing. You know our policy."

The city didn't pay ransom and it didn't give in to extortion demands.

The man continued, "We couldn't do what they're asking anyway. Whoever's behind this has no idea of what's involved. There're a hundred documents we'd have to put together. A nonprofit needs a three-person board, president, VP, secretary, treasurer, registered agent, and, Christ, a million approvals: the state revenue, IRS, EPA. Hell, a budget. Needs to be funded. We can't deed anything over until all that's done, which would take weeks or months . . ."

"Can you buy time?" Sachs asked.

"They set up that chat room on 13Chan. It's closed to the public, but we can post. I wrote that we need more time."

"They responded?"

"Two words. 'See above.' I'll show you." He recited a complicated URL and Sachs typed it into a nearby computer. A header for the site popped up, and in a private messaging window appeared a line drawing:

The mayor said, "No other response."

Sachs asked, "This the first time there's been affordable housing extortion in the city?"

"Protests, peaceful shit. Chaining themselves to jobsites, throwing eggs. Never violence."

Rhyme's eyes were on the wreckage. From a distance, the machines looked fragile. But the close-up images in the videos showed sturdy steel rods and support brackets.

Then again, had the Kommunalka Project actually been behind it?

"Timing?" he asked.

A pause. "How's that, Captain?"

"Did the demand come in before the crane fell or after?"

"Oh, you're thinking it was an accident and this group jumped on the bandwagon. It was ten minutes before the collapse."

Answering that question.

Sachs asked, "We're looking at the news. Nothing about the demand."

"No. We're not announcing. That'll mean panic. I've ordered all high-rise construction suspended for the time being and we're getting officers to every site where there's a tower crane."

"That's going to raise questions," Sachs pointed out.

In an off-hand tone, Harrison said, "Ah, I'll blame the feds or something. Hold on."

Voices, urgent, sounded in the background of the mayor's call.

"I have to go, Captain, Detectives. Please, do whatever you can. The city's resources? They're at your disposal. Liaise with the Bureau and DHS."

The call was disconnected.

Staring at the wreckage again. The blue of the tower was brilliant. Was it painted that way for safety? Or to advertise? Or simply cosmetics?

Sellitto poured some coffee from the carafe that had materialized. He walked to the computer monitor on the wall and squinted as he read the terrorists' note.

"So, they're not the brightest bulbs," he said. "Maybe we can use that."

"How's that?" Rhyme queried.

"Misspellings—'obsene.' And 'its' without an apostrophe."

Rhyme clicked his tongue. "Those were intentional, to make us think they're stupid. They're not."

"Yeah?"

"Other rules of grammar and punctuation're right. They use 'that' and 'which' correctly. 'That' restricts the meaning of the preceding word: 'the properties that are on the list below.' 'Which' is nonrestrictive—providing optional information. For instance: where they happened to have learned about the city's lack of redevelopment plans."

"Linc—"

"And they use 'since' correctly too, meaning 'from a point in time.' It *can* be used to mean 'because,' but that's not preferred. And see, they use 'because' in the proper sense a few sentences later. And the apostrophe before the gerund. 'Developers' building . . .' That's correct."

"Gerund?"

Rhyme: "It's a verb used as a noun. 'Running is good for you.' Or so I'm told. A gerund takes the possessive. Is no one else aware of these rules? Astonishing."

"Jesus, Linc, when your students make a little screwup on their papers, you give them shit like this?"

He frowned. "An F. Of course." A nod toward the post on the screen. "The chat room's anonymous. But the original email. Who sent it and how?"

Lon said, "Public IP address. A coffee shop in Brooklyn with no security camera. The Computer Crimes people think the perp wasn't even in the place. He must've been outside and hijacked their router."

"Well, one fact to note: they know computers. Or're working with someone who does." He added, "I think the mayor should announce. He'll have to before tomorrow morning. Give people a chance to stay clear of jobsites."

Sellitto repeated, "Harrison's right—there'd be panic. And he's gotta be worried about copycatting. Is that a goddamn gerund?"

"It would be if 'copycat' were a verb. Which *I* consider nonstandard. Even if some people don't."

Rhyme continued to study the footage of the twisted tower and the wreckage of everything in its path. It had fallen forward, not to its side, and the long tower and arm atop it extended from the concrete base in the middle of the jobsite between two tall buildings, which it had narrowly missed, to a park across the uptown-downtown avenue. Had it veered just a dozen feet right or left, it would have collided with glass high-rises. The death toll would have been far higher.

"How many cranes are there in the city?"

Sachs pulled out her phone and asked the question. She squinted as she read. "New York, all boroughs, twenty-six. We're low on the list. Toronto has over a hundred. L.A. about fifty."

That was all? Twenty-six? Rhyme thought there would be more. He didn't get outside much, of course, but when he did, it seemed the soaring towers were everywhere, the crossbeams balancing precariously atop the stalks.

Rhyme said, "I'll call Mel and get him up here. What's Pulaski doing?"

Sachs said, "Homicide's been using him. He's running a scene in Midtown."

Rhyme said, "When he's done, I want him here."

"I'll call," Sellitto said.

"And let's get a chart going."

Sachs moved aside the Unsub 212 board, but kept it near the front. They were expecting an update from the lead detective, who was on his way here presently.

In the cleared space, she tugged an easel and blank pad forward and started a new board. "How about naming the guy after the street. Unsub 89?"

"A perfect christening," Rhyme said.

She wrote this at the top of the chart in her fine handwriting.

Sellitto said, "Think it's a Russian thing? A cell. Given the name. Kommunwhatever?"

Rhyme shook his head. He was thinking back to a history course he'd tolerated years ago. He recalled that left-leaning movements in mid-twentieth-century America enjoyed co-opting Soviet terms: agitprop, kompromat, intelligentsia.

"Doubt it. The Russians may have a perennial interest in

destabilizing democracy, but I doubt the Motherland'd pressure the city to find housing for the proletariat. That's a Roman word, by the way. Marx stole it.

"But I agree with the mayor. We've got to coordinate with the feds. Maybe have Lyle handle that."

A recent addition to the ranks of NYPD detectives, Lyle Spencer was a former head of corporate security for a media empire. He was quiet, but interviewees tended to cooperate when he asked them questions. The man was massive, a bodybuilder, and his eyes were fierce. Rhyme believed he had seen Spencer smile once, but he wasn't sure.

Sachs left a message for the detective, detailing the situation and what they needed him to do.

Sellitto opened his briefcase and extracted a thick wad of documents. "This's from the foreman at the jobsite on Eighty-Ninth: blueprints, maps, SD cards from some security cams, a few other things he thought might be helpful."

Sachs tugged a worktable into the center of the non-sterile portion of the parlor, and Sellitto spread out the materials. From this sea of paper, she selected a diagram of the site and taped it to a whiteboard. The overhead view depicted the crane and the building whose construction it was part of. Surrounding structures were depicted in rudimentary sketches.

She looked at the TV screen, then drew an arrow on the board. "That's the way it fell. Between these buildings . . . All right, I'll get on the grid. Who knows, maybe we'll find a receipt from that Chinese restaurant in Queens where the wannabe Russian revolutionaries meet every Wednesday."

Sellitto gave a sardonic yeah-right laugh.

"Ah, it *does* happen." Rhyme was frowning as he looked at Sachs. "What was his name again? That serial killer. Staten Island. Dudley . . . ?"

"Smits. Dudley Smits." To Sellitto, she said, "He dropped a woman's business card when he was leaving a murder scene. Had his prints on it. We moved into her apartment and just hung out. Ten hours later he showed up with a knife and a roll of duct tape. The look on his face, priceless. Worth the wait."

4.

IN NEW YORK, no wilderness attracts birdwatchers like Central Park. Bigger forest preserves exist in the region, but the glowing green rectangle in Manhattan is home to the most fowl per square acre.

Wielding a pair of Nikon binoculars, the man remained motionless, gazing at a black-capped chickadee. He'd been to Central Park several times and knew the sizable inventory that birdwatchers could draw upon to fill out their collection lists.

He was dressed in casual, late-spring trousers (black) and a windbreaker (navy blue). Trim and athletic, thinning hair halfway to gray, but trimmed and combed carefully into place.

After a moment, the bird flicked away, and he recorded some observations in a small notebook. He continued to scan, slowly, south to north.

"Having much luck?"

The voice, a woman's, was directed at him. He turned. Pear-shaped and binoculared, she was glancing at the notebook in the man's hand. Her outfit was red and yellow, as if to make the point that camouflage was not a necessary component when bird-watching.

He said, "Saw an ovenbird."

"No!"

"I did."

"Did you put it on eBird?"

An online service that included rare sighting alerts.

"Not yet. You?"

She shrugged. "Not much. Just got here. I hear there's a mute swan. I'll check the ponds and reservoir later. Where was the ovenbird?"

"Near the museum."

She turned toward the Metropolitan, across the park, as if the two-tone warbler might be winging its way from there to here at this very moment. Then she turned back and regarded him glancingly. He was hardly handsome, he knew. And his appearance put him around fifty. But he was of fit build and had one special attribute that often appealed: a naked ring finger.

She said, "I saw an American widgeon near the boathouse."

"Did you?"

Silence fell between them. Then, suddenly, she blurted, "If I were a bird, that's what I'd be." She corrected. "Well, a water bird of some kind. Duck, swan, goose. It seems more peaceful. Not a pelican, though. They're kind of shits. I'm Carol."

"David." Holding the notebook in one hand and the Nikon in the other prevented a handshake. Nods sufficed.

A pause. She said, "I don't think I've seen you before."

Birdwatchers were a close-knit crew. Especially in Manhattan.

"Just transferred here." The man looked at his phone for the time.

"From where?"

"San Diego."

"Oh, love it. It's beautiful there."

He knew she'd never been.

Another pause. He said, "I better be going. Have a meeting."

"Nice talking to you. I'm going to go look for that ovenbird. Maybe I'll see you here again."

"I hope so," he said with a smile and turned west, following the sidewalk to another stand of the bushes that were ubiquitous in this part of the park. He gazed past the greenery, without the binoculars, and examined a building across the street, a brownstone—also common here.

He noted, on the sidewalk in front of it, a slim and balding man wearing a loose-fitting dark suit. On his belt was a gold NYPD detective badge. Climbing the stairs, he pressed a bell and looked up at the security camera. A moment later, the door opened.

Ah, there he is . . .

Beyond the officer, the man in the park could see into the dim hallway. And he now made a sighting far more exciting than any bird—which he had zero interest in anyway, other than as an excuse to be in the park with binoculars.

The person he could see, before the door closed, was of particular—you might say obsessive—interest to him. His name was Lincoln Rhyme, and it was he whom the faux birdwatcher, Charles Vespasian Hale, also known as the Watchmaker, had come to New York to kill.

5.

MOVE. FAST.

It's not too late, but it soon will be.

NYPD patrolman Ron Pulaski was thinking that there's that phrase you hear sometimes, about "the first forty-eight." Meaning that if you didn't get a solid lead within the first two days of a homicide, the case grew progressively more difficult to solve. That was crazy, as every cop knew, nothing more than a catchphrase from TV. It was the first forty-eight *minutes* that counted. After that, evidence and witness's memories started to vanish.

This death was well past that time—in fact, it was about two days old, smack on the line of the true-crime cliché.

Which is why he was moving fast.

Trim and blond and carefully clean-shaven, features hidden by the CSU Tyvek suit and mask, Pulaski was now gazing over the scene: a concrete floor, stained and pitted and cracked from ancient industrial machinery, long gone, whose design and function couldn't be deduced from the nature of the wear beneath his feet.

Water in shallow pools coated with a skim of deep blue and red oil. Concrete-block walls from which rods and pipes protruded. Rusty banks of shelves, empty, their paint largely gone. Mold was a chief design element.

Narrow windows were horizontal slats at the tops of the walls, typical of cellars like this one. Spattered and greasy, they nonetheless let in some light.

A defunct hot-air furnace of galvanized steel dominated one end of the space.

But was that one magic thing that would lead to the killer still here? Or had it evaporated or been digested by rats or dissolved into a billion molecules of obscuring matter?

There had once been that bit of vital evidence. At the time of the murder. It had absolutely been present.

According to a Frenchman who died in 1966.

Edmond Locard had been a forensic investigator—a criminalist—in Lyon, where he established the first forensic science laboratory in the world. His most famous precept was simple and has remained true to this day: it is impossible for a criminal to act without leaving traces of his presence either on the victim or within the scene.

Ron Pulaski had heard those words a hundred times—from his mentor, Lincoln Rhyme. He'd come to believe them.

And he knew that here, somewhere, had been the clues to find the person who had murdered the man who lay at Pulaski's feet in this dank cellar of a warehouse on the East Side of Manhattan. It possibly still was.

But that adverb was important.

Possibly . . .

Because after all this time—that infamous forty-eight hours— it might have vanished or morphed into something unrecognizable.

He knew the vital clue was nothing as tangible as friction-ridge prints or drops of the killer's own blood or a helpful shell casing. Those obvious clues were absent.

So it came down to "dust," Locard's charming word for trace evidence.

Pulaski glanced again at the victim. Fletcher Dalton.

In a gray suit, white shirt and dark tie, he was on his back, dead eyes on the black ceiling. The thirty-two-year-old was a broker at a trading house on Wall Street and lived by himself at 845 East 58th Street. He had not shown up for work yesterday and hadn't been found at home. His name and picture were put out on the wire. Two hours ago, an officer from Patrol happened to notice the door ajar in the deserted warehouse, which was scheduled for demo. He inhaled just one breath before he knew, and he called Homicide.

While Pulaski typically worked with Rhyme and Amelia Sachs, his crime scene reports and testimony at trial as a forensic expert had been noticed, and he'd recently been recruited to run scenes on his own.

Pulaski was pleased for the chance. He'd been Rhyme's and Sachs's assistant for some years, and both of them thought he should branch out. Forensic work proved to be far more engaging than street crime—the province of his official assignment, the Patrol Division. Another advantage: it made Jenny happier. The odds of her becoming a widow were considerably smaller when her husband's job involved picking up hairs with tweezers rather than confronting meth-addled gangbangers.

Another thing: he was good at crime scene work.

And the icing on the cake? He liked it.

How rare was it for what you love and what you excel at to come together?

Rhyme had told him that some people are born to crime scene work, while others simply do a job.

Inspired versus functional.

Artist versus mechanic.

The criminalist didn't exactly say aloud which camp Pulaski fell into, but he really didn't need to; with Lincoln Rhyme, you had to infer much, and the younger officer knew how to read him.

Another scan of the forty-by-fifty room. The nature of the killing seemed clear. Dalton was shot outside on the sidewalk and dragged into the basement—after the killer kicked the door open. Only one perp was present here; the dust on the floor told that story.

It was clear that the shooter had dragged the body from the door, straight to where he'd dumped it, with no detours—but of course Pulaski searched the entire space.

He used a pattern of his own: a spiral, starting at the center of the crime and walking in ever-expanding circles. He then turned and did the same in reverse, moving in shrinking loops. Lincoln advocated the grid pattern; with it, you search the scene back and forth, as if mowing a lawn. Then you turn perpendicular and search the same way, overlapping the same ground again.

Pulaski respected the grid, but he liked his own method better; the idea had come when his wife asked him to serve a spiral-cut ham at Thanksgiving.

He squinted against the glare from the half-dozen powerful halogen lights sitting on tripods strategically placed in the room.

It's here somewhere . . .

It has to be, right, Mr. Locard?

But where?

Find it, he told himself firmly now.

The clock is ticking . . .

His spiral-ham search completed, he concentrated on the most important parts of the scene: the path from the door to the body and the body itself.

And there, on Dalton's lapel, he found it.

The thing that fell into the vital category of evidence at a scene: different from everything else.

It was a dark blue fiber. A synthetic polymer. Because of that composition and its length, it had come from either a scarf or a stocking cap, which the officer knew because he had spent long hours studying scarves and stocking caps (and most other fabrics, for that matter), so that if he happened upon a sample at a crime scene he would have a good chance of identifying it in the field, rather than back in the lab, where the same results would have been attained, but after considerably more time.

Move. Fast.

Outside, Pulaski quickly stripped off the Tyvek, told the collection techs to get the evidence to the lab in Queens, and released the body to the Medical Examiner's tour doctor.

He then walked from the site of the murder to the subway station that Dalton—who had a MetroCard in his pocket—most likely would have exited from on his way home the night he died, three and a half blocks away (one did not bus one's way from Wall Street to the Upper East Side).

And here, along a stretch of warehouses and commercial buildings, he found what he was hoping for.

A Domain Awareness System camera mounted on a lamppost.

He placed a call to Central and was patched through to one of the DAS operators—dozens of them sat before banks upon banks of video screens, as they and their algorithmic partners scanned for bad guys and bad deeds.

Pulaski identified himself and gave the location of the camera, and the date and time Dalton would likely have passed by here.

"Okay," the man said. "You want it now?"

"Yeah, this number."

They disconnected. Soon his phone hummed and he called up the clip. Stepping out of the sun to see the screen better, he watched the video.

Ah, there.

A slim man, white, with a fastidious mustache appeared. He wore black slacks and jacket and his head was covered with a dark blue stocking cap, of exactly the same shade as the fiber Pulaski had just found.

As he walked east, his eyes were across the street, perhaps on Dalton; that side was not visible to the camera.

The man's hand was at his side—and once, he tapped his pocket. This he might have done for any number of reasons, but one would have been to make sure his gun was there, safely tucked away.

He was then out of sight. Fifteen minutes later he returned, quickly, and Pulaski formulated a theory of what had happened: somewhere along this street Dalton had witnessed something. It could not have been a recognizable crime; had it been, the trader would have called 911. Pulaski had checked: the only calls from this neighborhood that day had been reports of two heart attacks and a bad fall.

Whatever the crime was, Blue Hat could not afford to let Dalton live.

Pulaski called the DAS people back and asked if there were other cameras in the vicinity.

No, none.

Then he had an idea. He'd try something that he was sure would not work.

But he did it anyway.

He gave the DAS officer the time stamp of the tape where one could see Blue Hat's face the most clearly, and told him to take a screen capture and send it to another alphabet operation of the NYPD.

The department's FIS—Facial Identification Section—is not nearly the invasive operation that people believe it is. Its mission is to match pictures of possible suspects taken from security cameras in the field—or occasional bad-idea selfies—with mug shots or wanted-poster pictures in order to establish identities.

Pulaski had submitted about sixty images over his career, and no matches had been returned.

This one was different.

The officer he was on the line with said, "Well, guess what, Ron. That picture? FIS returned a ninety-two percent likely match."

"Is that good?"

"Ninety-two's pretty much gold." He laughed. "And I'll give you gold for another reason too. You're not going to believe who your suspect is. You sitting down?"

• • •

"Good morning, this is up-to-the-minute business news with WKDP. Investors came down with a bad case of the jitters following the collapse this morning of a crane at a construction site on Manhattan's Upper East Side. One worker was killed and a half-dozen injured. Evans Development and Moynahan Construction are the companies involved in building the luxury seventy-eight-story high-rise, where units will start at five million dollars. City officials report that the inspection certificates of all the tower cranes operating in New York are current, but federal regulators have urged that construction at those jobsites be suspended pending an investigation by the Department of Buildings and the federal National Institute of Standards and Technology. NIST has investigated the World Trade Center collapses and Pentagon attack on 9/11, and the Champlain Towers South building collapse in Miami. Stock in Evans Development, a publicly traded company, fell to an all-time low."

6.

THE LIGHTS LEFT little doubt as to where the incident had happened.

Hundreds of them, white, blue, red.

Sachs piloted her ancient Ford Torino, painted an urgent crimson, fast along the cross street toward the macabre spectacle, whipping through and around traffic. She nearly resorted to the sidewalk when several trucks refused to part and let her pass. At Third Avenue, the impatient honking resulted in a man's raised middle finger, which was instantly joined by its three companions and thumb to offer friendly greeting—the sort you'd give to a baby—when he saw the portable blue flasher unit and the NYPD placard on the dash.

Finally, a vehicular break, thanks to uniforms diverting cars and trucks elsewhere. She gunned the engine and made the finish line, skidding to a stop at the edge of the massive construction site on East 89th Street.

The vids on the news hadn't come close to depicting the carnage. The crane—made of blue pipes, much thicker than they appeared from a distance—lay between the two buildings it had narrowly missed, a tornado track of debris and damage extending from the base—a slab of concrete—to the park, where the tip of the boom had dug itself deep into the earth. Everything beneath it was flattened. The strip of disaster was a clutter of piping, metal parts, papers, slabs of cement, machinery, girders, concrete dust, bits of plastic, wire and cables, bent ladders and twisted stairs and landings. Apparently you didn't climb straight up to the top of a crane but ascended a ladder twenty feet or so, then turned and climbed once more, the rungs staggered so a slip-and-fall would be injurious but not fatal.

She looked at the cab, metal crushed and glass shattered. The damage was extensive. The operator would have died instantly— impact must have been at a hundred miles an hour—but what a terrible last few seconds he must have had, thinking of his fate as he saw the ground race toward him through the large windows.

Smoke rose, though there did not seem to have been a fire.

Like all New Yorkers, Sachs had seen hundreds of cranes in her years in the city, but had paid little attention to them. She'd heard of some accidents, but they were rare. To her, the machinery signaled another problem: they were flags of construction sites, which meant street lanes would be closed, further slowing the city's already decelerated traffic.

Another fact she knew about cranes from her job: they were referred to by organized crime triggermen and bosses as "headstones," because they rose over construction sites, which were popular places to dump hit victims when concrete was being poured.

She retrieved her crime scene gear from the trunk and started into the site, passing onlookers and a homeless man in a filthy brown three-quarter-length overcoat. On his head was perched a fuzzy hat, dark brown and orange, in the shape of those worn by Taliban warlords. Oblivious to the loss of life, he was nosing along the yellow tape, pointing his blue-and-white coffee cup toward the growing crowd and begging for change. But only half-heartedly. He spent more time looking over the debris. A scavenger, probably happy to pocket the dead operator's wallet or cash that had fallen from his pocket. Pathetic.

He glanced her way briefly, noting the badge and her cold glare, and moved on.

Sachs ducked under the tape and oriented herself, finding the base of the crane. Before she started toward it, a large woman in a yellow vest that read *Safety Supervisor* approached and handed her a white hard hat. She shook her head, thinking that the hat would, even if in a small way, contaminate the scene. "I don't—"

"Required." The woman steamed away to deliver another hat to someone who might be an executive or a government inspector. They were armed with a clipboard and briefcase.

Sachs asked a uniform, awkwardly trying to adjust a too-large hard hat, "Where's the IC?"

The uniform pointed to another officer, middle-aged, also in a hat, his yellow. She walked up to the incident commander.

"Captain."

"You're Sachs. Detective out of Major Cases, right? You work with Lincoln Rhyme."

A nod.

"These're weird." He tapped the plastic on his skull.

"Any more news on the injured?"

"Nothing new. One fatality, five in the hospital. Two critical. Oh, and one heart attack. He'll live."

Her phone purred with a text.

Lon Sellitto had written:

The Project sent a post to 13Chan. Said they think the city is trying to keep this quiet. Bad faith. So they posted publicly that the crane was sabotaged and more R coming down until the properties R transferred. The shits. F'ing panic.

Well, so much for blaming the feds for the shutdown.

Of course, panic would happen sooner or later anyway, so it was just as well word went out. The news might prompt witnesses to come forward.

Her eyes were on the tangled metal and mounds of debris. The tower of the crane was about fifteen feet square, with the bottom segment set in that concrete slab. All four feet were still mounted there; the tower had bent or snapped about thirty feet up.

She said to the IC, "Lon said he sabotaged the counterweights." A glance at the huge concrete slabs, lying sideways like discarded children's building blocks. "Have any idea how?" She scanned the trolley mechanism they were attached to. "No sign of IED residue."

"First thing I thought of, but I couldn't find any either. And nobody heard a bang. Waiting to talk to the foreman. He's been, you know, on the phone with the families. And corporate."

"Where is he?"

He nodded to a heavyset man of about fifty, in light blue slacks and blue shirt, whose pocket bristled with pens. His yellow hard hat was tilted forward at a jaunty angle and was covered with stickers from equipment manufacturers and unions.

She sympathized with him having to make the difficult calls to the family members, but she needed to start on the scene.

She approached. "Sorry, sir. I need to talk to you. Now, please." She held up her ID. He looked at her weapon first, then the fine print.

"I'll call you back." He disconnected and turned his red eyes toward her. From the smoke? From crying? Probably both.

"You know this was intentional."

S. Nowak—the name stitched on his blue shirt—was taut with anger, his teeth locked firmly together as he stared at the disaster. He nodded. "That officer over there told me, yeah. I can't believe somebody'd do something like this."

"Did you or anybody on your crews see anyone who might've been involved?"

He shook his head. "I've asked everybody. Nobody saw a thing."

She continued, "The detective you talked to earlier, Detective Sellitto?"

"Yeah, big guy. Brown suit."

"That's him. He said they sabotaged the counterweights. It threw the balance off."

"That's right."

"You have any idea how they did it?"

A shake of his head. "Somehow unhooked a couple of them. None of us can figure out how. They're made to stay on their tracks whatever happens. Impossible to fall. Except . . . I guess not." His eyes were staring at the slabs. "You know physics?"

"If it applies to car engines, yeah. Other than that . . ." A shrug.

"So you're aware of torque."

"Sure. Force that turns the drive shaft."

"And moment?"

"Moment?" she asked. "Like in time?"

"No. It's when there's force but *no* movement. Cranes stay upright because of moment. There's downward force on the front jib—the boom that carries the load. The counterweights in the back have to equal the force in front. That's moment—like balance. Maintaining moment is what operators—well, and the computers they use—do." He repeated almost reverently, "Balance. There's a trolley in the front that holds the hook for the load, and a trolley in the back with the weights. We're constantly moving the weights back and forth to counterbalance the load.

"Moment is so important that nobody ever screws up. It's like how pilots just don't forget to lower the landing gear. So that's what they attacked. Without the counterweights, there was no way the jib wasn't going down." He wiped his eyes. "What is this

I heard? Some bullshit about fair housing or something? Jesus Christ."

"*Affordable* housing."

"Hell of a way to pitch your cause."

"Could he have hacked into that computer?"

"Naw. You can't hack it. The system's not online. And that wasn't the problem," he said angrily. "They just disconnected the counterweights." His jaw tightened again as his eyes locked on to a cluster of rebar—the steel rods that reinforce concrete. These, a dozen of them, extended upward about six feet from the concrete slab they were anchored in. There was no mistaking the dried blood and tissue on them and the stains on the concrete.

Jesus . . .

Nowak was breathing deeply, fast, nearly hyperventilating. "He fell." A whisper. "All the way, headfirst. Hit the rebar. His body just . . . quivered. It wouldn't stop. He was stuck there, upside down. It took three firemen to get him free. Jesus. Three of them . . . I'll see that forever . . ."

So that was how the operator died. Not in the cab. He'd gotten out before it fell and tried to climb down.

Impaled . . .

"How could the suspect get up there?"

He checked back tears. "Climb, like everybody else. But nobody saw him, or them. We've got security during the day. A guard at night, but he'd be at the entrance. He didn't see anything. I asked him. As for the back, anybody could get over the walls if they wanted to." He nodded to the eight-foot-high wooden panels with holes cut in some of them for the curious to watch the building go up. "As for the tower, he'd have a hell of a climb, but my boys do it every day."

"You gave Detective Sellitto some SD cards of security footage. Did you find any others?"

"No."

"Could it've been an inside job?"

"What? You mean one of my people?" He simmered at the suggestion.

She didn't respond. It was a question that needed to be asked.

And she saw in his eyes the dawning understanding that the idea was reasonable and that he was considering it. Yet his reply was the very thing that Sachs was thinking: "Not impossible, I guess. But think about it. Somebody in this terror outfit joins a union, gets his card, works a site for weeks just to do something like this? And I heard they've threatened to do it again. So, what? They have inside people on other jobsites in town?" His voice faded and he took in the brown-stained rods again. Sachs couldn't help herself; she had to look too.

It took three firemen to get him free . . .

Then it was time for her to get to work. She had enough background of the scene. She began thinking forensically. Glancing around at the workers huddled together near the entrance, waiting for word if they could return to work or go home. The unsub would have worn what they wore so he could blend in: hard hat, work boots and gloves. Therefore, no latent prints and whatever boot prints he left would be mixed with hundreds of others.

As for facial recognition, the hard hats, dust masks and bandannas made that impossible—even if they lifted a clean capture from a video. And she noticed another problem with FR.

"A lot of sunglasses."

"You do beam work facing east in the morning and west in the afternoon, you need to see where exactly you're putting your boots when you're a hundred feet in the air."

Sachs looked at the counterweights.

"Where're the ones that fell first?"

They'd be the ones that the terrorists had sabotaged.

He pointed to a ragged hole in the wooden floor. "Temporary cover over the first basement. Went through it like butter."

Sachs walked to the hole and looked down. "Anybody down there?" She saw what might have been a flashlight beam.

"I sent somebody to see if anybody was hurt. I didn't hear, so I guess not."

So there'd be some contamination of the few things they knew for certain the suspect had touched—the cement blocks and the mechanism affixing them to the crane. But that was crime scene work—aiding casualties had to take priority over evidence.

"Hey, Nowak!"

They both looked toward the site's entrance. Two middle-aged women, crying, were standing beside another worker, the man who'd called.

"Family. I gotta talk to 'em."

He walked off slowly and Sachs joined the team from Crime Scene, a trio, standing behind the bus, gearing up. They were evidence collection technicians, civilian employees of the NYPD. The city had been using ECTs more and more in recent years. So much crime, so much to analyze, it didn't make logistical sense to tie up uniforms or gold shields with the grunt work that most crime scenes involved. Their training was arduous and they worked hard, many ECTs hoping they could join the department as officers.

After briefing them, she herself suited up in white Tyvek.

The hard hat was a contaminant, and it didn't fit under the hood of the jumpsuit. She set it aside—though not without the thought that Lincoln Rhyme's disabled condition resulted from him getting hit in the neck by a falling wooden beam at a construction site. Outside the suit, she strapped on a utility belt, which held a holster, and she snapped her Glock into the gray plastic. This too was a source of potential contamination, but one that was worth dealing with. Perps returned to the scene of the crime more frequently than one might expect. You constantly balanced crime scene integrity with survival.

After telling herself for the tenth time to stop looking at the bloody rebar, she tugged on gloves, picked up her personal collection kit, the one from her trunk, and walked to an opening that led to the first basement. A ladder was used to access the level and she climbed down it.

On that floor, she looked around the large empty space, dimly lit by ambient light from holes in the ceiling. She turned toward where the weights had fallen and her shoulders slumped. To get to them, she had to climb through a dark, narrow tunnel about twenty or thirty feet long, four feet high and three feet wide.

Of course, she thought wryly.

Amelia Sachs's greatest fear was enclosed spaces.

Well, get on with it. The scene's not going to search itself, and the Kommunalka Project is probably picking which crane'll be the next to come down.

Her throat suddenly burned and she coughed. The scents were what you'd expect: damp concrete, sawdust, motor oil and diesel exhaust. But there was something else: some kind of chemical. Astringent. Strong. When the counterweights landed, they must have crushed a drum of cleaning fluid. She pulled on a second mask, which helped.

Sachs stepped into the tunnel, walking awkwardly in a taut crouch.

One yard, two . . .

Give me a high-speed pursuit any day, she thought, the tachometer kissing red.

Give me a firefight with a tweaker in East New York, muzzle to muzzle.

Anything but this.

Three yards . . .

Well, damn it, the slower you go, the longer you're in here.

Finally she was out, and in a normal-sized corridor. At the end of this passage, she could see the weights, illuminated by light filtering through the hole they'd created. Dust floated around them.

Here, the chemical scent and the irritation, stinging both her throat and her eyes, were worse. Much worse.

Get to the weights. There was a chance that the unsub had left a dot of DNA or a fingerprint when he'd sabotaged the mechanism.

As good as a business card.

Dudley Smits . . .

She took one step forward and nearly tripped.

Shining her light downward, Amelia Sachs, the woman who rarely gasped, gasped now.

A worker—maybe the one the foreman had sent down here to check for casualties—lay on his stomach. A flashlight lay nearby; it was this beam of light she'd seen.

The man's eyes were open but unblinking, and it was clear he was dead.

And yet, wait. It seemed his hands were moving. She aimed the beam of her own flashlight at one of them.

And now another raspy intake of breath.

His skin was bubbling and dissolving. The appendage was settling as it liquified.

And the part of his face that rested on the concrete floor was doing the same. From chin to cheek, the flesh was being eaten away and bloody bone and flaps of muscle and ridges of gum were becoming exposed.

Sachs was coughing harder now.

She took a deep breath to clear her lungs . . .

Mistake.

Bad mistake.

It simply drew in more of the irritant, stabbing her mouth and nose and chest, and she began coughing in earnest.

The searing pain of fire. She had to escape. Fast.

Dropping her gear, Sachs turned and stumbled back into the tunnel. Now the dreaded passageway was her lifeline.

Lurching forward toward the ladder, she tried to push the Transmit button of her Motorola.

She missed.

Her vision was crackling, black on the periphery.

She staggered toward the ladder. The cough had grown into choking.

She took one step forward and, losing yet more of her sphere of sight, realized she was going down.

When she landed, she had a thought: That's weird. How can I smack the concrete so hard and not feel a—

7.

"**DETECTIVE.**" **RON PULASKI** was speaking into his phone. On the other end of the line was Lon Sellitto, who was—in the ever-changing structure of the NYPD—Pulaski's sorta-kinda boss.

But job hierarchy didn't matter at the moment. Pulaski had called Sellitto because Sellitto was senior and respected, and because the news Pulaski was about to share could not be ignored or lost in a report. Sellitto would make sure it was not.

"Pulaski," Sellitto said without waiting to hear what the patrolman's agenda was. "I left a message. Lincoln's going to need you on the crane case."

"Okay. But you gotta hear this. A scene I just ran?"

"Yeah, Homicide? East Side?"

Pulaski was outside the warehouse where Fletcher Dalton had died. The tape was still up. The emergency vehicles were gone.

"I have a probable ID. It's Eddie Tarr."

"Wait, you mean—?"

"The bomb maker. Yeah."

"Man. Wasn't he on the West Coast? That report on the wire,

the government building in Anaheim or someplace? Blew the shit out of it."

Pulaski said, "He's here now. Well, he's ninety-two percent here." He explained about the percentage likelihood of facial recognition. "But I'm thinking of it as one hundred."

"So the vic, the stock trader—this Dalton—was just a wrong-time/wrong-place guy."

"Looks like it. Saw something he shouldn't. Payment transfer, I'm guessing."

"Just the facial ID? That's all you got? Nothing else?"

"A maybe else."

"What?" Sellitto grumbled.

Pulaski reminded himself not to be cute with a veteran like the detective. "There wasn't any more DAS coverage in the area. But I found a security cam in a clothing boutique." The patrolman had thought it was a nice place. Normally, he'd have bought Jenny something in it—but not when the time was speeding past, the forty-eight-minute mark left far behind.

"I think Tarr got into a dark red sedan that maybe had Jersey plates."

"Tarr . . . I'm just looking him up on NCIC. Jesus. He sells his bombs all over the world. Doesn't matter what your politics are. You pay him enough he'll make you an IED, no questions asked. He doesn't plant them. He just makes them. The Palestinians've bought them to blow up Israelis, and vice versa. So, sedan you were saying? Maybe Jersey?"

"I rolled trace from where the tires were. Maybe that'll give me a lead."

"Wasn't it two days ago?"

"Like Lincoln says, 'The unlikely is better than nothing.'"

Sellitto muttered, "I think he said it better than that."

"He probably did."

Sellitto said, "I'm going to tell Dellray at the Bureau, and I know a guy at ATF. They'll want to jump on any leads to Tarr. Says here there're rewards on his head, half million."

"I'm going to follow up."

"The crane, though, Pulaski."

"I will. But I want this guy."

"He's terrorist enabled. And interstate. And international. That makes it fed all the way."

Pulaski said evenly, "No, not all the way. He killed a vic here. It's a homicide. And it's my case."

A pause. "Fair enough. Listen, something else. I need to talk to you. Won't take long. Maybe lunch today at Maggie's?"

"I can do a half hour. That's it, though."

"Good. Make it one o'clock?"

"Sure." Pulaski was staring absently at the door that Tarr—if Tarr *was* the killer—had kicked open after shooting Dalton in the back of the head.

"Oh, hold on, Pulaski . . . Got a notice coming through. About your Tarr case."

His heart thudded.

The detective continued, "Yeah, here it is. You want to write this down."

"I'm ready."

"They got a shitload of red cars in Jersey."

Pulaski started to say, "Very funny," but Sellitto'd already hung up.

8.

AMONG THE PLACES that Charles Hale had stayed were the Plaza Athénée in Paris, the Marquis Reforma in Mexico City, the Connaught in London, the weird but luxurious boat hotel in Singapore.

He'd chosen them, though, not for their ultra-posh décor and disciplined service, but because they were strategically important for his jobs: murdering a Saudi prince, discrediting a casino owner, stealing a valise containing something valuable enough for him to be paid one million dollars to pilfer . . . and assignments in the same vein.

Hale parked his SUV on a quiet street in Greenwich Village, walked a half block and turned into a dusty cul-de-sac. Here was his temporary New York City residence. It lacked the panache of any of those elegant, excessive places, but was perfect for his mission here.

It was a WillScot construction trailer squatting at the end of Hamilton Court, not far from the Hudson River. This was a spacious model, 480 square feet. A large central area and two smaller offices on either side, one of which was his bedroom. A bathroom—working, if small. Plenty of tables and shelves. It had been broken into months ago and some half-hearted graffiti decorated the walls, but otherwise there'd been no vandalism. Now, with the lights on much of the time, and security cameras aimed around the perimeter, anyone taking the trouble to slip down the cul-de-sac and peek would believe it occupied and depart, looking elsewhere for larceny or walls to spray-paint into bold art.

Hamilton Court was lined by partially demolished buildings or those scheduled to come down. New condos were planned, but construction was on hiatus for at least three months, according to court filings.

And Hale needed the place for only a day or two longer.

As he walked to the trailer, he stayed on the cobblestoned street itself; the sidewalks had been broken up with jackhammers, but the shattered concrete had not been removed. The paths looked like miniature rivers filled with jagged beige icebergs.

At the trailer, he opened the door's two electronic deadbolts and an unpickable chain key lock. He stepped inside and disarmed the security system. He doffed his jacket and put away the birdwatching gear.

The interior was sparse. Hale considered most decorations to be distractions and wastes of time. This prejudice did not apply to timepieces, of course, of which there were a half dozen: clocks and a reproduction of a clepsydra—the predecessor to the hourglass. But these weren't really adornments; they were associates. Friends. He had not brought them with him; the travel accommodations wouldn't have allowed for that. He kept them in a storage space downtown, but now he'd cleaned that out. He would not need it after this job.

Several of these timepieces he had constructed himself. His nickname, the Watchmaker, was not purely figurative.

Built-in fiberboard tables and metal shelves held paperwork, electronic and mechanical tools, instruments, several computers, a router, a coffeemaker, food and drinks. It was all arranged in perfect rows, as if Hale had used a ruler to place the objects. Any misalignment set him on edge.

The workings of a watch are order personified.

As is time itself.

No deviation is acceptable.

Two chairs sat in the center area. He'd also bought a TV, a terrestrial model with antenna, so he didn't need to subscribe to a cable service. While he had not seen an entertainment show for six years and three months, he needed the unit to collect news about any investigations against him. At the CIA and other spy outfits, the vast majority of the intel they gathered came not from disguised operatives or clever hacking, but from the media. Hale harvested information in the same way. The police, afraid of being seen as less than candid in the public's eye, always spilled too much.

On the shelves were a few books. Most were relevant to his projects here in the city, and several were devoted to Lincoln Rhyme. Some dealt with the topic of horology, the study of timepieces, but few about the physics of time. Despite Hale's obsession with the topic, lofty theory didn't interest him—the space-time continuum, black holes, wormholes, Stephen Hawking's chronology protection conjecture . . .

All of that was best described in TV's *Doctor Who*: "People assume that time is a strict progression from cause to effect, but actually from a nonlinear, non-subjective viewpoint, it's more like a big ball of wibbly-wobbly, timey-wimey stuff."

Hale caught a glimpse of himself in a wall mirror and the image gave him a jolt, even all these months after the surgery. Unlike every other cosmetic surgical patient on earth, Hale had paid, and paid a great deal, to turn his original self—handsome by most standards—into an older man, with a bunched-up and baggy face. This was necessary because his prior appearance was known (he'd even had a mug shot taken—thank you *so* much, Lincoln Rhyme), and anyone suspecting that he would go for plastic surgery would assume he would remove years, not add them. He'd given himself a balding pate too, which came from meticulous, painful plucking, not telltale shaving.

He made himself a cup of strong coffee. As he took the first sip, he received a text alert, accompanied by a flashing red background on the screen.

His security app—sensors at the chained-off opening of the cul-de-sac—had picked up a presence.

The slim figure was walking toward the trailer, keeping to the shadows on the east side of Hamilton, looking about cautiously. His hand was at his side, but it was easy to see that he was holding a gun. That metal did not reflect sunlight—it was flat black—but the gold NYPD detective badge on his belt certainly did.

Hale walked to the door and from a compartment hidden behind a framed certificate of inspection removed a similar gun—a Glock, though his was mounted with a silencer.

Just as the cop arrived at the door, Hale opened it and, glancing across the site to make sure he hadn't been followed, ushered in Andy Gilligan. This was the man Hale—as birdwatcher—had seen an hour before, walking through Lincoln Rhyme's front door.

The detective was well connected in the NYPD and smart and gutsy—and without his assistance, murdering the criminalist would be infinitely more difficult.

9.

RHYME HAD CALLED her twice, but Amelia Sachs hadn't answered.

Probably because she was concentrating on walking the grid at the crane collapse site.

Like Rhyme, Amelia became so focused on searching for relevant evidence that the external world vanished. It was one aspect of their lives that had drawn them together.

Still, he thought, she should have checked in by now.

The door buzzer sounded. Rhyme looked at the monitor, hit Enter and NYPD detective Mel Cooper walked into the parlor.

Trimly built, with a perpetual half smile on his face and the habit of pushing his thick black-framed glasses higher on his nose every few minutes, Cooper was the best forensic lab man in the city. Years ago, Rhyme had used all his negotiating skills (and budgetary cudgels) to steal him away from the small-town police department where he ran a crime scene lab. Cooper took seamlessly to urban forensics, though he occasionally expressed regret at not working crimes like the famous one in his hometown, involving a taxidermied fox, a sugar-maple log and a homemade rocket—a case he'd never gotten around to explaining to an intrigued Lincoln Rhyme.

Cooper had two passions: science and ballroom dancing, at which he and his mesmerizing Scandinavian girlfriend excelled.

He greeted Rhyme and Sellitto, who nodded distractedly, as he was on the phone.

After hanging his jacket, the tech took the Lipton tea Thom had brewed just for him (he liked to say he had simple tastes), then began to robe up. He looked around the parlor, frowning.

"I know. There's no evidence." Rhyme scowled. Then: "Have you heard from Amelia? She was on grid at the crane site and should've called in by now."

Cooper lifted a dismissing hand at the curious question; there'd be no reason for him to have heard from her.

"Is that anything?" He was now nodding at the documents that the foreman had provided: maps of the site, diagrams of the crane.

"Just backgrounder," Sellitto said after hanging up.

And Rhyme said staunchly, "Of. Zero. Evidentiary. Value."

Cooper looked over the chart on which Sachs had drawn the wreckage path. "Terrible. How tall was it?"

Sellitto said, "It's a self-erecting model . . ."

"A what?" Cooper asked, lifting a wry eyebrow.

The detective scoffed. "It's just what they call it. The tower expands by adding other segments. This one was at the maximum height they can go. About two hundred twenty feet."

And where the hell are you, Sachs? Rhyme looked to his phone once more, then grew angry with himself for the juvenile move.

Without evidence to analyze, there was nothing to do at the moment but a task he truly hated: scrubbing the security videos taken at the site.

He had a brief desire to fling the computer across the room.

Which he very likely might have done if he'd been able to. Lord knew he'd had enough temper tantrums when he was running CSU. Woe to anyone—brass included—who contaminated a scene or was too lazy to search or investigate as completely as they should.

More scrubbing.

Not a single goddamn frame of the person who'd climbed the tower to loosen or cut free the counterweights.

Nothing, nothing.

No-effing-thing.

"What was that?" Sellitto asked.

Rhyme, unaware that he'd spoken aloud, shook his head.

The doorbell rang and Rhyme looked at the video monitor. It was Sonja Montez, a talented evidence collection technician. He knew her diligence and savvy; she "got" crime scenes, understood them. She spoke to them and they spoke back. This might have been, she admitted candidly, because she knew the streets, having run with a girl gang in high school, though whatever they'd gotten up to, Montez had a clean record.

In her arms were two plastic bins like those that milk cartons are kept in. She'd hit the buzzer with her elbow.

Why had *she* brought the evidence from the scene and not Sachs?

Something was wrong.

He hit the door lock button on his keypad and the woman entered. No longer in Tyvek, Montez wore a bright green blouse and black leather skirt, and her heels clattered on the ancient oak floors. At her throat was a locket that contained pictures of her two young children, he knew; she'd showed them off proudly the first time she'd been here with a trove of evidence for him to analyze.

"Captain Rhyme. What's all this?" She stood at the X-ray machine and explosives and radiation detectors, and a small biotoxin chamber, in the front hallway.

"Just being careful."

A nod. "Can't have too much careful in this day and age," she said earnestly.

When Rhyme had learned a few months ago that an assassin was targeting him, he'd asked one of his most brilliant criminalist students to get into the attacker's mind and come up with the most logical way to kill Rhyme. The young man had decided the perp would exploit a weakness, something Rhyme loved and couldn't resist: evidence. He would plant a bomb or toxin in something from a crime scene.

So, until the assassin was identified and the threat eliminated, everything that came into the house from unknown origins was scanned.

Cooper and Montez greeted each other, and the lab man and Thom began feeding the envelopes and containers through the security machines.

Rhyme finally had to ask, "Sonja. I've called Amelia. She hasn't—"

The woman interrupted, frowning. "You mean you don't know?" She walked farther into the parlor until she was next to him.

Rhyme's heart began to pump furiously; given that he was insensate from the neck down, he knew this solely because of the throbbing in his temple.

"What?"

"She collapsed at the scene . . . She was in the basement of the jobsite, got exposed to something. Chemicals. The same stuff that killed a second worker."

"And is she—?"

"I'm fine," came a raspy voice from the doorway.

Amelia Sachs walked inside.

Rhyme frowned. She was carting an eighteen-inch green oxygen tank, to which was attached a clear tube, ending in a mask.

She clapped it onto her face, inhaled deeply and then nodded to a large glass jar in one of the evidence cartons. Inside was a small opaque plastic container. "That's it. In there. Be really careful. It's what he used to drop the counterweights. Killed one of the workers. Knocked me out. Medics got me . . ."

Her voice faded and he wondered if she were going to say "just in time." But that was a phrase too dramatic for Amelia Sachs. And her pause was simply so she could take in more oxygen.

Yet her initial pronouncement was not exactly accurate. She was not fine. "Fragile" was not a word that existed in her universe, but whatever had happened had—he sought a word—*diminished* her.

Inhaling more of the oxygen, she began to walk to the sterile portion of the lab, where she often stood to help Cooper navigate the evidence she'd collected. But now she diverted to one of the noisy—and unsightly—wicker chairs that had come with the town house and had yet to be discarded. She sat heavily and caught her breath.

"Sachs," Rhyme began.

She lifted an eyebrow briefly but remained silent.

Yet another way in which they were alike: minimizing physical maladies. Rhyme, for instance, as a quadriplegic, had blood pressure concerns—autonomic dysreflexia—that needed attention. The remedy was simple—nitroglycerine two percent paste, or some other drugs—but he tended to slough off symptoms and stay focused on the job. She suffered from arthritis and simply ignored the pain and popped pills—over-the-counter ones only—and continued on with the investigation.

The faint motion of her head told him she was doing this now, refusing to acknowledge her present condition. Her eyes told a different story.

She inhaled yet again and turned to Sellitto. In a low voice: "I had to send in a bomb squad robot to collect the sample. And whatever that crap is, it melted the tires and dissolved the camera lens. They're going to send Major Cases a bill. Just to warn you. It won't be cheap."

. . .

As she uploaded the crime scene photos she'd taken, Sachs explained about the second death, the worker who'd gone down to where the counterweights had fallen, in the first basement. He'd apparently been overcome and stumbled into the substance, which began eating away his skin. He crawled about thirty feet before he died.

"Those were the fumes that got me."

After a soft coughing fit, she added that when she hadn't responded to Sonja Montez's radio call, a med tech had hurried to the scene and found her at the foot of a ladder that led to the basement. A team got her out and on oxygen right away. They wanted her to go to the ER, but she declined.

Montez was needed at another scene. Sachs thanked her. The women embraced, and with farewell nods to the others, the ECT left the town house.

Sachs seemed to have had enough of sitting. She rose, wrapped the tube around the oxygen tank and was going to set it aside. But with some irritation she hesitated, unraveled the tube and took more breaths through the mask.

"Jesus, Amelia," Sellitto said, "lie down for a bit."

"Later," she said absently.

And again ignored Rhyme's look of concern.

She turned to Mel Cooper, who had taken the collected samples and was setting them out on a workspace in the sterile portion of the lab.

"That jar." She nodded toward it again. "The fire marshal said to use neoprene gloves, an apron and a respirator."

Rhyme noticed her hollow eyes staring at the photos on the

large monitor above the evidence boards: images of the victim in the basement, the melting skin, the bubbling of tissue and blood.

Then she turned away and back with them, in the lab. Fully back.

Cooper found the appropriate PPE and donned it over his lab jacket and slacks.

Another brief bout of shallow coughing from Sachs, a wince at the pain, then: "There just wasn't much to collect, Rhyme. Sonja found boot prints at the base of the tower, where the ladder started. It was the only way up. But they matched the operator's. I had the morgue send a picture. Our unsub must've worn booties at the crane and then pulled them off when he walked back into the site so his boots'd look like everyone else's.

"How he did it was he got a device on the counterweights trolley rail. Can't really tell what it was. The stuff dissolved it almost completely."

She explained that the substance, whatever it was, had begun to dissolve the concrete of the weights itself. "Made them lighter and the crane began to tip forward. The operator did what he could, but finally two of the weights dropped free, and that was it." Her voice sounded husky and tired, and she paused for more oxygen. She coughed hard several times and wiped her mouth with a tissue, then glanced unobtrusively at it. Rhyme could see no blood, but his view was masked; he wondered if she could.

She repeated what she'd told him earlier—about all the workers in gloves and boots. Dressing like them, the unsub might as well have been invisible.

Murder in a construction site . . .

"The precinct's got a dozen uniforms out canvassing stores and offices nearby. See if anybody got a look of someone carting a box into the site."

Rhyme grimaced. Videos and witnesses, yet only enough evidence to fit into—not even fill—two small milk crates.

Ridiculous.

Sellitto looked toward Cooper, who was running samples through his equipment. "You found out what that shit is yet, Mel?"

Eyes on the crime scene images, Rhyme gave a brief laugh of surprise. "Well, we *know* what it is. The only question is can we find out where the unsub got it."

"You know just by looking at the pictures?" Sellitto asked.

"Of course. That, and Amelia's symptoms."

"And?"

"Take radioactive toxins and botulinum out of the equation, and it's the most dangerous substance on earth."

10.

"HEY," SAID ANDY GILLIGAN in greeting.

Charles Hale nodded and through the curtain in the door window scanned Hamilton Court once more.

The cop snapped, "I looked. Nobody was following. I know what I'm doing. Not my first circus."

Wasn't the expression "rodeo"?

Hale closed and locked the door, then put the gun back into the compartment, feeling no urge to explain his caution or to comment on the fact that Gilligan himself had been clutching a firearm as he approached the trailer.

They moved to the center section of the mobile construction headquarters and sat at the table. "Coffee?" Hale asked.

"No, I'm good."

"It went all right?"

The detective clicked his tongue. "Perfect. None of them suspect anything. Now, here's this," Gilligan said, as if about to deliver a Christmas present to a buddy. He withdrew several sheets from his inside jacket pocket. It was quite the nice garment. The detective, Hale had learned, had several sources of income—all of it tax free—beyond what the NYPD paid him. Hale himself had put $100K into an offshore account for Gilligan this year alone.

"What is it?"

"Lifted it from a file at Rhyme's. It'll be helpful."

Hale opened the sheets and scanned the list of eighteen names. Most of them were crossed out.

"You'll want to talk to the others, the one's I haven't checked off," Gilligan said. "Might be a witness."

"What's the climate like there, in Rhyme's?"

"The crane thing's got them occupied. Totally. My case is on the back burner."

He was referring to the Department of Structures and Engineering theft. The possessive pronoun "my" was true in two senses: it was Gilligan's case because he was lead detective on it—but also because he was the thief, the man who'd broken into the building and stolen the documents and drives.

He was the man Rhyme and Amelia Sachs had nicknamed Unsub 212.

The stolen DSE materials were what now covered the table in front of the men.

"Anything new I should know about Rhyme's security?"

"No. Still just the parcel X-ray machine. The biotox frame. The detectors for bombs and radiation."

When the detective had first reported to Hale that there was a uranium detector, Gilligan had laughed. "Rhyme thinks somebody's going to nuke him?"

Hale had not bothered to explain that dirty devices—which spread radioactive material—are a far more realistic danger than a nuclear reaction.

"And still no metal detectors?"

"No."

"The video you took? The card?"

Gilligan seemed hesitant as he handed Hale an SD card. "I didn't get much. I didn't want to, you know, be too obvious, taping."

The detective had worn a body cam with a button lens on the occasions he'd been to Rhyme's. Some of this was to allow Hale to see exactly what the defenses were like in the town house.

Hale also wanted to see the criminalist himself. Like a herpetologist needs to observe his favorite species of snake in its own environment.

He called up a movie-viewing program on his laptop, loaded the card and scrubbed through what Gilligan had recorded.

The quality was good for the most part. The detective had stood still and panned slowly. He did, however, cover the lens with his sleeve frequently—out of fear of being detected, probably.

Hale now froze a frame, leaning toward the screen.

He was looking at a particularly clear, well-lit capture.

And studied the image intensely.

Lincoln Rhyme is a handsome man, with a prominent nose and thick, trimmed dark hair. Those confined to wheelchairs sometimes gain weight or grow gaunt. Rhyme has done neither. He exercises, it's clear.

His dark eyes are keen, and a comma of hair falls over his right forehead. His brows are furrowed as he looks toward the portion of his parlor sealed off by a glass wall. It is the sterile side of the room, the laboratory. This hermetical sealing is similar to the finest watchmaking facilities, which are kept breathlessly clean, out of fear that dust—or far worse, a bit of sand or grit—might make its way into the works and render the timepiece useless.

Interrupting Hale's reverie, Gilligan now said, "You want, I can still try for the mike." A brief pause. "I'd have to charge you more because of the risk, of course."

They had debated sneaking a transmitter into the room.

Without a metal detector at the door, it would be easy to smuggle in a bug. But Rhyme or someone else would probably sweep the place—especially now that he knew he was the target of a killer.

"No."

Hale pushed the Play triangle once again.

Now Gilligan has turned from Rhyme and is walking along the row of bookshelves. The camera pans across the titles. Some are books on the law and police procedure, but more are titles devoted to the sciences, notably chemistry, physics, geology and other environmental subjects. One is *The Analysis and Classification of Mud on the Eastern Seaboard*.

The camera pans back. After mundane footage, the video goes black.

Hale wished Gilligan had gotten a scan of the evidence boards, but he was apparently too nervous to do so.

As Hale sat back, reflecting on what he'd just seen, sipping coffee, Gilligan was looking at the timepieces.

The clepsydra, in particular, grabbed his attention. The instrument was about eighteen inches high. The frame was of ebony and the top and bottom disks featured brass buttons depicting the signs of the zodiac.

"You make that?" Gilligan asked.

"The clepsydra? No. I found it at an antiques store and liked the lines."

Gilligan asked, "Clep . . . what?"

"Clepsydra. Predecessor of the hourglass. Same principal, measuring the passage of time, but with dripping water. They predate the sand models by two thousand years. There were problems with them—they couldn't be used on ships because of the rocking. Condensation was an issue too. Hourglasses like those"—he pointed to two on a shelf nearby—"came about around eight hundred AD. They were inventions of the church, for timing mass and services."

"It doesn't look like sand." Gilligan was squinting.

"No, most of them didn't use sand. Pulverized marble or burnt eggshell were more accurate. This one? It's tin oxide. Hourglasses gave us the term 'knots,' for speed."

"Yeah?" Gilligan asked. "I've got a boat. Nice one."

Which I might have bought him, thought Hale.

"Sailors tied knots into a rope and then fixed it to a log. They threw the rope overboard and used an hourglass to see how many knots flipped through their fingers for a given period of time."

"Cool. I'll tell my boating buddies."

Hale finished his coffee, washed the cup and dried his hands. "You spare fifteen minutes now? I have an idea—it'll be good for both of us—and I want your thoughts."

Gilligan looked at his digital watch. Cheap. No judgment from Hale. A watch like this might drift .5 seconds a day; a million-dollar mechanical model typically loses twice that. "Sure, I guess."

Hale once again checked the monitors. Clear. He slung his backpack over his shoulder and the two men stepped outside. Hale set the locks and they continued down the dusty cobblestones.

"Graveyard," Gilligan muttered.

"What?"

The detective waved his arm, indicating the dilapidated buildings lining the cul-de-sac. "They look like big tombstones."

They walked around the chain barrier and onto the quiet street, so typical of this part of Greenwich Village.

"Better if we take one car. Yours?"

Gilligan said, "I've got to be at One PP in a half hour."

"I have a meeting too, uptown. I'll take the train."

They climbed into the sweet-smelling Lexus, which was spotless. The mileage would be low. Maybe Hale had bought him this, rather than the boat. Maybe a portion of each.

As Gilligan started the engine, Hale asked, "The GPS is disconnected, right?"

"Yeah. I made sure."

"Head south. Then east. We're going to Webber and Blenheim."

After twenty minutes of negotiating the narrow downtown streets, which grew increasingly deserted, they arrived at the intersection. A vacant lot took up half the block. Mostly dirt, some clumps of grass. A dead tree. Trash. In a few places, the sunken brownstone remains of tenements, typical of nineteenth-century Lower East Side.

"What's here?"

"Part of my plans for Rhyme."

The detective pulled the sleek car to the curb—carefully; he'd be afraid of scratching the wheels. "He really is an arrogant son of a bitch, you know."

"No doubt about that."

They climbed from the car and walked to the six-foot-high chain-link fence around the lot. The gate had been stretched open, so it was easy to slip through.

Hale pointed to a row of abandoned tenements on the other side of the lot.

Gilligan said, "I was thinking about Rhyme."

"Yes?"

"My brother and me, we hunt. Have all our lives. We're fucking good shots. Rhyme gets out of the town house some."

Hale was thinking: Rhyme goes to the Manhattan School of Criminal Justice for the courses he teaches. Tuesday and Thursday and every other weekend. The school was two thousand, three hundred feet from the town house. Usually, his aide drove him in the disabled-accessible van, but on nice days he sometimes motored his way to and from class.

"I could get up on one of those buildings. Two shots. That'd be it. A third for his aide, so he doesn't try any lifesaving shit. I'd only charge an extra fifty K. What do you think?"

Hale was silent. Then: "No, I think we'll stick to what I've planned."

Gilligan laughed. "We negotiating? Okay, *thirty* K."

"The plan."

"Like building a watch," Gilligan said. "You don't change the design halfway through."

"Just like that."

Hale had slowed and Gilligan walked ahead a few paces. When he turned back, he found that he was looking at Hale's hand, which held a silenced weapon pointed his way.

His eyes revealed shock.

Disbelief too, as if having seen Hale put his Glock back into the compartment beside the trailer door, it was impossible to fathom the concept that someone could actually own *two* pistols.

II.

LON SELLITTO: "So what is it, kryptonite?"

A pop culture reference, Rhyme guessed. Maybe some weapon used by a villain in a movie.

"An inorganic acid. Hydrofluoric. HF's the chemical symbol. Technically it's classified as a weak acid."

Sachs scoffed and Sellitto grumbled, "Weak? Tell *him* that." Nodding toward the pictures of the dead construction worker.

"That only means it partially dissociates in water. It's an ion issue. It can be as corrosive as any other acid. But with HF, corrosion isn't the real problem. It's the combination of the elements that makes it so deadly. It's a one-two punch. The H—hydrogen—burns through the top layer of skin so fast you hardly feel it . . . Though you definitely do an hour or two later. Then, once it's in your body, the F—fluoride—attacks internal cells. The result is liquefaction necrosis. And the name of that condition pretty much says it all. Poisoning occurs by contact or inhalation. Breathe it and it'll burn all the way through your lungs. Dyspnea, cyanosis, pulmonary edema."

This description coincided with Sachs hitting the oxygen once more.

"Jesus," Sellitto muttered. "Does it take much?"

"No, a few drops'll kill you. There's no antidote. And you can't wash it off. All you can do is try to treat the symptoms. Massive pain and infection." He called to Cooper, "Anything else in addition to the acid in the sample?"

"Fragments and sludge of industrial concrete, sand, steel, a little iron, all in states suggesting they were dissolved by the acid."

"What's the concentration?" Rhyme asked.

"Thirty-two percent."

"That's a mistake. Run it again or recalibrate the equipment."

"Done all of the above. Thirty-two percent."

The highest concentration that Rhyme had ever heard of was twenty, and that was just for shipment and storage—in very specialized containers. The product was then greatly diluted for sale to end users. On the market, it was, at the most, two to four percent. A concentration that Sachs had collected at the scene would quickly eat through anything but the very few materials impervious to it, and gas released when it was exposed to air could kill within minutes.

She had been very fortunate to have missed any more exposure in the tunnel beneath the jobsite.

He glanced her way. She was only half listening. She was inhaling more oxygen and staring at some pictures of upturned rebar rods. They were rusty, but two were darker. Dried blood.

The operator must have landed on these when he fell from the sky.

Rhyme nodded at another one of her pictures on the monitor, depicting the counterweight trolley. The acid delivery device was a smoking discolored blob.

"Damn it. He got it up there *somehow*. The top of the crane.

We'll have to work on that. Once it was in place, how was it activated?"

"The detonator," Cooper said, holding up another clear plastic container. Inside was what appeared to be a small board of solid-state electronics, also deformed and charred by the acid. He was speaking with the respirator on, through the attached mike.

"Small charge, probably just pulled open a half-dozen big-caliber rounds for the gunpowder."

"Antenna?"

"Hard to say."

Rhyme grumbled, "Of *course* it's hard to say. It's melted into oblivion. But if you had to *guess*."

"Not remote. Timed."

As Rhyme had figured. "Is it off the shelf?"

"No. Homemade."

So, impossible to trace.

"How much acid?"

Cooper shrugged. "At this concentration, two liters. Maybe three."

Sachs coughed, a snapping, painful sound. She discreetly lifted a tissue to her mouth once more. A fast glance. With yet another bout of irritation, she stuffed the wad away in her jeans pocket. A hit of oxygen, then she said, "He knew what he was doing. He'd have to calculate how much weight he'd need to remove from the counterweights to make the crane unstable. There's this thing the foreman was telling me about. Moment. It's—"

Rhyme said, "Moment equals force times distance. Expressed in units of newton-meters."

Sellitto was nodding. "So he's got a degree in engineering. Put that on the chart."

"No," Rhyme said dryly. "Put down that he stayed awake in high school science class. Everybody knows that formula."

Lon Sellitto rolled his eyes. "No, not *everybody* . . . But there *is* one thing we do know."

Rhyme and Sachs looked toward the detective.

"He's in good shape. Climbing that."

"No elevator?"

"No," Sachs said. "Ladders." She walked to the diagram the foreman had provided to Sellitto—a side view of the crane before it fell—and tapped various places as she spoke. "Up here, he got into the slewing room, where the turntable is. Then up another ladder to go out onto the top, then down another ladder to the jib on the back."

Rhyme could see a flat walkway that ran to the rear. It ended at a three-foot-high barrier, on the other side of which was the counterweight trolley. Up to that point were handrails and cables so workers could hook on as fall protection. But beyond that he'd have to tightrope walk—or crawl—along a narrow track two hundred feet in the air to get to the counterweights.

He *really* would have wanted this crane to come down, going to that risk and effort.

Rhyme repeated his earlier comment. "We need to source the acid."

Sachs said, "I'll get some people at the lab in Queens on it."

"Tell them to look for suppliers who sell thirty-two percent or higher concentrations. You can dilute it, but you can't make it more concentrated, not without a lot of time and effort."

She placed the call, and after some deep inhalations, began a conversation with an officer on the other end of the line. Mel Cooper continued to examine the evidence that Sachs and the technicians had collected. Cooper called out the results, which were discouraging. The soil samples from the routes the unsub probably took to get to the crane tower base all matched the dirt throughout the jobsite. What they wanted was soil that *didn't* match, which meant it might, possibly, have been left by the unsub and, if unique and traceable, could lead to his house or hideout.

After Sachs disconnected her call, she asked, "The videos you've been going through? Anything?"

Rhyme scoffed. "Nothing. The damn cameras all point down, ground level."

The security system was meant to capture thieves, not acrobats sabotaging equipment in the sky above the jobsite.

He glanced at a digital wall clock. Twenty-two hours till the next crane came down.

On one of the murder boards was a map of New York—all five boroughs. The city's construction permits department had provided a list of all the tower cranes presently in use. Thom had helped out by marking them with red X's.

Which of these would be next?

Sellitto received a text. He looked at the screen. "Crap. It's the mayor. He wants an update."

"You've been here the whole time, Lon. We've learned that the unsub uses acid whose source we have no clue about yet, that he didn't leave any discernable body or other trace at the scene. We're in the dark completely about race, age and build—other than that he's got strong legs and a good sense of balance."

"Then I'll tell the mayor that. They just need a bone." He read another missive and said, "Hoped that announcing it was intentional might bring out some witnesses. But nobody's come forward."

Not a surprise.

"And where's Ron?" Rhyme asked, his voice edgy. "We need him here. Isn't he done with the homicide scene yet? How long could it take?"

Though even as he asked the question he was aware of what he told his students. *You search until there's nothing left to search for. One hour, ten, seventy-two.*

"Turns out there's a little more to it. The kid's got a big win. He may've linked it to Eddie Tarr."

Well, this was interesting. The Dublin-born former industrial engineer who put his considerable skills to work making clever devices that destroyed the structures that equally clever men and women designed and built. Wanted in dozens of jurisdictions, the careful and reclusive Tarr reportedly lived off the grid somewhere in the Northwest. Was he here for a job or to collect in-person payment?

"He'll be here, but I know he wants to run down a lead or two on Tarr."

Rhyme and Sachs shared a look. He could see that she too was happy for their protégé. With this, the brass would be taking notice of him.

Rhyme's phone hummed. It was Lyle Spencer, who'd been following up with the feds on the housing terrorists and the demands they'd made.

"Lyle."

"Lincoln. I have something on the crane case. I can't find anything about the Kommunalka Project. Not through NCIS, Homeland, the Bureau. I even checked with the CIA and NSA about traffic including the name. Zip. Even at their Russia desk.

"But there's software now, websites, where professors can check to see if students have plagiarized papers or had an AI system, like ChatGPT, write the stuff for them. I plugged their letter to the mayor into the web, and some language from a few years ago got returned. The Kommunalkas lifted it verbatim from blog posts by somebody advocating for affordable housing. And this guy was arrested for political protests and vandalism."

Good thinking on Spencer's part. Now the equally important question: "Any chance we can find him?"

"Oh, a pretty good one." Spencer sounded amused. "It's Stephen Cody."

"No shit," Sellitto muttered.

"And that would be?" Rhyme asked impatiently.

A pause, probably suggesting a measure of disbelief. "The U.S. representative."

Like sports, politics was irrelevant to Rhyme, unless the subject came up in an investigation, and it rarely did. "Never heard of him."

"Really? He represents your district, Lincoln. In fact, his office is right around the corner from you."

• • •

"I'm Amber Andrews with the midday business report. The stock market continued its slide into negative territory after terrorists claimed credit for the collapse of a construction crane on New York's Upper East Side, resulting in two deaths and a half-dozen injuries. The real estate market as well is predicted to slump, with commercial and residential developers closing down jobsites, since more attacks are threatened. The group, the Kommunalka Project, is demanding the city create more affordable housing and approve fewer permits for luxury high-rises, like the one sabotaged today on Eighty-Ninth Street. The police and federal authorities are investigating. Residents are being asked to avoid any construction sites with cranes."

12.

HE WAS BACKSTAGE.

All two hundred and forty pounds of him.

Standing with arms crossed over his massive chest, he kept returning to the question: Was the man he was looking at a killer?

Lyle Spencer was listening, somewhat, to the words from the stage. The debate was within his range of vision, forty feet away, but he was experiencing the event on a monitor. You could see the expressions better this way. Lyle Spencer liked expressions, he liked angles of heads, enfolded or dangling arms, hands making fists, hands splayed. As for legs, he liked legs still and legs tapping.

He really liked tapping legs.

In this instance, the kinesic analysis—body language—was tricky. The truth, he suspected, was in camo, as the debate was between two politicians.

Spencer leaned toward the monitor. A man was debating a woman, who was giving her closing argument. Spencer paid no attention to her. He continued to study her opponent, who was on the right of the stage to the audience. Tall, with a build like the former football player that he was (Spencer had done his homework—always). He wore dark slacks and a blue business shirt with sleeves rolled up. No tie. Thick black hair, tousled intentionally, Spencer was sure. He seemed good at cultivating a Look.

Ah, looking earnest and thoughtful.

But was he a killer?

Unlikely, but hardly impossible. When Spencer was upstate, he'd collared murderous grandmothers and kindergarten teachers and a particularly bad minister. They were pictures of innocence. You never really knew until you started digging. And began checking out evasive eyes and, yes, tapping legs.

The site of this verbal fencing match was an august performing arts center on Manhattan's Upper East Side. Onstage were the candidates for U.S. representative for a district that embraced parts of Manhattan and the Bronx: the incumbent, Stephen Cody—the man Lincoln Rhyme had never heard of—and the challenger, a Manhattan businesswoman in her fifties, Marie Whitman Leppert.

Cody jotted a note.

Killer? Not a killer?

Well . . .

That minister had tortured his victims, killed them and then went upstairs to write sermons that were both poetic and inspirational. Love thy neighbor was a theme. They were quite good.

Applause signaled the end of the opponent's concluding remarks. Spencer knew little about the woman.

The moderator, a white-haired, red-frocked woman from public broadcasting, said, "Last word to you, Representative Cody. You have one minute."

"Thank you, Margaret. And thanks to everyone at the Ninety-Second Street Y for hosting this event." He paused. Dramatic. "Now, this afternoon was supposed to be a debate. That, to me, means give-and-take and addressing one participant's position with an opposing one. But all I heard was attack, attack, attack.

My opponent was quick to point out what she claimed were problems with my proposals. But did she address the dangers and injustices that those proposals are meant to cure? No."

He turned to the other podium. Close-up, his eyes were fervent. "You attacked my climate change plans but didn't offer any alternatives—even though, like I proved, according to the experts, half of New York City will be underwater by the end of the century. You—"

The opponent apparently couldn't restrain herself. "The way you'd pay for it is pure fantasy and—"

"Ms. Leppert. This is Representative Cody's final statement."

"You were happy to tear down my proposal for creating a path to citizenship, but said nothing about how *you* would help the millions of hardworking individuals who came to this country—like your and my ancestors did—to escape oppression and find opportunity for their families. You questioned my plan for free or subsidized tuition for community or four-year college if the students agree to work programs after graduation that benefit society. You said nothing about addressing the obscene wealth disparity like I did, with my three-point tax plan—"

"Which robs the middle class."

"Please, Ms. Leppert."

"My opponent talks about her law-and-order record, spending years as a federal prosecutor in Texas jailing cartel members. And I give her credit for that. God bless her for her service. But that job did not prepare her one bit for the problems we face here: throwing first-time offenders for minor drug misdemeanors in prison—"

"Time, Representative Cody."

"—effectively ruining their lives. Now, on—"

"Representative?"

"On my website, you'll be able to see in clear, specific detail what my proposals are, which I've only been able to sketch out in broad brushes this afternoon. They'll help everyone—bus drivers and deli counter-people and nurses and businessmen and -women. And if you honor me with reelection, I pledge that I will tirelessly fight to make each and every one of those proposals a reality. Thank you."

Applause—somewhat louder than for the opponent, though Spencer wasn't sure. He suspected that most of the audience members were by now thinking of where to go afterward for tea or alcohol.

The debaters shook the moderator's hand. Leppert walked backstage first, passing by Spencer with no reaction to his presence, and began speaking with a young female assistant, who gushed about her performance in a sycophantic way that Spencer deduced irritated the candidate. Probably soon to be replaced.

After a brief conversation with the moderator, Cody entered the dim, matte-black space behind the stage. He was about as tall as Spencer, well over six feet, but weighed forty or so pounds less. Now that the two politicos were freed of the constraints of behaving in front of an audience, would fur fly in a big way?

But no.

"Got me good there," Leppert said with a cheerful frown. "Didn't have my Post Toasties in order on HB three seventeen."

"Eh. If you had, I'd've gone down in flames. Took a chance. How's Emily?"

"Healed nicely. Thanks." Leppert grimaced. "Out for the season, though."

"That'll hurt more than the wild pitch."

"Already filling up her schedule with other stuff—which means *my* schedule. As chauffeur." Leppert declined the makeup wipe from the intense assistant; a glance in the mirror apparently told her that she'd keep the paint job the pros had done. She picked up a Coach backpack, removed a diamond necklace and ring, and placed them around her neck and on her finger. She had ditched the posh accessories for the debate, and kept fixed the collar button on her blouse, which she now undid.

She had a Look too.

The conversation rolled into the absent pleasantries of a chance cocktail party encounter.

The businesswoman offered a breezy "See you at the breakfast Tuesday."

"Stab me with a stick," Cody muttered as she vanished out the door.

Then he turned to Spencer. Cody *did* snag a makeup wipe and went to work. "Wasn't sure who you were here to see. I guess I win. Who're you with?"

A flash of Spencer's badge.

The representative rolled down his sleeves, pulled on a jacket. He nodded after Leppert. "Did you hear her say 'Thank you' at the end?"

"I wasn't paying attention."

"I wasn't either. I don't think she did, but *I* did. In public speaking, you're not supposed to thank your audience. You're doing the audience a favor by appearing. They should thank *you*. I keep forgetting." He grimaced. "I get riled up."

"You both thanked the moderator."

"You *have* to thank the moderator. Even the bad ones."

"A close race?"

"I'm way ahead in the polls, but it ain't over till, et cetera. Marie's got some momentum. Devoted following. She's not rags to riches. More JCPenney to riches and she earned it herself, and she really did put cartel punks away. All right. What can I do for you, Detective?" From a case, he removed eyeglasses with bright red frames, replacing the black, apparently believing the midday audience would prefer a more studious and less stylish candidate.

"You study public speaking?"

"Not study. Debate club. Moot court."

"How many of these do you do a year?"

"Maybe a dozen."

"You know the crane incident?"

"Of course. Terrible. My colleague was on the scene. His district. They're saying it's intentional. Sabotage."

"That's right."

"Domestic terrorism?"

Spencer nodded.

Cody said, "Right wing? Neo-Nazis? Racists? Plenty of those around, but people forget that the left have been pretty fast doing the bad stuff too. A horse-drawn cart blew up in front of J.P. Morgan in 1920, killing thirty-eight. Anarchists were suspected."

"This is about affordable housing."

Cody received a text, read, sent a brief reply. He looked up. "Housing."

Spencer continued, "That's one of your issues. I saw it on your website."

"A serious problem, housing. Who are these people?"

"They're calling themselves the Kommunalka Project, after a public housing plan in Soviet Russia."

"Never heard of them."

Spencer watched eyes, hands, legs. The trick in kinesic analysis is to get a baseline—how one behaves when telling known truths—compared to behavior when asked investigative questions. Hence, Spencer asking him about his history of debating—to which he knew the answers. Now he was looking for deviation.

"Either they're new or they're deep underground. We can't find them. And they're only communicating via the dark web."

"What was their point with the crane?"

"Extortion. They're demanding the city turn a couple dozen old buildings into housing units."

"And if not? More cranes?"

"That's right."

"Sick." Then he was nodding. "All right. Detective, let's get to it. That's why you're here. I have a history of housing activism. And an arrest record, as you probably know. But that wasn't for housing. It was environmental."

"You vandalized a planning and zoning board office and a corporation accused of polluting an upstate river. You chained yourself to the gate of an oil depot construction job in Brooklyn."

"Didn't have to search very far for that. It's on my website. And there's nothing in the Constitution that prevents a criminal from holding office." A chuckle. "Some would say it's a prerequisite. You think I'm involved in this. Though I can't help but notice you still have your handcuffs tucked away."

"I read transcripts of your last three speeches. You don't mention affordable housing once."

"Like I'm trying to distance myself from the Kommunalka-ists."

"That's the impression." He added, "In their note, making the demand for the housing, they used a quotation from you."

"Ah. That's it."

"'The city is the largest landowner in the area. It holds three hundred and seventy million square feet of property and its obsene how little of that is devouted to affordable housing.'"

"'Devouted'? Didn't read my statement *that* carefully, I guess."

"And they misspelled 'it's' and 'obscene.'"

Cody asked, "How'd you find it?"

"A cheating website."

He frowned. "Ashley Madison? That dating thing for married men?"

Spencer had to laugh. "Cheating on term papers. A professor uploads a student's work and the software looks for previous published writing to see if he stole any of it. Or if a chatbot wrote it."

Cody nodded. "I used ChatGPT to write a speech for me. It wasn't bad."

A large, somber man wearing a black suit stepped into the area. "Sir. The Alliance?"

"I'll be right down." The makeup was nearly gone. Cody examined his face, wet a paper towel and finished the job. "Detective, have to ask: Using one's own public quotation in an extortion note? Doesn't that seem pretty stupid?"

Spencer shrugged. "Are you in touch with affordable housing activists? From your website's position paper, I'd think you have to be."

"You want me to ask about this group?"

"Would you?"

"I will."

Spencer handed him a card. The politician pocketed it.

Cody said, "When did you get here today?"

"Twenty-five minutes ago. Thirty."

"So you missed my pledge to introduce federal legislation that would guarantee affordable housing to families making fifty thousand a year or less."

Oh.

"I'm not avoiding the issue, Detective. I guess what I'd say is: so many problems, so little time."

13.

"WATCH THAT PHALANX."

Ron Pulaski waited, tilting his head slightly.

Lon Sellitto explained by pointing. A flock or a gaggle—or, apparently, a *phalanx*—of pigeons was headed their way fast. A naïve—some would say idiotic—tourist was tossing seed on the ground nearby.

They were in the square outside of One PP, where they'd met, and were on their way to Maggie's, a New York diner in the old-school mold. A feeding trough for cops.

"What is a phalanx, exactly?" the younger officer asked as the two continued along the sidewalk.

"Greek for 'shitload.'"

"If I'm ever on *Jeopardy!* that might help."

"Rachel and me? We play trivia. We compete. A bar. You?"

"No."

Sellitto pushed the door open. "Keeps your mind active. Until you have a beer. Then it deactivates."

They got a booth and Sellitto pulled off his wrinkled brown raincoat, revealing a wrinkled brown suit.

Pulaski couldn't help but think of the fine suit—pressed flat as a tabletop—that stock trader Fletcher Dalton had died in.

And where the hell was the green-eyed, red-headed bomb maker who had ended his life?

A shitload of red cars in Jersey . . .

The beige-uniformed waitress approached.

"Lon, Ron. It's the younger -on and the older -on. See, I said older. Not old, Lon."

"You're a dear, Tally."

Forever armed with a coffeepot, she poured two mugs without their asking. If you didn't drink coffee, you didn't come to Maggie's.

"Anything else?"

Muffin for older -on. Younger picked a grilled cheese sandwich.

"So, you do trivia. What does phalanx *really* mean?"

"No clue. So." Sellitto lifted a palm. "Good job with the lead to Tarr. They're over the moon about it, the task force. Which, by the way, is something else I don't get. *Over the moon,* I mean."

A massive corn muffin arrived. Pulaski recalled Sellitto had said that corn muffins weren't as bad for you because they didn't have the sugar that blueberry had. And corn was nutritious. Pulaski didn't know enough to dispute or agree. And why do so anyway? Everybody loved corn muffins.

The sandwich landed too. A lot of cheese. Pulaski took a bite.

Sellitto asked, "How'd you do it? With Tarr? I never heard."

Pulaski explained about the blue fiber and the DAS footage.

"Damn." Sellitto laughed out loud.

The younger officer frowned. "I keep checking the intel sheet for IED chatter or jobs in New York. Threat assessment's the same as it's been all month."

"You're on intel? You got clearance?"

"Yeah."

"When?" Sellitto was impressed.

"I don't know," Pulaski replied after another bite of the imposing sandwich. "Six, eight months ago. Was a hassle. Man, they look
into everything. Talk to your friends, family. Polygraph. Thought
they were going to ask me if I was a Yankees fan. And the truth'd
come out. I'd be busted."

The detective laughed.

Odd, Pulaski was thinking: It seemed Sellitto'd been paying
close attention to him. Really close. Studying him, sort of. This
wasn't uncomfortable, but was on the line.

The younger officer continued, "I checked some folks who
might be Tarr's potential customers. There's that militia outfit.
Those assholes from Westchester? They don't like the governor. So maybe they hired him."

Sellitto was now concentrating. "I don't know about that one.
How can they afford Tarr? I hear he's expensive as hell."

"Right, makes me think it's not them. They're strip mall, and
Tarr is galleria." A shrug. "There's talk of a turf war, M-42s against
that Jamaican crew, in Spanish Harlem."

"Naw, they shoot, they don't blow up."

Pulaski considered this. "I guess so. I talked to ATF and they're
looking into chatter. Might be hard to find anything, though. At
his level, you know. He's careful."

With all the data snooping nowadays, the smart bad guys were
increasingly using handwritten notes and in-person meetings to
communicate and pay for services. That philosophy extended bin
Laden's life for over a decade. And wire transfers, crypto and even
cash were out—too traceable. Diamonds and gold were becoming
the preferred form of wages.

"So," Pulaski said, "I'll hit all the trace I found where that red
car was. And canvass the scene again."

Back to the sandwich. The thing about grilled cheese is that the fourth bite isn't as much fun as the first, and it goes downhill from there. Too much of the same.

More coffee arrived. It really was the best in the city.

Sellitto sipped. "Ow. Hot, careful."

Somber now, the detective asked, "Ron, any chance Tarr or somebody could place you on the scene? Well, either of them—the basement scene, or the street where you tipped to the red car?"

"Maybe. But the hit was two days ago. Why would Tarr come back today?"

Of course, if Tarr was keeping tabs on the warehouse, it wouldn't be impossible to find the lead officer on the case.

"Well, keep looking over your shoulder. Now," he said, moving on, "the crane thing. Linc and Amelia want you on it."

"I'll juggle. I'll get up there right after this."

And that word, "this," was intentional, because it signified that Pulaski knew the lunch was about something other than lunch and he was impatient to hear what.

The detective got it and pushed the corpse of the muffin away, a surprising gesture; food—especially pastries—were meant to be finished in Lon Sellitto's world. His eyes were suddenly evasive.

"Okay. Here's the thing . . . You know, things happen sometimes."

Pulaski nodded, not so much in agreement with the detective's pretty much meaningless comment, but solely to encourage the man to get to the point.

"Nothing really lasts forever." This pronouncement was equally solemn.

And ambiguous.

What was this about? Pulaski was suddenly alarmed. Sellitto wasn't getting divorced, because he and Rachel weren't married. They could be breaking up, but the detective and he weren't so close they'd talk about it.

Anything else he might be talking about? Retiring? Couldn't imagine that. Sellitto as a security guard? Fishing? Playing bocce? Ha!

"You know we got the biggest crime scene operation in the country, after the Bureau?"

"Sure."

"Only, we got something that makes it special. It's Lincoln that sets us apart. And I don't just mean he's sharp. Naw, it's that he's independent. No politics, no squabbling, no game playing. He runs a case, gets the evidence, presents the evidence, and not a single goddamn other thing matters."

Pulaski felt his heart beating faster than it had a moment ago. *Nothing really lasts forever . . .*

"We gotta keep that . . . What would you call it? That *model*, you know? Keep it intact."

"Detective?"

Yes, there was bomb maker Tarr to catch and there was a crane killer to stop. But mostly Pulaski needed the man to spit out what he was afraid was coming next.

Maybe the man detected the concern in his eyes. "This isn't about anything more than a question. There's nothing I know, okay? But . . . If anything was to happen to Lincoln, could you take over?"

"What do you know?"

"Nothing. I mean it. All, what do you say, hypothetical."

"He's not sick?"

"Naw, what I said—nothing I've heard. It's just we want to know we can maintain what he's got going. This's been talked about upstairs. We've looked at your record, your reports, your wins."

A pause. "I had that . . . thing. A few years ago."

"We know about it."

He said nothing more about the subject.

Which Ron Pulaski thought about at least once a day.

Then Sellitto was on to pitching his case again.

"You think like Lincoln, you act like him." A faint laugh. "And you're not a prick."

Which might have been comparing him to some individuals in the NYPD—but definitely was comparing him to Lincoln Rhyme, who, occasionally, was.

Pulaski: "Lincoln's a civilian. I don't want to quit."

"Naw, you'll be blue. Payroll, benees, everything. It's just you'll have, what's the word? Autonomy. Completely independent. Like him. You keep your rank." He scowled. "And can get your gold. If you ever schedule the damn test."

"Been meaning to." He had always wanted to be a detective, but studying for the test took time he rarely had.

"You'll keep your years in, everything."

Tally swooped in with the coffee. Sellitto shook his head. Pulaski did as well. And like a skipping stone, she was on to other patrons.

After a moment, Sellitto said, "You thinking this is going on behind his back, Linc's? No. It was him brought it up."

"He did?" Almost a whisper. "What about Amelia?"

A pause. "Her too. We all talked about it."

"Why wouldn't she take over?"

"Not her thing. She walks the grid great; you know that. You'd want her with you in a firefight or a high-speed chase. We want a thinking cop. Subway stations and blue fibers and DAS and red sedans. All right, I said my piece." He frowned. "Is it p-i-e-c-e or p-e-a-c-e?"

"No clue."

"Do you care?"

Pulaski shrugged. "Not unless some terrorist wrote it in a manifesto and it'll help nail his ass."

Sellitto gave a big smile, as rare for him as leaving a half-eaten muffin.

He waved for the check and he paid.

The men stepped outside and Pulaski looked up. No birds in phalanxes or other formations. Just a few solitary pigeons and a lone gull.

After a moment, Pulaski turned. "Don't like to think about anything happening to Lincoln, Lieutenant. But if it does, or he retires, or whatever, yeah, I'm in."

Then something happened that had not occurred in all the years the men had known each other. Sellitto stuck out his paw of a hand and gripped Pulaski's, and they shook firmly.

"Why don't we make it 'Lon' at this point."

14.

THE THING SOARED above her and she thought: Reminds me of something. What?

From years ago. When I was a kid.

At a fast glance, the crane resembled a creature from one of those Transformers movies. But it wasn't that. She wasn't much of a moviegoer. Something else.

A huge American flag was attached to the crosspiece, two hundred feet up, and it flapped madly, snapping and fluttering.

She frowned. Was the whole boom thing swinging back and forth?

Yes.

Interesting.

Like a weather vane, it rotated slowly so that the massive crosspiece faced into today's steady breeze. This happened automatically, it seemed. The mechanism apparently loose. No one was in the cab. In fact, no one was in the jobsite, other than a few men at the entrance. Guards. The mayor had ordered all construction sites shut down until the terrorists were captured.

Could it be this one is targeted next? Simone wondered, recalling the deadline was ten tomorrow morning.

Looking up once more.

And what *did* it remind her of?

She was close, but the memory remained elusive.

She turned her attention back to what she'd just unloaded from the rental van. A half-dozen open-top boxes containing packets and canisters and jars and other smaller appliances. Sealed cartons. A heavy box, on whose side were the words: "Kitchen-Aid Bread Maker Deluxe." These sat on the sidewalk beside the van.

This was a familiar sight. She came to the city infrequently, but one observation she'd made was the many moving boxes stationed in front of apartments and town houses throughout the city, waiting for Allied Van Lines, for Mayflower, for brothers-in-law, for sorority sisters to assist in a relocation.

Some people would be moving up. Others, hard with luck, down. Some out of the five boroughs altogether. New York City can gut you, she supposed.

Simone lugged the hand truck from the back. It dropped to the concrete with a clang. She shoved the lip of the cart under the big appliance and strapped it to the back with a canvas tie-down. She began rolling it toward Number 744. This unit was identical to the other structures on this largely deserted avenue on the far West Side. A former industrial block, it was now filled with empty lofts, raw space. Seven Forty-Four was 2,200 square feet of beautiful, ancient oak floors, a working toilet and sink, an overhead bank of lights and zero else.

"Hey, neighbor."

She turned to find herself looking at a man in his late twenties walking slowly down the stairs of the structure next door to hers.

He was handsome, with sculpted features, thick hair rising confidently skyward, a popular look. Jeans and a T that said something, but had been through the wash a dozen too many times for legibility.

"Hi." A smile. One of her more *entrancing* features, she'd been told. She looked past him to his apartment. "The broker told me none of the other places on the street were rented yet."

"Well, here I am. Your lucky day." Not quite a flirt. He was being cute. His voice suggested he'd been raised in New England.

He flexed and unflexed his right hand. He seemed born to team sports. "Moving day. Cool."

"Just a few things I had at my old place. Uptown. The big push is next weekend."

He subtly examined the blond hair, twined into a perfect braid, the lengthy fingers (bearing no jewelry), the trim figure—though with hips a touch more ample than she, on a bad day, would have liked. He would get nowhere in a scan of any other part of the physique, as she sensed he was inclined to do; she was covered from waist to neck with an excessively large, deep blue Royals sweatshirt. He settled for her heart-shaped face. One of Simone's avocations was poetry, writing as well as reading, and there was certainly an element about her that suggested a demure Elizabethan literata from England's Lake District. Mary Shelley, Annabella Byron . . . She nurtured the look.

Even in the sweats she was a shining lamp for men like this one, particularly those a bit younger than her. And he hovered close, right on the edge of that invisible but well-defined comfort perimeter that surrounds us.

He looked up at the building she was parked in front of. "Yours raw too?"

"Empty as a . . ." A laugh. The poet within her failed at simile. "As Shea Stadium in October."

Sports, right. That's what she got for wearing a team sweatshirt.

He became the enthusiastic tour guide. "Up the street, the corner, there's Chinese. It's okay. Nothing to write home about. Next to it there's a deli, Mideastern. And two Indian places."

Her eyes revealed interest. "I love Indian. I dated somebody from New Delhi. That man could cook."

Orientation had been established, pleasing him no end. As did the fact that the boyfriend was affixed to a past-tense verb.

"How 'bout a gym?" she asked.

"You totally work out," he said. An excuse to scan her, top to toe. "Yeah, not bad. . . . Health club, I mean."

She gave no response to the unwieldy flirt, and he continued, "When're you going to start the buildout?"

"Getting estimates. You?"

"Three, four weeks. Lemme help."

"You don't have to. Seriously."

He assumed a grave look. "I'm afraid I'll have to insist."

"What're you, a lawyer?"

"Broker."

She frowned. "Do they do much insisting?"

"What we do for a living. You can't say no to a broker."

"Just be careful, please."

He took over on the handcart and rolled it, step by step, up the stairs—yes, carefully. Simone carried boxes up behind him. At the top, she unlocked the door and swung it open. She followed him inside.

"So you bake?" A nod at the big box.

"Hobby."

"An attractive neighbor who bakes. Jackpot!" He looked around, taking in the scabby walls, the soot-covered ceilings, a rusty metal pillar. "You got some work ahead of you." Pointing to a patch of green on the floor. "Watch the mold."

"I have somebody coming. First call I made."

"I can picture it now. You totally have to put your bed there."
He pointed to a corner.

"That could work."

Did he give her a slightly coy smile?

She locked up and they returned to the van.

"You heard about those attacks?" he asked, looking up at the crane.

And what *did* it remind her of?

"Yeah. Scary. Terrorists or something?"

"Assholes."

She frowned. "If it was going to fall, would it come this way?"

He studied it. "I don't think so. But, you know, the next attack's supposed to be tomorrow morning."

"I heard. Ten o'clock."

"They might have some other shit planned too." As he gazed upward, he was doing some fast calculations. "You want, just going to throw this out. You want, maybe we could maybe get out of town for the day. I've got a BMW. M8. Ragtop. It's sweet." His eyes glowed.

She smiled at the nice try. "Rain check?"

"Deal."

Simone said, "Beer?"

He blinked.

"Sure."

She supposed he was thinking bar, but she walked to the back of the van and climbed in. He followed into the dim space. They were both ducking. A cooler was behind the driver's seat, bungee-corded down. She dug through it and handed him one.

"Woman after my own heart."

They twisted the tops off and they drank.

He downed half of his right away, which was good. It took only seconds for the drugs to hit him. He dropped the bottle to the bed of the truck, convulsed for a few minutes and then lay still.

Pulling on latex gloves she slipped his bottle into a trash bag and mopped up the laced beer with paper towels. This went inside too, along with her open but still full bottle.

Simone never drank on a job.

She climbed out. Before drugging him, she'd scanned to make sure no one was present. That was still true.

Ah. She gave a fast smile.

She had her answer.

A praying mantis.

That's what the crane reminded her of. One summer, she'd discovered a creature on a railing of her family's back porch. It was largely motionless, but swayed ever so slightly when ants wandered past filled with their driven but unknowable ant purpose.

She then closed the door of the van and walked to the driver's side, climbed in. A look at her watch. She had a flirtatious neighbor to dispose of, and a vehicle to burn down to the rims. She'd have to leave now to get to the meeting on time.

15.

Explosives, gasoline, poisons, and gunpowder are like fingerprints. Unique. Each sample discovered at a crime scene has characteristics that can lead directly back to a place of manufacture or sale, wholesale if not retail. And at that location, you might just find a portal to your unsub . . .

A passage from a chapter in Rhyme's book on forensic analysis in which he discussed tracing substances by studying chemical composition. He went on to give an example. Gasoline.

It is around five percent alkanes; three percent alkenes; twenty-five percent isoalkanes; four percent cycloalkenes; twenty to fifty percent total aromatics. Then there are the additives: blending agents—anti-knock substances, antioxidants, metal deactivators, lead scavengers, upper-cylinder lubricants, detergents and dyes—there are literally a thousand different substances in any particular brand of gasoline.

Unique . . .

Not so with the substance that Unsub 89 was using to bring down the city's cranes.

Hydrofluoric acid contains hydrogen and fluoride. And, when diluted, water. No garnish.

If there was anything that might guide their search for a source, it was the concentration.

Yet even that qualifier was not paying off.

The canvassers in Queens, along with Cooper and Sachs, had found eighteen companies in the tri-state area that sold the chemical in the rich concentration of the substance their unsub had used.

She cleared her throat yet again, glanced toward the oxygen, but decided against it. Rhyme was keeping an eye on her. HF exposure through the lungs, as he'd told those in the parlor not long ago, acts more immediately than through the skin. But that's not to say that there wasn't a residue of the acid slowly working its way through the small tubes of bronchi and the even tinier bronchioles.

"Sachs? Did they X-ray?"

"No."

Of course they wouldn't, not in the field . . . But that wasn't really the meaning of his question. He was asking her if it wouldn't be better to go into the ER and *get* one done in radiology.

She turned her attention back to the phone.

"Found two more suppliers," Cooper called from the other side of the glass partition. He recited the names and addresses, and Sachs recorded them elegantly on the murder board.

Nineteen, twenty . . .

Wonderful, thought Rhyme, in his most sardonic mode.

And then too, he reflected, even if they found the supplier, the perp would've taken precautions to hide his identity, paying cash.

Soon the tally hit thirty-seven and finally stalled.

Rhyme said, "Didn't know it was *that* common."

In the sterile portion of the parlor, Cooper, reading from one of the most reliable sources in law enforcement—Google—said, "It's one of the fastest-growing industrial products on the market." He went on to explain that the demand for HF acid rose about ten percent a year and would soon top a billion dollars in revenue. "It's used for more things than you'd think. Etching, cleaning, refining gas, making Teflon and fluoxetine—Prozac. You ever get depressed, Lincoln?"

"No time."

"To get depressed?"

"No time for your trade association's up-with-HF spiel."

So it was as impossible to isolate a source of the acid as it was to source an unregistered Smith & Wesson on the street.

He scanned the chart. Albert Industrial Products to Zeigler Chemicals . . .

Hell.

Rhyme took a call from Lyle Spencer.

"Lincoln."

"What did you find out about the politician that I should know everything about but do not?"

The man gave a brief laugh. "I'm convinced Representative Cody didn't have anything to do with it. The Kommunalka Project just dug up a statement from a paper he wrote years ago. His body language? It told me that the attack was a surprise to him."

Unlike witnesses' observations and psychological profiling, kinesic analysis done by an expert was more or less reliable, Rhyme felt. A colleague in California, Kathryn Dance, working for the CBI, had proven to him on several occasions that techniques were reliable in painting interrogees credible or not.

So, the congressman was off the persons-of-interest list.

Spencer continued, "He said he's never heard of any violent side to the affordable housing movement. But he knows activists. He's going to contact them."

"All right," Rhyme muttered. Another dead end. Or at least a badly wounded one.

After they disconnected, Sachs wrote the detective's conclusions on the whiteboard, then took a call. "Detective Sachs . . . That's right . . ."

Rhyme's eyes strayed out the window. From this narrow view alone, he could see three cranes lording over the East Side, all motionless. The stillness was eerie.

Sachs tucked her phone away and, after a blast of oxygen, said, "Downtown. Maybe a witness from the jobsite. I'm going to talk to him." After another blast of oxygen, she pulled on her black leather jacket and walked into the front hall. A pause. She returned and, without a word to or glance at anyone else, grabbed the tank and hurried outside. A moment later, Rhyme heard her car's throaty engine fire up. The gruff sound reminded him of her voice, with the acid exposure.

The sound had just disappeared when Rhyme's phone sounded. It was Sellitto.

"Lon."

"Gotta tell you, Linc. Just heard."

"Another one? A crane?"

The deadline in the demand was tomorrow, but extortionists and kidnappers are known to improvise.

"No. It's Andy Gilligan. He's dead. Shot."

Rhyme and Mel Cooper shared a glance.

"Details?"

"Could be a pro job. Double tap, chest, then face. Vacant lot, Lower East Side."

"What was he doing there?"

"No idea. Supervisor doesn't know either. No wits and the respondings said his wallet, cash and car keys—to a new Lexus—were on him. The car was there too."

"And his caseload?"

"Some minor OC stuff. A jacking or two. Some missing shipping containers. Then what we're working together: Structures and Engineering."

"Where's Pulaski?"

"He's on his way to you right now."

"Text me the address of the Gilligan scene. Pulaski too."

"You got it. Oh, and Linc. I talked with Ron about what you and me were saying? He's okay with it."

"Good to know."

The men disconnected and Rhyme ordered his phone to call Pulaski.

One ring later: "Lincoln. I'm on my way—"

"There's a scene I need you to run. Lon's texting you the address."

"The crane case?"

"No. It's Andy Gilligan. Looks like a professional tap."

The officer was silent. "Kind of a coincidence . . ."

"What is?"

"The DSE theft—documents about the city's infrastructure. Maybe Unsub 89's the shooter. He wanted the files for the crane attacks. Gilligan got a lead and Eighty-Nine tipped to him, took him out. What do you think?"

"Only one way to find out."

"Run the scene."

"Call in with what you find."

16.

"MOVE ALONG THERE."

An easy job.

Guard duty, basically, but even easier.

Guarding something nobody would want.

Dennis Chung, a twenty-eight-year-old patrol officer out of a neighboring precinct house, had been one of the uniforms picked to keep an eye on the wreckage at the jobsite on 89th Street.

In regulation blues and a wool jacket, the slim, fit officer was standing near the police-line tape at the north side of the site. The crane had fallen in this direction and taken out all the fencing, two bulldozers, two flatbeds and a shitload of supply pallets. Plaster and concrete dust were everywhere.

Chung's job was easy, yes, but he still had to be on top of his game. The nobody-would-want part referred to the fact that all the valuable supplies that thieves might walk off with had been secured on the other side of the site, near the main entrance. If you were inclined to perp a sheet of plasterboard or two, you could find some here, but why risk getting collared for what you could get at Home Depot for twenty bucks?

"Move along, please."

The real risk was one that wouldn't have existed twenty years ago: selfies.

And apparently—he wasn't into social media—it was popular to get them at the sites of disasters. And the closer to the wreckage you got, the better. Nobody cared about the police tape. The *Do Not Cross* words in stark black type apparently translated to "Come on in and take all the pix you want."

So, he wasn't stopping thievery; he was saving people's hides. Most of the acid that had been used in the attack was neutralized—the FDNY had sprayed gallons of some crap on the counterweights and the rear boom of the crane. But there were unstable piles of wreckage and rubble and beams and other spilled chemicals that would guarantee a trip to the emergency room.

And yet here people were taking selfies . . .

Which raised something Chung had come to worry about in recent years. All the damn pictures people took.

So far, he guessed, he'd been in two or three hundred while on duty. Some people asked him to be in their pix. He declined, of course, but he often ended up in the background inadvertently. The patrolman did a lot of work for the Street Crime Unit, which took on some of the tougher crews in the city. Not all of them were morons, and he guessed they were plenty familiar with computers. Maybe they would scan people's Facebook pages and Twitter accounts and run pictures of cops in those background shots through facial recognition programs to get their names and addresses.

Maybe far-fetched.

But with all the technology nowadays . . . nothing seemed impossible.

"Hey, move along."

The two kids were leaning over the tape to get some shots of the rebar rods that the worker had landed on in his fall from the top of the crane. Two hundred feet in the air. The teens looked privileged. Westchester, maybe? Or Connecticut? And Chung hoped they might start to lecture him on the First Amendment.

At which point he would detain them for trespass.

But, too bad, they simply tucked their phones away and left.

Another scan of the grounds.

A text from his wife about her parents coming for dinner. He was to get dessert after his watch. That was fine too.

He put the phone away.

Which is when he saw motion within the yellow tape. Well within. Not far from the base of the shattered crane, which rose straight up for about thirty feet before it bent and cracked from the fall.

Chung squinted.

Yes, there was somebody moving from south to north—from the direction of the main entrance toward where workers were cutting apart the fallen crane with torches and diamond-edged power saws.

Well, damn.

It was somebody he'd seen before.

A homeless man. He'd walked right past Chung a half hour ago.

He wore a gamy hat like that of a French revolutionary or an Afghan warrior. It was brown and orange, striped. His other garments were a torn and dirty brown overcoat that looked way too warm even on a day like this. Baggy and stained pants. Mismatched shoes. His face was smudged and under his nails were black crescents, particularly troubling to Chung, who had a thing for clean hands.

How had he gotten inside?

Probably just ambled into the site, by virtue of the fact that he was invisible.

All homeless people are.

And Chung thought this fellow was particularly sad. Mid-fifties, wan skin beneath the smudges. Sick, maybe. Likely no family, or a family he was estranged from.

Still, he was trespassing. Chung wouldn't have thought of citing him, much less bringing him in. But he needed to get the guy out of the site before he got himself killed. The holes in the building floor that the counterweights had crashed through were merely marked with orange caution tape. There was no fence around them—which Chung would have done. One wrong step there, and it'd be a thirty-foot drop to concrete.

And there was rebar down there too.

"Hey, you!"

The man was fifty or sixty feet away, and with the sound of the electric saws grinding their way through steel, the officer guessed his voice didn't make it to the fellow's ears.

Chung thought: Oh, hell. He ducked under the tape and, after wagging a finger at a couple of tourists perilously close to an unstable piece of the mast, he started through the wreckage toward where the homeless guy was plodding along.

He called again, and this time his shout came during a pause in the screeching cry of the saws.

The man looked his way and froze.

Chung waved toward the street, but the man just stood there, staring blankly. Drunk, maybe.

When the man stayed put, Chung started for him. He had to duck under some of the fallen crane structures. They seemed sturdy, but each one weighed tons. An unlikely collapse could squash you just as dead as a probable one.

Because the officer had needed to duck, he momentarily lost sight of the homeless man. When he emerged and rose, he scanned in the direction he'd last seen him.

Nothing.

No, wait. There he was. He hadn't exited, but was in a portion of the site where the operator's cab had come crashing to the ground.

Goddamn it.

If I break a leg, you're going to detention, asshole . . .

The man glanced back at him and now made his way north once more.

Then Chung noticed something else about him. When he'd seen him earlier, he was holding one of those blue-and-white deli coffee cups, begging for money. He still held this in his left hand, but in his right was something shiny, metallic. That's what he was doing here—not taking an odd shortcut, but scavenging the grounds for items of value. Had he found something that had belonged to the dead operator? Chung could add larceny to the trespass count.

Scavenging from a disaster site. Didn't get lower than that.

The homeless man now saw Chung coming his way, and he moved more quickly, surprisingly fast. In a few minutes he was climbing through a gap in the shattered fence.

Chung continued after him, but he slowed, minding the booby traps of the wreckage, and when he finally emerged from the site, the man was not to be seen.

One thing remained: the blue cup. He must have dropped it climbing through the fencing.

Had this been a real crime, Chung would, of course, have collected the cup in gloved fingers to preserve it until Crime Scene arrived.

But, while he was pissed at the guy, there was no way he was going to start a case.

He snagged the cup, and after taking the change—he'd give it to a Ronald McDonald House, or some other charity—he tossed it into the back of a garbage truck filling with debris.

Wondering: What had the guy found that was so valuable he didn't care about what was in the cup?

Chung headed quickly back to his original station, where a group of teen girls had breached the yellow tape. The quartet was well within the site, doing—for God's sake—a coordinated dance for TikTok, or whatever, in front of a cell phone they'd propped up on what must have been a convenient photo tripod: a porta-potty crushed into a small cube by the weight of the huge mast.

17.

RON PULASKI PULLED up to the assembly of emergency vehicles, lights flashing—white and blue and red.

Blue, like patrol uniforms.

Red, like blood.

White, like a corpse.

He told himself to can the soft thinking. He climbed out, hitched up his gun and looked around the site where Andy Gilligan had been murdered.

A dozen vehicles, two dozen emergency workers.

All right, Mr. Locard, what do you have in store for us here?

Orienting himself, he happened to gaze up the street, blocked off by a squad car. On the other side of it, pausing in the middle of the north-south avenue, was a sedan. The windows of the dark-red vehicle were tinted and Pulaski couldn't see the driver clearly. It might have been merely pausing, like many others, to check out the excitement.

Then again, the minute he squinted, focusing on it, the driver sped away.

Watch yourself . . .

He proceeded past the CS bus, calling, "A minute" to the pair of evidence collection techs from Queens Crime Scene.

On the street, near the yellow tape, was the gold shield Lon Sellitto had put on the case. He was directing two uniforms to storefronts nearby, for the canvass. Pulaski'd never worked with Al Sanchez, but he knew of him. Out of One PP, the stocky man, with thick, wavy hair, was senior in Homicide. Sellitto had picked a senior investigator, Pulaski supposed, rather than a gold out of the local house, because of the victim—NYPD detective.

Joining him, Pulaski identified himself.

Sanchez said, "Yeah, Lon said you'd be running the scene. You work with that Lincoln Rhyme."

"I do."

"I gotta meet him some day. Okay. Let me show you what we got." They walked under the yellow tape and ducked through a chain-link gate. Soon they were at the body. Sanchez clicked his tongue. "Pro. Three rounds. Double chest, one face." He shrugged. "Don't know why he was down here. Don't even know what he was working on."

"Some minor OC stuff. Mostly the DSE case."

"What's DSE?"

"Department of Structures and Engineering. Perp stole charts, diagrams, maps, construction permit requests, inspection schedules. Stuff like that."

"Why?" He looked as perplexed as anyone would be at a theft that didn't involve money, diamonds, trade secrets or the like.

"No idea."

"You have an unsub?"

"Not yet. But . . ."

Meaning that Gilligan's death might get them closer to one.

Sanchez scoffed. "You steal a bunch of paperwork, then triple tap the gold shield who drew the case? That's a septic system of bad."

Pulaski looked around. "Funny place for a hit. Not the street. And how'd the shooter get to him?"

Rhyme had taught him that there is no single crime scene.

The body—if we're talking homicide—is the hub of the wheel. The unsub had to get there and then he had to leave. Those spokes're as important as where the deed was done.

The body was in almost the direct center of a bulldozer-cleared field, beside a pit that would have been the basement of an old tenement, of which there were plenty in this neighborhood. Pulaski had checked on the property and there were no plans to do anything with it. No permit requests—not since 1978. And the developer never finished the paperwork.

The perp could have come at him from the gate, a half-dozen buildings across the field, a pathway that led to the next east-west street a block away. It was barred with chain-link, but at six feet high that fence would stop only the most out-of-shape killers.

"That's his car?"

A white Lexus sat at the curb.

"Yeah."

"ME?"

"Released him. You're good."

"Canvassing?"

"Got a half dozen on it."

"Reports of shots?"

"No."

Not unusual. Only a fraction of those within hearing distance actually called a report in. Why volunteer to report a person who was, obviously, armed with a deadly weapon?

"Nothing from ShotSpotter either."

This, however, was odd. The gunshot detection system the

NYPD used could triangulate on the sound of a gunshot, give the approximate location and tell if the shooter was in motion—sometimes even determine which direction he was headed in. The system was active in Manhattan, though it didn't cover all neighborhoods with equal accuracy.

Pulaski reminded himself: *Move. Fast.*

He walked to the ECTs, a young pair, two men, with the short hair favored by techs of the male variety, in the belief there was less of a chance of shedding one of their own strands at a scene.

The latter seemed pleased to be working a case with Pulaski. His eyes radiated—what was it? Admiration?

Probably. And the source was because he worked with Lincoln Rhyme.

Here he was on their case, Lincoln's protégé.

And successor?

Pulaski's gut did a flip with this thought.

He put the subject aside and nodded his acknowledgment. "Let's move."

"Yessir."

"I'm going to run the car and the corpse. You two take that path to the fence—and comb the fence real good. And then those two buildings there. Ground floors have views of the site." They would have been perfect spots from which to stalk Gilligan.

Doing whatever it was he was doing.

The two donned their space suits and set to work, while Pulaski too garbed up. He had just started toward the corpse when Sanchez called, "Uh-oh."

The detective nodded toward a shiny black sedan that had just parked nearby, the occupant of the backseat now climbing out. He was in his late fifties, in a nice-fitting charcoal suit. Silver-haired. A long, stern face. He looked over the crime scene and then scanned the press—a half-dozen reporters and camerapeople behind yet another line, some distance from the scene.

Sanchez said, "Everett Burdick. Dep inspector, One PP. You know him?"

"No."

"We call him Anchor Amber."

Pulaski chuckled. Cops' irreverence was legendary. Amber Andrews was a popular newscaster for the local affiliate of a national network. Her broadcasts were always far more about her than the story. Ah, so Burdick was an airtime hound—the sort who ran unnecessary press conferences displaying stacks of cash and packages of drugs seized in raids.

Sanchez added, "Ego and talent, you know. They're not—what do they say?—mutually exclusive. He's not a bad cop. Was good on the street, and he's good at One PP. He just has to let everybody know it."

Burdick strode up to Sanchez, ignoring Pulaski.

Fine with him. He had work to do. He slipped through the gate and began vacuuming up trace on the way to the corpse and then started on the body, collecting from the victim's clothing, scraping fingernails, taking a hair sample, looking for the slugs, which turned out to be still within the body. The autopsy doc would remove them and have them sent to ballistics in Queens. Aside from the huge Desert Eagle .50, or the tiny .17 HMR, it's hard to tell the caliber of the slug from the wound. Most guns are in the 9mm, .380 or .38 range—all basically the same. And these rounds appeared around that size, but there are thousands of weapons with that caliber, so it was pointless to speculate what the make and model might be.

The absence of exit wounds was intriguing. The accuracy meant the shooter was not far away when he pulled the trigger. Normally at that range, the bullets would likely have penetrated the chest cavity, if not the skull, and exited. That this didn't happen meant he'd possibly used a silencer, which dramatically reduces not only the sound but the velocity of the shot. This theory was born out too by the absence of 911 calls reporting gunshots or of ShotSpotter alerts. Despite what you see in the movies, silencers aren't that common. Muggers and your average thieves rarely have access. Organized crime and professional triggermen, yes.

So, as Sanchez had speculated: the shooter was likely a pro.

No spent shells. The gun might have been a revolver, which would leave none—and despite the gap between chamber and barrel, it was somewhat quieted by a silencer. A semiauto, conversely, would have ejected brass. Then again, pros always took the empty shells with them. He found, however, where the brass would likely have ended up—to the right of where the shooter stood—and six to eight feet away he took samples of the dirt from where the flying shells would have landed.

Gilligan's own weapon, a common Glock 17, was on his hip. No extra mag on the opposite side of his body, which told Pulaski that he didn't do much fieldwork. You never ventured out of the office without at least one extra magazine.

Pulaski then began on the spiral ham. His comprehensive search.

There were a half-dozen footprints, but much of the site was hard-packed clay and gravel and grass, none of which yielded any impressions.

He dropped off what he'd collected at the bus and proceeded to the Lexus.

And what will you have for Mr. Locard and me?

The interior contained the typical: an empty coffee cup, two water bottles, DMV and insurance documents. The vehicle was only a month old. There was paperwork in the door and center console. Car stuff mostly. No more toll receipts nowadays. That information, often helpful, was available with a warrant only, from the bridge, tunnel, and toll road authorities.

He found several restaurant receipts, some recent, though none from this morning.

He lifted soil samples from the carpet, passenger seat and back-seats, latents from the wheel, touchpad screen, other controls and surfaces, and door handles, both sides.

In the trunk was a laptop. He bagged this too.

Finally, a search of the seats. Under them, of course, but also *in* them: a place that no evidence-collecting book—even Lincoln Rhyme's—suggested searching. But Pulaski patted down the supple leather, as if frisking a suspicious-looking gangbanger for drugs or weapons.

And here he found it, behind a slit cut into the side of the driver's-side backseat.

Something that put Andy Gilligan's murder in a whole new light.

18.

A LOT OF people had second phones—the providers courteously offered great deals to suck you in—but Gilligan's was a burner.

You could tell because it was a brand name, but an older model—three years out-of-date, yet in good shape, no scuffs or chips. Pay-as-you-go companies bought up inventories of older phones like this, selling them to a diverse crowd: those with limited means, teenagers learning how to budget and . . . to murderers and drug dealers.

As he placed it in the evidence bag, Pulaski was reflecting that a cop could certainly have a burner for legitimate reasons. So he could talk to CIs or suspects and not give away his personal number. Maybe Gilligan did some undercover work.

But why hide it so carefully?

If he was worried about it being stolen, there was the trunk or the glove compartment.

So Pulaski seized on the idea that Gilligan was involved in something illegal and the phone was one he used to communicate with a partner, Mr. X.

Think, he told himself.

Had he come here to meet that person, who had ambushed him?

Pulaski looked at it logically. Gilligan had died facing the shooter. If it was a stranger coming at him in a random attack, the detective would at least have reached for his own gun. But, based on his posture in death, that hadn't happened.

So then, assume they *were* partners and met here for some reason. Think! Speculate!

Bold . . .

He walked to the street and examined the asphalt in front of and behind the Lexus. No recent tire prints. Maybe Mr. X had parked some distance away.

He walked to Sanchez. "I think they knew each other. Gilligan and the shooter."

"Really?"

"Think so. I need to know where the perp parked. Not near the Lexus, but let's check along here. Could you clear the street?"

"Sure. I'll back everybody out." Sanchez called to the officers on-site and gave the order.

One young woman officer said to Pulaski, "Sir, you want me to ribbon the whole place?"

Sir? They were the same age.

"Yeah, thanks."

With a flip of her blond ponytail she turned, fetched a roll of yellow tape and started to work.

The two evidence collection techs returned to the gate.

"Find anything?" Pulaski asked.

They replied that they had not.

Which supported his theory that the men were together and had entered the site from this side of the lot.

Maybe it was a hit, pure and simple. Neither Gilligan nor the shooter had any business here, other than the second one's murdering the detective.

He walked to the CS bus and snagged new evidence bags.

He was about to start his search for recent tire treads, when Sanchez approached. His face was not happy. "He's not going to do it."

"Who's not going to do what?"

"Burdick. He said there's no need to expand the scene. That that's what Crime Scene people do when they don't know what to look for."

Pulaski frowned. "What does that even mean?"

"I'm just telling you."

He glanced toward the deputy inspector and, behind him, the reporters.

Phalanx . . .

The blond officer, holding the yellow roll, looked toward Pulaski uncertainly. The DI had apparently told her too to stand down.

Pulaski approached. He took the roll from her. "I've got this."

"Sorry . . ."

"No, it's good."

He turned toward Burdick and said, "I'm going to have to ask everyone to move back to the intersection. I'm sealing the street."

And, armed with the tape, he waited for them to migrate.

A few reporters did, but paused when Burdick said, in a voice louder than necessary, "Officer. Like I just explained. Not necessary." And looked at him with a pinched face that was the gaze of somebody smart talking to somebody less smart. He said, "It's unprofessional. Might as well tape off the whole neighborhood."

And for the millionth time, Pulaski had that brief flash: I'm screwing up. I'm doing something wrong.

I had that thing that happened . . .

Then he kicked the thought aside.

"Based on the evidence I've found, I need it sealed."

"What evidence?"

Pulaski wasn't going to respond. "The entire block."

"That's ridiculous."

Pulaski supposed that whatever nonsense the man was spouting about the size of the declared scene had nothing to do with the size of the declared scene. This was about Deputy Inspector Burdick appearing in charge.

Amber Andrews . . .

He might just as easily have said, "I want to shrink the perimeter by six inches." Or something equally nonsensical.

Pulaski said, "Can I talk to you in private, sir?"

The answer apparently was no.

Burdick stood his ground and spoke more loudly yet for the reporters happily witnessing the intramural squabbling. "Look. I've been an investigator longer than you've been on the force. You don't need to expand it." He looked around and pointed across the street to an abandoned tenement, which he seemed to have picked at random. "And you need to search that building. It's critical. I know it. Instinct, I can tell."

A structure that had been boarded up for months if not years and in front of which was a dusty sidewalk and entryway that showed no evidence of foot traffic in recent days.

Pulaski lowered his voice. "Are you sure you don't want to take this private? Just step over to the van."

Burdick's icy voice: "You're Patrol, right?"

"Correct."

"You're not in uniform."

"I'm temporarily assigned to Crime Scene."

"Name?"

"Pulaski, Ron."

"Well, Pulaski, Ron. I'm a deputy inspector. You don't take me out behind the woodshed. I take you."

"Seniority isn't the issue. I need the street cleared. There could be evidence that everybody's walking over right now."

"You do not need the street cleared. You need to search that building."

He happened to be pointing to the structure next door to the building he had previously indicated. He'd mixed them up.

Pulaski said firmly, "This's my crime scene. I control it. I need you to move forty feet in that direction."

The look of astonishment was remarkable.

In a finger-snap, it turned to rage. And then a snide smile appeared. "Thin ice, Patrolman."

He'd embarrassed the dep inspector in front of the press.

A cardinal sin.

Pulaski whispered in response, "We had the chance to keep this between us. Now I'm going to ask you once more to move back. And if you don't, I'm detaining you for obstruction of justice. And I'll use restraints if I have to."

Burdick called, "Detective Sanchez! Detective Sanchez!"

The man ambled up. "Sir?"

"I'm suspending this officer effective immediately. You'll keep the scene secure until another CSU officer arrives."

Sanchez glanced from Burdick to Pulaski and back again. "It's his scene, Deputy Inspector. He makes the calls."

"But not if he's being incompetent. And insubordinate. I'm relieving him of command."

Pulaski frowned. There was no procedure for this that he'd heard of. Sanchez's face revealed that the idea was alien to him as well.

"Can't do it, sir. You know he's working for Lincoln Rhyme."

"Yeah, yeah, yeah. I'm not impressed."

Keeping his insincerely smiling face as calm as possible—the cameras were clicking—he waited for Sanchez to move or at least for Pulaski to back down.

Like Sachs had taught him, Pulaski wore his service belt outside the Tyvek so his weapon would be easily accessible.

The handcuffs too, which he now reached for.

"You can't be serious," the man blustered.

The standoff lasted only a few seconds. Then Burdick gave a faint nod. He said in a louder voice: "Oh, you're saying there might be an active shooter nearby?"

Burdick turned to the press. "This officer has informed me that we've just learned a shooter might be nearby. It would be safer if we moved to the end of the block. You should've mentioned that sooner, Officer."

Pulaski summoned up a my-bad frown. "Sorry, sir. My mistake."

The DI gestured the reporters back—as if he were saving their lives—and Pulaski quickly ran the tape around the light poles at the far end, and those across the street. He handed off the roll to one of the officers to finish the job at the other end of the block.

Pulaski stepped onto the curb and walked along the entire length of the street, head down, searching for the recent tire tracks—the shooter's—which he knew were here.

Except there weren't any.

Oops. Got that one wrong.

But the conclusion was even better than finding the shooter's tire treads. It meant the killer and his victim drove here together.

Pulaski confirmed this by taking electrostatic impressions from the street beneath the driver's side and the passenger's side of the Lexus. The first matched Gilligan's. The second matched the shooter's.

He returned to the CS van and looked over the vacant lot. The number cards, yellow with black type on them, placed where every bit of evidence had been found.

He realized he was stalling.

It had occurred to him some moments ago what he had to do. And he was dreading it.

Was there an alternative?

No, not given his rule on the first forty-eight minutes.

He needed to push the case forward immediately and there was only one way he could make that happen.

He walked to a cluster of uniforms nearby. "Anybody help me? Need some gum."

One patrolman nodded. "Juicy Fruit."

"Great." It was in fact his favorite. He took the stick and began to chew. Then he turned to the blond officer, who had started to string the tape. He nodded to her purse. "I hope you don't think this's an insult. But I've got to ask you a question."

19.

LINCOLN RHYME WAS looking into the sterile portion of the parlor, at the cartons Ron Pulaski had just brought in from the Gilligan scene.

Mel Cooper was taking the samples, logging them and starting analysis.

"You scored a burner phone," Rhyme noted, looking at the evidence bag in Pulaski's hand.

Lon Sellitto grumbled, "So? It'll be locked. They're always locked."

"This one's not," Pulaski said.

"Yeah? Careless of him."

"It *was* locked. I unlocked it."

"How?"

A tightening of his lips. "Wasn't the most pleasant thing in the world. I washed the blood and brains off Gilligan's forehead, stuffed some chewing gum in the bullet hole and knocked a few pieces of bone back into place. Then I borrowed some makeup from one of the uniforms. Was afraid I'd insulted her, you know, like she's a woman, of *course* she'd have makeup. But she was cool with it."

Rhyme barked an uncharacteristic laugh. "You tricked the facial rec lock."

Sellitto glanced toward Rhyme. "The chewing gum–makeup trick. Put that in the next edition of your book, Linc."

The young officer continued, "Once I was in, I shut off the password security."

"Always thinking, Pulaski. Always thinking. Well, let's see what's on it." Rhyme called, "Thom? Thom!"

The aide walked into the room. "Yes?"

"Glove up and play cop. Give me everything that's on that phone. Call logs, voice mails, texts. Let's hope we can see emails without a password."

"Me?"

"Amelia's on a lead."

"Hm. Do I get a raise?"

"No, you get not fired."

"I'll organize a strike later." He pulled on latex gloves and took the evidence bag containing the phone.

"And don't forget . . ."

"Chain of custody," he called as he disappeared into the dining room to begin excavation.

Pulaski gave the men his theory that Gilligan and the shooter knew each other.

"Gilligan? Corrupt?" Rhyme, not pleased, looked around the parlor. "If so, not a great idea, us inviting him in."

Sellitto said, "But remember, Linc. We didn't. He came to us."

Even more troubling . . . He wanted to be here. Why?

Cooper continued itemizing what Pulaski had found: A laptop.

Trace from Gilligan's shoes, from the corpse and around it, from the logical path the victim and the shooter had walked, from the street beneath the doors, from the Lexus. Fingernail scrapings too and several items from the car.

"Slugs?"

Pulaski said, "Still in him. I think the shooter had a suppressor."

"Video?" Rhyme was looking at the SD card Pulaski was feeding into a computer.

"Found a receipt for a diner Gilligan ate at yesterday. I stopped by on the way here. They copied their security cam footage for me around the time he was there. Great baklava, by the way." He called up a player program, loaded the security footage and began scrubbing.

While he searched, Rhyme said, "Mel, the trace. And, Lon, can you do the honors?" A nod at the whiteboard.

"Yeah, with my handwriting? Sister Mary Elizabeth didn't give me rave reviews in grade school." But he took the marker and smoothed the top sheet on the easel with his hand, like Picasso ready to draw.

Cooper began calling out the conclusions reached by that workhorse of all crime labs: the gas chromatograph/mass spectrometer, which isolates and identifies unknown substances.

The bulk of what Pulaski had collected near the body and in the field were sand and loam soil. This matched the control samples, which meant that they were of no probative value.

But then he discovered trace that did *not* match. It had come from a source other than the field where Gilligan died.

Mel Cooper reported: "Silica, alumina and magnesia, iron, potassium, sodium, and calcium. Alkaline earth. Decaying organic material. Hydrous aluminum phyllosilicates."

"Really? Interesting."

Sellitto's eyes made a wide and sarcastic circuit of the ceiling. Rhyme ignored it.

He asked, "Where was it collected?"

"On the victim's shoes and footprints where he and the shooter walked. Most abundant under the passenger's and driver's doors, and the car's front seat carpet, both sides."

"Ah, excellent! They picked it up *before* they got in the car. But where? That's what we want to know. The shooter's hideout? Maybe the house of some OC head? I want to know more. Mel, 'scope a sample. Optical."

Another basic tool in crime labs, a compound microscope—so named because it had multiple lenses—was nothing fancy. Its job was simple: to make little things look bigger.

A moment later, images of particles appeared on one of the monitors near Rhyme, mirroring what Cooper was looking at through the eyepiece of the Mitutoyo microscope, a precision instrument that came in at $10K.

"Put a scale up," Rhyme instructed.

A grid appeared. The smaller particles, tan in color, were about .002mm or smaller.

He said, "All right. With particles that small, and those ingredients? It's clay."

One of the six basic categories of earth soils, along with shale, loam, silt, peat and chalk.

Cooper continued, "Ground calcium, consistent with shellfish shells, very old."

"Clay and shells?" Sellitto mused. "Narrows it to near a shoreline, right? Why the sour face, Linc?"

"Because, yes, you're right. Shoreline. And New York City has more than five hundred miles of it. More than Boston, Miami, L.A. and San Francisco combined. What else? I want something *unique*."

Cooper went on, "Charcoal. Decaying bits of wood coated with varnish, fibers from deteriorating leather and wool. Copper, iron. Then isoamyl alcohol, n-propyl alcohol, epicatechin and vanillin. Everything's old, very old."

Rhyme regarded the results as Sellitto wrote in his C– handwriting. "The last? Some kind of liquor. Antique. Hm. All right. Now, that trace came from a different location. Where . . . ?" He drew the word out. "Pulaski, did you—?"

"No GPS in Gilligan's car. Disabled. Was that what you were going to ask?"

"It was. His other phone? His main one?"

"Wasn't there. Assume the shooter took it."

After writing this down, Sellitto offered, "Man is getting guiltier by the minute."

Pulaski got a text. He read it, and his face tightened with minor disgust.

Sellitto lifted an inquiring eyebrow.

"I had to shepherd a dep inspector out of the way."

"So? It's your scene."

"Yeah, well, I kind of threatened him with obstruction. In front of the press. Nearly cuffed and detained him."

Rhyme's reaction was amusement and a bit of pride. He'd done the same thing on several occasions and actually put an NYPD captain in the back of a blue-and-white for an hour.

"Who?" Sellitto asked.

"Burdick."

Sellitto said, "Oh him. Yeah, well, he's got an excuse."

Pulaski was frowning. "What's that?"

"He's a dick."

Cooper called, "I've got the shoes. Both're size eleven. Smooth soles. No manufacturer's ID."

Naturally, one of the most common. And shoe size has only

a tangential correlation to height or build. "Wear patterns?" he called. Heels or tips worn down in certain ways can reveal professions.

"Gilligan's're worn more than the shooter's, but neither of them tell us anything."

Cooper, bent over the microscope again, called, "More trace from the mystery location. Fibers that have the cellular structure of horsehair. Like the rest of it, old."

"The computer?" Rhyme asked. "It's Gilligan's for sure?"

Pulaski told him, "Yep. His name and number are on a label on the back. If found, please call et cetera. His prints too. Only his. And it's his personal one, not PD issue."

"How do you know?"

Pulaski said, "It's a Core i7. With an Nvidia graphics card. Too expensive to be PD issue."

"It's *got* to have something we can use. Please tell me it's not locked."

A few keystrokes. "Nope. Password."

Pulaski said, "And it doesn't have a fingerprint key to unlock it." Print readers on electronics don't optically read the ridges, furrows and whorls. They sense conductance—electric charges—in the ridges. Conductance quickly decreases after death, though. The computer would remain locked for the time being.

"I've got him on the deli video," Pulaski called.

Rhyme was looking at a fish-eye high-definition scene of the interior of a diner. He couldn't help but be impressed. The kid—no, the young man—had gone the extra step to drive to the restaurant and get a copy of the recording. What was significant about this was that he was mixing crime scene work with field investigation. That was unusual—and, some would say, against protocol. Usually a forensic officer handed off findings to a detective, who would then follow up. This two-step process often resulted in delays. Pulaski wasn't having any of that. He wanted crime scene leads followed up on immediately. And that meant doing it himself. He'd told Rhyme once about this theory he had—the forty-eight-minute rule in closing cases. The criminalist couldn't disagree.

In the video they watched Andy Gilligan as he entered; the lighting was good. He was led to a table off to the side, where he sat with his back to the camera. He ordered a meal, a cup of coffee. He ate and drank quickly and made no calls and sent or received no texts.

"That's odd," Pulaski offered. "Nobody by themselves in a restaurant doesn't hit the electronics. He's just staring out the window."

"Because he feels like a shit for what he did." Rhyme added, "Or thinking of ways to spend whatever the shooter paid him."

Then he fell silent and squinted. "There's something . . ."

"What's that, Linc?"

"I want to see it again. From the minute he enters. Regular speed."

Pulaski manipulated the controls. "You have something?".

The answer was: not exactly. But the images had triggered a vague association.

A memory.

Was it the restaurant?

No, he'd never seen it before.

The view outside?

No, just any city street.

Maybe it was something about Gilligan himself . . .

After all, the man had spent some hours here in the parlor on the DSE break-in case. He'd been here just this morning.

But, no, it was in a context different from the crime scene work they'd done together in the town house.

Clothing?

No . . .

A mannerism?

Then: "Yes!"

All three men in the lab looked his way.

What was familiar was the man's stride.

And Lincoln Rhyme knew where he'd seen it before.

"Mel! I want the security cam of the DSE break-in. Put it on the second monitor."

Rhyme motored closer to that screen. Come on, he thought impatiently. Come on.

"I'm getting it."

Apparently, he'd spoken out loud.

Soon, a security video was playing, a case number and date appeared, glowing yellow, on a black screen. The scene came to life and they were looking at what a subtitle explained was the west hallway, first floor, of the Department of Structures and Engineering building. Unsub 212 was walking away from the camera toward the exit, the stolen file folders tucked under his right arm.

"Look at Gilligan's walk at the diner. Look at the thief's walk at DSE."

Sellitto was whispering, "The fuck? They're the same."

Many law enforcement agencies were using gait-profiling software to identify perps and witnesses. It wasn't yet admissible at trial in most states, but comparing how a known individual walked with an unknown individual in security videos like this could help investigators tentatively ID the perp. Rhyme didn't have a program for this in the lab, but he hardly needed one. The two men were clearly the same.

"And his ear," Pulaski said.

Ah, yes. In both videos he lifted his left hand and compulsively tugged the lobe, a nervous habit.

There was no doubt. Andy Gilligan was Unsub 212.

Sellitto said, "The hell is this about? The detective running the DSE theft case is also the goddamn perp? Somebody explain that to me."

At that moment, Mel Cooper's voice came through the speaker clearly. Normally placid, he sounded energized. "Well, we have something here. Where the shooter's shell casings landed in the field and he picked them up? Guess what I found in the trace?"

"Mel!" Rhyme exhaled noisily. He wasn't in the mood for dramatic setups.

Unfazed, the tech turned to them with a smile. "Hydrofluoric acid."

"Jesus," Sellitto muttered. "So, the shooter's been to the crane collapse—or he's Unsub Eighty-Nine himself."

Rhyme said, "Too much of a coincidence for him to happen to have been at the scene for no reason. No, he's the mechanic, either with the Kommunalka Project or hired by them. And he needed an inside man in the city government. He pays Gilligan to get him a list of the properties they want turned into affordable housing. That's where the list came from. And he wanted charts and maps of building sites in the city so he can figure out which cranes are the best to sabotage."

Sellitto helped himself to a cookie from a tray that Rhyme had not noticed earlier. Thom, a talented baker, was forever leaving out treats that visitors enjoyed but that his boss had little interest in.

Eyes back on the board, Rhyme whispered, "And the mystery man, the mechanic . . . Who the hell are you?"

The answer to that very question came just a moment later.

Thom Reston stepped into the parlor. "There isn't much on Gilligan's phone. No data, no downloads. Just records of calls. Some local—probably to other burners—but there were some to and from a number in England. I checked the exchange. It's in Manchester. If that means anything."

Rhyme was silent for a moment, letting the shock settle.

He said, "It means everything. Unsub Eighty-Nine, the crane man? It's the Watchmaker."

20.

AS HE WAITED for the couple who were soon to die, Charles Vespasian Hale wondered if they had children.

He didn't want the children, if any, to die—and didn't want them not to die. They were irrelevant. All that mattered was the *husband* die because of what he'd seen, and that his wife die because he might have told her what he'd seen.

If that meant the kids grew up as orphans, so be it.

Unless they were accompanying their parents now and entered the house with them.

In which case, they wouldn't grow up at all.

Hale eased back into the foliage of the small park across the street from their modest bungalow in Queens.

The house was owned by a worker at the jobsite where the crane had fallen. His name had been on the list that Gilligan had stolen from Rhyme's apartment that morning. Hale had called the workers Gilligan had not gotten to, and only this man turned out to be a witness, having seen something "odd" at the site. An SUV parked where it shouldn't have been.

It happened to be the vehicle Hale had driven there, to sabotage the crane.

Well, he'd ditched the Chevy already, but what was troubling was that the man had seen the *contents* of the SUV.

And so, the man had to die.

Hale hadn't known that Moynahan Construction workers had a special lot. He'd parked on the street and left a hard hat on the dash. This is what caught the worker's attention.

And signed his death warrant.

Hale had hurried to the man's house here and, finding no one home, slipped inside and left the present for them.

Hale now remained behind the brush and weeds and waited.

Beside the park was a lawyer's office. The attorney might or might not have been talented in court, but he or she was definitely a skilled linguist. A sign in the window reported that Spanish, Greek, Armenian, Turkish and Chinese were spoken. Hale had heard that soon the country would be minority white. He occasionally received calls from potential clients wishing to hire him to assassinate someone because they were of one of the "lesser races."

Yes, that term had actually been used.

He always declined such offers, because, yes, he found such jobs distasteful, but also because those who held such views were invariably stupid—and that quality, in any criminal venture, was an undeniable liability.

Now a car slowed and pulled into the driveway. The couple got out. No children. That answered that question. Though, wait . . . The woman was roundly pregnant. So a partial yes.

His targets seemed to be an average couple. Average build, average hair, average gait. They walked quaintly arm in arm. No . . . That wasn't accurate. He was gripping *her* arm for support. He was likely one of the half dozen injured when the crane collapsed. There'd been only two deaths, which was a disappointment. Not that he was sadistic by nature—hardly (sadism was inefficient); no,

Hale simply wanted the attacks to splash. He needed the city to focus.

The two—in their late twenties, he guessed—walked through a white picket gate and past the—yes—average lawn and garden that dominated their front yard.

The man, athletic and solid like most construction workers, paused and gazed down at a bush with yellow petals. Hale knew some flora, but only those important in his work. Those that were poisonous or irritants or narcotic.

Then they continued to the front door, painted a bold red. After unlocking the latch, the man gestured gallantly for her to enter.

She did; he followed, limping, and swung the door shut for what would be the last time in their lives.

Assured that they were in the kill zone, Hale started up the street to his new SUV—a different color and make from the first. This was a black Pathfinder. As he walked, he placed a phone call from his burner. Inside the couple's house, the receiving cell phone circuit silently took the call and began a countdown that would, after giving Hale twenty minutes to be nowhere near, set off a small packet of explosives. The charge would be so light that they would hear only a faint crack.

That the sound was gentle, however, did not mean that the consequences would also be. The explosion would shatter a container of hydrofluoric acid.

The liquid form is one of the most deadly surface toxins on earth, but anhydrous HF gas is worse. The resulting fumes—materializing spontaneously when the liquid met air at room temperature—would spread fast from the source and would flow through the entire house in less than a minute, as Hale had turned the HVAC fan up to high when he'd rigged the device.

And the deaths? Unpleasant, yes. HF on the skin was, ironically, not especially painful at first. Gas wafting into lungs and eyes and mouth and nose, though, caused instant unimaginable agony. But it wouldn't last long, not with the quantity he'd filled the device with.

Now the threat posed by the inquisitive SUV voyeur had been eliminated. It was time to return to what was next on his agenda.

It was, indisputably, the most important aspect of his mission.

And the one about which he was the most curious.

21.

"DON'T THINK I'VE seen you looking quite so surprised, Linc."

Which was a mild way of putting it.

"I've been expecting Hale," Rhyme said slowly. And he reminded them of a communique that he'd not long ago received via a rather circuitous route. The British Government Communications Headquarters—an innocuous name for one of the most effective snooping agencies in the world—had been listening in on terrorist traffic and coincidentally heard that anonymous actors, one of whom was in Manchester, England, were plotting Rhyme's death. They'd gotten word to the FBI, which in turn alerted the criminalist.

Manchester was Hale's temporary base of operation.

"He was going to get here sooner or later—killing me is not the kind of job he'd contract out. But how the hell is he involved with the cranes?"

"Well, I guess the Kommunalka Project hired him, didn't they?" Sellitto asked.

Rhyme's eyes went from the evidence boards to the windows. "Maybe. But his being here, it opens up a lot more possibilities. It might explain why nobody's heard of our resident communists. Thinking about it, a radical underground group, affording Hale's fees? Not impossible, especially if the Kommunalka's a front for a bigger operation, but not necessarily likely. Maybe he's up to something else entirely.

"And good job, Pulaski. Without the facial reconstruction trick, we never would have known."

But the young officer seemed not to hear the compliment. He was staring at the board. "You know what it means, right? Gilligan's death? Hale's going to move on you soon."

"True. Gilligan was here to check out my security. If Hale killed him, he's learned what he needs. He'll act before I change anything."

Sellitto was shaking his head. "So, Andy Gilligan was bought. That's tough. But not completely a surprise. You know he's got a brother?"

Rhyme said, "I didn't."

"Yeah. Mick Gilligan's connected. A crew in Brooklyn. We knew it, of course. And they saw each other some. Andy was up front about it. He told his commander. All he said was he wouldn't be involved in any operation against Mick. The brass let it slide." A scowl. "Andy was a damn good cop. He closed cases . . . But now? We've got to go back and check out every one he ran. Look over the recovered drug and cash inventories. See if anything got skimmed."

Rhyme was thinking of the phone calls to and from England. He called to Thom, "When was the last one?"

The aide looked over the sheet he'd logged the calls on. "Three days ago."

"That's when he left the UK and came here. But how'd he get into the country? Man's on a dozen watch lists." Rhyme told his computer, "Send Zoom invite. Fred Dellray. Schedule a meeting now."

The computer did as told and a few moments later the FBI agent was on the screen.

"Lincoln, Lon, and there's young Pulaski dwelling in the corners." Dellray was in his office in the federal building in downtown Manhattan. It was a perfunctory place with government-tan paint on the walls, a bookcase behind him filled with carefully ordered volumes. A desktop computer.

Another phone rang and he held up a bony finger, dark as the brown leather of his desk chair. He took the call and muted Zoom.

Though Dellray had advanced degrees, there were no certificates or diplomas on the walls. The only decoration was a poster of a disheveled man in a toga, beneath which were the words:

Luck is what happens when preparation meets opportunity.
—Seneca

Beneath it sat a copy of Title 18 of the U.S. Code. The federal criminal statutes. Post-it notes protruded. They were pink, blue and yellow.

Dellray was wearing a very un-FBI suit in powder blue, along with the equally nonconforming yellow shirt and pink tie. He could get away with offending J. Edgar Hoover's ghost because he was the best runner of undercover agents and CIs in the Bureau— and he got out into the field himself from time to time to play the role of an obscenely rich warlord or arms dealer or the corrupt government official with a gambling problem eager to take a bribe from a contractor.

He disconnected the call and returned to Zoom. "So. Anything interesting on the crane situation? I'll tell you, all I have to do is peek outside my window and there's one there, looming. All our counterterror people decided to decamp to the other side of the building in case it does a Humpty Dumpty. It's. A. Distraction. What do you need?"

"Any unauthorized entries into the U.S. three days ago, or so, of a male, white, forties. Originating in the UK, but he might've transited anywhere in the world. And I've sent a picture. Mug shot."

"I'll do some rings here, Lincoln. I'll get back. Who's this arch vill-i-an?"

Rhyme had tried to categorize Dellray's syntax, grammar and patois. It was not possible.

"The Watchmaker."

A silence descended. A rarity with Dellray. "Well . . ."

"Yes, Fred. I know what he's here for."

"Keep this line open. I'm headin' west, where my fearless colleagues're hiding out from falling cranes. Be right back."

The lanky man vanished.

22.

ABBY WAS WATERING the gardenias, in a hanging basket on the porch, when she heard the noise.

What was that?

A pop.

It was coming from the neighbor's house.

The forty-four-year-old mother of three and part-time librarian looked across the narrow strips of side yards to the bungalow that was almost identical to the one she and her husband owned— identical to many of them, actually, in this part of Queens. Only, the next-door couple had gone with red trim, not yellow.

Abby decided she liked red better, but would never go to the expense of painting something that didn't need to be painted. How stupid was that? Besides, that'd look like she did it because the neighbors had and even though that was true, she didn't want anybody to *think* it was true.

Pop.

Her eyes on the bungalow, wondering about the sound. She was thinking what a time they've been through, the folks who lived there. The poor husband, the construction worker who'd nearly died in that terrible crane incident that morning.

Abby's hubby, Tim, was a mechanic at Harbey's Automotive—yes, not Harvey's—and had never been in any danger even during the fire.

And the pregnant wife? Going to drop at any minute.

What a time . . .

One pour for you, she thought to the largest of the hanging plants—secretly her favorite.

One pour for you.

Good drinks, everybody.

Abby loved her plants. She talked to them and believed they did better because of the conversation.

She looked at their house once more.

Wait, what was that?

She was alarmed. Smoke? Was there a fire?

Grabbing her phone, she started to dial 911. Then she paused. No. She realized she was looking at the bathroom. It was steam. A few wisps slid from the partially open window and vanished quickly. And there was no smoke anywhere else.

That's all it was. Steam.

She herself just loved hot baths.

Abby walked into the kitchen and filled her watering can once again. She walked through the house, careful not to spill on the carpet, and out the door to the front porch, where four more plants waited.

"One pour for you," she said. And turning to the others, she whispered, "Just be patient. It's almost your turn."

• • •

As they waited for the lanky FBI agent to return, Rhyme noted some other aspects of Dellray's office: photos of his wife and three children. So the couple had had another youngster . . . Then again, maybe he'd had three the last time the subject of his family came up.

The criminalist was perpetually short on knowledge of his colleagues' personal lives.

Sellitto began to ask something. But Rhyme held up a finger as he stared forward—not at the evidence whiteboard, but out the window. Branches and leaves and clouds, and some striking blue sky beyond.

Dellray returned. He dropped into his chair. "Gotcha one for the ages, Lincoln. Didn't come across my desk 'cause I'm spending my precious hours and brain cells putting some racist skinheads away. Now, this is most interesting. Three days ago, incident at JFK. No collateral intel, no chatter, no hot box alerts. Not. A. One. We all together on that?"

"I will be when you tell me what you found out."

A chuckle. "Triple Seven on an international flight. Parks at the gate, everybody hightails it off the big steel bird, passengers, flight crew. Now, this is where it gets good.

"Next flight, few hours later, the first officer does a walk-around. What they have to do. Checks out the plane, kicks the tires, makes sure the wings're bolted on. And she looks into the nosewheel well. And guess what that woman finds? You can't, so I'll tell ya. An oxygen tank, big enough for an eight-hour supply, a mask, and a thermal sleeping bag heated with a twelve-volt battery."

At thirty-five thousand feet, temperatures can reach −70 Fahrenheit, though you won't feel unpleasant for very long. Hypoxia—lack of oxygen—will kill you before cruising altitude.

One for the ages . . .

"Departed where? Manchester?"

"Yes indeed."

Sellitto muttered, "The Watchmaker, just the sort of grand entrance he'd go for."

"Evidence?" Rhyme asked.

"PERT bundled it up and took it down to Quantico."

The Bureau's Physical Evidence Response Team was good. And the lab in Quantico was perhaps the best in the world.

"Can they pull a print now? I . . . We have to know for sure."

"Name's Hale, right?"

"Charles Vespasian Hale."

"Hold on."

A green and yellow flash as he disappeared.

Rhyme's eyes slipped out the window once again.

A crane stabbed the sky . . .

In his mind, the pieces were lining up.

But he needed the critical confirmation from Dellray.

Who was back, two minutes later.

"It's your boy, Lincoln. Nothing big in the surprise department—Hale was smart enough to wear cloth gloves in the plane, but must've figured that'd be suspicious inside the terminal. They lifted a print on the door handle for the baggage crew. So the Watchmaker is the crane man."

"Looks that way. Let Homeland Security know. He's on their list too."

They disconnected.

The Watchmaker. The man whose plots Rhyme had foiled several times in the United States and Mexico. The man Rhyme had actually arrested and incarcerated, though he'd managed to escape from a prison that was very difficult to escape from.

The man who was, to use the overly romantic and inartful term, Rhyme reflected, his nemesis.

Now it was Sellitto who was peering out the window. "He's here. But where?"

Rhyme reflected for a moment. "That's what I've been thinking about, and I have an idea."

23.

IT WAS A twenty mph zone.

Amelia Sachs was doing sixty, and irritated that she had to slow for intersections.

She had dash flashers on the grille, but no siren. She'd have to look into that.

Hell. Speed bump. Down to forty.

Thud, bang.

Ouch . . .

Then faster.

Sachs was piloting her Torino, engine raging, down a trim residential street in Queens, a block of small, detached single-families. Red brick, beige stone, a few framed, painted in sub-dued colors. Not unlike the Brooklyn neighborhood she'd grown up in.

One reason for the speed: an earlier delay. A coughing fit had forced her to pull over, lower her head and breathe the sweet oxygen through the mask until the spasms ended. She actually pulled into the parking lot in front of a hospital's emergency room.

Debating.

But then she'd controlled it and continued on to meet with the witness.

A brief coughing fit now, filling her with anger at the man who would use this shit as a weapon.

Anger at her own lungs for not resisting better.

Forget it.

Drive.

Once through an intersection, her right foot dropped hard and the car jerked ahead, speeding faster yet.

She was hands-free on her cell phone. Com had arranged a patch from the police radio frequency. The line was open to responding officers answering to the address in Queens, where the witness lived.

"Detective Five Eight Eight Five, come in. K."

"Go ahead."

"We're on-site. Looks like a fire."

"Negative. It's acid fumes. Keep back. One whiff'll kill you. I've called FD. They're bringing the hazmat team."

"Roger, Detective. It's all over the place now, the smoke or fumes or whatever."

"Just keep it secure. And stay back. I'd tell you to look for the perp, but we don't have ID. He could be around there, waiting to see what happens."

She coughed once again and glanced at the oxygen tank on the passenger's seat.

No.

No time to stop.

"You all right, Detective?" the officer asked over the line.

"Fine."

"What's this all about?"

"Homeowner was a wit in the crane collapse this morning. Unsub got his address. Planted an IED—the acid, not explosives. I mean it, don't get close."

"Roger that."

A skidding turn.

"I'll be there in fifteen," she said and disconnected.

Then she turned her head slightly and said to the passengers in the backseat, "How you doing there?"

The woman, sitting directly behind her, said, "I think I'm going to be sick. I'm sorry."

"We're almost there."

"Okay."

"And you, sir?"

"I'm fine. I like your car."

In the rearview mirror, Sachs could see the couple. She looked peaked. He was gazing over the interior of the Ford as if he were a prospective buyer.

The man was the workman—the witness—the unsub had just tried to kill.

The call Sachs had received in the town house had come from him. He identified himself as one of the workmen at the site that morning. She decided to interview him herself and drove to Queens.

She had been nearly to the house when she'd placed a call.

"Hello?" It was the voice of the witness she was on her way to meet.

She identified herself. "I just want to make sure you're home. I'm almost there."

There'd been a pause. "Well, didn't he call you?" the worker asked.

"Who?"

"The other detective. He called me after you did. I assumed he'd tell you I gave him a statement, you know. There's no need for you to come."

Jesus . . . Sachs felt the jolt in her belly. Ignoring a sharp urge to cough, she had slammed the accelerator down. "Get out of your house. Now."

Of course: the call had been from the unsub or an associate—somehow, they'd gotten the worker's name and number and learning that he'd seen something, the man had to die. She knew the cast investigating the crane attack, and nobody would have called a witness without coordinating with Sachs.

"What do you—?"

She had said, "It wasn't a cop. It's the killer. You're in danger. He knows you're a witness. Get out now!"

"Oh, Lord."

"I'm almost there. Go out your back door, walk through the yard of the house behind you to Twenty-Fourth. I'll meet you there."

How would he come at them? she'd wondered. No idea, so she called in both ESU—NYPD's SWAT team—and reported an IED to Central and Bomb Squad.

She had then just arrived at the address and, scanning for any hostiles, skidded around the corner onto 24th. There they had clambered into the backseat—to the extent that an extremely pregnant woman could clamber—and Sachs spun tires, released ghosts of blue smoke.

Now she was en route to the local precinct, where she'd leave them in protective custody and then she herself would race back to the bungalow to walk the grid there.

And confront the fumes again; she'd been right about the MO; Unsub 89 had left an IED in the house. An acid bomb.

And with that thought, her lungs ironically began another bout of coughing.

She hit fifty again, balancing urgency with the conditions of one of her passengers: both the pregnancy and the nausea.

In the lot of the precinct, she stopped near the front door, turned to them.

"It's poison?" the wife asked. "Acid?"

"That's right."

She began to cry.

"And you're sure he put it inside?" From the husband.

"Yep, it's detonated. It's all through your house. Officers've seen the fumes."

"Christ," he muttered. "If we'd been inside . . ." He then asked, "This is all because I saw his SUV? That's what I told him I saw."

"Could you have gotten a look at him planting the device he used to sabotage the counterweights?"

"Maybe. I don't remember anything like that."

"How close were you to the crane?"

There was hesitation as the husband and wife glanced each other's way. Apparently, her question surprised them, as if she were missing some detail that they both knew.

The man said, "Well, pretty close. I was the operator."

24.

SACHS SAID, "I thought the operator died."

"What?" Garry Helprin's face was confused briefly. Then it went still. "That was Leon Roubideaux who died. Beam man. Nobody better." A grimace, laced with anger. "He was in the building, the twenty-first floor. Tried to run a plank to the tower, to rig an arresting cable. It was crazy. Wouldn't've worked. But . . . He was a friend."

"I'm sorry." The image returned: the rebar, dark with blood, flecked with bits of flesh and brain. "You climbed down before it fell?"

His wife, Peggy, said, "He rappelled."

Sachs lifted an eyebrow.

"Rock and mountain climbing're my hobbies. I keep three hundred feet of line in the cab. Just in case. I mean, the just-in-case I was thinking of was that the stairwell got damaged or there was a fire. Never thought I'd have to bail out of a crash."

"Can you tell me anything about the man who called, claiming he was a detective?"

"Not much. No foreign accent, or accent from here, like Southern or Boston. Said his name was Adams, I think. Didn't really say anything about himself."

"Caller ID?"

"It said 'NYPD.' No number. That's why I didn't think anything of it."

"Easy to set up a phone to do that. Happens all the time. And what did you tell him? That vehicle you mentioned?"

Her pad was out and a pen.

"A beige SUV, I don't know what kind, with Connecticut plates parked at the side of the site. Why I noticed it, it was parked in a funny place, not the lot reserved for workers. But I knew it was one of the crew 'cause there was a hard hat on the dash. We sometimes leave 'em there so the traffic cops know we're working and give us a break."

"What else did you see?"

"In the back there was a cardboard box, three feet square, eighteen inches high, maybe. No markings I remember. Some serious black gloves that went up to your elbows, a pair of what looked like expensive binoculars—I don't know what brand—and a paperback book. Couldn't see the cover very well, but it was bright: red and orange. Only one letter of the jacket you could see: 'K.' The last letter of the title."

"You've got good eyes."

"Crane operators—always looking."

"Any drink cups or cans?"

"No. Or food wrappers."

"Bumper stickers?"

"Don't think so."

What about Garry's sighting bothered the unsub enough to try to kill him?

Gripping his wife's hand, Garry asked, "When can we go back inside?"

"You can't go back. I want you to leave town until he's caught. Disappear. I want him to think you're dead."

The man nodded. "So he won't know I told you what I saw."

"Exactly."

"Just leave?" his wife whispered. "No clothes? No money, nothing?"

"Whatever's in your wallet or purse. That's it."

They looked at each other. She said, "Benji can pick us up. We can stay with them in Syosset."

Garry was staring out the window. He said in a low, angry voice, "He killed her."

Sachs lifted an eyebrow.

"Big Blue. That's what I named her. After Paul Bunyan's ox. We put up thirty-four buildings together."

Sachs said, "Come on, let's get you inside."

Inside the precinct house, Sachs handed the couple off to the community relations officer, a kind-eyed woman of about fifty. She led them to the watch room.

The wife embraced Sachs hard—if awkwardly, because of the woman's near-bursting physique.

The detective returned to the car and sat with her head back—which seemed to help the coughing. Some oxygen. A new sensation—stinging—in her chest.

The ER?

X-ray?

No.

She sat up, cranked the engine and texted Rhyme.

Unsub was at witness's house. Queens. He got their name. Set an IED. They're safe. Will canvass neighbors to see if anybody saw him.

Sixty seconds after she sent the message, she received a reply.

She felt a blow in her gut as she stared at the words.

Get statement but we have an ID. Unsub 89 is the
Watchmaker. Gilligan working for him but dead now.
Evidence at scene where you are? We need it. You
okay to search?

The Watchmaker . . . Well, this changed everything.
Her response was simple:
Yes.
A fast hit of oxygen, then she rolled the canister onto the
passenger-side floor and slammed the transmission into first.

25.

WHILE HE WAS never uneasy, as anyone else might use the word, anyone *normal*, an intense hum of edgy anticipation now pulsed within him.

Charles Hale's entire plan hinged upon what was about to happen.

He wasn't concerned about security; the associate he was meeting had been vetted multiple times and there were precautions in place. It was simply that, as with a timepiece, the slightest deviation from tolerances would make the difference between functional and useless. And he needed this person's role in his plan to work out perfectly.

Like when he was making watches he had to depend on a metalworker in Germany to make the springs—an art in itself.

A third-party expert.

Just like now.

The traffic here in Harlem was thick and swam along the streets like a school of fish that were simultaneously uncertain and assertive. He pulled the Pathfinder into a slot near the City College of New York and walked west through St. Nicholas Park, along a winding pathway glistening from a recent sprinkling. He smelled earth, car exhaust, a floral scent from a row of yellow flowers that were nonlethal and, as he'd reflected not long before, of little practical use to him. They were, however, pleasant to look at. Hale had little time for aesthetics, but he was human, after all, and could be moved, provided the emotion wasn't a distraction or dilutant.

He broke from the park and started along 139th Street, part of Strivers' Row, a nineteenth-century residential real estate project by David H. King Jr., the man responsible for constructing the 1889 *New York Times* building, the base of the Statue of Liberty and the second Madison Square Garden. The brownstone, yellow-brick and limestone town houses here, many of them trimmed with terra-cotta, were gems. They had been marketed to middle-class whites, the predominant demographic in Harlem when they were built. The project failed and the foreclosing financiers let the units sit empty for twenty years before reluctantly agreeing to sell to Black purchasers.

Hale knew this fact about the neighborhood because there was something else here that appealed to him, and he saw it now: an outdoor clock, jutting over the sidewalk.

Six feet in diameter, dating to just after the Harlem Renaissance of the 1920s and '30s, the timepiece was affixed to the façade of the Baker and Williams Building. The structure had at that time housed a musical instrument manufacturer, brass their specialty. Proud of their neighborhood—and more than a little aware of publicity—the owners decided to commission the clock.

Another motive for adding the attraction dated to the time that Baker, who was Black, was, for no fiscal reason, denied a loan by a vice president at Merchants Bank and Trust on Wall Street, over whose front door hung a similar clock. The timepiece that Baker ordered built and installed in Harlem was exactly one inch larger than the bank's.

The company was long gone and the building had been converted. It featured a coffee shop at street level with apartments on the remaining eight floors.

The clock was simple—there were no complications, not even a day-of-the-week function. But the one thing that it featured, which many others did not, was a transparent face. You could see the workings perfectly. If he happened to have a job in New York, it was one of the half-dozen or so outdoor timepieces to which he made a pilgrimage.

This was perhaps his favorite. Both for its construction and its history, which was proof that time exists wholly independent of race, gender, national origin, orientation. It had, you might say, no "time" for such human constructs and the division that resulted from them.

An interesting philosophical question, and one he might think about further.

Though not, of course, at the moment.

. . .

"Borrrrrring."

"Uhm. We're sitting on our asses with Cubano sandwiches and coffee. What, you want to be running tweakers to ground?"

"We're watching it being hung is what we're doing."

"What?"

"Watching wallpaper being hung." A pause. "Instead of paint drying. I was trying to be clever. Didn't work?"

"Hm."

The young detective who'd slung out the botched metaphor

stretched and sipped more of the sweet, powerful brew. He was in the driver's seat of the plumbing van—confiscated during a drug bust and now used for stakeouts and surveillance. It had a vague scent of metal, which probably came from metal, but might also have come from blood, which the Vehicles crew at NYPD hadn't sufficiently scrubbed away.

Assigned to the nearby 32 House, he and his partner, who was lounging in the passenger seat, resembled each other vaguely. They were both short, athletic. The noticeable difference: the driver was blond, the other brunet.

"We have to listen to that?" Brunet, slightly older, asked with an unnecessary glance at the radio. It was disgorging soft rock.

"So change it. Whatever you want. What're the odds he'll show up here?"

"You're not saying that you really mean what're the odds. You're saying it like you mean this's a waste of time."

Blond: "Ex-act-ly. No, that's country. Find another station."

"You said whatever I wanted. I changed it to country."

"Hip-hop."

"I could do hip-hop."

The NYPD unwritten rule was that on stakeout it was okay to listen to music because that tended to keep you awake. Sports were forbidden because games distracted from your mission of observing bad guys doing bad things. This was tough. Nine-tenths of the force loved sports. The rest were assholes.

The cultural compromise ironed out, they sat back and continued to watch the street.

"Uhm. Where'd this come from?" Brunet asked the question.

He hadn't been at the briefing. Blond had snagged him for the detail because they got along pretty well and agreed on most stuff. Important stuff. Teams and politics. Music didn't count.

"You know that guy in the wheelchair? Ex-cop."

"Who doesn't? Rhyme. Captain. Crime Scene."

Blond told him, "There's somebody got into the country. Terrorist or something. Snuck in in the wheel well of a plane. From England."

"Calling bogus. You couldn't do that. Impossible."

"A hundred bucks?" Blond reached into his pocket and pulled out bills. He counted. "Eighty-seven bucks?"

Brunet grew cautious. "Put it away. But how the fuck?"

"Oxygen tank and a heater."

"No shit." Brunet was both impressed at the feat and relieved that he hadn't lost the price of dinner for him and the wife.

"So this guy's the one behind the crane this morning."

"And Rhyme's running the case? How's that work? He's a civie."

"Sellitto out of Major Cases, downtown? He's lead."

"Oh, the sourpuss."

"But Rhyme kind of runs it."

Moments passed, more scanning the street. Brunet said: "So, he really can't walk? Rhyme?"

"Sure, he can walk. He runs marathons too. He just sits in a wheelchair all day 'cause it gets him sympathy."

"I'm only saying."

Sipping more of the Cuban coffee, Blond looked at the printout once more, then scanned the street again for a sighting of the man depicted on the sheet.

Charles Vespasian Hale.

A more ordinary-looking man you could not find.

One thing was key: the suspect would probably pay a visit to one of the legendary outdoor timepieces of the city.

He'd actually said that, Sellitto had said. "Legendary timepieces." Most of them in the watch room struggled not to snicker.

There were five of these Rhyme had picked and the PD had undercover teams on them all.

Brunet sat forward, scanned a passerby. Blond checked too. The pedestrian wasn't him.

Blond kept coming back to the end of the briefing Sellitto'd done, when he asked what the teams should do if he was spotted. He'd replied, "Call it in, follow. Keep watching. He makes you, or he moves on somebody, you take him." Sellitto had then hesitated and grumbled, "Standard procedures apply, but . . ."

The qualifier he ended his sentence with was a tough one.

He was talking about deadly force, while not really talking about it.

Officers can kill a suspect only when their lives or someone else's is in direct danger.

But . . .

With that one word, Sellitto was suggesting that Hale fell into a different category.

Meaning, without saying: take him out at the *least* presentation of threat.

But it wouldn't come to that.

Blond had decided that Sellitto was wrong. No way would Hale, if he really was that smart, risk getting collared or shot just to see a fucking clock, legendary or otherwise.

Especially the one they were parked across from. The timepiece that jutted out over the coffee shop in the Baker and Williams Building up here in Harlem was, the detective concluded, really just so-so.

26.

CHARLES HALE WAS moving through the crowded streets, just another man in Harlem, on his way to eat, to an ad presentation, to see a cousin who'd moved here recently, to meet his mistress for a fast lunchtime, to meet his wife for a real lunch.

Not jaunty, not cautious.

Walking in New York City mode.

Purposeful yet distracted.

Eyes ahead of him on the Baker and Williams clock.

"Excuse me."

He turned to see a woman in her thirties, blond hair pulled back, taut. She was tanned from the out-of-doors, not a machine. (Having tinted himself for various jobs, he knew the difference.) She wore a skirted suit of navy blue, a white blouse, pearls. She held a shopping bag from an upscale 58th Street boutique.

She displayed her phone. "I'm trying to find this mural." On the screen was a picture of the street painting depicting the poet Langston Hughes, a native son of Harlem.

He looked down at it. Then he drew his phone and called up a map. She looked at *his* screen.

Green dots appeared in the upper right-hand corner of both phones as the retinal scans did their duty. This form of proving ID had the lowest false acceptance and false rejection rate of all biometric security measures.

"There," he said, and they turned away from the huge clock and walked into the shop behind them, sat in the window. He ordered black coffee. It was chamomile tea for her.

"Did you get out to the Hamptons I didn't even bother the train the cab I wasn't sure if she'd get fired but sure enough and not a minute too soon the bottom line was a disaster . . ."

The rambling conversation, unrehearsed, ceased when the drinks arrived and they'd each assessed those sitting nearby were no threat.

Turning her deep blue eyes his way, she said, "Brad told me you've subbed out work to him before."

Brad was the leader of the crew she worked for much of the time. They were, in effect, mercenaries, though the half dozen operated far more subtly than the camo-wearing, inked and bearded grunts one thought of when hearing that job description. When Hale had contacted Brad Garland with his needs, the man had instantly recommended the woman who sat in front of him now.

"That's right." Hale didn't need to say the results had been good. If they hadn't been, she wouldn't be here now.

She sipped tea and sat back. "To let you know. Somebody saw me at the drop site."

A dialectologist would situate her somewhere between the rust belt and cornfields.

"Yes?"

She went on to explain that the real estate agent who'd leased her the drop had lied or been mistaken. The buildings on either side of hers were supposed to be unoccupied, but the one to the west had been sold. A young stockbroker had seen her and insisted on helping her move some things into her space.

"Would have been too obvious to refuse. But it's handled." She added matter-of-factly, "I gave him a beer laced with thiopental and midazolam. My recipe. I know the dosage. He'll be in a coma for four, five days. I drove to the South Bronx to get rid of the truck and dumped him on the way. Not a high-traffic area, but he'd be spotted. Wall Street boy buys drugs in a bad area, ODs. Nobody'll think it's more than that."

"Are you sure he'll wake up?"

"No." Nothing followed that stark assessment but a sip of tea.

"What name are you using?" he asked. Pseudonyms were common in this line of work.

"With you, my real one. Simone."

"And Charles."

But they would stick to first names only.

He glanced at her ringless fingers and noticed that her right index pad seemed calloused. This happened occasionally when one practiced repetitively with handguns, firing hundreds of rounds a session.

"Did you build it yourself?"

"Some of it. Not the software. I can code, but I needed somebody special. I hired a good kid. He's an expert at reverse engineering source codes. You need to know Assembly for that."

Which told Hale nothing. He never burdened his mind with facts or skills that he didn't use in his jobs. He had once read that Sherlock Holmes did not know the Copernican theory of the universe, and assumed that the sun revolved around the earth—and, why not? If a case could be solved by knowing that mornings saw the sun in the east, and evenings in the west, well, who needed more than that?

In this, Hale and Lincoln Rhyme were very similar.

He'd done a great deal of reading about his counterpart.

He set his coffee down and noted that she was studying him, and not obscuring the fact.

She knew his age and had probably seen pre-surgery pictures. He would have thought she'd be startled and put off by his aging and uglifying himself. But that did not appear to be the case.

Her head turned to her left, slightly.

"The plumbing van. Police or FBI?"

"NYPD." The vehicle, which was on stakeout duty a block away, across from the Baker and Williams Building, had regular commercial plates, not government, but Hale had run them; it was registered to the city of New York. Confiscated.

"They're there because of the clock?"

"That's right. It means Lincoln knows I'm in town. That's one reason I wanted to come here—to the clock. To find out."

How this had happened, Hale couldn't guess. The criminalist never failed to surprise him.

She handed him the bag she'd brought. Inside, there might be silk socks or a Brooks Brothers tie. Definitely there was an envelope, containing an address and a key.

He reached into his breast pocket and handed her an envelope. It was light, but contained a quarter million dollars in diamonds, those without microscopic registration numbers, which—people would be surprised to learn—nearly all retail gems contain.

A few clients accepted offshore wire transfer payments. Nobody in this business took crypto. If a client proposed it, Hale dropped them instantly.

She said, "That clock. The big one?"

He nodded.

Neither of them looked.

"You can see all the gears. It's interesting."

"They're not called gears."

"No?"

"They're wheels."

"Even with the teeth?"

"Yes. Gears're what's used in transmissions. In timepieces they're 'wheels.' The mechanism's called the wheelwork. Or train."

"Are you making one now?"

"A watch? Not here."

She cocked her head and said, "There's a crane above the drop spot."

He didn't look into the bag for the address. "Where?"

"West Thirty-Eighth."

Hale offered a faint, and rare, smile. "No, that's not the next target. Though it would be ironic. We should leave." He set money down for the bill. "That mural on your phone. Why Langston Hughes?"

"Poetry's an interest."

"So you really want to see it?"

"Yes."

So the trip to Harlem was a pilgrimage for both of them.

She rose. Hale did too. The script required a pressing together of cheeks and a sincere "Thanks"—for the birthday present belatedly delivered.

He said, "I'll text you about the next step. Tomorrow."

Her eyes still on his, she offered, "My time's yours." Then she turned, blending seamlessly into a throng of passersby.

27.

COUNTDOWN: 16 HOURS

SACHS WALKED INTO the parlor, carrying what was not even a carton full of evidence. Just a few bags with chain-of-custody cards attached.

She vetted everything through the security devices in the lobby, then handed the material to Mel Cooper. After a hit of oxygen, she explained to Rhyme, Sellitto and Cooper, "The crane's operator lived. It was another worker who died."

Lon Sellitto asked, "How the hell?"

She set the tank aside and gave a faint laugh. "Rappelled from the top just before it went over. Apparently, the man loves his heights. A rock climber, mountaineer."

"Lord," Mel Cooper murmured, flipping through the evidence bags. "Heights."

She continued, "The unsub, well, the *Watchmaker*, found out he was a witness and set a device to take him and his wife out."

"Did any neighbors see anything?"

"No. One saw some mist coming from a window, but she thought it was steam. Nothing else."

"How'd Hale get his name?" Rhyme asked.

"A detective called this morning and asked if he'd seen anything suspicious. He was canvassing all the workers. He had a list. Which I'm sure Gilligan swiped when he was here and gave to Hale."

Rhyme nodded, then asked, "Well, what did the operator see that nearly got him killed?"

"A beige SUV parked where it shouldn't've been. Inside, a hard hat on the dash. A three-by-three-foot-by-eighteen-inch box in the back. No markings that he could remember. Gloves that were probably neoprene. Binoculars—nice ones—and a book, paperback with an orange and yellow cover. Letter 'K'—the last letter on the cover. No other information."

Rhyme said slowly, "All right. Maybe he's worried about the SUV, but I'm sure it's gone now. The Watchmaker wouldn't use the same vehicle twice. The cardboard box, gloves, hat? Nothing there that Hale'd worry about. The binoculars or the book could be something. Why doesn't he want us to see them?" No answer presented itself. He asked Sachs, "Get into the operator's house?"

"No. The battalion commander wouldn't release the scene. Too much acid and fumes. But I got a look through a window. The device had dissolved. Just like at Eighty-Ninth Street, on the counterweights."

It was good she hadn't pushed it. The exposure she'd had was bad enough. Any more might have knocked her into the hospital—and with their prey now being the Watchmaker, he couldn't have her sidelined.

"And that?" Rhyme nodded to the carton Mel Cooper had taken.

The exceedingly *minuscule* carton.

"I got shoe prints and trace, front and back doors."

A moment later Cooper called, "The shoe print's ninety percent likely the same as what Ron found at the Gilligan homicide scene. I'm looking at the trace now . . ." Eyes on the GC/MS screen, he called, "Same trace as earlier—the clay, bacteria, rotting wood and cloth fibers. Liquor. Again, old, old, old . . . But an addition: ammonia and isocyanic acid."

"Urea," Rhyme said.

Sellitto shrugged. "He walked through where somebody peed. Doesn't tell us anything."

"Walked through where somebody peed a long, long time ago. Those are what urea degrades into."

Sachs wrote the discovery on the whiteboard.

By comparison, yes, Sellitto's scrawl was terrible.

The detective looked at his watch. "I'm getting home, shower and dinner. You need me, call. Why do people say things like that? If you need me, of course you're going to call."

He steamed out of the town house. Mel Cooper said he was doing the same.

Ron Pulaski was downtown. He'd switched temporarily to the Eddie Tarr case and was tracking down a lead on the red sedan that the bomb maker had supposedly driven when he killed a witness on the Upper East Side. Apparently, though, the lead had not panned out and now he was returning to the city to accompany Sachs in making the rounds of construction sites that contained the tower cranes they considered the most likely targets. This was mostly to check security—but it was possible that they might happen upon the Watchmaker in the act.

Stranger things had happened.

Thom appeared in the doorway and asked, "Dinner?"

"We'll get to it," Rhyme said absently, staring at the murder boards.

At that moment, an email appeared on Rhyme's computer, a Zoom request.

The name on the sender's email matched a name on the board: Stephen Cody, the U.S. representative currently in a race for reelection. The man Lyle Spencer had interviewed earlier in the day.

That man Rhyme had never heard of, despite the fact he was the criminalist's advocate in Washington, DC.

He said, "Sachs, let's see what he has to say."

She sat down at the computer attached to the largest monitor in the room and typed. A moment later they were looking at the man, businessman handsome, thick hair a bit mussed, the sleeves of his light blue shirt rolled up. He wore no tie and his collar was open. His eyeglasses had dark red frames. Rhyme wondered, in passing, if the color affected how he visually processed what he saw. Interesting idea. He'd do a study to see if frame color had any effect on visual acuity. Something to consider at crime scene searches.

"Representative Cody. I'm Detective Sachs."

"Detective. And, Captain Rhyme, an honor to meet you."

Rhyme nodded.

Cody explained he'd been a federal prosecutor before seeking office and had learned of Rhyme through that job. He'd also read some of the books in a series about Rhyme—some of the more famous cases he'd worked on. Rhyme had always wondered why the author bothered.

"Detective Spencer was asking me about the attack on the crane, some affordable housing activists. Housing's one of my platform planks. A real problem everywhere, especially in New York. There's something to their demands: we have so much square footage the government could put to good use, but there's resistance. Major resistance."

"Hm. A shame," Rhyme mumbled and Sachs cut him a glance, which unfolded into: don't be sarcastic, we might need him. His response was to lift an eyebrow in concession.

"But I'm sure you're not interested in lectures. I'll tell you what I found: None of the organizations in the affordable housing world know anything about this Kommunalka Project. And no one's ever heard of affordable housing terrorism. When you think about it, it's not a cause where violence really works. You can burn down ski resort developments, you can spike trees in lumber forests, you can monkey-wrench land-clearing bulldozers. But those're directed against an *enemy*: the oil companies, the developers. Affordable housing's goal isn't to stop anybody from doing anything. It's just to make living quarters available to people who can't otherwise afford it."

"Helpful," Rhyme said. And it was true. He had not thought about that.

"If I hear anything else, though, I'll be in touch."

Sachs thanked him and they ended the meeting.

She said, "You going to vote for him?"

"I don't know. When's the election?"

"November. It's always in November."

"Is it? Who's he running against?"

"Her name's Leppert, former prosecutor too. She went after the cartels in South Texas. I like her."

"Really?" he asked absently. "So, I think that confirms it. Affordable housing? It's just one of his complications."

Charles Vespasian Hale was a killer and a scam artist and a burglar and a mercenary.

But he was something else as well: he was an illusionist. He took his lead from the concept of complications in watchmaking: any function of a watch or clock other than telling the time. Complications could be hidden within the instrument, like a bell-striking mechanism; or they could be visible on the display, such as dials indicating the phases of the moon, tides, seasons. Watches with many such features were called "grande complications."

The term could also be used to describe Hale's plots.

Rhyme had done considerable research into the subject of horology, to better understand his adversary. He'd learned that the watch with the most complications is the Franck Muller Aeternitas Mega 4. Thirty-six features and nearly fifteen hundred parts.

He wondered if Hale owned one. Maybe he'd made a watch himself with even more complications than that.

"All right," he said slowly, "we'll put affordable housing off the table temporarily. Then who hired him and what's he really got planned?"

Sachs asked, "If it's something else, then what does that do to the deadline?"

In thirteen hours, the Watchmaker had promised, another crane would come crashing to earth.

"We assume he'll keep going. Whatever he's up to, the sabotage is part of it."

The front door buzzer sounded. Rhyme and Sachs both looked at the monitor, each with an at-this-time-of-night? expression.

A nondescript man, Black, middle-aged, was looking up at the camera. He wore a dark suit, blue or black, and a white shirt with a tie. On his belt was a gold badge.

"Yes?"

"Captain Rhyme. Lawrence Hylton. Internal Affairs. Sorry to bother you this late. Can I speak with you?" The accent was Caribbean, Rhyme judged. Jamaican, maybe.

Rhyme let him inside and Sachs went to greet and usher him into the parlor.

When he stepped inside, he scanned the impressive laboratory and then focused on Rhyme. Once again, a visitor's face glowed with minor adulation.

Rhyme's own expression was clouded. Not because of the man's presence, or the somewhat irritating awe, but because of his learning just now that he had absolutely no idea what the Watchmaker was up to.

Thom swung through the room, surprised there was a guest. He asked about coffee or another beverage—missing, or ignoring, Rhyme's frown meant to discourage anything that kept Hylton here a moment longer than necessary.

But the detective declined with a grateful nod.

Sachs stifled a cough and motioned to a chair.

Bad news. He sat. The stay might be longer than Rhyme had hoped.

"We understand Detective Gilligan was behind the Department of Structures and Engineering theft and was working with the man behind the crane attacks."

"Yes, that's how it appears."

Hylton removed a well-worn notebook from his inside breast pocket, a gold pen too. He jotted something at the top of the small sheet. Date and place, most likely. In the old days, when he was a line detective, this is what Rhyme did too. Even then, though, he found himself taking more notes about the evidence at the scene than what the witnesses had to say. He sometimes missed their testimony entirely.

"And who is that other man?"

Rhyme had alerted One PP and the mayor's office the minute they learned that Hale was in town. He supposed Internal Affairs wasn't kept informed of cases out of their bailiwick, though given Hale's reputation and his history of jobs in New York, it seemed odd that Hylton didn't know.

"Charles Vespasian Hale. Professional criminal. He's got a file, NYPD and FBI, if you want to read more."

"Is he the one who killed Detective Gilligan?"

"We believe so."

Notes were jotted, examined, and then added to. "And the reason for that?"

"Unknown at this point."

Hylton's eyes returned to the lab. He seemed about to ask a question regarding it, but then sensed Rhyme's impatience. He gave a near smile and turned his eyes back to the criminalist. "What evidence do you have against Detective Gilligan?"

Rhyme nodded at Sachs and she explained what they'd found.

More jotting, and then Hylton was frowning. "I mean, all this to make housing available for the poor?"

A shrug. "We've decided that Hale is up to something else," said Sachs. "We don't know what at this point."

"Though we do know one item on his agenda," offered Rhyme. "To kill me."

The gold pen paused.

"Some outfit has a contract on you? OC—the mob?"

"No. It's personal. And that's one of the reasons Hale hired Gilligan. To get inside here and find out what kind of security I have."

Hylton looked at the X-ray and the nitrate detector. "I wondered about those." He then asked, "You have any idea where this Hale is now?"

"No."

If we did . . .

"Did Detective Gilligan give you any clues about associates he might've been working with? Either on this case or any others?"

Rhyme and Sachs regarded each other. She shook her head.

The detective put the pad and pen away, buttoned his jacket, and with a last look around the parlor started for the door. He paused and turned back. "So, this Hale wants to tag you, and Gilligan was working with him. I don't know whether it's important or not, but there's something maybe you should know. After we got the paperwork on him, we pulled Gilligan's activity report. Last week he went to Emergency Service and checked out six flash-bangs and five C4 breaching charges.

"Put 'em together and there's more than enough bang to be fatal. We've searched his office and house. We didn't find them."

Hylton glanced at the scanner in the front hallway. "You get any packages from people you don't know, well, make sure you take a close look. And don't drop 'em accidentally."

28.

CHARLES HALE GAZED up at the tower crane that Simone had mentioned as they sat in the Harlem coffeehouse.

The jib was weather-vaning in the wind; the slewing plate had been released so it could turn and keep pressure from the wind off the mast. A huge American flag flapped noisily two hundred feet up. He'd think that might affect performance, but it wasn't his concern.

He turned and glanced at the building west of the one Simone had rented as a drop site. He'd half-expected the police, investigating how the young man who lived there had come to overdose on an anesthetic cocktail.

But no. He had the street to himself.

With the key she'd given him in the "gift bag," he opened the door. Coincidentally, the key was the same as he used in all his safe houses, including the one here. It was of an unusual design, a short length of chain. The lock it fit into was as unpickable as one could be.

Inside, hand near a weapon in his waistband, he clicked on the green-tinted overheads and walked to the box containing the device she'd had made. He looked down at the printing on the cardboard side.

KitchenAid Bread Maker Deluxe

He was amused at the camouflage. He knelt and opened the lid, looking inside.

The device was of quite the compact design, resembling a generator of the sort you'd buy at a home improvement store. A burnished metal base, on top of which sat an array of metal and black carbon fiber boxes and tubes and fixtures and wires. To one side were large batteries. The top was the business end: a brushed aluminum tube, two feet long and six inches in diameter.

Most devices of destruction appear haphazard. True IEDs are just jumbles of wires and circuit boards and chunks of explosives. No order, sloppy and tangled.

What Simone had created, however, was stylish, elegant, even sensuous. German Bauhaus design of the early twentieth century came to mind.

He ran his hand slowly over the top, regretting the necessity for latex gloves. He would have liked to feel its texture on his skin.

As a watchmaker by avocation, Hale was talented with tools and had the ability to construct any number of things—the acid delivery systems for the cranes, for instance, or the one that killed the witness in Queens.

But this was different. This was special, beyond his skills.

All the more reason for respect. Then he sealed the box back up and wheeled the bulky thing out to the back of the SUV. He wrestled it in.

He then returned to the apartment and found the cardboard box that Simone had mentioned in the note she'd given him in Harlem. Inside were what appeared to be a bag of flour and a can of Crisco. Hale dumped the contents of the bag—a metallic-shaded powder—onto the floor near where Simone's device had rested. He opened the can and poured the brown gelatin inside over the floor in a trail from the door to the powder.

The last thing he extracted from the box was a Fourth of July sparkler.

At the doorway, he turned and lit it, dropping it on the gelatin, which ignited immediately. The mix of gasoline, naphthalene and palmitate—napalm—caught fire immediately and began to burn toward the powder, which was iron oxide rust and aluminum, also known as thermite. The napalm burned at about 1,000 degrees Celsius, hot enough to do considerable damage, but the thermite would reach a temperature of 4,000 degrees, guaranteeing that not a molecule of DNA remained.

Hale returned to the SUV and drove down to Greenwich Village. There, near the Hamilton Court cul-de-sac, he left the vehicle in a garage one of his companies had rented and returned to the trailer.

His security app told him that no one had breached either the cul-de-sac nor the safe house, which he entered. Closing the door, he shut off the security system, then walked into the bedroom, stripped off the outer garments he was wearing and hung them in the small closet. The suit jacket and trousers had been specially made and had neoprene linings. He was always careful when planting the acid but, of course, accidents happen, especially with such an unstable chemical.

In the minuscule bathroom, he opened the medicine cabinet door and removed the jar of Penotanyl, prescribed by the doctor who had done the cosmetic surgery. Unscrewing the top, he rubbed the white substance on his face from forehead to chin. The slicing and rearranging to alter him had been so extensive that the ointment was necessary to keep the skin from drying and cracking.

Hale was a man of iron discipline, but even he found it hard to resist rubbing during the bouts of itching.

Another glance at the stranger in the mirror. Still startling.

He replaced the medicine and then dressed in jeans, a black T-shirt and a sweatshirt. His sidearm, a smaller Glock, a model 43, went into the holster inside his belt. No silencer for this weapon. In close combat, you want noise.

Logging on to his computer, he typed in a local news station's URL. Hale was one person who did not regret the demise of print journalism. Oh, he read news voraciously. He had sixteen anonymous subscriptions—ranging from the *New York Times* to the Bulgarian *State Daily*—but he needed the immediacy of online editions.

DECORATED NYPD DETECTIVE KILLED ON LOWER EAST SIDE

The story reported that Andrew Raymond Gilligan, a sixteen-year veteran, had been shot gangland style. It was likely that the killer had been a mob enforcer, shooting Gilligan to stop an organized crime investigation he was working on. The police, though, had no suspects in mind.

"He was a good cop and a good man," his brother, Mick Gilligan, 43, said. "He didn't deserve this."

He continued to scan several other sources and found nothing of the acid attack on Garry Helprin and his wife. Which meant they were dead. Their bodies would be discovered eventually; with luck, though, he'd be gone by then.

Hale closed out of the site. He brewed a cup of coffee and, after scanning the security monitors, sat back and sipped the hot beverage.

He reflected on the story about Gilligan's death. It was illuminating. The theory that he'd been killed by an OC hit man was nonsense—a murder like that bought gang leaders far more trouble than it prevented. No, the story was floated as a smoke screen. And *that* meant that Lincoln and the others knew about the connection between Gilligan and him, and that Hale was the shooter.

This was unfortunate, but not unexpected.

He tried to anticipate what Lincoln would do with that connection.

That remained a mystery.

But Hale's plan was unfolding quickly; he would finish up here and soon be gone.

More coffee. Drinking it slowly. Hale had an idea for a weight-loss program. The key thing to count? Not calories or carbs or fat, but *time*. The slower you ate, the fuller you felt and the less you took in. And you enjoyed the act of indulging longer. Another creative idea he would never put into practice. Every once in a rare while, he regretted striving for perfect anonymity.

His eyes were on the clepsydra that had so interested the late Andy Gilligan. The ancient Romans relied on sundials and obelisks for most of their timekeeping, but on overcast days and at night, they used hourglasses like this one.

Hale had once read a story about the emperor Caligula. A fascinating man, he was the world's first Photoshopper, having a sculpture of his own head affixed to a statue of Jupiter. He was also completely mad, vindictive and paranoid. He got it into his demented head to kill a number of Jews who were not worshipping him with sufficient adulation. But an advisor convinced him that the clepsydra in his chambers was magic, and that it had transported him back in time. He'd already murdered hundreds in the Jewish community, so there was no need to kill any more.

Caligula believed the man and would spend hours playing with the timepiece, convinced that with it he could move back and forth in time.

As he sipped the coffee, finishing the cup, he let his thoughts wander away from imperial Rome—and away from Lincoln Rhyme.

A minute later he picked up an unused burner phone.

"No," he told himself and set it down. He'd actually spoken aloud.

Then he lifted the unit once more and tapped in a number.

29.

DRIVING NORTH THROUGH Tribeca, Ron Pulaski was on the phone with an Alcohol, Tobacco, Firearms and Explosives supervisor.

"I'll tell you, Officer, we've been talking." Nate Lathrop was speaking loudly, as he'd done throughout the conversation. This happened occasionally with those in this particular profession. Because of the explosives side of the outfit's business, a number of agents' hearing had suffered over the years.

Pulaski was on Bluetooth earbuds and lifted the phone to turn the volume down.

"Go on, Nate."

"What?"

Pulaski shouted, "Go on!"

"Us and the Bureau and Homeland? No trace of Tarr on any of the wires. No intel on any target. We think he was transiting."

"So he's not priority?"

Nate shouted, "So I have to tell you he's not high priority."

"All right, but you've got the red sedan out, don't you?"

"The sedan? Yeah. But—"

"I know there are a lot of them, but I sent you the likely time he hit either the bridge or the tunnel to get back to Jersey. I just want somebody to look over the vids."

"Yeah, it's in the system."

Pulaski almost added, "Did your meeting include the discussion that, target or not, he had probably murdered someone?" But what was the point?

They would care, of course, about a homicide in Manhattan, but they wouldn't care as much as Pulaski.

He thanked the man in a shout and disconnected.

In truth, he didn't really mind how it was turning out—the investigation into Tarr was his alone. He didn't have to answer to the feds, who could be overbearing at times. A lot of jurisdictional turf wars in this business. Tarr was his and his alone.

Good.

He turned and negotiated his way through the warren of streets in this part of Manhattan—old, and designed when horses and wagons were the means of transportation. The lead had not paid off. A video camera had recorded a red sedan at the entrance to the Holland Tunnel, but the official camera had not been working properly and it didn't record the tag. Pulaski had canvassed other cameras and finally gotten a number.

It was registered to a man who was a salesman for a drug company. He checked out.

Now time to get back to the Watchmaker and the cranes. He and Amelia were going to hit possible target sites.

He glanced at the time. Late. He'd hoped the search here, near the Holland Tunnel, would go faster and then he'd get a brief dinner with Jenny and the kids.

As he drove he reflected on Sellitto tapping him to be Lincoln's replacement.

This, he did not count as a victory, because in order for it to happen, the criminalist would have to retire or . . . Well, no desire to finish that sentence.

He'd tell Jenny, of course. He'd tell his brother, Tony, a twin, who was Patrol, out of the 6 House in Greenwich Village.

He was debating where to go for a beer to talk about it. Next Thursday—the night he and Tone went out alone for drinks and dinner.

His mobile hummed. The caller was from Queens, the crime scene lab.

"Hello?"

"Officer Pulaski?"

"That's right."

"Hey," the woman's voice said, "sorry to bother you this late."

"That's fine. Go ahead."

"I'm logging in the evidence from the Dalton murder? That you ran this morning?"

"Okay."

"There's an issue with chain of custody, I—"

A blaring horn filled the night and Pulaski's car slammed full speed into an SUV that materialized in front of him. The Hyundai that he'd hit spun in a full circle, while the Accord that Pulaski was driving—their personal car—jerked sideways and flipped over onto its roof, skidding to a stop against a lamppost, which came tumbling down. Two pedestrians leapt out of its way.

Stunned, he blinked away the shock and began to assess if anything was broken. No. He was functioning okay. Fumbling for the phone, he glanced at the other vehicle. He had to get out and see about their condition.

But as he popped the belt and crumpled hard against the ceiling, he smelled the powerful, astringent odor of gasoline. And with a whooshing roar, orange and blue flames appeared as fast and as shockingly as the SUV had.

They danced around him, a bright and playful display that was in stark contrast to the monotone nighttime street.

30.

"COMPLICATED," HALE SAID.

The light in this portion of the trailer, the office converted to a bedroom, was unenthusiastic, but he was close enough to make out the details of what he gazed at.

"When did you learn to do it?"

The two lay side by side on the weak mattress covered with pristine sheets and a down comforter, all of which were underneath their naked bodies at the moment.

Simone replied, "Young. I was young."

He examined her handiwork once again, leaning closer, and in doing so, smelled her smells, and his. Saw a scar, of which she was not self-conscious in the least: a ragged slice under her left breast. Another was just below the rib cage.

She bore some tats too: a 5.56mm round, in silhouette, on one shoulder blade, and Chinese characters on the other. He didn't know the meaning.

"May I?" Perhaps an ironic request considering how they had just spent the past hour. But it seemed right.

"Yes."

He lifted her tawny braid and studied the twined strands.

The symmetry, the perfect intervals between turns . . . they touched Hale on some visceral level and gave him unusual pleasure.

"Your mother, she teach you?"

"She wasn't part of my life."

"Then how?" Maybe her father. Why only a mother could teach her child to braid hair was a thought from an older era. But if the topic of her maternal superstructure was off-limits, then paternal might be as well. "If you're okay with it," he said.

"Of course. It was my mentor. A former nun. She delivered food in sub-Saharan Africa. The outpost kept getting hit by a warlord. He told her to order twice the food she was allotted by the charity running the place and give it to him. If she didn't, he and his men would take girls from the village instead. He ended up taking more than half and some girls anyway. She prayed they would stop. When that didn't work, she quit the church. The warlord didn't survive till their next encounter. He was gunned down."

"And how did she become your mentor?"

"I found myself in Africa too. I was there with someone." A pause. "Circumstances changed. I needed work suddenly. One of the men she paid to deal with the warlords turned on her. I found myself in a position to remedy the situation."

Hale too used such euphemisms in his work.

Remedy . . .

"It seems I had a talent."

She was not inclined to elaborate on this aspect of her biography either. He sensed there was nothing in the tale that was troubling or too sensitive to share. It was more that the narrative was tedious to her and, therefore, to anyone else.

Their original topic, though, enlivened her: "Braids have a

history. Archeologists found figurines and statues that're more than twenty-five thousand years old. Africa and France. Asia too. I do a different one every few days. They could be this."

It was a single strand.

"Or a fishtail, a five-stranded rope, a French, a waterfall. Some I make up as I go. In some cults—even today—women are required to wear them. Their husbands insist. A sign of subservience. I like the irony."

"You can also pin it up quickly if you need to fight."

Her expression said that she had done just that.

The strands ended in a blue ribbon.

She rolled toward him. Her breasts, compact, pressed into a crease. He mirrored her pose and his hand went to her shoulder, near the bullet ink. The muscle was solid, which he knew not from this touch, but from their fierce joining. Legs too. He supposed she ran. Was it an attempt to bleed away some tension, some concern, some fire within her? She presented calm, to the edge of blasé. He didn't believe it.

He had examined her scars. Now she looked at his. With the trigger-calloused index finger she touched the raised skin over a bullet wound. Then a longer one. It had been created some years ago when an IED meant to kill him had not, though it had turned a Coca-Cola can into an improbable but efficient piece of shrapnel.

Touching the braid again.

He had not been with a woman in this way—without paying—for several years. He found it consuming. And for Charles Hale to be consumed was a rare thing. It could be dangerous.

She seemed aware suddenly of the ticking of a clock, a Royal Bonn porcelain, which sat nearby on a shelf. Her eyes were on it and swung slowly to him. "I've followed you. When Brad told me he'd gotten your message, I told him I wanted the job. I wanted to work with you."

He made a gesture toward his face, his scalp. "Wasn't exactly who you were expecting, though, was I?"

Her face tightened and she scoffed, meaning she had no interest in what he looked like. He recalled their first meeting, at the coffeehouse, she'd glanced at his face quickly, out of curiosity at the surgery, and then focused for the rest of their time together on his eyes.

"I've wondered. Why clocks?"

"When you build watches, boredom is not a possibility."

"Ah, boredom." A very faint tightening of her lips. She understood.

He told her what he rarely thought of any longer: his childhood, in the Arizona desert, absent parents. Long hours to fill. "Time dragged. I was drawn to what marked the passage. Studying watches, collecting watches, *making* watches. It made those hours bearable.

"But then timepieces . . . they weren't enough. I needed to put the theory behind them into something bigger. Just as complicated, just as elegant. But more intense.

"I got the answer when a friend's life was destroyed. A drunk driver. He ended up in a wheelchair."

"Like Lincoln Rhyme."

"Hm. The driver? No remorse. None. I decided to kill him. But I realized I'd need to plot it out as carefully as a watchmaker plans his timepiece. It's not hard to kill someone. You—"

"Hit them over the head with a pipe."

He paused. His very words, with the exception that the weapon in his illustration would be a brick.

He said, "No elegance."

"And then there's escape."

Hale offered, "It worked. He died. I got away. The line was crossed and I knew I'd never go back."

"What's next for you?" she asked.

"Underground. For a while, at least. With Lincoln's death, there'll be people after me."

She said, "Always happens with a public target."

"You?"

"A kill. College town. No one connected to the school. An OC informant. But I'll use the faculty as a cover. I'll be a poet."

Hale couldn't fathom how the wheels and springs of *that* plot would work.

Simone eased onto her back and tugged the sheet up to her armpits. Not from modesty, but because the trailer was drafty. "You must have hundreds of clocks and watches. Is there a favorite?"

"Always the next one, the one I'm working on at the moment."

She nodded; she understood this too.

"But of those I've made in the past? A clock made out of meteoric iron."

She said, "Kamacite and taenite. Alloys of nickel and iron. For one job, I had to be a geologist."

"The only naturally found metallic form of iron on earth. Meteorites."

She was considering something, eyes on the ceiling. "But . . . springs? Iron wouldn't have elasticity."

"No springs. I used a weight escarpment. I carved a small chain out of the iron. Another favorite? Not one I made. I acquired it. Made out of bone. It does have some metal. But I think you could make a tension device from bone that could power it."

"Human bone?"

"I don't know. I suppose it could be tested. Maybe there's some DNA left."

"Who made it?"

"A prisoner in Russia. Political prisoner. He was on a work detail and they let him have tools. It took him a year. He made it as a bribe for one of the guards to let him escape. It could be sold for thousands. In dollars. You couldn't carry enough rubles to buy it."

"Did it work?"

"The clock worked fine. His plans didn't. The guard took it and shot him."

"How do you know the story?"

"The horology world is small."

"All the clocks you're talking about are analog. Wheels, springs, weights, chains. No interest in digital ones?"

"I respect them but, no, not really. Other than one. The atomic clock."

"I've heard of it. It sets universal time, right?"

He nodded.

"Even when working perfectly, mechanical and electric and electronic clocks're affected by temperature, solar flares, magnetic fields, altitude changes. The highest level—nearly faultless—are ones that measure time according to the resonant frequency of atoms. In the U.S., the National Institute of Standards and Technology uses cesium atoms cooled to near absolute zero."

"*Nearly* faultless?"

"They lose or gain one second every three hundred million years."

"Does life need to be that accurate?"

"Business meetings, luncheon dates, theater curtains, weddings, no. Airline scheduling, trains, timing of radiation bursts in cancer treatments, yes. Outer space? A timing error of a billionth of a second can mean nearly a twelve-inch positioning error on reentry. And your spaceship disintegrates. Atomic clocks are being replaced by optical. Even more accurate. Do you collect anything? Poetry, I suppose."

"And miniature steam engines. They run on alcohol."

"Don't know that I've ever seen one."

"I find them hypnotic. The blue flame, the smell of the fire."

"What do they do?"

"Turn wheels and belts, spin governors. There are a few that're practical. One can run a generator in a safe house I have that's off the grid. Steam can do just about anything electrons can. Charles Babbage had a design for a steam-powered computer, the Analytical Engine, he called it—1834. It was never finished, but I've always thought I might like to get the plans and do it myself. Were there ever any steam-powered clocks?"

"One, also the eighteen hundreds, Birmingham, England. It was essentially a promotion piece for the values of steam. Here and there nowadays, some tourist attractions."

"Are they accurate?"

"As accurate as the escarpment. The steam doesn't turn the hands. It lifts weights that drive the wheels. There's one in the Midwest. Instead of chiming the hour, it blows a whistle."

"Why do you want Rhyme dead?"

"When a horologist builds a clock or watch, the rooms are as clean as scientists making a space telescope. Not a single bit of dust or a hair or grain of sand. The room I use, in Europe, has negative pressure."

"Like a biohazard lab."

"Lincoln is a grain of sand that keeps ending up in my wheelworks. We've been on a collision course for years. There was a job I wanted, last year. An oligarch. London. Highest security in the city. More than for the king."

"Dmitry Olshevsky."

"That's him. Five million." He felt the irritation once again. "I was passed over. Pierre LeClaire got the job. The buyer didn't say, but I think it was what Lincoln had done to my reputation."

"And you're *his* grain of sand. Because he may have stopped some projects, but you're still free."

True. But little consolation.

Hale happened to glance at the security camera monitor. Someone—a man, he believed—stood at the mouth of the cul-de-sac just on the other side of the chain barring entry. Had the man gotten closer, the alarm would have sounded.

This was not unusual. People were curious about the demolition site.

Was this just a passerby who'd noted the crumbling buildings? A potential buyer of the land?

A potential thief?

A precursor to a raid? If so, he had an escape plan prepared—Gilligan's theft of underground passage maps in the city had been helpful. And anyone breaching the trailer would not live long enough to find any evidence of where he had gone.

He rose and pressed a button, which turned on a spotlight affixed to the building beside where the watcher stood.

The sudden bath of illumination seemed not to bother him at all. Even in the wash of light, his features were not distinguishable, and Hale could tell only his race, which was white, and a medium build. His head was covered with a baseball cap. The clothing was casual, not business attire. The visitor was behind a pile of construction rubble, so nothing below his chest was visible. He stayed in place for a moment, then turned and left.

She looked up at his still face.

"Nothing."

She rose and began to dress.

Hale gauged his reaction to her impending departure. A definitive conclusion did not materialize.

Simone said, "He's not well, Rhyme. I was reading."

"He's disabled. There are issues. But nothing to make me think he'll die of natural causes anytime soon."

Her eyes on the ticking clock as she buttoned her blouse with deft fingers. "He's had a good run, you could say. Better, I think, for him to go out on a high note."

This would be her poetic side speaking. Sentiment was not an aspect of Charles Vespasian Hale. He was, in this way too like Lincoln Rhyme.

The way he would describe the endgame fast approaching was simpler: time eventually runs out for everyone.

31.

AT 10:15 THAT EVENING, Amelia Sachs announced, "I want to get out to the sites. Still haven't heard from Ron."

She sent another text, as she'd done several times earlier. Pulaski had not responded. Not like him.

In jeans and a black T, she was gazing at the map of the city, on which the tower cranes in operation in the five boroughs were indicated with red X's. She rocked back and forth on her low black boots. With her phone she took pictures of a half dozen, to record the addresses. She didn't need to explain her selection. These were the tallest, the ones that would do the most damage when they tumbled to earth tomorrow morning, if the Watchmaker stayed true to his promise.

Rhyme could see she was restless, frustrated. The leads were not moving them forward, and this made her grow tense. She worked on curbing those habits she used to eliminate stress—the nails digging into her cuticles, digging into her scalp. She told herself to stop. The commands worked occasionally.

"I'll go on without him." She Velcro-strapped a plate of body armor over her torso. A check of her weapon and extra magazines. This was beyond redundant; he'd personally seen her check the equipment twice today. But this was his wife: both edgy and calmly, coldly professional. These are not mutually exclusive characteristics.

She caught him watching her clip two magazine holsters onto her left hip and place another in her left front pants pocket.

"I stumble across Hale, and it comes down to it? I'll only wound him."

Rhyme shrugged.

NYPD forbade shooting to wound. Weapons were made, and carried, to kill. They served no other purpose unless, on a breezy day, you needed a paperweight.

But this was the Watchmaker.

Rhyme wanted him alive.

Jacket back on, she pulled her car keys from the shelf. There were two, one for the ignition, one for the trunk, the Torino having been born in an era before the miracle—or curse—of digital electronics. The bits of metal jangled like tiny bells.

Rhyme could certainly see in her eyes the fire to find the killer. But tonight, that intensity was diminished by something else: her labored breathing, her unsteadiness.

The coughing.

"Sachs."

She looked at him.

"It's a good plan. But, no. Not you."

Her lips tightened.

"No chest X-ray, all right. Your call. But get some rest."

"It's *him*, Rhyme. The Watchmaker."

"Tonight, you're talking guard duty. Anybody could handle that. Spencer."

And helping make his argument: her breathing stuttered and

she reluctantly took some more hits from the oxygen. He noted only now that it appeared to be a new tank. She hadn't mentioned swapping the first one out for another.

"If we can't find out where the next attack's going to be, there'll be a scene to search tomorrow. That's where we'll need you."

Did she bristle at the hint? That he was a superior officer. If you took the relationship out of the equation, the marriage, that's what he technically was, even if retired. He was a captain, she a mere gold shield.

The fraught moment might have become something harsher.

Except it did not; her eyes explained she knew he was right.

She didn't move for a moment, then her shoulders sagged. "All right."

And it seemed to Rhyme that relief washed over her. She dropped into a chair and placed a call to Lyle Spencer, telling him of her plan to hit several of the most likely target sites tomorrow and make sure guards were in place . . . and look for the Watchmaker himself, on the off chance that he was preparing one of the tower cranes for tomorrow's attack.

After disconnecting, she nodded upstairs. "Early bedtime."

He offered a half smile and was about to respond when there came the sound of the front door opening—the visitor would have the number pad code—and the brief rush of traffic before the door closed.

Ron Pulaski appeared in the arched doorway to the parlor.

Pale, eyes wide, he stopped and winced, then looked from one to the other.

"Ron, are you all right?" Sachs asked.

"There was an accident. Downtown. I hit somebody, another car."

"But are you *okay?*"

"Just stunned. The other car, it caught fire, the driver—a kid, a student—he's in the hospital. I went over there myself to see how he is. They couldn't tell me. Or wouldn't. Not family, you know."

"Get to a doctor, Ron," Sachs said.

"They checked me out at the scene, the EMTs. I'm good, just stiff."

Rhyme said, "The word is Tarr doesn't have any targets. It's not that urgent, Ron. A day to rest won't hurt."

"Yeah," he said, and his voice was bitter. "Looks like it's going to be more than a day. They ran the standard post-accident blood panel. I tested positive for fentanyl."

Rhyme and Sachs glanced each other's way.

The criminalist asked, "Did you happen to—"

"Yeah, I sure did. Tried to save a banger in this crew we'd just taken down. Didn't have gloves on." He grimaced. "Stupid, with fent."

Rhyme knew the dangers of the drug. Some first responders had passed out simply by touching an overdose victim. Several nearly died. Now the opioid antidote Narcan was carried by every responder—for themselves as well as for victims.

"I'm on administrative leave till the inquiry."

"It'll be a formality," Sachs said. "This's happened before."

"Yeah, well, I'm not sure how good it's going to go." He sighed. "I screwed up. The whole thing was my fault. I ran a red light."

Sachs said, "All right, Ron. Get yourself a lawyer. The union'll set you up."

He nodded, his eyes flat. "Yeah."

Rhyme said, "Get on home. Get some rest."

Sachs asked, "You have wheels?"

"Got a pool car. The director took pity. Have to return it tomorrow. I don't know, I'll . . . I'll rent one, I guess." He seemed dazed. "Just wanted to let you know . . ."

"Call us tomorrow."

"Yeah, sure. 'Night."

And, shoulders slumped, he walked slowly out of the town house.

Sachs said, "That's going to be a tough one. Drugs and running a light and an injury? He'll beat the narc, but the optics're bad. Cops I know've been fired for less. And, Jesus, there're reporters already looking over the blotter. They love stuff like this almost as much as an officer-involved shooting."

"We'll make some calls," Rhyme said, though he was thinking that his political pull in the NYPD extended only so far, as his official connection with the department was about the same as that of a Rite Aid clerk or Uber driver.

Sachs said, "I'll go upstairs."

They kissed good night, and carting the oxygen tank, she trod up the stairs, not conceding her condition to the extent she'd take the elevator.

Rhyme nodded, and after she left, his eyes settled on the murder board. Where the top had once said *Unsub 89*, it now read merely *Hale.*

Lincoln Rhyme was thinking:

Bishops and rooks and pawns . . .

I can see the movement of the pieces in our chess game, Charles.

As always, they're moving with your, yes, clockwork precision, economical and unhesitant.

Moving on squares black and squares white.

Bishops and rooks and pawns . . .

One space at a time, two, ten . . .

But, Charles, what eludes me is your strategy. How can I counter this move or that without having a clue as to how you're going to conquer my king?

Unless and until Rhyme could figure that out, his failure—and he felt it keenly—would have mortal consequences to the citizens of New York.

And, of course, to Rhyme himself. He was very aware of a note

Hale had sent to him, a prelude to his trip here, a note that left no doubt what his intentions were:

> *The next time we meet—and we will meet again, I*
> *promise you—will be the last. Farewell, for now, Lincoln.*
> *I'll leave you with this sentiment, which I hope you will*
> *ponder on sleepless nights: Quidam hostibus potest neglecta;*
> *aliis hostibus mori debent.*
>
> *Yours, Charles Vespasian Hale*

The Latin translated into: "Some enemies can be ignored; other enemies must die."

II

A GRAIN OF SAND

32.

FROM THE EARLY-MORNING shadows of an alley across from his next target, Charles Vespasian Hale was looking over the jobsite.

Specifically, his attention was upon a cluster of men near the entrance—there were two other ways into the place, but they had been sealed with four-by-eight plywood sheets.

The men were engaged in a lively conversation. Sports? Streaming TV shows? Women?

But, having been transformed from craftsmen to guards, they were observant, surely hoping for the chance to whip the hide of the man who'd pissed on their sacred profession.

Wearing jeans, a dark windbreaker, a black baseball cap, he studied them now, these stocky men in brown overalls, yellow and orange vests and yellow hard hats. Their hands were blunt, their brows broad, faces tanned. The job would pay well, and Hale supposed they, like the late Andy Gilligan, owned boats for weekend diversion. One smoked—furtively, breaking a rule—while another sipped coffee. The third occasionally lifted a brown paper bag to his lips. Hale had learned that a surprising number of skyscraper workers drank, especially those doing beam work. Their deaths from falling were underreported.

These three looked about occasionally, but being amateurs at the security business, they missed much.

Including Hale himself.

He gazed skyward to the Swenson-Thorburg AB tower crane soaring into the sky, the tubing like blood-coated bone, the company's signature crimson hue.

The slewing unit—the massive turntable—was unlocked and, like the one he'd seen yesterday at the dead-drop site, the jib swiveled slightly in the wind.

The crane was, from this base view, a brute of a creature. But from his research for the project here in New York, Hale had come to see them as devices of great subtlety. Their development in fact paralleled the evolution of timepieces.

From shadoofs—pivoting levers that held buckets to scoop up well water—to derrick cranes (named after Thomas Derrick, the famed Elizabethan hangman) to the towers of the 1970s, cranes, like clocks, drove the engines of industry, and therefore society. At some point, cities could no longer grow geographically and remain cities. Horizontal expansion did not work. It was cranes that made cities seek the skies, drawing more and more population, and grow increasingly powerful.

To Hale, though, there was one immutable difference between cranes and clocks. While he could not conceive of destroying any watch or clock (other than IED timers, of course), he could without any twitch of concern bring one of these monsters crashing to its knees.

And this particular tumble, in a few hours, would be spectacular.

The crane itself was only slightly higher and heavier than the one he'd brought down yesterday. But the difference was this: there was no operator in the cab to heroically point the jib where it could do the least harm. When the Swenson-Thorburg AB died, so would many people. The building the jib towered over was 1960s construction: the superstructure, of course, was steel. But much of the rest was soft aluminum and glass—which would explode under the impact like a thousand hand grenades made of sharpened shards and collapse upon itself. Layer upon layer of building material, bone and blood.

He looked at his watch.

The time was 7:03 a.m.

There remained, of course, the question of getting the acid delivered to the device's counterweight trolley. This would be a bit trickier than the first one, given the guards.

Whose eyes diligently scanned the street, the sidewalk, pedestrians, passing vehicles—especially those that slowed as drivers and passengers shot fast, nervous glances at the spidery red legs of the crane, which reached to a hazy sky.

Could any of these be the crane killer?

But after a few minutes of observing the impromptu guards, Hale decided that the risk of his being discovered in the act of sabotage was minimal.

The trio was keenly observant, yes. But they were looking everywhere except where they should.

33.

NO LUCK WITH the acid manufacturers.

No luck finding who might have hired the Watchmaker, and why, now that housing terrorism seemed unlikely.

No luck with the FBI's finding leads from Hale's front-of-the-airplane accommodations on the flight to JFK.

No luck with the dirt that Pulaski had collected at the Gilligan shooting, supplemented by what Sachs had found at the Helprins' house in Queens.

Then Rhyme grew irritated that he'd even thought the word "luck," a concept that had no place in forensic science, or any other branch of serious study—despite the Seneca poster in FBI agent Fred Dellray's office.

Lyle Spencer's hunting expedition last night had confirmed that every tower crane site he stopped at was guarded by at least three individuals, either workers volunteering for the job or rent-a-cops. All the exits were either sealed off or guarded, and floodlights turned on to illuminate the ground around the crane bases.

At 7:30 this morning, however, they did catch a break.

The NYPD's Computer Crimes operation had called. They'd been notified that a computer found at a crime scene needed to be cracked. The division itself didn't have supercomputers to break passwords, but used an outside service that could. Sachs—who appeared better this morning—agreed to meet the Computer Crimes detective there with Gilligan's laptop.

With some *luck*, Rhyme thought acerbically, they might find information on it that could lead them to the Watchmaker's safe house or reveal the next target.

After she'd left, the computer in one hand, the green tank in another, Rhyme happened to be looking at a nearby monitor. The news was on, a local station. Thom had, irritatingly, left the unit running when he'd brought breakfast into the lab. Rhyme rolled forward for the remote to shut it off. But then he happened to focus on the present story.

Eyes sweeping from the TV to the map of the city, defaced with the red marks indicating the cranes.

"Thom! Thom!"

The aide appeared, eyebrow raised. "You sound . . . I don't know. Alarmed."

"Hardly. I should sound *urgent*. There's a difference."

"Well, what's so *urgent*, then?"

"Your new mission." Eyes still on the map, he said, "You get to help solve the case—and, even better, you get to do it just like I do. Sitting on your ass."

• • •

"Investors this morning are moving out of the mortgage market and into equities and corporate bonds following the attack yesterday by domestic terrorists on a crane on Manhattan's Upper East Side, with threats of more to come unless demands for affordable housing are met.

"*The jobsite where the first attack occurred is where Evans Development is constructing a luxury high-rise that will ultimately soar eighty-five stories into the air. With the three lower floors devoted to retail and commercial, the rest of the building, designed by Japanese architect Niso Hamashura will contain 984 co-op units ranging in size from eighteen hundred square feet to thirteen thousand.*

"*Developers in the city have suspended construction while the police and federal authorities hunt for the terrorists. Reggie Novak, president of the Tri-State Developers' Association, has warned that member companies might face bankruptcy if the stoppage continues for more than a few days. Stocks are trading lower this morning.*"

34.

NOT THE NERD Sachs had expected.

Walking toward her in front of Emery Digital Solutions' downtown headquarters, on cobblestoned Marquis Street, Arnold Levine nodded. He wore polished shoes, a pale blue shirt, a navy tie and a navy-blue suit. The only clash in his couture was that the gold badge holder was brown and the belt it was hung on was black. Hardly a sin.

Didn't computer guys wear hoodies and sweats?

Levine was a supervisor in the NYPD Computer Crimes Unit, one of the country's premier agencies battling cyberterrorism, child exploitation and fraud.

No, nothing nerdish about him at all.

Until he started to talk.

Shaking her hand enthusiastically, he rambled, "I lobbied One PP for a supercomputer. I could find a reasonable one: an HPE Cray SC 250kW NA with a liquid-cooled cabinet. A bargain—two hundred and thirty-five K. They said no. So we have to farm out the work." A nod at the building. "If anybody can do it, it's them."

She inhaled, smelling the exhausty, damp-pavement scent of mornings in Manhattan. The breath controlled the impending coughing spell, but the sting was still there. She thought about the green tank in the car, but decided to leave it there. It somehow represented a sign of weakness.

They walked past security vehicles—a police unit and an unmarked sedan with U.S. government plates, both parked with a good view of the building. Then, inside, they were met by two more guards, large men, armed, who looked at their IDs closely and then regarded a computer for their names. They were nodded through a magnetometer and then emerged, collecting their metal on the other side.

"Wait here," said one of the guards. "Mr. Emery'll be right out."

Levine, in full nerd mode now, said with a conspiratorial whisper, "Oh, that Cray? The super box I mentioned? I told them we could lease out the time when we weren't using it, but it was no to that too. A security thing, they said. But anybody could write script to firewall it. I could do that; *you* could do that. What they didn't want to do—"

"Was write a check for two hundred and thirty-five K."

"Exactly right."

He wore a wedding ring, and she wondered if he inundated his spouse with nonstop tech recitations. Maybe she was a nerd too.

He continued to ramble, she continued to not listen. The time was 8:10.

The Watchmaker's next deadline loomed.

A minute later, the door leading into the interior of the company opened with an electronic lock click, and a tall, lean man in his mid-thirties stepped out. He was gangly and dressed in orange jeans, a rust-colored T, blue running shoes.

"Detectives Sachs and Levine? Ben Emery."

They shook hands.

She couldn't help but notice that Emery's eyes grew intrigued as they took in her face—then wistful when they arrived at her left hand and the wedding band. He gave the tiniest of shrugs and gestured them back into the bowels of the operation.

The place was cold and dim and filled with workstations dominated by monitors and pale beige boxes, all sprouting a million wires. The purposes of the devices were an utter mystery to her, and she was sure, even if Levine or Emery had explained the point of them, she would have understood nothing.

He led them down long corridors, offering details of what each department did, as if they'd asked. Levine nodded knowingly from time to time and asked enthusiastic questions.

Soon they arrived at a workstation in the back of the facility, that of a large man in a Hawaiian shirt, cargo pants and black flip-flops. He was Stanley Grier and he was the one who would be doing the forensic analysis and cracking the passcode.

She handed him the warrant she'd just gotten from a night-court magistrate. He scanned it, then pulled on latex gloves and took the bag from Sachs, checking the serial number of the computer to make sure the paperwork was in order. He extracted the unit, set it squarely in the center of his immaculate workstation. He put his name and signature on the chain-of-custody card.

"It's been swept for explosives and radiation," she said.

"Well, figured that. Okay. I'll get to work and see what's what. I'll make a mirror, but I may have to open it up and pull the hard drive out."

"That's fine," she said. "Though if it comes to trial, you may have to testify that you didn't disturb any data."

"Been there, done that," Grier said.

A coughing fit took her and all three men glanced her way. It seemed that Levine and Emery were concerned for her, while Grier's frown suggested that exhaled breath and spittle might infect the servers, as if she were spreading digital, not physiological, viruses. She didn't explain about the toxin but concentrated on controlling the spasms.

"Are you . . . ?" Emery began.

"Fine," she said, a snipped word, though offered with a smile of thanks. "How long, do you think?" she asked Grier.

"No way of knowing. Was the owner a good guy or a bad one?"

"Bad."

"Then he probably made the password rigorous." A frown. "They tend to do that."

She said, "We need to get the data. And ASAP. The vic—the victim—was working with the man who sabotaged that crane on Eighty-Ninth Street. There might be something in there about where the next attack's going to be."

"Well. Shit. That's at ten, right?"

She nodded.

"I'll get to it." He grabbed a handful of cables and began plugging them into the laptop and his own workstation.

Emery saw them out of the building and with a last regretful look at the unavailable Amelia Sachs, he wished them a good day.

Outside, she took a call from Rhyme and nodded toward Levine, who reciprocated, walked to his PD car pool sedan and drove off, headed downtown.

"Rhyme."

"I didn't hear, so no miracles?"

"The computer? No. They just got started."

"You okay to handle something?"

"Yes," she said firmly.

He said nothing more about her condition. Then in a voice she thought was uncharacteristically mysterious he added, "Just to let you know: it's a little odd."

35.

A NEWS STORY.

Lincoln Rhyme had been inspired by a report on cable TV, which Sachs found amusing since he never watched the tube. And with Thom's help, he'd formulated the "odd" task for her.

She now was playing it out, cruising slowly into a parking garage on the Upper East Side.

A hostile attendant approached, seeing the rattling muscle car, the garage being a fiefdom where renegade wheels were not welcome. Upon viewing the shield and ID, he retreated, though the scowl remained. She wondered if, on exiting, he'd charge her the $28.99 per hour. She guessed he would, her public service notwithstanding.

Rhyme's theory had to do with who had really hired the Watchmaker for the crane sabotage, now that they believed it had nothing to do with striking a blow for reasonably priced housing.

Real estate, however, *might* be involved.

The news story he'd seen was about how the freeze on construction was affecting the market. He'd explained, "I like the idea of the Watchmaker coming up with a plan to game the system."

"How?"

"Hale's hired by a developer. He comes up with a plan to tip cranes over. The market plummets. The anchors love that word, don't they? 'Plummet.' I heard it four times this morning. Then they buy up the devalued property. Or buy shares in something called REITs. Real estate investment trusts. Thom found out about them. They're like a mutual fund for property, not stock. And one story said that with the work stoppage, builders're going to fall behind schedule and miss milestones. The financing bank can foreclose. Then the perps buy up the property for cheap."

Thom had come up with a list of six developers, four in Manhattan, one in Queens and one in Brooklyn. Their companies were private, more likely to break the law than publicly traded ones.

Rhyme split the list, half to Sachs, half to Lyle Spencer, and sent them out for reconnaissance.

She now motored into the garage attached to the high-rise office building where the man first on her list had his company. Rasheed Bahrani—worth only $21 billion, falling low in the net-worth catalog.

As she cruised up and down the ramp in the expansive garage, she was searching not for the man, but for his car.

She'd borrowed an MPH-900 license plate reader from the Traffic division and mounted it—with duct tape—to the driver's-side window of her Torino. The lens of the LPR scanned each plate as she drove past.

Bahrani owned four cars and she certainly could have manu-ally looked for the make and model of the vehicles. But that would be slow—and given the deadline, they couldn't afford the time. The LPR could read the plates instantly and so she could drive as fast as the geography of the garage would allow and still get a ping when the device spotted one of the tags.

The engine growled loudly under the low ceiling as she pushed ahead in second gear. And as in every garage on earth, any turns produced an alarming—and, to her, addictive—squeal.

Two levels, three, seven, ten, twelve . . . She caught a whiff of scalding tire tread.

She got to the top floor, skidded in a smoky circle and started down, foot off the pedals, letting the gears do the braking.

At floor nine, she had a hit and skidded to a stop.

There it was.

Bahrani's Bentley Mulsanne. One of the most luxurious cars in the world.

She didn't roll in those circles, but guessed the tag was north of a quarter million dollars and the iron under the hood topped 500 horsepower. A turbocharger *had* to be involved. There were probably ways to break into a new Bentley, but the technique would surely need the computer power of Emery Digital Solutions. Picking a mechanical lock—the relatively easy way of breaking into her Ford—was not an option.

But without access to the interior (she had no warrant anyway), she would settle for the dirt on the ground under the four doors—in the places the developer and any passengers, ideally the Watchmaker himself, had stood upon climbing out of the vehicle.

She shifted into first, killed the engine and set the parking brake, fixing the car in place on the steep incline. A few hits of oxygen. From the backseat she took a backpack. Concerned that, if Bahrani were behind the sabotage, he or a security man might be keeping an eye out for just such surveillance. She walked to the fish-eye lens camera covering this level and blasted it with nitrogen gas. The frosting would last about ten minutes and then thaw. She'd be gone and the system would be functioning once more to protect against muggers and carjackers.

Latex gloves on, she hurried to the car and used electrostatic sheets to pick up footprints, and, with a portable vacuum, collect trace. These samples went into four separate bags—one for the concrete beneath each door. She jotted the make and plate on each bag and the location of the samples. She took samples too from under the trunk. The bags all went into a milk crate she kept in the back.

Then on the trail again.

There were no other hits in this garage, and fifteen minutes later she was on to Suspect Two. No luck here. The Mercedes, Rolls and Ferrari he owned weren't in the lot that serviced the office of Willis Tamblyn (who came in at a respectable $29B).

She pulled into traffic and headed to the Upper West Side to hit the third suspect's building, the richest of the group. It seemed incongruous that any of these men, as wealthy as they were, would come up with a deadly and destructive plan like this for the sake of earning yet another hundred million or so.

But maybe the perp didn't have as much money as the press and Wikipedia reported. Look at Bernie Madoff.

Or maybe collecting property and wealth were a compulsion to him. And he was like any other addict, always needed more, more, more.

She happened to glance at the car's clock, which sat to the right of the amp gauge and above the oil.

The time was 8:50.

An hour until the next attack.

And where, Sachs wondered, would that be?

36.

ON THE EIGHTH FLOOR of St. Francis hospital, in a room midway along Ward S, Dr. Anita Gomez is calling, "Almost there," reassuring sweaty MaryJeanne McAllister, who is huffing and grunting in pain. "Eight centimeters. Won't be long. You're doing fine." Labor started early; her husband is out of town, hurrying back, and MaryJeanne is on the phone with him. Apparently, he's concerned about the sounds issuing from his wife's mouth. MaryJeanne says, "He wants you to give me some meds. There's too much pain." Dr. Gomez refrains from explaining that the level of pain MaryJeanne is experiencing seems perfectly normal. Plus, her patient didn't want an epidermal or spinal, afraid, wrongly, that it might affect the baby and Dr. Gomez tells her this. "He wants . . ." A grunt. "Holy shit! . . . To talk to you." And offers the phone. The doctor takes it, shuts it off and drops it on a table. "No!" the patient rages. But then she falls silent, apart from the breathing. Both women frown. They hear a curious noise. Low in pitch, from outside. What *is* that? Dr. Gomez wonders, but then it's obscured by the mother's unearthly wail. She hits nine centimeters. "Call my husband," she rages. Dr. Gomez cheerfully replies, "Get ready to push."

On the seventh floor, directly below ob-gyn delivery, neurosurgeon Carla DiVito is preparing to repair an aneurysm in the brain of Tyler Sanford in surgical suite 11. The patient presented with what he described as a searing headache, the "worst he'd ever experienced." Tests of the condition—the swelling of a vessel in the brain—revealed it had not yet ruptured, but the ballooning was sizable. DiVito, the anesthesiologist, two nurses and a resident are present in the room that is, of course, spotless and sterile, but is tiled in the bile green that designers in the 1960s felt, for some unearthly reason, that patients and physicians preferred. Sanford is unconscious and a small portion of his skull has been removed—the burnt smell from the saw lingering unpleasantly as always. Since the aneurysm is large, Dr. DiVito will be using a flow diverter rather than clipping off the vessel. "How do you like it?" a nurse asks. He is nodding toward the Aesculap Aeos robotic microscope hovering over the open brain. "Heaven," the doctor replies. In the past, most neurosurgeons suffered significant ergometric problems—back pain, primarily—from bending over a patient for hours. The microscope allows her to remain upright and view the incision and procedure on a vertical 4K screen. Whereas she could only do one such procedure a day, now she can easily do two. She glances up to her team briefly. "Let's get started."

On the sixth floor, directly under suite 11, is recovery room 3E. The wife and adult son of Henry Moskowitz are sitting beside the bed. "We can have it in the pavilion," the son, David, says. He's raised the topic of the venue for his daughter's sixteenth birthday party, eight months away, not because it must be planned now, but because it will, he hopes, distract his mother from her husband's condition. She's always on board for party planning, as he well knows. She considers. "The pavilion's good. They didn't trim the grass very well for Edna's." "No," her son agrees. They both stare at the unconscious man, the wealth of machinery around him. The surgeon has assured them that the quadruple bypass went well, and he should be coming out of the anesthetic soon. David now cocks his head, hearing some groaning from outside. Thunder? No, the day is clear. But the brief sound put him in mind of the party venue. "We should see what size tents they have. October can be rainy." "Yes," his mother says. "It can."

On each of these three floors—and for that matter, every floor in this building—near the middle is a room roughly twenty by twenty. The doors are double-locked and covered by large signs: *FIRE HAZARD* and *No Smoking*, the latter of which, of course, dated to a different era, but had remained, perhaps because the message still imparted a historical, almost genetic, urgency. Inside these rooms are scores of tanks of oxygen, carbon dioxide, nitrogen, nitrous oxide and regular air. Some of these are stored, some fitted to hoses that feed into wall sockets. Also present are tanks of sevoflurane, an anesthetic. While nonflammable in itself, fires and explosions can occur when this gas reacts with an absorbent used in anesthesia procedures, barium hydroxide lime, of which there are several containers here as well. In addition, here are receptacles of cyclopropane, divinyl ethel, ethyl chloride and ethylene. These facilities are known among staff as the Dynamite Rooms.

And eighty feet above this stack of suites and rooms sits the jib of a Swenson-Thorburg AB tower crane. Like all the others in the city it is no longer in service, temporarily halted because of the sabotage. Since the only weights on the front jib are cables, the trolly and hook, the counterweight blocks had been shuttled close to the cab and locked in position. Until a few minutes ago, moment—balance—had been achieved. Now, though, the jib is ever so slowly leaning forward toward the hospital. This is because of what is known in the industrial world as an "acid attack," a term of art having nothing to do with tossing a caustic solution at a political rival or a cheating lover. It merely means there is a chemical reaction in progress. In this case, hydrofluoric acid was released from a plastic container and is presently engaged in, first, acting on the calcium hydroxide in the cement to turn it into a paste of calcium silicate hydrate, and, second, liquifying that resultant. A slurry of this mixture is sloughing off the blocks, along with bits of the rear trolley and brackets holding the blocks to it. This residue is sprinkling down to the jobsite—the place being deserted—though none of the skeleton crew at the entrance notices. Several of them thought they heard a moaning or groaning. This is the sound of the slewing plates binding as the tower mast leans forward. But since they've been guarding the entrance and are convinced no one could sabotage *their* crane, they put the sound down to the wind or an aircraft or a distant truck and return to their argument about a recent draft pick in the NFL.

37.

COUNTDOWN: 1 HOUR

SO. IT'S BACK to this.

Reviewing damn security videos. What security guards do, looking for kids who shoplift necklaces and candy bars at Walmart.

But, with a perp who has the inconsiderate habit of dissolving the most important physical evidence with acid, there was little else to do.

An irritated Lincoln Rhyme scrubbed the video into the far past and then back to the not-so-far.

He was not alone. Mel Cooper was doing the same at a nearby computer.

Two forensic analysts—the best in the city—with no evidence to analyze.

Though not happy with the task, he acknowledged the possibility of finding a nugget or two this way. While it was true that he didn't trust witnesses, even the most cooperative, he did trust his own eyes—all the more because he believed that after he'd been robbed of so much by the accident, his other senses had been enhanced. Perhaps his imagination, but he'd come to believe that if he saw something himself it was the truth.

As he searched, he was thinking of the question that had dogged them from the beginning: How had the Watchmaker gotten the hydrofluoric acid onto the counterweights?

They knew he was somewhere near the crane yesterday morning when it came down—because Garry Helprin, the operator, had seen his beige SUV nearby.

And that meant he was probably present somewhere on video too, captured when he made his way to the tower, climbed it and planted the device. The operator started work at 9:00 and probably would have seen an intruder make the climb, so the device was planted prior to that. But how much prior? He knew from the discovery in the wheel well of the jet at JFK airport that the Watchmaker had been in the country for only a few days, which at least set a limit on the footage to search. This still meant, though, that Rhyme had to scrub through hundreds of hours of video, from multiple sources. He had footage from seven cameras.

Five of these were private security cameras with fair to poor resolution. Two of them were better, being newer additions to the Domain Awareness System.

"Nothing," Cooper muttered.

Rhyme glanced at the clock on the wall nearby.

9:14.

Then a look at the map and a fleeting thought: Which one is your target, Charles?

He returned to the screen and scrubbed more quickly, focusing on the night before and the morning of the attack.

But the only person climbing the crane tower, at any time before the incident, was Helprin, just before 9 a.m.

The cameras were blocked occasionally by trucks stopping at lights or making deliveries at the jobsite or to nearby office buildings and apartments. Of particular irritation were advertising trucks, flatbeds toting large billboards. Most were cigarette ads—forbidden on TV—and for medicines to treat maladies whose nature was not clear from the content. Also, a number of campaign ads. Two, Rhyme noted, were pushing for voters to cast a ballot for Marie Leppert, the cartel buster running against the man who was Rhyme's own representative in Washington, former activist (and criminal) Stephen Cody.

At one point, a large black bird nearly slammed into the camera, startling him.

When no clear suspects were evident, Rhyme turned his attention to the spectators, aware that perps do indeed return to the scene of the crime occasionally. He took note in particular of those who had visited the site on two separate occasions, if he could find them.

The most curious of these was a small, hunched-over homeless man in a bizarre orange and brown hat, like a nineteenth-century soldier's, and a dirty brown overcoat. Rhyme noticed him because of his odd costume, yes, but also because of the man's obsessive interest in the site. He held a blue-and-white coffee cup to collect change, but wasn't doing much solicitation. He actually walked right past a businessman offering him a bill. He moved around the perimeter until the fire department's Biotox unit arrived to neutralize the acid and they cleared everyone away.

Rhyme saw that he returned a couple of hours later. Most of the construction crew had gone home, so he just walked onto the site.

He seemed to be looking for something. Scavenging for valuables? Probably. He'd found something; there was a glistening metal object in his hand. If he spent much time there, maybe he'd be somebody for Sachs to talk to. If he could be located.

The second person who visited the site twice was memorable only because he was a musician. He carried a pale blue-gray guitar case, the word "Martin" printed on the side. Rhyme had learned from an investigation years ago that this was one of the best acoustic brands in the world. The man holding it at the jobsite was of medium build, white and bearded, a dark baseball cap with no logo tugged down firmly on his head. He wore sunglasses. He was in a black leather jacket and blue jeans.

His first visit was an hour after the collapse, then he returned four hours later. Rhyme could not deduce the man's purpose in being present. Unlike the homeless man, who was drawn to the wreckage, the musician was constantly scanning the crowds, as if he were planning to meet someone.

He made two circuits of the site on his second visit. Apparently not finding what or whom he sought, he turned and left. Rhyme could have captured an image, but the sunglasses and the low brim of the hat meant facial recognition wouldn't work.

His presence, like that of the homeless man, was probably nothing. Coincidence.

He continued to scrub, three days ago, two, yesterday. Daytime. Nighttime. Nobody approached the base of the mast except the operator.

He reflected: You'd think they'd make an algorithm that could spot perps doing all kinds of things—like climbing tower cranes.

Algorithms. Computers, data . . .

A thought occurred: Today there was a new type of Edmond Locard's "dust" in the criminalist's world digital bits and bytes. The ones and zeros that could lead you to your suspect's home or office as efficiently as soil samples and bloodstains.

Except not in this case.

He sighed and returned to the monitor, scrubbing through the near bird strike.

But wait . . .

He froze the playback and reversed, frame by frame.

The black thing filled the screen.

It wasn't a bird.

"Mel. Is this what I think?"

The technician looked. "It is. A drone." Cooper flew "unmanned ariel vehicles" as a hobby and knew them well.

The stopped image had caught two propellers in motion.

"Goddamn. That's how he did it."

Drones could not legally be flown in the city, but misdemeanors would be no deterrent to the Watchmaker.

"Would it be big enough to carry the payload?"

"A commercial model, yes."

"They're tracked aren't they?"

"Right. FAA, the Bureau and Homeland Security. But the last two're the most active."

Rhyme instructed the phone, "Call Dellray."

The FBI agent answered on the first ring.

"Lincoln."

"Fred. The cranes. We think the Watchmaker might be placing the device on them with a drone. Mel says you and DHS track them."

"Oh, yeah. We're the boys 'n' gals for you. Our Counterterror folk. They're lookin' for birds all. The. Time. I'll patch you through to a buddy—still hiding out on the other side of the office, by the way. No end of trouble I'm givin' them for that. Hold tight."

Rhyme's eyes drifted to the map of the cranes in the city. He was thinking back to the early hours of the morning. Lyle Spencer had returned from his visits to the towers that they'd decided were most likely to be the next target. He'd reported that the bases of the cranes were all well guarded.

With a drone, those precautions were useless.

Then a baritone voice sounded into the phone. "Mr. Rhyme. Special Agent Sanji Khan, Counterterror. How can I help?"

Rhyme explained that he believed the device used to sabotage the crane on the Upper East Side was put in place with a drone. "You monitor them, right?"

"We do. FAA and DHS too. We coordinate findings. Radar and RF—radio frequency. If there's a UAV—unmanned ariel vehicle—anywhere, we get a location. GPS from the RF is best. Radar's dicey in the city."

"Have you had any alerts lately?"

"Alert? No." Khan added, "There's an algorithm that only scrambles a response if the thing is near a high-profile target—airports, government buildings, embassies, concert halls, parades, that sort of thing. If the flight's under ten minutes and it's a low-threat location, we just log the details and don't go after anybody. Usually it's somebody gets a birthday or Christmas present and starts playing with it without knowing the law."

"If I gave you the time and location, could you let me know if a drone was there? And—this is important—if it's been logged again anywhere in the city?"

"Sure . . . If he's flying the same unit. They have unique profiles."

"Mel, give him the details! Agent, this is Detective Cooper on the line."

The tech looked up the information and recited it into the speakerphone.

No more than sixty seconds later—the gap filled with Khan's hard-pounding keyboarding—the agent said, "I've got it here. There's a log report of a flight just where you describe it, Eighty-Ninth Street, early in the morning before the crane came down. Flew over the site, hovered, and then went dark on East Eighty-Eighth."

Where Hale's SUV was parked. The box in the back that Helprin had seen would be what he stored it in.

"We profiled it in the Carter Max4000 line."

"Big enough to deliver a few liters of liquid?"

"Easy."

"Now, other flights by the same one?"

"Yessir. Three of them. Classified as probably random and not acted on either."

"Where?"

"One was in the four hundred block of Towson Street, Brooklyn. Another in front of an office building, Manhattan, 556 Hadley, between SoHo and downtown. East. The last one was 622 East Twenty-Third. It's been quiet since. But it's on the wire now. If it goes aerial again, we'll be on it and get tactical involved. You want to be included?"

"Yes," Rhyme said absently. He was staring at the map. No cranes, that block of Brooklyn. No cranes near Hadley. But East 23rd, there was one. A bright red circle.

"Mel, what's at that address, on Twenty-Third?"

Rhyme glanced at the clock. Just over a half hour until the next attack.

The tech typed on a nearby keyboard and a crisp picture appeared on the screen in front of Rhyme. It was from a satellite image database.

In the middle of a U-shaped complex of yellow-tan brick buildings sat a massive crane, with a yellow cab and jibs atop a red tower.

The buildings made up the St. Francis Hospital Center.

"Mel, call their security and the local precinct. Evacuate the place. And get Amelia over there. Now."

38.

AMELIA SACHS ARRIVED at the hospital and skidded to a stop, the crane looming in front of her.

It was in the middle of a jobsite, the jib hovering over the main building—the north side of the U that the complex was configured in. The hour was not yet ten, but the device was tilting and the counterweights were shedding bits of concrete and drips of liquid—the HF acid was already at work.

Moment had been compromised.

Her eyes were drawn upward. The bright red color, the shade of fresh blood. When the thing fell it would strike the middle of the top floor, about eight stories up. The front jib was eighty or ninety feet higher than the crest of the building. Upon impact, the many tons of metal would accelerate as they fell and slam into the structure with incredible force, slicing through at least the top three or four floors.

This was a crane that Lyle Spencer had checked last night. He had found guards at the base of the mast and the entrance to the site. But Rhyme's text a few minutes ago explained why his efforts had been a waste of time; Hale was using a drone to plant the acid.

Sachs looked at the oxygen tank on the seat beside her. Without the mask on, she inhaled deeply.

Some sting, some coughing.

Was the goddamn stuff eating away at more and more parts of her lung, like the counterweights in front of her?

A hit of oxygen.

Glancing around the scene that was, like the first collapse, a circus of vehicles and lights and people in uniforms of all shades and styles.

She closed her eyes and lowered her head as she inhaled from the tank a half-dozen times.

Good enough for now. Go.

Climbing from the Torino, she spotted the NYPD incident commander, a gray-haired uniformed captain of about fifty. He was as thin and pale as the man beside him was dark-complected and stocky, the FDNY battalion chief, who was in black slacks and a white shirt under a fire department jacket, dark with yellow stripes. The firefighters didn't need hard hats, of course, they had their own helmets, in classic firefighter shape, yellow. His had a crest of a badge on the front topped with a large *CHIEF* and his number below. His name was Williams.

She tilted her belt badge toward them. "Sachs. Major Cases. I'm one of the leads on this one."

"Oh," the police IC said, *O'Reilly* on his breastplate. "You're with Lincoln Rhyme?"

She nodded, her preferred response to a question that could be answered several ways.

Looking up, "Can it be turned?" If the jib was rotated 90 degrees, it would face the street, which was cordoned off and a fall would cause little damage.

The battalion chief said, "The minute we got that call from Captain Rhyme, that this was the next one to go? I asked the foreman that. But it's frozen in place. The turntable plates are already buckled."

She looked over the building it was aimed at again. The hospital looked fragile. It had been constructed in the 1960s and was made of aluminum and glass and metal panels, blue in color and rusting around the edges. There'd be a steel superstructure, but little else to stop the massive knife of the jib.

Some patients, visitors and staff sprinted out. But many ambled, simply unable to move quickly. They limped, they wheeled in chairs. A few wheeled their IV units beside them, as if they were robotic companions from a science fiction movie.

"Evac progress?"

O'Reilly told her, "Well, we've got out a lot of the ambulatories, visitors and nonessential staff. Floors one through five. The problem is, above that, it's aimed at rooms where there're procedures going on. I mean, patients open, on tables in operations. Open heart. Brain surgery. Giving birth. You can't just wheel them out. They're closing up the patients they can and rigging lines and life support to the beds to move them. Some're pretty, what's the word? Fragile."

"Can't they just get them to lower floors? The thing's not going to crash through the whole building."

"No, we need everybody out entirely," Williams said. "The thing is also aimed for the gas supply rooms. Hundreds of canisters and wall lines. Oxygen and flammable gases. Hospitals're like grain elevators. A spark and that's it."

A groan sounded from the base of the tower as it tilted and the jib eased downward another few feet.

The battalion chief added, "I had some people rig tethers." He pointed to cables attached to the mast about halfway up and connected to the girders on the addition that was being built. "I don't know if they'll do any good. Doesn't look like it. They're already bending the beams they're attached to. Maybe bought some time."

After a coughing fit, Sachs gazed up at the precarious structure. She asked, "Is the operator here?"

"The crane operator?" the IC asked. "No reason for him to be. The site's shut down. Why?"

"Maybe he'd know some way to, I don't know, shift the weight? Or to shore it up somehow we're not thinking of?"

"Well, there's nobody here."

And a thought occurred.

She ripped her phone from her pocket and scrolled for a number. It was the mobile of the operator from the first collapse, Garry Helprin. She tapped it.

Buzzing, buzzing . . .

Thinking, Please answer.

Please . . .

But he didn't.

Voice mail.

Hell.

She cleared her throat. "Garry, it's Detective Sachs. There's another crane coming down. It's aimed at a hospital. We want any thoughts you have about slowing it. They're rigging tether lines, but I don't think they'll last. Call me or Lincoln Rhyme."

She gave both numbers, then turned to the incident commanders. "I'm going to help with the evac. I'll call you if I hear back."

Another glance at the crane. It had sagged another two degrees. How much longer?

No point in speculating. She grabbed the oxygen tank from the Torino and a Motorola from the coms van, then ran toward the entrance.

Inside the dim, chaotic lobby, she saw the elevator doors open and the lights above them blinking. Of course, risk of fire. They'd been put in fire service mode. She looked at the stairway, people streaming down.

Stairs.

Steep stairs.

Eight flights.

Oh, man.

Three deep hits of sweet O, and she slung the green tank over her shoulder and started up.

Gasping for breath with every step.

39.

THE SCENARIO UPSTAIRS was worse than she'd thought.

On the eighth floor, the top, thirty patients, visitors and staff remained, clustered at the east and west exits at the far end of the hallway. But then, wait—she had to supplement the count by doubling the number of patients; it was the ob-gyn and delivery ward.

These narrow fire exits were the only routes that could be used since the main exit—the elevators—was not available. The backlog was due to the number of patients who were not ambulatory. Mothers who had given birth minutes before, C-section patients, and several, she was told by a nurse, who were here not as ob-gyn, but had been moved to recovery rooms from downstairs, presumably because of space shortage. The latter two groups were confined to beds. Several were still unconscious.

Sachs joined the other rescue workers, wheeling to the exits chairs and beds of patients who couldn't walk.

Out the window facing south, the tower was clearly visible, the tubes glowing in the morning sun. It was not very close, but that structure itself was only half of the risk. When the collapse came, the mast would cut through the side walls of the hospital, the jib the top.

As she looked, it eased forward another few feet.

Were the tether straps holding?

Not very well, apparently.

Sachs learned, to her relief, that the evacuees didn't need to get all the way down to the street. They only had to get to five, where there was a bridge to the east building. There, the elevators were working.

One aide called, "Detective, can't we just stage everybody where they are? In front of the exits?"

"No. Out of the building. Fire risk." Nodding to the room directly behind her: the gas storage and supply room the battalion chief had told her about. The *HAZARD* sign was small, the *No Smoking* one big, the *Danger Flammable Substances* the largest of all.

She spotted a new mother and her swathed baby in a wheelchair, in the corner, alone. She was crying as hard as the newborn. Sachs gripped the handles and hurried the pair down the hall and got her in the queue for extraction down the stairs. "Can you walk?" she asked.

In broken English she said, "I can. I wanted to. They say I can't. I asked. It's against the rules."

Sachs smiled to her. "Today's different." Sachs helped her up, and led her to the exit, where she handed her off to a nurse who had just crested the stairs. He took the patient by the shoulders and they descended. "One step at a time. You're doing fine. Boy or girl?"

Their voices were lost as they disappeared into the dim stairway.

Chatter cascaded through her radio.

"LeRoi. I'm on seven. Cleared all the theaters but three. They can't move. Two are on heart-lung machines, the other is halfway through a kidney transplant. And there's a brain surgeon refuses to move. She says it would kill the patient. Cutting staff to minimum and getting unnecessary workers out."

The sixth-floor workers reported similar problems. It was a post-op recovery ward, with a number of patients who were unconscious and in precarious condition from surgery.

Somebody shouted through the coms, "I got twelve fucking beds here the size of double-wides. I need bodies in 6-W to carry 'em down. Now!"

Sachs sped one more mama and infant to the exit and then noticed some activity beside her—in a recovery room, cut off from the corridor with a frosted-glass window. Inside were three patients, sleeping off the anesthetic. An elderly woman, an older man and a teenage boy. Also a half-dozen family members or friends, who had refused to leave those they were visiting.

Or simply didn't believe the announcement of impending disaster.

Like the others, these beds were on wheels, but they were connected to a half-dozen instruments mounted on the wall and racks. Nurses and orderlies were frantically in the process of detaching the devices and setting them directly beside the snoozing patients.

A groan from outside.

Sachs looked out the window.

The mast was tilting farther.

"You need to go now!" Sachs grabbed some big plastic instrument, probes attaching it to the patient via colorful wires. She shoved it into the hands of one of the male visitors. He sagged under the weight. "You." She pointed to a woman of about thirty. "Time to put those health club muscles to work. Take that one." She pointed to another bulky device. It seemed to weigh thirty or forty pounds.

"I don't know—"

"Take it!"

She did, and managed.

All the equipment was on battery power, so Sachs unplugged the units and pointed.

The three beds cruised slowly toward the western exit, the one with the least backlog.

Coughing, spitting, Sachs trotted along the corridor, checking rooms.

All empty.

Until she got to S-12.

She walked inside to hear a wrenching sound: a groaning scream, if there was such a thing. An extremely pregnant woman lay on her back, pillows behind her head, her feet up in stirrups. Her doctor—the name tag read *Dr. A. Gomez*—was bending forward and calling, "Push."

The woman was sweating, her dark hair plastered to her head, uttering unearthly sounds and occasionally firing off some heartfelt swear words.

Assuming Sachs, as a woman, was cognizant of all things obstetrics, the doctor said, "She's ten centimeters."

"Okay?"

"I lost my nurse . . . Push!"

So they really said that.

Sachs had a coughing fit.

"You sick?" the doctor asked.

"No, acid exposure."

The woman slapped her stethoscope on Sachs's chest. "Breathe."

Sachs did.

"Again."

Once more.

"You're all right."

"What?"

"You're fine. I know lungs."

Just like that . . .

"Now, I need your help."

"Look, you better find somebody else."

"Oh, who?" the doctor asked, genuinely mystified.

This portion of the corridor was empty.

"Did they teach you this in cop school?"

"I missed that part."

"Well, Detective, there're eight billion people on earth and they all got here the same way. It's not that hard." A fast smile. "You'll do fine. Clean gloves." Then to the woman: "Breathe. Push!"

"Jesus Christ!" the woman wailed.

"Is she . . . okay?"

"Ah, yes. She's good."

Sachs ripped off the blue latex and grabbed clear surgical gloves, thicker than what she wore at crime scenes. It's nearly impossible to pull them on moist fingers, so she blew hard to dry them.

Once gloved, she turned to the doctor, who said, "I need the vitals. That monitor there. Call them out. Temperature, pulse, respiration, blood pressure. That's all I need for now."

For now? What the hell was coming next?

Another scream, apparently.

Brother, the woman had lungs.

"I want some fucking drugs!"

"You're doing fine. Push!"

Sachs was calling out numbers.

The patient: "I want—"

At that moment came an explosion, a cannon shell, from outside. The room next to the one they were in disappeared in a blast of glass shards and plastic and metal and Sheetrock.

Sachs glanced through the glass wall.

It was the steel restraining cable the battalion chief had ordered rigged; the thing had snapped and shot into the room, blown the door off the hinges and embedded itself deep in the hallway wall.

Those in the corridor screamed, though it seemed no one had

been hit. Had they been, the metal would have sliced through their flesh and bone effortlessly.

Seeing, briefly, bloody rebar rods . . .

How many more tether cables were there? She believed she'd seen a half dozen.

"Drugs, I want some drugs!"

"Push!" From the doctor.

Another metallic groan from outside. The tower bent closer.

"I want some—!"

Sachs leaned close to the patient. "Shut up and push!"

40.

"I WENT TO see him. They wouldn't let me up."

The detective sitting across from Ron Pulaski nodded at the patrolman's words.

"I just wanted to wish him the best. I brought some candy. Who needs flowers? But they wouldn't let me up."

"Probably a legal thing. You being the driver of the car that hit him."

"Just felt so bad about it. Guess I looked pretty miserable. Nurse took pity on me and told me he'll be all right. Some burns, concussion, but he should be out in a few days."

The interview Pulaski had been summoned to was being conducted in the office of Internal Affairs detective Ed Garner, which made Pulaski feel more or less comfortable, since it was cluttered, the desk piled high with case files and rows of Redweld folders on the floor. The family pictures revealed that he and his wife had two children about the ages of Pulaski and Jenny's. The whole family liked to fish, it seemed.

Both men wore dark suits and white shirts, Garner's collar and cuffs contrasting with his dark skin. Pulaski's tie was red, Garner's deep green, and Pulaski thought they both could have walked out of Police Plaza and gone straight to a funeral.

The IA detective had a notebook open in front of him and a digital recorder sitting next to it, the red Recording dot illuminated.

"Now, Officer Pulaski—" Garner was speaking.

"Ron is fine."

His last name sounded too official. Like he'd already been convicted of negligent operation of a vehicle under the influence and was about to be sentenced to prison by a stern judge.

"Okay, Ron," he said in a friendly voice. "Good. Let's go that way—I'm Ed. Now, you're pretty freaked out. Of course you are. But we'll get through this as fast as we can. Get you back home. Just some preliminaries we have to get out of the way. Today we're just taking your statement for an internal review. This is *not* a criminal investigation. The sole point of my questions're to see if NYPD administrative and procedural rules were followed in the incident on Parker Street."

Pulaski was looking at a file folder. His own. It wasn't thick—a quarter inch. Maybe less.

"Officer? Ron?"

He hadn't been paying attention. He'd been looking at the folder.

"You understand you have a right to an attorney."

"I've called some. Nobody I talked to was available yet. And I want to get back on the street ASAP."

Eddie Tarr and his red sedan were out there somewhere.

"So." He lifted his palms. "Here I am."

"Our report will go to the accident review board. You're—"

"Familiar? Yes."

"The board'll determine if there's been a breach of procedure. And if there has been, what action should be taken. Now, I said this wasn't a criminal case, but there's the possibility it could become one. Badges from the local house've run the scene, canvassing. That's a separate thing. If the facts warrant, the findings'll be referred to the DA's office. So, two investigations. You follow?"

What was there not to? "Yes."

"Now, you have the right against self-incrimination in the *criminal* investigation. But since this, here, is administrative, we can compel you to talk to us. If you don't, you'll be subject to department discipline. Failure to cooperate."

"Okay. But what I say here can't be used in any criminal investigation."

Garner nodded with a smile. "*If* there is one. Correct."

Pulaski noted that Garner hadn't asked him if it was all right to record. There was probably some fine print in the *Patrolman's Handbook* that said when you signed on, you consented to having red-eyed space monsters record your statements.

"Okay, all that crap's out of the way. In your own words, tell me what happened." Then the detective gave a half smile. "Though who the hell else's words'd you use?"

Pulaski didn't laugh, but the IA cop's comment took a bit of the tension out of the room. He took a breath. "Okay, I was driving back up to Lincoln Rhyme's town house after checking out a lead to a case I'm running for Major Cases. And this SUV just was *there*. Just appeared. I didn't even get to the brake. Just bang." He fell silent, seeing the vehicle, hearing the sound.

"Do you recall how fast you were going?"

"Not really, maybe forty."

"What was the speed limit?"

"Last sign I saw was thirty-five."

"But you're not sure that's what it was when the collision occurred."

"I . . . No, I'm not sure. No."

"Do you remember where exactly in the intersection the

accident occurred? I mean, was the other vehicle in the right or the center turn lane of Halmont?"

"I don't know."

Garner consulted a sheet of paper.

"You were on your mobile. That's what the phone logs show."

"Yes, I was. Crime Scene in Queens had called. Question about a scene I'd run earlier in the day."

"Where were you on Parker exactly when you got the call?"

"I don't really remember. I'd guess fifty feet from the intersection."

"Now you're approaching Halmont. How many pedestrians did you see in the intersection?"

"I don't remember. I wasn't paying attention."

"And cars?"

"Again, no clue."

"And as you approached, you didn't see the light turn yellow, then red?"

"I . . . I guess I didn't. The last I looked it was green."

"And when was that?"

"I don't know. Like everybody else. You glance up. It's green. You keep going." A shrug. "The signal? Did anybody check to make sure it was working okay?"

"Oh, yeah, Traffic checked it out. It was working. Could you have been looking around, concentrating on the call?"

"I was listening, you know, but not really concentrating."

Garner lifted an eyebrow. "You climbed out and jumped through those flames to get to the SUV. Took some balls."

"Wasn't as bad as it looked."

In fact, it wasn't even a decision. He'd rolled through the open window of his car and, seeing the flames from the ruptured gas tank of the SUV he'd hit, just instinctively charged the vehicle to help the occupants, though the only one—the driver—was by then out and lying on the pavement.

"All right, good, Ron. Now, the positive drug test. That sets off alarm bells, you understand. Do you do recreational drugs?"

"No, never. Well, to be honest, I tried pot once. Hated it. It was years ago."

Garner said, "I smoked some in college. Just made me drowsy. Fell asleep in English—which had this professor that made you sleepy anyway. That happen to you?"

"Don't really remember. I think it did."

"But no drugs since then?"

"No."

"Alcohol?"

"Wine or beer some. Two, three times a week."

"Now, describe how you think the fentanyl got into your system."

"As near as I can figure, I ran a dealer collar. Biggy with the M-42s in East New York. When we cleared the place I found one of his lieutenants, he was lying face down, and, you know, unresponsive. I rolled him over, administered Narcan and started chest compression. But he was gone."

"You didn't wear gloves?"

"I know it's procedure, but I wanted to move fast. I thought I could save him." He shook his head. "His crew, they knew he was there, dying, and they didn't do anything. Not a thing."

"At least you put the assholes away."

"Yeah . . . This does happen, right?"

"What's that?"

"Failing a drug test because you touched somebody at a bust?"

"Oh, yeah. The board's been here before. How would you describe your physical state?"

"A stiff neck."

"Oh, not from the accident. In general."

"Good."

"No injuries?"

"No."

"All right, Ron, your colonoscopy's over. Oh, just one other thing, could you draw a diagram of where you were in the intersection when the accident happened?"

"Draw?" He exhaled a brief laugh. "I'm no artist. My daughter should do it for you."

"Ha. In our house, it's my son. Just do the best you can." He handed Pulaski a sheet of paper and pen, and a file folder to set the paper on; the desk was too cluttered to write.

He gave it a shot and handed it back.

Pulaski was silent, eyes on the picture of Garner and his family. They remained there a long time.

"Ron?"

Apparently Garner had asked him something.

"Sorry, what?"

"I said, 'That's it.'"

He rose. "I guess we're going to get sued."

"Oh, yeah, big-time. But we've got insurance. And good lawyers. Speaking of which, whatever the board does, you gotta lawyer up too. You'll be named in the suit personally."

Pulaski didn't respond. He was picturing himself as a defendant in court.

His tone sympathetic, Garner said, "We've got psychologists on call. I'd recommend talking to one."

"I don't really need that. I already have somebody."

"Really? Who?"

"My wife."

41.

AMELIA SACHS ASKED urgently, "Aren't you going to slap her?"

"What?"

Sachs nodded to the bloody, damp and wrinkled little form lying in a blue square of cloth in the doctor's hands.

"You know, slap her on the butt? Make her breathe?"

"Oh. We don't do that anymore. Not for years."

Dr. Gomez suctioned some gunk from the nose and mouth and rubbed the infant with the cloth. Yes, she seemed to be breathing fine and was crying softly.

Glancing at Sachs: "Have to get the cord. I need your help."

Right. Has to be cut. That much she knew. Sachs pulled from her back pocket the sleek Italian switchblade she always carried. Hit the button. It snapped open.

The doctor stared.

Sachs said, "We can sterilize it."

The woman frowned. "I just meant could you hold her while I clamp?"

Oh.

She put the knife away. And carefully took the baby.

In less than a minute the cord was clamped and severed and, to Sachs's relief, the infant was in the arms of her mother, who was sobbing—maybe in fear of another cable strike or the falling tower, though possibly from the birthing experience. Both, probably.

"Can she walk?" Sachs asked.

"Bleeding, a chair's better."

The mom: "*Bleeding!* You didn't tell me I'd be bleeding."

A cheerful response: "Yes, I did, ma'am. You'll be fine."

There was a wheelchair in the corner. The doctor and Sachs got the mother into it.

Sachs pushed the chair into the corridor.

Hell, both exits were now completely backed up. The severed cable had panicked everyone and that caused a crush. Several people had tried to carry the massive beds down the stairs but hadn't been strong enough and pieces of furniture were sitting on the tops of the steps, jamming the doorways.

Rescue workers were trying to calm everyone and free the beds. This wasn't working.

Sachs thought back to her promise to Rhyme that she would only wound the Watchmaker.

She now changed her mind.

She pushed the mother and baby toward the closest exit while Dr. Gomez, noticing with a frown that a nurse at the opposite exit had fallen, hurried toward her.

"I want a pain pill!" the new mother demanded.

Sachs ignored her.

Just then another cable broke free and exploded into the window where Dr. Gomez was walking to the injured hospital worker. The woman disappeared in a cascade of dust and glass shards.

No . . .

"Doctor!"

She couldn't see if the woman had been hit. She parked the

wheelchair next to the west exit and started toward where she'd last seen Gomez.

She still could see nothing of the strike's aftermath; the smoke and dust were too dense.

Then she noticed something odd and paused.

On the linoleum floor in front of her, a shadow appeared and began to move.

What . . . ?

It filled the floor, a latticework of black lines.

The shadow of the mast.

She turned to the window just as screams filled the corridor.

"It's coming down!" someone cried.

Sachs dove to the floor and rolled against the wall, which she figured would provide some protection. Unless of course the crane simply caved in the entire floor, burying them all under a breath-stealing andiron of debris . . .

Claustrophobia . . .

At least she wouldn't have to suffer that horror for very long; the collapse would ignite the gas and flammable solvents and burn everyone here to death within minutes.

And she noted too: the coughing had stopped.

Waiting for the crash . . .

Waiting . . .

For the crash that didn't happen.

Instead of the deafening sound of collapsing metal and glass, another noise grew evident and then increased in volume.

Thump, thump, thump . . .

She rose and made her way cautiously to the window. She turned to her left and saw Dr. Gomez was on her feet and walking to the injured worker.

The crane was still looming in sight. But no longer moving their way.

Thump, thump . . .

About forty feet above the mast was a helicopter. A hook had been lowered from a winch above the open door and had snapped onto the front jib.

The craft was big, but hardly meant to lift weights like the crane, and a worker sat strapped in the doorway, his hand on a control on the winch. If the mast finally gave way and fell freely, he would have to release the cable so it didn't pull the craft to the ground with it.

But so far the chopper was handling the load. The mast sank slowly.

Down, down, slowly . . .

Twenty feet from the top of the building.

Then ten.

With a resounding metallic clang, the mast came to rest against what would be the steel girder of the crown. The helicopter remained in position.

The cable slacked, and the tower and jib were stable.

The worker pulled the pin, releasing the cable. It fell, shimmering in a band of sun, and dropped straight down as the helicopter hovered for a moment, like an angel's halo above the genuflecting crane, and then rose slowly into a faultless sky.

42.

SHE WAS OUTSIDE the main building, watching crews run cables from the tower and jib to rebar rods set in the concrete foundation of the addition.

Reminding her of what amounted to the murder weapon that had killed the operator's friend in such a horrid way.

Here, at least, a better ending.

Crews were also atop the main building, dismantling the jib and lowering the segments to the roof where, she supposed, another chopper would remove them.

Her phone purred.

"Rhyme."

"I heard. It got lassoed."

She explained that Garry Helprin, the operator, had gotten the message she left, learned of the impending disaster and called the head of his company. The boss had scrambled their heavy-lifting S-64E Sikorsky—which was doing a job on West 55th Street and the Hudson. The pilot had dumped the load and sped to the hospital. It took only two attempts to hook the mast like a bass.

Rhyme told her, "And Counterterrorism at the Bureau found two other drone flights. But not near any jobsites. A residential block in Brooklyn and an office building, Manhattan. We're trying to find the connection. Walk the grid, Sachs. I need evidence. And get me all the video footage you can."

"What?" The word was uttered as an astonished whisper. "*You* want video?"

"It's all right, Sachs. Locard has given me dispensation."

He disconnected.

She waved to the evidence collection techs who were suiting up on the perimeter of the site. She walked their way, diverting briefly to talk to two uniforms, young, possibly recent additions to the Patrol roster. "Canvass hospital security and nearby offices and stores for video. SD cards, though it's better if you can upload it. Here." She handed them one of her business cards, which included instructions on secure uploads to her NYPD database for video evidence.

A whole new world . . .

"Yes, ma'am," they said simultaneously . . . and a bit eerily.

They walked off briskly, and Sachs joined the trio of collection officers. Rhyme wanted his evidence, but there wouldn't be much. They had to wait until the mast was stable enough to climb, and even then the only prize would be the melted delivery system. And what would that yield?

They'd identified the drone, Rhyme had told her in a text, but it was a common model, with more than a thousand units sold in the past year. Oh, the Watchmaker might have been nearby to fly the UAV to its perch but, then again, he could have sat in his living room a mile away and directed the machine to the crane.

A voice intruded. "Miss? Policeman? Woman?"

She turned to see the patient whose baby she'd just helped deliver. She was in a wheelchair; an orderly had pushed her here.

"I'm MaryJeanne. Two n's. McAllister. We never met, not

official." They shook hands. Her dark hair, flyaway earlier, was pulled back in a taut ponytail.

Sachs looked down at the tiny child, swaddled and snoozing. You can't really say they're cute or pretty at this stage, so she didn't. She asked, "How are you both doing?"

"She's good. I still hurt. But I can't take anything. Not with . . ." She nodded downward. "You know, I'll be nursing. I was . . . a little loud. Sorry about that."

"You were fine, truly."

"You see that thing?" she whispered, nodding at the crane. "I thought it was over."

"So did I," Sachs said. "You have somebody coming to take you home?"

"My husband. The baby was a surprise. Well, I don't mean *that* way. I mean she was way early. He was out of town, but he's driving back now."

"You need another blanket?"

"I'm good. You know, we never came up with a girl name we liked. We had a dozen for boys. Troy, Erik with a 'k.' Tate . . . But nothing for girls. So. How would you feel, I mean would it be okay if we named her after you?"

Sachs couldn't help but smile at the charming gesture. "My name's Amelia."

MaryJeanne cocked her head, then she frowned. "No. Don't like it. Got anything else?"

Sachs's smile became a stifled laugh. "My last name's Sachs, and you don't want that one. Hey. How about something a little different?"

"What?"

"My husband's last name. Rhyme."

"Like what songs do?"

"That's right."

"Yeah. I like that one. Rhyme McAllister. I could go with that."

Sachs looked a final time at the baby. The tiny thing was quiet, no longer crying for the moment, and completely enwrapped in naïve sleep and in the enviable ignorance of the evil that had been a part of her arrival on this earth.

43.

AMELIA SACHS WAS watching a crane—a mobile one, not a tower—lift to the ground detached segments of the mast and jib that had been leaning against St. Francis. Soon the portion of the trolley that had been largely melted by the HF acid would be accessible.

The odds of collecting helpful evidence?

Not great, but maybe they'd get a brand name of a circuit board, or they'd find that this acid concentration was unique—and therefore easier to source.

Her phone sounded.

"Rhyme," she answered.

"Sachs, where are you?"

"Hospital. Near the crane. Should be able to get some samples pretty soon. Pictures too."

"Let the techs run the scene. I've got a lead. Have to move fast."

"Tell me."

"The samples you and Lyle took? In the garages? We had a

positive hit. One of the developers we targeted left HF trace on the ground under the passenger door of his limo."

"Which car?" She wondered if it was the Bentley.

"It's a Mercedes that Lyle sampled. It's owned by one of the biggest developers in the area. Willis Tamblyn."

The one she tried to find after the Bentley but hadn't been able to.

"No record, but Lon checked city logs. He's been in the Structures and Engineering building a dozen times in the last year."

So his theory was making sense: this developer hired the Watchmaker to devalue property so he could pick it up cheap.

"We've had it on the LPR wire and they had a hit on the Merc five minutes ago. About three blocks from you."

"So he's here, looking over Hale's handiwork. And he's probably pissed we stopped the collapse. Where's the Merc?"

He gave her the address. "I'm sending you Tamblyn's DMV picture."

She glanced at her phone. In his fifties, thinning hair, stern face, like smiling would be painful. He looked like . . . a real estate developer.

"I'm on my way."

They disconnected. She ripped off the cumbersome white Tyvek overalls and pulled on her black sport jacket once more. A lead had come up, she told the three evidence collection techs; they should continue with the scene. She'd be back soon.

A jog wasn't a pleasing proposition, given her battered lungs and windpipe.

But Dr. A. Gomez had declared her fine, so jog she did.

Thinking of an old expression of her father's, one that she lived her life by:

When you move, they can't getcha . . .

. . .

Patrolwoman Evelyn Maple, a ten-year vet on the NYPD, was keeping selfie takers out of the scene.

Yes, the crane was stabilized and dismantled.

Yes, the crews looked like they knew what they were doing.

But she, a mother of two, was keeping *her* damn distance. Because you never knew what could happen. Why wasn't everybody else doing the same?

"You, you can't be on that side of the rope."

"It's tape, technically, Officer." Snotty little blond cheerleader sort.

The officer was not tall, about five-four, and petite, so she lacked the intimidation factor she wished she had.

On the other hand, she had a badge and a gun and an extremely cool gaze, and the combination tended to get people to do what she wanted.

Tape, not rope . . .

You, move along. It's not safe. It's private property. You'll get squashed like a squirrel in Larchmont . . .

She squinted toward where the concrete counterweights of the big bright red crane were dangling as the acid or whatever it was ate through the brackets that held them to a metal trolley on the rear end of the boom.

Was someone *there?*

Yes.

Seriously?

Somebody was walking around the base of the crane, a massive concrete slab. He was looking down and picking things up.

A scavenger.

Maple ducked under the tape herself and made her way toward him. He was clearly homeless: dirty brown overcoat, squat orange and brown cap, shoes that didn't match, no socks.

Trespassing on a crime scene.

Looking for spare coins or valuables from victims?

Disgusting.

"Sir, excuse me."

He turned around, surprised.

"You have some ID?"

He looked at her with mad—though not, in her opinion, dangerous—eyes.

He said passionately, "New York has been transformed."

"Let me see some ID."

"Don't have any. But don't you think the streets are wider than they used to be? Sidewalks're cleaner. The geraniums hanging from lampposts, the trees are more obvious."

Oh, man.

One of those.

Maple had heard that the terror attacks were all about housing and getting people off the street. People like this.

He waved his arm. "See, they're hiding in their homes, they're afraid of those things." His palm ended up aimed at the crane. "So who do we see on the streets? Statues! Famous leaders. And department store mannequins. They're all correct shades now. Have you noticed?

"And how quiet it is! No jackhammers, no dynamite warning horns, not much honking. A siren or two, but they're pretty rare. You don't need a siren if there're no cars to get out of your way headin' for that shooting or the coronary, right?

"Transformed. Cranes come down, and the city's gone back in time a hundred years. It's 1900, except no a-*ooo*-ga squeeze horns on internal combustion vehicles and no clop clop of horses. And the shit! New York used to have a hundred thousand horses in the city. They produced two million pounds of shit a day."

Hm. Never thought about it. But she was tired of him now. "Sir, do you have a shelter you stay in?"

"Downtown."

"Why don't you just go on down there now. This place isn't safe."

He rattled his cup. "This woman. She gave me a handful of pennies. Pennies! But the joke was on her. She had to go to all the trouble. And I still got twenty-four cents." He cocked his head. "Like twenty-four hours in the day. That means something. Do you believe in signs, Officer?"

"Why don't you just head on home now?"

"All right, all right." He made his way back to the sidewalk and turned in the direction where Maple had seen that detective disappear just a few moments ago, moving quickly.

Amelia Sachs. Long red hair.

Tall.

Ah . . .

The homeless man stopped and turned back. "What do you think they did with it?"

"What's that, sir?" Maple asked, weariness in her voice.

"Two million pounds a day."

He continued down the sidewalk.

He had to be completely nuts. A businessman glanced at him and tried to slip a bill into his cup. He missed and it fluttered to the ground.

The homeless man glanced back—it looked like it was a ten or twenty—and just let it lie there as he continued down the sidewalk once more, walking with what almost seemed to be an intense purpose.

44.

SACHS WAS BREATHLESS as she strode along the sidewalk to where the license plate number recognition system had placed the Mercedes owned by Willis Tamblyn, the developer who had possibly—likely?—hired the Watchmaker to create chaos in the New York real estate market.

She called, "Rhyme, you there? I'm on my way."

"How far?"

"Three, four minutes. Odds that Tamblyn came here to meet the Watchmaker?"

"Don't know. And I'm thinking," Rhyme added slowly. "It might be a setup. Maybe Hale's one step ahead of us. Or thinks he is."

"And the car's a trap?"

"Possibly."

"The flash-bangs and breaching charges that Gilligan stole? An IED in the Merc."

Rhyme said, "Or more HF acid. If there's nobody in it, stand down and wait for Bomb Squad."

"K. I'm almost there."

She signed off and changed to the tactical frequency.

"Detective Five Eight Eight Five. ESU. Further to the attempted incident at Twenty-Third. Over." The words came out between gasps. She might have been fine, but her lungs didn't completely believe the assessment.

A clatter then: "Amelia. Bo Haumann. K."

This time the operation warranted the chief of the Emergency Service Unit himself, not just a captain commander.

"Bo."

"Where are you?" he asked.

"Three minutes out. On foot. And you?"

"Six or seven." The man's voice was raspy, and she'd always wondered why. As far as she knew, he didn't smoke. At any rate, the lean, grizzled man certainly looked the part of someone with a voice like this. "What's the scenario?"

"Got a car owned by a Willis Tamblyn. Real estate developer. Possible he hired Charles Hale—"

"The Watchmaker."

"Right. To take down the cranes."

"Why?"

"Money."

"One motive that never fails."

"I'm about there, Bo. I can see the vehicle. I'm taking a look. Over."

"K."

Ahead was the long, gleaming black limo. Fast, sleek, intelligent. But like that luxurious piece of machinery she'd seen earlier in the day, the Bentley, the Mercedes drove by electronics, not heart, and she wouldn't have owned one for the world.

Sachs slowed to a casual businessperson lope as she crossed the street onto the block where the vehicle was parked, then caught her breath. This was a stretch of wholesale shops and warehouses, so there was minimal foot traffic. It was a good location for a takedown—low risk for collateral damage, though there was a downside to the sparsity; she and other officers, even in street clothes, would be more obvious to the observant Watchmaker, whose survival skills were legendary.

If this was a trap, though, she doubted he would spring it when she was outside the vehicle. The amount of explosives Gilligan had stolen was not nearly enough to create a big enough bang to injure anyone unless they were in the vehicle itself.

It would take a huge IED—pounds of C4—to create a blast radius that large to kill officers merely nearby the car.

Still, she moved up slowly.

When she was even with the car, she casually looked inside and noted that it was occupied. So, not a trap.

A large man, complexion nearly as dark as the car's paint job, sat in the driver's seat, reviewing texts, or playing a game on his phone. He was in a black suit and a white shirt. In the backseat was a brown suitcase, a wheelie model. It was closed.

Before the man looked her way, she veered left and stepped into a store that sold buttons, of which there had to be a hundred thousand on display.

An Asian woman in a flowery dress called, "Wholesale only."

Sachs, a former model, remembered the days of fashion shoots, when a product manager for the designer's house would send a very nervous young assistant scurrying off to a store just like this to find an accessory for a gown because he didn't feel the existing one "spoke to his vision."

She held up her ID. "Police action. Go in the back. Stay there."

The wide-eyed woman blinked and then turned one-eighty and headed for the door.

"And don't make any calls."

The clerk dropped her phone on the counter as if it were on fire and disappeared into the back.

She radioed, "Bo. I'm in Feldstein's Buttons and Fixtures. Vehicle is occupied. Black male, thirties. He's muscle. Couldn't tell about weapons. He didn't make me. Suitcase in the back, closed. I don't think it's a trap, but the luggage is making me nervous."

Haumann said, "Bomb Squad and Fire's on silent roll ups, six, seven minutes out. We're there in four."

The driver tapped his earpiece and sat forward slightly. The Merc's engine turned over.

"Bo. Driver took a call and's starting the engine. And he's looking behind. Tamblyn's on his way here. Maybe with the Watchmaker. I'm going to get the muscle out of the vehicle."

"Can you wait for backup?"

"No time. They're going to be leaving. I'll get the driver inside the store, restrained. Tamblyn gets here, looks in the driver's seat. I come up behind. If the Watchmaker's with him, I get both down on their knees. Wait for you."

Haumann hesitated. "All right. We'll speed it up. Out."

He didn't say "Be careful" out loud, but his tone offered the sentiment.

She eased outside.

Another glance up and down the street.

A half-dozen people, but no Tamblyn.

Approaching the car, she noted the driver was reading his phone's screen.

ID in her left hand. Her right was near her weapon.

Was detaining him legal? she wondered.

It might be iffy constitutionally—a tiny bit of HF acid trace on a shoe print in a commercial garage supporting probable cause? Maybe Tamblyn, but the driver? That was a close call.

But she'd worry about the law later.

Catch 'em first.

This *was* the Watchmaker they were after.

As she moved up to the window, about to rap on it—and draw

down, if necessary—she realized that somebody among those she'd noted on the street had come up directly behind her.

She glanced back and saw a homeless man. He was in a stained coat and wore a weird hat, like a Middle Eastern warlord. He was vaguely familiar. Yes, he'd been at the first scene!

Amelia Sachs had made one of the fundamental mistakes in an arrest scenario: focusing on the obvious suspect and dropping her defenses with the apparently innocent.

But then she was looking past the hat, the coat, the tattered shoes, the dirty face, and she realized she recognized him from someplace other than the 89th Street scene.

From the DMV pictures Lincoln Rhyme had just sent.

Clean the face, comb the hair . . . and it was Willis Tamblyn, the developer, the man who, they now believed, had hired the Watchmaker to bring New York City's cranes tumbling down to earth.

45.

AFTER CLOSING AND double-locking the door of his home in Queens, he kissed Jenny and called hello to the children, a greeting they might or might not have heard, as they were upstairs with their phones and computers. The parents had decided to keep them home today because of the publicity their father had garnered from the accident and the suspension.

And—though they didn't share it with the children, of course—the threat that the Eddie Tarr investigation might or might not pose.

The dogs arrived, as always upon his entering, to greet him enthusiastically. Auggie was a dual citizenship canine—a mini Australian shepherd, aka American shepherd. He ran to Ron with the remnants of a stuffed toy he had recently eviscerated.

"Thanks," he said, taking the limp thing, a dragon, and tossing it into the hallway, where the dog collected the hide and began chewing again. He seemed pleased of the acknowledgment and ripped and chomped all the harder.

Daisy was a kaleidoscope of genes: papillon, sheltie, Aussie, Jack Russell, and Chihuahua. The children sometimes reminded the sweet thing that her ultimate ancestor was the wolf. To no effect.

He noted that Jenny wasn't wearing her usual household sweats but a flaring black skirt and red blouse. The slim woman looked like she was headed out for a night with the girls. "Book club?" he asked.

"Nope. Stayin' home with my man."

A smile, another kiss.

Her freckled face grew serious. "Reporter came by. Wanted to know my reaction to my husband being investigated. Distracted driving while under the influence."

Ron frowned. He'd supposed the accident would get reported, but how had the fact he'd been on a phone call at the time even come up?

"I sent him away, tail between his legs. You can't pepper spray reporters," Jenny said, "I have that right?"

"They have laws against it."

"Somebody in Albany needs to get that off the books."

He kissed her again, this time her forehead. She was a foot shorter and this portion of her face was a frequent landing spot for his lips. Her appearance was much the same as it had been when they'd met years ago . . . Her hair was now a bob, which had the curious effect of changing the shape of her face, emphasizing different angles. He liked her hair short, liked it long. She was beautiful to him and had always been. Always would be.

He was then aware that the accident had made him sentimental and he kicked *that* emotion out the door.

"Lunch!" she called.

Seconds later, Martine and Brad descended the stairs like stunt-people. It was apparently a race, with older Brad beating Martine by a nose. Preteen fashion dictated hoodies, both light gray. And, of course, baggy shorts—plaid in Brad's case, bright orange in his sister's. She was always the bolder in fashion choices and had already—to Ron's horror—wondered aloud if tattoos hurt.

The two children, both blond and dusted with Mom's freckles, knew their mealtime tasks—pouring water and soda and milk and bringing out the serving dishes of cold cuts, potato chips, pickles, salad, sliced watermelon. Ron sat down in his customary chair, the one with arms. He didn't do this because he was the head of the family. It was because it was the most uncomfortable chair of the dining set. He could buy a new one. Another thing he now had time to get around to.

They dished up, they ate, they talked.

Like, Donovan? Going to the Mets? And Boston. It's going to suck . . . Totally. Can I go to the retreat? . . . Luis and Harvey're going . . . Near West Point. They have a tour. There's some military museum there. I'm tired of the flute . . . Morgan's got a guitar. Her father bought her a Fender . . . Oh, where we went last summer, Lake George? . . . There's this TikTok video . . . A cat . . . After dinner . . . The test? Yeah, it went okay . . .

The conversation jogged and flowed everywhere—except to the subject of why Dad would be staying home for a while. Children are ever curious and fiercely perceptive. Much of their life was their soccer teams, their virtual worlds, their hanging with friends, their texting—but they also had news feeds and forums and they were as conversant on the topic of their father's suspension as anyone. Probably more than ninety percent of NYPD personnel.

And so, when the eating dwindled and plates were clean, Ron decided it was time.

"All right. Family meeting."

A concept not regularly exercised in this household. His own father had convened get-togethers once or twice a year, and Ron and Tony, his twin brother, would sit down on the carpeted floor while their mother took her rocker and Dad would talk about downsizing and what a move to Queens from Brooklyn would mean or that Grandad Bill had passed or that the doctor had found something and he needed to be in the hospital for a while . . .

So Ron had understandably come to associate the idea of an official family conference with unhappiness and had never convened one.

Until now.

They moved to the living room.

He took an armchair so that Jenny couldn't sit beside him, which, for some reason, he felt would magnify the gravity and upset the children more.

"You know a little about what's going on. But I'm going to tell you everything."

He explained to them about the crash, how he was going to be ticketed and maybe even charged for running a red light and hurting somebody. The person he'd hit was going to live. Because of the police department rules he had to take some time off.

He and their mother would make sure they'd be fine. This was just a temporary thing. Their lives would hardly change at all.

And there was no way to hide or buff it:

The drugs.

About which the children were, sadly, conversant, given the school's health curriculum.

He'd explained about the sticky, potent nature of fentanyl. How he and their mother had never done anything recreationally except a little pot (tell them everything, just not too much of everything).

That part was a mistake. That part would get straightened out.

They nodded that they understood.

But did they wholly?

And, for that matter, how convincing could he be when he wasn't sure that it *would* get straightened out?

The one part of everything that did not make it into the final version: that he might be arrested and go to jail.

A bridge to be crossed later, if required.

He asked if they had any questions.

Brad asked: "Are we going to have to move?"

"No. Absolutely not."

Martine wanted to ask something, but didn't. Ron—like all parents, a psychic—said, "There's no talk of me losing my job. And if I did, I'd get a new one. Easy-peasey."

Relief flowed into the girl's face.

A sensation that her father absolutely did not feel.

At the thought of leaving the only job he had ever wanted, or keeping the badge but being desked, Ron's gut tightened, his heart stuttered. He controlled the urge to cry. Barely.

Brad, the more reserved of the two, said, "Maybe we should, like, stay home."

Ron reached out and gripped the boy's forearm. "No, we go on with our life. We live it normally. We don't let things like this affect us. We rise above it. You ever hear that expression?"

They nodded.

"Now, are you okay with this?"

They said, "Sure" and "Okay."

But the words were flimsy. They were confused and shaken and, possibly, afraid.

This broke Ron Pulaski's heart.

But he fired up a smoke screen of his own: "Clear the table, finish your homework. Then Monopoly with dessert."

Their smiles were genuine. Their favorite version of the game was Dog-opoly. Which would give them the chance to resume the ongoing discussion of adding a canine to the household.

"Homework?" Ron asked again.

Martine, in grade school, didn't have any.

"Mine's done," Brad said.

But he said it in a way that Ron had heard gangbangers on the street say, "Ain't got nothing on me."

"All of it?" Ron asked.

"Kinda."

"Kinda?" He laughed. "Either the light's on or it isn't."

Lincoln Rhyme, when hearing a phrase like "most unique" would say, "Either it's unique or it isn't. Like being pregnant." Ron thought the table lamp metaphor more appropriate.

"Maybe this paper. But it's almost finished."

"Well, maybe you can finish it later. Go get the game."

The boy's face brightened.

The children readied the table in the rec room and brought their ringers—Auggie and Daisy—with them. Ron and Jenny walked into the kitchen to finish the cleanup. Wiping the counter, Jenny said, "How does this affect what you told me yesterday? Your talk with Lon?"

About taking over for Lincoln Rhyme.

If he got fired, nothing would stop him from being a consultant for the NYPD like Lincoln. Except his credibility as an expert witness would be destroyed. And that meant he'd never be hired.

Indicted and convicted . . . Well, that was something else.

"Depends on the findings."

"They'd be idiots to let you go. Look what you did at that scene yesterday. Getting that lead on the bomber. The task force must've been in heaven."

Over the moon . . .

"There's politics, there's optics."

"How did the interview go?"

A shrug. "The IA cop, he was decent. Didn't go half as bad as I thought it would."

Thinking back to the half hour with Garner.

And staring out the window.

She walked close and put her arms around him, her head against his chest. "Whatever happens, we'll get through it."

Ron resisted the gravitational tug to look toward the mantel above the fireplace.

"We're ready." Brad's voice.

"Daddy, what do you want to be? I'm the cat and Brad's the mailman."

He called, "I'll be the fire hydrant."

"That's gross."

Nobody wanted to be the hydrant in Dog-opoly, but Ron couldn't think of the other pieces.

And then he paused, looking out the window once again.

"What is it?" Jenny was looking at his focused eyes.

He kissed her forehead. "I'll be right in. Have to make a call."

As Jenny took a half gallon of ice cream from the freezer, Ron stepped outside onto the back porch.

Pulling out his phone, he looked up a contact number and placed a call.

"Hey, Ron," Lyle Spencer said. "How're you doing? I heard. Man, I'm sorry about what happened."

"I'm okay. Thanks. Listen, can you spare a few minutes now?"

"For you, absolutely."

46.

AMELIA SACHS HANDED his ID back.

The man in the homeless garb was indeed Willis Tamblyn.

Now that she could look past the costume and smudged face, it was clear that he was the man in the DMV picture Rhyme had sent.

Tamblyn was worth, she recalled, about $29 billion—though that was according to a Google search anyway, so who really knew? He had been a real estate developer in New York City and New Jersey all his professional life. He'd been born poor. In the press about him, the word "bootstrap" appeared frequently. And once or twice the phrase "with a conscience" in such a way that the reporter penning the story seemed surprised to be including it in the same sentence with "real estate developer."

Nearby was Bo Haumann and one of the ESU tactical teams. The threat assessment was low, but low wasn't nonexistent.

Tamblyn's driver checked out too. He was a former NYPD officer, who'd tripled his salary—and maybe extended his life span—by going private. He had no record and the concealed-carry for his weapon was in order.

"We found evidence that links you to the first crane collapse."

"Well, obviously it would. I was there." He gave a breathy laugh. "You even saw me. But you don't remember."

"No, I do."

Tamblyn tilted his head slightly. "What evidence exactly? I'm curious."

"Trace evidence." Give your subjects something that keeps them talking, Sachs thought, but never anything they can use.

He frowned more wrinkles into a wrinkled face. "Ah. You vacuumed up, or whatever you do, dirt outside my car. No, *all* the big developer's cars. Who else, I wonder. Liebermann? Frost? Bahrani? And assumed one of us hired a hit man with a hacksaw to tip cranes over for fun and profit. A cruiser spotted this." A nod at the Mercedes. "And called it in. Do you say, 'Calling it in'?" He nodded broadly. "I know. It was the acid! In the news. That's the trace. Bad stuff. I steered clear."

She wished *she* had, though the lungs were clearly on the mend.

"Okay, sure I was at the collapse on Eighty-Ninth Street. And the hospital." A nod north. "*And* the Bingham construction site where the elevator dropped sixty feet and broke a workman's back. I was at the Richard Henderson development on the Hudson. The big glass tower? Construction waste wasn't secured. A ton of scrap lumber was blown over the side. It fell six hundred feet and hit three workers at a hundred miles an hour. One was killed. Another lost an arm."

He nodded to his cell phone, which she'd removed from his overcoat and placed on the hood of his car. "I video the sites, then I write reports on how the accidents could've been prevented. Laborers' International, Brotherhood of Carpenters, Plumbing and Pipefitting, Sheet Metal, Painters and Allied Trades . . . All the unions report incidents to me. I play detective." He cut his gaze toward the shield on her belt, almost as if he wished he had one.

"You're a crusading developer, saving workers' lives."

He liked the phrase.

"I meet regularly with the mayor and the director of safety at Structures and Engineering."

Explaining why he'd logged in there.

The man had removed the odd hat and overcoat. They appeared grimy, but that was all part of the stage acting, it seemed. The dirt and grease were spray paint. While she'd originally expected an unpleasant odor, all she detected was a faint lavender scent. Maybe shampoo, though Tamblyn seemed like a cologne kind of guy.

"Why the disguise?"

"I'm like a restaurant reviewer. The companies and developers know me. If they were to see me and there's unsafe conditions, they'd cover them up. Or manhandle me off the site. Sometimes I'm a tourist, sometimes a street musician. Homeless is best. I'm invisible." He scoffed. "I got right behind you, didn't I? If I'd been the man behind the collapse, you'd be dead."

Couldn't argue with him there.

"And when you act insane, they just want you to go away." He told her an officer had just detained him at the hospital scene. But once he started to ramble, she got tired of him pretty fast and sent him along.

"Frederick," he said, looking to his driver. "Water, towels." He turned back to her and she nodded okay.

The driver walked to the back of the vehicle and removed the requested items from the trunk, which Sachs and ESU had already cleared. He handed his boss the bottle and the cloth towels—which looked sumptuous. She'd never seen towels that thick.

Tamblyn rinsed the dirt off his hands. The water splashed and flew. He didn't care who or what got wet. Sachs stepped back. When he was done, he dried, and then began removing the crud from beneath his nails with a file portion of a pair of clippers. "Dirty nails. You want somebody to think you're an unfortunate soul, if you ever go undercover, you need dirty nails."

She didn't respond, but decided it was not bad advice.

He studiously cleaned each fingertip, rolling the residue into tiny balls and dropping them on the sidewalk. "Are you believing me? Ah, your face says not exactly . . . All right. Call this number."

He recited one and she dialed. The line rang once and was picked up. "Hello?" A man's impatient voice.

Sachs asked, "Who is this?"

"The fuck. Who is *this* and how did you get this number?"

"Detective Amelia Sachs, NYPD. I'm with Willis Tamblyn. Who am I speaking to?"

"Tony Harrison."

The mayor of New York.

"Is Willis all right?"

"Yes. Let me call you on the City Hall line," she said.

"Are you—?"

She disconnected and called the main number and in ten seconds was speaking to the man once again.

He grumbled, "Your conspiracy bones satisfied, and my authenticity established, Detective Sachs?"

"Yes." Maybe a "sir" might be in order. She wasn't in the mood.

"Mr. Tamblyn has been at several of the crime scenes involving the crane collapses."

"I know. That's what he does. Anything more?"

"No. I—"

The line went dead.

She said, "The collapses were intentional. How can you guard against that?"

He shrugged. "Wind happens. Metal failure happens. Terrorists happen. Contractors have to be ready for anything. Look at what we learned on Eighty-Ninth. The operator had a rope in the cab. A hundred dollars' worth of rope saved his life. That went into my report. And the hospital? I'm going to recommend the city doesn't approve freestanding cranes. They have to be attached to the structure they're building."

She asked, "Did you see anyone at either of the sites who gave you the impression they were involved?"

"No. Just a bunch of jackals who wanted selfies at a disaster. Now, can I go?"

Her phone buzzed.

She told Tamblyn, "Not yet." Then, to the phone: "Rhyme. I've got him. Only, it's not quite what we thought." She explained about Tamblyn's mission, and the mayor's confirmation.

"Homeless . . ." Rhyme said. "I saw somebody earlier, on one of the videos. Let me check something . . . Ah, yes, it's Tamblyn. That's what he was holding, a cell phone." He fell silent. "Put him on speaker."

She tapped the button and moved the unit closer to Tamblyn. She said, "It's Lincoln Rhyme. He's—"

The developer said, "I know who he is . . . Mr. Rhyme."

"Mr. Tamblyn. We could use your help. Let me run a few ideas by you and see what you think."

"I suppose. If it's urgent. I have an engagement." And started on the nails of his right hand.

Rhyme said, "Urgent, yes. We just checked the countdown clock. It's been reset. Only this time whoever's behind it has upped the deadline. Another crane comes down in just a few hours."

47.

"SENATOR, FOUR O'CLOCK."

Not a reference to time.

Position of threat.

The two men were in Lower Manhattan, east of Wall Street.

A glance to his right and behind.

He noted a fortyish man in jeans, dark baseball cap and a sweatshirt, no logo, navy blue. The kind favored by street thieves. Toss-aways, they were called. You mug somebody, run and throw away what you were wearing to fool those searching for you.

"Why's it a threat, you think?"

Peter, the tall, broad "personal security specialist," replied, "Paused when we waited for the light, made a call that might not have been a call. It looked fake." The sun flared off Peter's naked scalp.

"You see him earlier?"

"No."

"We'll keep an eye out."

Edward Talese, a U.S. senator from New York, had just met with his party's presidential campaign manager. The meeting between her and Talese had gone well and he'd come away with a list of donors to cuddle up with.

Talese was fifty-nine years old and sturdy of build and he wore his blond hair in a crew cut, which deemphasized the lack thereof. Not that he cared. His face was bulldog scrunched, though the jowls echoed a different breed—a bloodhound. Talese knew he was sometimes described in canine metaphors, and that was okay by him. He owned four: a wolfhound, a Malinois, a bluetick and a Chihuahua. Some people were amused that of the quartet the only one he himself had brought into the family was Buttercup, who weighed in at six pounds, three ounces. And that, only because she was overweight.

Normally he and Peter would be in the limo, which was bullet resistant (a phrase that, for some reason, amused him, as if the car merely *disdained* lead projectiles). But the first meeting had been at campaign headquarters downtown and to get to the next, with a donor at the Water Street Hotel, it was far more efficient and faster to walk than to negotiate the impossible Financial District traffic.

He wondered now if this exposure was a mistake.

He looked back once more.

He couldn't tell if the man was still there; the lunchtime crowds were thick.

The day was clear. Strong sunlight slanted downward and replicated itself in a hundred windows, the reflected beams dimmer and cooler than the original act, but still glary.

Ahead he caught a glimpse of City Hall, impressive as ever. They would normally have cut through Steve Flanders Square, in front of the elaborate structure, but it was closed off, sealed with yellow police tape.

"What happened there?" the senator asked.

"Look." He pointed to a construction site where one of those cranes was being built. The site was deserted.

"Oh, that affordable housing gang, or whoever."

The crane was only sixty, seventy feet high. But, Talese supposed, could do some damage if it came down. Affordable housing—that was their gripe. He sympathized—he'd discussed the issue with the head of Housing and Urban Development—but killing people to make their point?

"That way." Peter pointed and unbuttoned his jacket to reveal his firearm.

After some minutes of serpentine travel—dodging people who were glued to their phones—Talese and Peter emerged again into the sun. They crossed the busy street to the hotel, a structure impressive if you loved metal and glass. The word "cozy" need not apply.

"See him?" Talese was looking back.

"He turned. Probably nothing."

In the bright, functional lobby, he expected to be greeted by the campaign donor himself, an impossibly wealthy hedge fund manager. When he didn't see the man, he pulled out his phone. Before he placed the call, though, a tall man in a dark suit and white shirt walked directly up to him. Peter stirred.

"Senator Talese."

Not a question. Anyone with a TV knew who he was.

"Mr. Roth won't be able to take your meeting. But there's someone else who'd like to see you."

Peter said, "We'll see some ID."

He produced it.

Noting the man's employer, Talese lifted an eyebrow.

The meeting, it seemed, was going to be considerably different from the one he'd had planned.

48.

IN HIS TOWN HOUSE, on the line with Willis Tamblyn, Lincoln Rhyme was saying into the phone, "The person actually sabotaging the cranes is a hired gun. Charges millions for jobs like this."

"My."

Rhyme thought Tamblyn seemed unimpressed. Millions to him was probably just a private jet budget.

"We want to know who hired him. We find that out, we find him. So we need a motive."

He imagined Sachs was nearly smiling to hear him say the disreputable M-word.

Rhyme continued, "First, it was what you might've heard in the news: activists forcing the city to convert old government property into affordable housing. But we've discarded that."

"Well, I'd think so," he said sardonically. "You should've called me right up front. I'd've told you. There are plenty of shits in the affordable housing movement and most of them are stupid. Naïve, at least. But extortion? Not their thing. And they couldn't pull together a fee like that anyway."

Rhyme said, "Then we were thinking of—"

Tamblyn interrupted. "An amoral real estate developer. Like me."

"Yes. Driving down the market to pick up properties for cheap."

A scoffing exhalation. "And how exactly would that work?"

Rhyme said, "REITs, for one."

Tamblyn seemed perplexed at the very thought. "They're long-term. And valuation is based on funds from operations, and interest rates. Not *New York Post* headlines. Next?"

Sachs came in with: "Manipulating the stock market?"

Now an outright laugh. "You can't be serious. You want to play *that* game, you pick one stock, go short, get an anonymous blog, post fake stories about the dangers of electric cars or a dermatology drug, and cash out when the price dips. Then go to jail, by the way. The SEC's been there. Falling cranes? Wall Street may hiccup, but they've forgotten about it come cocktail hour."

Rhyme tried: "Delays in construction. The projects go bankrupt. A developer moves in—"

"And buys them for a song? Where did you hear that?"

"A news story . . ."

"Oh, oh . . . On the *news*. Of course it *has* to be true . . . Well, the last thing banks want is to own property they hold the mortgage on. The construction milestones? Nobody takes them seriously. It gets worked out."

Rhyme's eyes were taking in the evidence boards. He glanced absently toward the sterile portion of the parlor, where Mel Cooper was analyzing yet more trace Sachs and Pulaski had collected. His expression explained he was finding nothing new.

"Sachs, show him a list of the properties that were on the Kommunalka Project demand list."

Tamblyn grunted. "I'm meeting someone."

Rhyme said, "Five hours. Till another crane."

"It's Lucien's. Do you know how long it takes to get a reservation?"

Sachs said, "I've got it."

"Mr. Tamblyn?" Rhyme prompted.

"I'm reading, I'm reading."

"Is there any strategic reason our perp would want *those* properties transferred to a corporation? Some're former government installations. Maybe there're records stored there? Research facilities? Some geographic reason? They're adjacent to critical locations? Or, maybe, to keep them off the market?"

In a distracted voice, Tamblyn said, "You have quite the devious mind. Impressive. But . . . no."

Rhyme asked, "Why?"

"Ninety percent of them ain't going anywhere anytime soon. They're frozen. On no-transfer lists."

"No-transfer?" Sachs asked.

"They're toxic. Literally. A couple're Superfund. The others? Cleanup'll take years. He had to've known that. Sounds like he closed his eyes and picked some property that was city owned without thinking about it."

Rhyme asked, "So your opinion—your *expert* opinion—is that these crimes have nothing to do with real estate?"

"Well, this guy is *your* million-dollar killer, not mine, but on what you've given me, that's correct. He has something else in mind entirely."

49.

"MR. PRESIDENT."

"Edward."

Senator Talese stepped into the parlor. The exterior and lobby of the hotel may have been bland, but these rooms were decidedly posh.

But, then again, it *was* the Presidential Suite.

The commander in chief rose from a couch that was surrounded by a sea of paperwork and strode forward over the off-white sponge of carpet to grip the man's hand. President William Boyd was a tall, angular man whose mixed-race heritage showed in the soft tone of his skin. He was known for his ready smile, which he flashed now.

Talese was senior in the opposing party and he wondered what Boyd would think if he knew that he'd just spent the last two hours strategizing about removing him from office come the election in November. Then decided the man wouldn't care. It was all part of the game. And in fact he and Boyd had worked together frequently, beating down partisanship when they could and getting compromise legislation hammered out.

"Senator." The tall, regal First Lady stood in the doorway.

"Mrs. Boyd."

"How're Emily and the girls? The grandchildren?"

"All well, thank you." Talese noted the First Daughter, ten years old, was also in good form, fervently tapping her iPad screen.

"I'll leave you to it." The woman closed the double doors behind her.

The men sat. Boyd said, "Sometimes, this business, don't you feel like a magician? Sleight of hand, misdirection. Do you know any card tricks, Edward?"

"I do, sir. I play hearts with my grandkids and I watch my loose change vanish. So the hedge fund manager I was supposed to meet—it was a disappearing act."

"I'd hardly dig up a rich man to fund my opponent's war chest, would I? Caught you off guard."

"Yessir."

The man stretched. Despite his apparently robust health, he looked tired. But then Talese had worked with three presidents and they were perpetually tired. The job simply tuckers you out.

"The polls . . . It's going to be a coin toss in November."

"Close. Yes."

"Good CEOs don't last—business or government. And I don't mean good as in talented and efficient. I mean as in doing good." Boyd rose and poured himself coffee. He lifted an eyebrow. Talese shook his head. "You ever see the movie *Fail Safe*, Edward?"

"Long time ago. Our bombers get a message by mistake to nuke Moscow. Are we worried about war?"

"No, no. I'm thinking of that scene where the president asks the American ambassador in Russia to sacrifice himself, so they'll know that Moscow's been destroyed."

"He stays on the phone until it's destroyed in the blast. The Russian ambassador in New York does the same."

They traded the two cities to avoid all-out war. Like swapping queens at chess.

A chilling flick.

Talese continued, "Melted ambassadors. This is not a very auspicious conversation, Mr. President."

"My infrastructure bill, Edward . . ."

"Ah." And Talese saw what was coming and was suddenly aware of the concept of seeing his life pass before his eyes. In this case, his political life. "Only just a bit more popular than nuclear holocaust, I'll give you that."

A laugh.

Boyd's legislation would be a massive overhaul of the country's roads, bridges, tunnels, airports, railroads and the like. Improving safety and employing tens of thousands of workers.

Opponents, all of them vehement, said that bill might bankrupt the country.

Talese was looking down at the bird's-eye maple coffee table.

Boyd: "You've read the drafts. What do you think?"

"In theory, it might work."

With a coy tone in his voice, the president said, "I've heard some feedback . . . Off the record, of course. You like the idea."

Where *did* the man get his intelligence?

"Edward, help me get this off the ground."

"Mr. President . . ."

Boyd leaned forward. "Your clean water legislation? I'll make sure it happens."

Jesus.

That would be a miracle . . .

The senator sighed. "Dinner the other night? I mentioned that the water bill was coming in at one point two billion. And Sammi said, 'Guess somebody left the faucet running.'"

A chuckle. "We need more twelve-year-olds in Congress."

Just like Boyd to know the names and ages of his oppo's grand-children.

"I vote for it, it'll be the end of my career."

"Ah, you're not up for four years. Voters'll forget."

"My party won't. After this term I won't be able to get any job short of dogcatcher."

Talese looked out the window as the sun cast its relentless light on the magnificent city.

Not impulsive as a politician, not impulsive as a husband or father or grandfather, Senator Edward Talese of New York did not act impulsively now. His quick mind ordered facts and conse-quences and said, "I'll do it, sir. You've got my vote."

Dogcatcher . . .

The president rose quickly and took Talese's hand in both of his.

"I've been thinking of a title for when I write my autobiogra-phy," the senator mused. "Or, when my ghostwriter does. I've got it now: *The Devil's Bargainer.*"

The president laughed his famous laugh.

The two walked to the door.

Talese said, "That movie? The one where the two ambassadors got nuked? At least they avoided World War Three. That was something."

50.

LINCOLN RHYME'S EMAIL inbox flashed with a Zoom request to join a meeting five minutes from now.

The host was the homeless billionaire Willis Tamblyn.

This would be a follow-up to their prior conversation a half hour ago.

After the developer had shot down their theories about the Watchmaker's motives, Rhyme had wondered if the developer could help in another way.

"Six months?" Tamblyn had muttered.

"What?" Rhyme had asked.

"How long it takes to get that reservation at Lucien's."

Rhyme had asked, "Will it still be in business six months from now, do you think?"

There'd been a pause. "Jacques won't be happy. What do you need?"

Rhyme had said, "A developer has to know a lot about the history of the city, its geography, I assume."

"Are you joking? Someone once wrote that nobody knows more about New York City than Willis Tamblyn. I took offense. Saying 'nobody knows more.' That puts me on an equal footing with every Tom, Dick and Loser of developers. The right way to say it is simpler and doesn't involve a negative. I know more than any other living person about the city."

"Then maybe you can help us find a location. It's where the co-conspirators met in the crane attack."

"Conspirators," Tamblyn had said slowly, savoring either the word or the concept itself. Perhaps both.

"This is what our officers found in the soil." And he had sent a picture from the murder board.

- *Andy Gilligan, homicide*
    - *clay soil*
    - *oyster shells, old*
    - *decaying substances, all probably several hundred years old:*
        - *wool*
        - *leather*
        - *varnished wood*
        - *liquor*
        - *horsehair*
        - *charcoal*
- *Garry Helprin, attempted homicide*
    - *clay soil*
    - *oyster shells, old*
    - *decaying substances, all probably several hundred years old:*
        - *wool*
        - *leather*
        - *varnished wood*
        - *liquor*

- *horsehair*
- *charcoal*
- *ammonia and isocyanic acid*

"Let me look into it."

This is what Tamblyn was now going to be Zooming about.

Rhyme clicked on the invite.

Tamblyn's face appeared, wide-angle, from his phone camera. He was at a fancy dining table.

Lucien's? He'd gone after all, it seemed.

The developer suddenly muttered to a man in a white jacket. "I know I'm on the phone. I know it's against your policy. I also know I could write a check for this place on the spot and turn it into an Arby's franchise. The maître d' will tell you who I am. Now go away. Mr. Rhyme? So, that evidence you found? The best I can do is tell you that when foundation crews dig up anything that might be historical, they have to tell the city. And the construction comes to a halt, and the bleeding hearts get court orders to preserve the site for further inspection. Screw it if the company goes out of business and hardworking men and women get fired."

He calmed. "Well, I've seen these items you found before. A military connection. Revolutionary War. The wood is from gun stocks, horsehair from, yes, you guessed it. The liquor's key. Did you know that soldiers back then fought drunk? I saw a show on cable. Makes sense. Would you go charging up against musket balls and bayonets sober? I myself wouldn't."

"That still leaves a lot of possibilities, though. Battlefields, training sites, camps. The army and navy've always been stationed here. The clay and oyster shells probably mean downtown Manhattan, southwest Brooklyn, north Staten Island, eastern Jersey down to Newark. But I don't know that does you a lot of good."

More than five hundred miles of shoreline . . .

Rhyme's eyes rose to the ceiling, considering the man's words.

And the thought emerged.

Military installations . . .

Ammonia and isocyanic acid.

Urea.

Which is the main source of saltpeter—sodium nitrate, used in the manufacture of gunpowder.

A student of explosives, like all forensic scientists, Rhyme knew that in the nineteenth century gunpowder was always in short supply and manufacturers—desperate for saltpeter, the main source for which was pee—would pay preachers so they could collect dried urine from church pews, where it accumulated after parishioners remained in their seats to listen to sermons that stretched on for hours, and let their natural functions simply occur—rather than risk the wrath of God or, more likely, the appearance of irreverence by slipping away to the outhouse.

Rhyme asked, "Is there anywhere you can think of where gunpowder was *manufactured* in the area back then—and in a place where construction might've been halted?"

"Ah, that's easy. There's a current job on hiatus because excavators found an old military installation where gunpower was made. Late seventeen hundreds. Down in Greenwich Village. It used to be known as Gunners' Row. They changed it years ago. Now it's called Hamilton Court."

• • •

Before him, rising two hundred feet into the air, was an Engström-Aber tower crane, a self-erecting model.

Bold yellow with a blue cab, this model, he'd learned, was a workhorse in the city. Hale couldn't help but admire it. The mast measured twelve by twelve feet, and the forward jib—made of eleven sections—totaled two hundred and seventy feet, while the counterweight jib extended sixty-nine. It could heft fifty-five thousand pounds. Not surprising, it was expensive to rent; few construction companies owned tower cranes; to justify the expense, a unit would have been used weekly, and not many contractors did high-rise jobs that required them. The E-A came in at $15,900 per month.

And the meter was ticking. Sitting unused did not excuse the rent, and a crazy man who might tip it over was not an act of God under the rental agreement.

He now parked a half block from the site. Gazing about and seeing no one, other than drivers of vehicles oblivious to him and his SUV, he tapped to life his tablet and found the diagram that was among those that the unfortunate Andy Gilligan had stolen from the city's DSE department. He looked from the glossy surface to the grounds around him.

Yes, there it was—a four-foot-wide concrete tunnel that would be used to channel rainwater and snowmelt runoff to a drainage system under a nearby road and ultimately to the Hudson River.

All was good. Yes, the workers-turned-guards were diligent and took their task seriously. Their coffee and cigarettes did not distract from their vigil.

Of course, the danger they were looking for, like air-raid wardens in World War II England, was coming from the sky, they believed.

Searching for one of the acid-toting drones.

And once again the amateur guards were looking everywhere but the place they should be looking.

Climbing from the vehicle, he donned the hard hat—yellow like the other workers wore—and zipped his Carhartt overalls up tight at the neck. He walked to the back, raised the liftgate and pulled out the heavy backpack.

He made his way to the tunnel and began to shimmy through. At the end, some fifty feet away, he climbed the steel rungs set into the concrete as a ladder and emerged near the crane's base.

Above him the jib loomed. The wind was up and there was a faint whistle as it streamed through the yellow tubing and black support wires. The operator had released the clutch so that the jib weather-vaned safely.

He examined the base of the mast. The drone was resting in peace, but his plan didn't call for that anyway. Nor was any of the lovely HF acid involved.

This crane incident would be different.

In a few minutes, the packages had been delivered and he returned to the tunnel and made his way back to the car.

In the driver's seat he tossed the helmet into the back, began the drive back to his safe house on Hamilton. As he left, he examined the site once more.

He supposed that this particular crane, while towering, garnered less attention than others. The area around it had been completely cleared in a four-hundred-foot circumference. So if, for some reason, the terrorist, or pyscho, sabotaged it, there were no apartments or office buildings to crush.

Which didn't mean there was *no* target within the crane's reach.

The most important one in fact of his whole project.

51.

DETECTIVE LYLE SPENCER—a full foot taller than Ron Pulaski—stood at the door. He wore a black suit and white shirt, no tie. Pulaski looked up and shook the man's meaty hand.

They stepped into the living room, and Ron introduced the detective to Jenny. They too shook hands.

The children, at the Dog-opoly board, looked up. Jenny said, "And our children. Martine and Brad. This is Detective Spencer."

"You're big."

"Brad!" she said.

Spencer laughed. "Not a worry." The detective's eyes looked around the comfortable room: affordable furniture, pictures, vacation souvenirs, sports uniforms, family relics going back generations. Then the accessories that make a dwelling a home: video game cartridges, magazines, recipe cards, soccer and softball gear, mismatched running shoes, pretzel and potato chip packets.

Jenny cast her husband a playfully exasperated look, and he realized he'd forgotten to tell her there'd be a houseguest calling.

"We'll be out back."

"The game!" Martine called.

"I won't be long."

"Coffee? Beer?"

Both declined Jenny's offer.

Brad called, "Detective Spencer? Were you like Special Forces?"

"SEALs."

"Man . . . Team Six?"

"No."

"But did you do secret missions?"

"Oh, you bet. But I can't talk about them."

"Cool!"

Ron nodded to the kitchen and the two men walked through it, and onto the back porch. The covered rectangle, unscreened, overlooked a patch of lawn ringed with planting beds in which nothing had been planted. They were weed free, though, and filled with fragrant mulch, which Ron and the children had spread themselves. It was not that long ago—less than a month—though that pleasant Saturday afternoon might have been a decade ago.

Ron noted the big man's somber expression, not present when he'd arrived.

They looked over the grass.

Filling the silence, Spencer asked softly, "When did it happen?"

It . . .

"Or we can move on. Just wanted to ask."

"No. It's okay. A few years. How'd you know?"

"Your wife said 'our children.' Not 'two of our children.' And I met an older boy and a younger girl. But there were pictures on the mantel of Brad and an older girl."

The man was, after all, a detective.

And looking at the face, big and tough, but tinted with pain,

Ron Pulaski knew another fact about Lyle Spencer. They had something in common.

Ron said, "Cancer. Happened fast. Man, you do everything . . . and sometimes everything isn't enough."

"I'm sorry."

"Over the years we must've had a hundred people over, Jenny and me. Probably looked at that same picture. Nobody made the leap. Maybe they wondered and didn't want to ask. But I don't think so. They just didn't notice. And your situation?"

Looking out over the yard, the man said, "Wasn't that different. We had a daughter too. Then . . . It was an orphan disease."

Ron shook his head.

"Term of art, our doctor said. A rare disease. In the U.S., the definition is less than two hundred thousand people have it." He gave a dim laugh. "I told Lincoln. And you know him. He said the word 'orphan' comes from the Greek. And it doesn't mean just a child without his parents. It can mean a parent who's lost a child.

"There're sometimes drugs to treat orphan diseases, but the companies don't develop them on scale. Not profitable. A single pill might cost a quarter million dollars."

"No!"

"That's what she needed. I was upstate, at a small sheriff's office. I helped myself to some drug money to pay for it."

Ron knew that Spencer had had a convoluted route to becoming an NYPD detective. He'd heard about a conviction, but the governor had pardoned him and expunged his record, which allowed him to join up. He'd wondered what had happened.

"It work at all, the drug?"

"For a while. Then it didn't."

If there ever was a justifiable crime, it was the one Spencer had committed.

Spencer asked, "Lincoln and Amelia know?"

"No." There was no discernible reason for not telling them. He just hadn't. "You? You said Lincoln knows."

"He deduced it. He wondered why I was about to play high dive off the side of a building, that Locksmith case we worked, little while ago."

So, the detective had considered killing himself. He must have been a widower, or his wife might have left him after the daughter's death and his arrest. Ron knew too that after his spinal cord accident, years ago, Lincoln had found a doctor willing to rig a setup so he could end his life.

After his daughter's death, Ron had never considered anything that extreme. He had the rest of his family to be there for. But that wasn't to say that he—and Jenny—didn't die in a way. Part of them would forever remain lifeless.

Spencer said, "One of the hardest things. Bug—our nickname— she knew. Knew everything, and it was like, she just accepted it, got on with life while she had it. 'What's for dinner?' Or, 'Dad, like really? You forgot the Netflix passcode again?'"

Ron was nodding and, just barely, keeping the tears banked. "Same thing with Claire, yes. I never knew if it was courage or de-nial. Or something else." A deep breath. "Never figured that out."

Their grief counselor had said, "You need to embrace the mem-ories and then do what she would have wanted for you two: to move on."

But he and Jenny agreed that was bullshit. What Claire would have wanted was to cry at Disney movies, to gossip with other girls, to flirt with boys and fight with Mom and Dad when she turned thirteen and pick a college and meet the right person and maybe, someday, have children of her own.

That's what the girl would have wanted.

Her parents' state of mind wasn't—and shouldn't have been— a thing she considered at all.

So they had mourned then, and they mourned now. They would always mourn.

Jenny had said it best earlier: They had gotten through it, yes. But move on? Never.

Finally, Ron asked, "So. What I was asking?"

Spencer took a notebook from his sport coat pocket. "Did some digging. And hate to break the news, Ron, but you've got yourself one hell of a problem."

52.

COUNTDOWN: 3 HOURS

AS GOOD A tactical solution as she could put together under the circumstances.

There was little cover on the cul-de-sac street, Hamilton Court, which was lined with buildings in various degrees of human-made destruction and natural decay. The short avenue had been a commercial area at one point, presumably devoted to wholesale food—the Meatpacking District was not far away. But developers had seen the glow of Manhattan profits and had scooped up the block.

Then, as Willis Tamblyn explained, the project crashed, thanks to a few pieces of old armament and traces of rum.

She was at the chained-off entrance, surveying the two hundred feet of cobblestones before her.

The evidence suggested that the Watchmaker and Gilligan had spent time here. The question, however, was whether this was the killer's safe house, or simply a random spot they'd picked to stop at and have a conversation.

Except Rhyme and Sachs didn't think it was the latter. Aerial views of Hamilton Court showed a trailer, the sort used as head-quarters on construction jobs. It was dusty and battered and invisible from the main streets. A good safe house.

Sachs had also speculated: The street is old, the buildings are old. Which would appeal to the Watchmaker psychologically, as the place was from a different moment in time.

An analysis she did not, of course, share with Lincoln Rhyme, who maintained a negative view of psych profiling.

As she directed the three entry teams into place, she noticed something else that suggested the trailer was his temporary home: a video camera at the mouth of the cul-de-sac, facing inward and hidden in a pile of bricks. She could understand security cameras on the trailer itself, but why cover the street leading to it? The logical answer was: to give warning of officers approaching.

She and one of the dynamic entry teams, four persons total on each, were now staged behind this pile of rubble, out of view of the camera.

"This is Car Seven. We're ready. K."

Her earpiece clattered loudly. She turned the volume down. "Roger, Seven."

Two plain-clothed detectives in an SUV marked with the logo of an actual real estate company were parked on Hudson, fifty feet away.

At Sachs's word, they would drive up to the entrance of Hamilton and turn into the mouth of Hamilton, blocking the camera.

"Five Eight Eight Five," she radioed. "Teams Two and Three, report. K."

"Team Two. In position behind 208 Hamilton. Back entrance breached. Clear route to trailer."

"Roger, Two. Three?"

"Three, we're second floor 216 Hamilton. Clear view of target premises. Sniper and spotter in position."

"Roger."

She charged her M4. The weapon could be fired fully automatic, burst or semi, and she moved the selector to auto.

I'll try to keep him alive, Rhyme. But I'm not risking a single soul on my teams.

Her heart tapped at just above normal velocity, and the slight elevation was not from concern about the operation itself or its success. It was the pleasure she felt at moments like this. The pure joy swelling within her just before a tactical operation. Her palms were dry and, for a change, she felt no urge to dig a nail into a cuticle or her scalp, a compulsive habit that persisted from her youth. Her nerves were presently at rest.

A deep breath. The faintest trace of congestion. Hardly noticeable.

You're fine . . .

She glanced back at her team, two men, one woman. Younger than she. Their eyes still. Their bodies coiled. They crouched— and she envied them their youthful knees.

One of the men gripped his weapon with tight fingers. He was gazing at the ground, his lips pressed hard together—the only portion of his face, other than the eyes, that was visible, due to the Nomex hoods. He realized she was looking his way. When he met her gaze, she nodded.

And he came down from that troubled place where he'd momentarily perched. It would be his first time out.

"Three," she called. "What do you see? K."

"Shades are down. No visual. But we have a heat signature."

"Human?"

"Likely. Right temp. And in motion."

So, the Watchmaker *was* inside.

"K. Team Two, move to the front of 208. Advise. And, Zillow Girl, pull into position."

A laugh from the detective in Car Seven. She said, "On the move."

The SUV now drove past Sachs and Team One, then pulled into the mouth of the cul-de-sac, blocking the security camera. The stocky woman, made a bit stockier by the body armor under her floral dress, climbed out and grabbed a stack of file folders from the backseat. A prospective buyer of the property—also an ESU detective—stepped from the passenger side and looked around, as if assessing whether this was a place he wanted to sink half a billion dollars into.

"Three, any response to the presence?"

"Negative. He's in the middle of the trailer. Not moving anymore. Maybe at a table."

"Five Eight Eight Five to Two. We go in first, you're behind."

"Roger. K."

"All teams. Remember the briefing. Special rules of engagement. One call to surrender, if it's ignored and there's the least threat signature, lethal force is authorized."

They confirmed.

She took a deep breath, smelling wet stone and pungent exhaust from the SUV. Her weapon's safety off, finger outside the trigger, muzzle aware.

"Team Two, we're on the move."

A glance behind her, nods from the team.

Then the four were out of cover and jogging toward the trailer, crouching.

"Three, heat signal?"

"Moved a foot or two. Away from the door. Slow. I don't think he's onto you."

"K."

Thirty feet from the door.

The Watchmaker, she was thinking . . . Would this be their last confrontation?

Twenty . . .

Team Two, led by Sharonne Brown, a woman she had worked

with for years. The ESU officer was built like Sachs, slim and tall, one difference being that Brown was in the gym at least an hour a day and could bench-press two hundred pounds without shedding a drop of sweat.

Sachs nodded and Brown's team fell in behind hers, staggered, for better firing coverage—and to minimize cluster damage from a shooter inside.

Ten feet away.

"Three, we're here. Signature?"

"He's moved a few feet again, but still not near any windows."

She had a passing thought: Gilligan had stolen and delivered to the Watchmaker the DSE documents, some of them maps of underground passages, of which most in the city were here and farther south. Did he possibly have an escape route planned through a tunnel?

Maybe, but they had the element of surprise.

Anyway, there were no tactical variations possible, given the layout and the urgency.

Sachs pointed to the windows, and Brown directed two of her officers to cover them. Hale wouldn't try to escape that way, but they were perfect firing stations. He might even have mounted steel plates behind the blinds and would fire from a small porthole.

Three reported, "Moved a few inches, but not toward the windows. He doesn't know you're there."

Or he's holding a submachine gun pointed at the door, waiting for the first person in.

Then they were at the trailer.

This was no-knock. The breaching officer moved up fast and quickly mounted a C4 charge on the lock plate. Double wad.

They each carried gas masks and neoprene smocks, to protect against HF acid and gas. But she had decided they shouldn't wear the gear during the assault. That would be dangerous, limiting field of sight and movement of weapons. If he was inside, there wasn't much risk of exposure to the stuff.

Even as she thought this, though, she pictured the construction worker lying in the tunnel at the first scene, his skin dissolving, blood bubbling. This image had replaced that of the gory rebar rods.

She scanned the team. They nodded. The breaching officer lifted the detonator pad, but refrained from a "Fire in the hole!" They didn't want to give the Watchmaker the slightest indication of their presence.

Sachs nodded.

The packet exploded with a sharp crack, and she started forward.

53.

RON PULASKI UNFOLDED the document Lyle Spencer had produced.

Spencer said, "I called in a marker, and got that. It's a draft. They're still working on it."

Ron looked down at the sheet in his hand.

> *Throughout the interview, it appeared that Subject Pulaski—*

"Subject?" he whispered. "*That's* what they're calling me?"

> *—had only a vague recollection of the accident, even though it just happened, and he admitted he'd been only lightly injured. He used the phrases "I don't know" and "I don't remember" frequently. He admitted he was not concentrating at the time of the collision . . .*

On the goddamn phone call. *That's* what I wasn't concentrating on.

*At one point in the interview he was staring into space
and did not even hear the interviewer's question.*

Because I was looking at the picture of Garner's family and
thinking about my dead daughter . . .

*He admitted to using drugs and admitted that they
made him sleepy.*

What the hell? Half a joint twenty years ago?

*He could not say definitively that he saw whether the
traffic light he was approaching was green.*
*He was deceptive regarding injuries. Significantly he
sustained a head injury on a case, which apparently
required considerable rehabilitating work. The injury
resulted in memory loss and confusion. There's little in his
NYPD personnel file on his condition. I suggest we locate
the original medical report and append it to any
recommendation by the full Officer Involved Accident
board.*
*His rendering of a diagram of the scene was childlike.
He could not even draw a straight line.*

Because you intentionally sat me down in front of a cluttered
desk. There was nothing else to write on but my lap. Christ . . .

*My conclusions are that while the quantity of drugs in
his system was negligible, given the presence of narcotics
and the totality of his confused and memory-impaired
responses, it would be prudent for the department to either
terminate Subject Pulaski or assign him to an
administration position in the NYPD. I do not think the*

*department can afford to risk Subject Pulaski creating
another life-threatening situation.*

*Respectfully submitted,
T. J. Burdick, Deputy Inspector*

Burdick.

Hell.

"It's all out of fucking context," he muttered, using a word that
rarely escaped his lips, and had never done so in his family home.
"For all I know, they doctored the tape to make me sound like a
zombie."

Spencer asked, "The injury they're talking about?"

Eyes on the lawn, he paused and said, "It was a job. The first
one I worked with Lincoln and Amelia."

He explained how he'd turned a corner of a building while
searching for an unsub, too close to the wall, and the perp, who'd
been lying in wait, caught him in the forehead with a billy club.

The lump went away not too long after, but the brain injury
remained. He'd lost memory, lost his ability to make decisions and
to work out the simplest of problems.

His parents, Jenny, his brother, had all been there to support
him and help with the rehab. They also encouraged him to get
back into his uniform.

Which he couldn't do.

He wasn't afraid. Like the old adage about getting back up on
the horse after a fall. That meant you'd been hurt once and were
worried about getting hurt again. He couldn't even remember the
attack, let alone any pain he'd suffered.

What troubled him: He was worried about endangering a
partner, a bystander.

Worried about hesitating when he had to act.

Worried about not unpacking a situation properly and making the right decisions.

And so he avoided the risk altogether. Though it killed him to give up his beloved street patrol, he chose to hide. He sat at home, he walked, he drank coffee and watched games. He wrestled with taking other lines of work. Maybe programming on a computer in the NYPD's statistics department. That was important, he told himself. You needed accurate figures when it was budget time.

Then came Lincoln Rhyme.

And with his trademark bluster and impatience, he told Ron what everyone else was tiptoeing around: Get over it.

"Everybody's got *something* wrong with them, Rookie. Hm?" And didn't bother to glance down at his useless legs.

Two months later, the day after his last head injury rehab session, Ron donned the uniform once more.

Now, looking over his tiny backyard, Ron said to Lyle Spencer, "This's a hit job."

"Why?"

"Burdick was contaminating my crime scene. We could've had a private conversation, but he was grandstanding in front of the press. I threatened him with obstruction. Nearly cuffed him."

"So he sent Garner after you." He shook his head. "Personal vendetta? Man, that's low . . . And, I've gotta say, it took a lot of effort. He must really have it in for you. And those medical records of yours. They're going to be a problem. Hell, they might even change them. Make it seem worse. Maybe say something like there's permanent damage."

Medical records, Ron Pulaski was thinking.

Medical records . . .

"Listen, thanks, Lyle."

"Anytime. I've got zero patience for bullshit. Especially when it's coming from our team."

He walked the man around the house to his car. He said, "And, you know, anything you want to talk about."

Spencer nodded, understanding Ron was not speaking of Burdick's setup. "Same goes for you."

They shook hands and Spencer got into his unmarked, the Dodge listing to the left under his weight.

Standing on his trim lawn, which he so enjoyed tending, Ron stared down the street, watching the detective's car disappear.

He was again thinking, Medical reports.

And then thinking one more thing, which he now just couldn't get out of his mind.

Personal vendetta? Man, that's low . . . And a lot of work.

54.

"I COULD SMELL IT, RHYME."

Amelia Sachs walked into the town house carrying the oddest bit of evidence he'd ever seen: a metal door, sealed in cellophane wrap. Where the hinges had been were nothing but clusters of bullet holes.

The gloves, he noted too, were not standard latex. They were black. Neoprene probably, which told Rhyme precisely what smell she was referring to.

"The construction trailer? After we breached the door, I could smell it. I aborted and backed out. He had a trap—charges on a couple of drums of HF. The place is gone."

"Injuries?"

"No, the teams're good."

She'd explained that Hale had fooled them yet again. The heat signature "proving" that he was inside was only a lantern or heat lamp set at about 98 degrees, placed on a Roomba.

"A what?"

"Vacuum cleaner you can program to move on its own."

Such a thing existed?

"At least the charges were small. If there had been a half ki of C4, and it blew the canisters, *that* would've made things awkward."

Amelia Sachs tended toward understatement on the topic of risk to her person.

"And that?" he said, pointing at the door she carried.

"I wanted *something*," she grumbled. "Got my mask on and emptied two mags into the hinges and ripped it off just before I had to dodge the acid." She added an exasperated, "I'm pretty pissed. I'll need to do an FDR. They won't waive it. I checked."

Any time an officer's weapon was fired, even accidentally, he or she had to fill out a Firearms Discharge Report. They were lengthy. The city took guns seriously and firing them even more so.

She handed the tech the door. "Mel. Here."

Cooper stepped from the sterile portion of the parlor, and in his own neoprenes took the thing from her.

Rhyme said, "The knob."

She was nodding. "I'm betting he didn't wear gloves all the time, and he was probably pretty sure that if there was a breach, the acid'd not only kill the intruder but would melt the knob into sludge, along with any trace he'd left there."

Fifteen minutes later, they had answers. The Watchmaker's fingerprints were on the knob. A few grains of sand, similar to those in the lot where Gilligan died and more of the trace that led Tamblyn to give them Hamilton Court. There was also a short hair with the bulb attached, so DNA could be run, but that would be a formality, as the fingerprints left no doubt.

"And traces of silicone," Cooper called.

Rhyme's brow troughed. "Hard to source. One of the most common substances on earth. There are hundreds of suppliers. You create trimethyl, dimethyl and methyl chlorosilane from the element silicon. Do that, add the 'e' and you've got flexible, heat- and cold-resistant stuff that's used in, well, a million different things: lubricants, food processing and medicine, caulks, gaskets, sealants. And don't you love this: it has excellent release *and* adhesion properties. Imagine a contradiction like that."

Chemistry was never far from the mind of Lincoln Rhyme.

Cooper called through the intercom, "So, too many possibilities to figure out what he's using it for."

"Hm," was Rhyme's confirmation.

Sachs asked, "Used something made out of silicone to store acid?"

"Probably not. HF'll degrade it. And if this is on the doorknob, it was a gel or liquid."

Had she risked her life for nothing? Rhyme was wondering.

Yet he kept in mind what he told his classes: a finding of flour alone doesn't tell you much. But traces of yeast, egg yolk, milk and salt could lead you to a murderous baker.

And here? What else had they discovered that might help narrow the search? He scanned the whiteboards. And saw no answers.

The lab phone buzzed.

The caller was Dellray on his mobile.

"Fred."

A British voice responded. "Unfurled an interesting fact here, Lincoln. Quite interesting."

Who the hell was this?

"Is that you?"

"Undercover. I'm Sir Percy Thompson, a London casino owner and playboy. If they still have playboys. I need to stay in character.

Accent's a bit tricky. I mean dodgy. I'm aiming for Covent Garden."

"What's so interesting?"

Fred Dellray was not a man to be rushed, but he chopped off some backstory and subplotting. "Has to do with your drones. No reports since the hospital. But have something interesting about the prior sightings."

Rhyme recalled. Two flights were logged, but they had not been near any construction sites. "Where were they again?"

The FBI agent told him: "The four hundred block of Towson Street, Brooklyn. Then the office building, 556 Hadley, Manhattan. I was wondering what kind of family relationships the two flights shared. Might they be siblings? Cousins?"

The typical Dellray jargon was utterly absent. It was disorienting. Sachs had made him watch a few episodes of a show called *Downton Abbey* (not bad, he'd assessed), and Dellray sounded exactly like one of the characters.

He continued, "I found nothing obvious to me. But I've been playing with a new toy we have here. It's called ORDA, which people might call an acronym, but we know—"

"It's only an acronym if it spells a real word."

"Quite. This one stands for Obscure Relationship Data Analysis."

"Familiar with it. Used it myself."

"You, the emperor of evidence?"

Rhyme had originally been skeptical of the software, which processed trillions of bits of data taken from two or more things— maybe places, people, events—that seemed to have nothing in common. But the software was capable of finding the most ethereal connections.

"And?" Rhyme asked.

"And the electronic brain came back with the aforementioned

interesting *thing*. A certain individual lives on the block that was strafed in Brooklyn. And his office is on the block it flew by in the city."

Rhyme and Sachs eyed each other.

He asked, "And who is it?"

"This would seem to be quite the day for your civics lessons, Lincoln . . ."

55.

IT WAS CRAZY, what he was doing.

Breaching the barbed-wire fence of party affiliation and voting for the president's infrastructure bill.

Doing good . . .

As Senator Edward Talese and Peter, his bodyguard, were walking to a media interview, he was speculating what would happen to him when he voiced the vote on the Senate floor.

Goodbye to the good committee assignments.

Dogcatcher . . .

He had to smile.

Thinking of his affection for Buttercup, all six pounds and three ounces of her.

They walked for another half block and Talese realized he was hungry. "We'll stop at Ross's deli."

"Yessir. Good."

At times of stress, what was better than a "mile-high" pastrami sandwich, slammed down on the counter in front of you by surly carvers, who only reluctantly would hand over an extra pickle as if you were a bank robber demanding small bills?

Talese loved the place.

They walked in silence for a time, dodging the pedestrians and traffic downtown, similar to their walk in the opposite direction not long ago. Though there was one difference. The radiant sunlight was now gone, obscured by a layer of imposing clouds.

He was looking forward to the interview, which would probably focus on his clean water legislation. And with that a burst of pure happiness within him—he now had Boyd's support. The bill would surely pass. Other topics would come up, of course, but at this stage of his career, so many years of elected office under his belt, so many days of political battle, he was confident he could answer or evade any question aimed at him by the probing, but easily anticipated, journalists.

"No sign, sir."

Peter would be referring to the man in the throwaway attire they'd seen earlier. Probably just another citizen on the streets of Manhattan. One of millions. A worker, a professor, a tourist.

But then it occurred to him that if anyone knew of his conversation with the president and was inclined to make sure that he did *not* cast the vote for Boyd's bill, someone with issues with a huge infrastructure spending bill, that individual might just resort to efforts a lot more serious than lobbying.

If he died, the governor would appoint a new senator to finish out his term, and that man or woman would absolutely not support the president's plan.

Just then he happened to notice someone across the square looking his way. He was big and dark-complected. Not of mixed race, it seemed, but Anglo with olive-tinted skin.

Looking down at his phone, he strode forward along a route that would soon intercept the two men.

His suit jacket was a touch too large, and the senator wondered if the man was armed.

"Peter."

"I made him too, sir."

"He alone?"

"Can't tell. On the street, yes. But somebody else in a building? Don't know."

Too many windows for a shooter to fire from.

Was he a colleague of the man who had followed him earlier?

And, if he was, and Talese was their target, what would their mission be here in public?

Although, thinking back to some of those cases he'd run as a prosecutor, it was astonishing how many professional killers had gunned down someone in the middle of a crowded street and even the most seemingly cooperative witnesses saw nothing helpful.

The large man was getting closer and ignoring Talese and his guard—or so it seemed. His eyes taking in the area, the people, the windows, the cars . . .

Talese felt his heart thud at triple the usual pace.

He slowed.

And then a sharp voice sounded behind him.

"Senator?"

Talese turned fast.

Was this it? A bullet?

Peter spun about too, his hand inside his jacket.

But the man who approached wore a gold shield on his belt. NYPD detective.

Talese's face tightened into a querying look. He glanced around, noting that the man on the intersecting path was getting closer yet.

"Detective, there's—" Talese began.

But the cop cut him off, saying, with irritation, "Your phone's off."

"My . . . Oh." He fished in his pocket. He'd shut it off, per the rules of meeting with the president—so it could be used neither as a recording device nor as a homing tracker to guide a Hellfire missile.

"I'm Lon Sellitto."

Peter said, once again, "I'll see some ID, please."

Talese expected the bulky man, in a wrinkled raincoat, to gripe. He was wearing a badge, after all. But without hesitating, he offered a card.

The guard examined it and sent a text. In a matter of seconds, the phone hummed. He nodded to his boss. "Legit."

"Look," Talese said, nodding over his shoulder, "there's somebody—"

He didn't need to finish the sentence because Sellitto was lifting a hand in greeting to the very person the senator was referring to.

The big somber man joined them and displayed his own badge. It resembled that of an old-time sheriff.

"I'm U.S. marshal Michael Quayle, Senator. Your phone's off."

"I know, I know." Talese revived the unit and it immediately began chiming with texts and reports of voice mail messages.

"All right, Detective, Marshal. What's this about?"

Sellitto said, "After we're out of the open, Senator."

"I really want—"

"Out of the open," Quayle echoed in a tone that would accept no argument.

A black SUV pulled to the curb and squealed to a stop. The marshal gestured for the senator to get in first, which he did. This vehicle seemed a lot more than merely bullet resistant.

When the men were inside, Sellitto said to the driver, "Federal building."

"Yessir."

The Suburban galloped off, bounding hard on the uneven streets. No one wore belts and Talese had to grip the handhold firmly.

"Okay." The senator looked pointedly at the detective.

Sellitto said, "You're familiar with the crane accidents in the city."

"Sure. A domestic terror outfit wants affordable housing units."

"No. That was a cover. To keep us focused away from what the unsub's really got in mind."

"Which is?"

"You dead."

Talese nodded slowly. So perhaps his concerns today were not so paranoid after all.

"Who is it?"

"We know the identity of the mechanic. But not who's hired him."

"My family . . ."

"They're safe. We have a team in your house."

"He's . . . This man? The mechanic? Where is he?"

"We don't know. We're looking for him now."

"How did you find out?"

"The cranes were sabotaged with drones. DHS gave us a map of other flights. He flew one over the block you live on, in Brooklyn, and also near your office here."

"Jesus."

Peter said, "You should know, Detective. An hour ago, little longer, we were on our way to a meeting and it looked like somebody was following us. I made him and he turned down another street."

Sellitto pulled out a notebook, a battered one like detectives in TV shows always use. "Description."

Talese and Peter gave it to the detective.

"Is there any reason somebody would want you dead? Whistleblowing? Any old prosecutions that may've come back?"

"No . . ."

But he was looking out the window, reflecting: Was what he'd thought of earlier possible? That someone wanted him dead because of his vote for the tax bill?

"I have no idea. I mean, yes, I put a lot of bad guys away. It was years ago. But a few of them were sociopaths. I can track down their names and see if anybody's been released lately."

Sellitto looked his way for a moment, then tucked the pad away and pulled out his phone.

Talese said, "I'm scheduled to go on TV in an hour. Can we stop at the studio?"

"No."

"But it's CNN," Talese said.

Still texting, the detective said, "The answer's still no. And do me a favor and sit back."

"Sit back?"

"Yeah, away from the window. You're putting me in the line of fire too."

56.

"TALESE'S AT THE FEDERAL BUILDING."

Lon Sellitto's voice was coming through the speaker into the parlor.

Rhyme asked, "The theory? Who wants him dead and why?"

"He says he doesn't know. But he was like sixty-eight percent he doesn't know."

Rhyme asked, "Can you up the dial?"

"I can try. He's a politician. Either they're evasive or they lie. Give me a mob enforcer any day. They sing like chickadees."

"You stopped at the tech department, right?"

"It's the weirdest thing I've ever done for you, Linc."

"But you did it?"

"Yeah."

"More on that later."

As soon as they disconnected, his phone hummed again.

"Rhyme here."

"Detective, I'm Ben Emery. Emery Digital Solutions? Two of

your officers dropped off a computer for us to crack. I wanted to give you an update."

Ah, good. Rhyme still hoped emails on Gilligan's laptop could reveal who'd hired Hale, for what purpose and where future attacks might be. Maybe even an alternative safe house now that his primary one had self-destructed.

"Do you have anything?"

"Afraid it's moving slowly."

Wasn't this the day and age of supercomputers? Couldn't teenagers hack into a laptop while texting and playing video games simultaneously?

Emery continued, "We're brute forcing, but he used an SHA-256 hash."

"Which is?" Rhyme's voice betrayed his impatience.

"Secure Hash Algorithm 256."

A sigh. "And 'hash' is?"

"Software that turns one string of data into another one. To passcode protect something, you create a password, right? Then you feed it into a hash generator and it becomes a string of data. Let's say the password's your name: Lincoln Rhyme. Loved that book about you by the way . . ."

"Mr. Emery," Rhyme muttered.

"All right. Well. I just sent you the hash of your name. It's on your phone."

A text arrived.

49b14a858f2c023331d308310de984acad
097cd510ed2e5cb0185fab284be511

"All right. The passcode's your name. Somebody needs to crack it. It's easy to find the hash—there's no reason to hide it, since hashes only go one way. You can't turn it back *into* the password. Like you can't turn ground beef back into a sirloin. But what you *can* do is start typing characters into the hash generator. Randomly, hoping for a match. And after a few hours of typing words in you decide to try *Lincoln Rhyme*—"

"And bang. You see that that hash matches your password hash. And you're in."

"Exactly!" He sounded pleased Rhyme got it. "That's what we're doing now. Inputting words and characters, hoping to find a hash that matches. Not typing them in, of course. It's all done automatically. We're running about a trillion hashes a second."

"Excellent. So, you'll crack it soon? A few hours, you were saying?"

A pause. "Well, Detective Rhyme, that was just an illustration. Why I'm calling . . . If we don't have it now, that means he's probably using a mix of uppercase, lowercase, numbers and special characters like question marks and percentage signs."

Rhyme frowned. "You're saying it might take a day or more?"

This pause was longer. "Uhm. If he's got a fifteen-character password, which isn't unusual, about two hundred million years."

"Is that . . . Are you joking?"

"Uhm, well, no, sir," said the man who, it was clear to Rhyme, probably never joked about computer matters.

"You have to have a faster computer there."

"Doesn't matter. Even with Fugaku, in Japan"—he said this almost reverently—"you might shave off a few hundred thousand years is all. But maybe we'll be lucky and he used something short."

Ah, the damn L-word again.

Rhyme added another unnecessary: "Let me know the minute you find something."

"I'll do that, sir. Oh, just one question?"

"Yes?"

"That Detective Sachs. Just checking. She *is* married, right?"

Was he really asking that?

"Uhm. Yes."

"Okay. Thanks."

They disconnected.

He ordered his phone, "Call Pulaski."

A moment later: "Lincoln. How's the case?"

"Taken some turns. It's not real estate. The cranes're a misdirection. He had us focus on the drones delivering the acid, when he was really using them to check his real target. Hale was hired to take out a U.S. senator. Edward Talese."

"Why?"

"Not sure yet. And Gilligan's computer's a bust. The expert says it could take two hundred million years to crack it."

"How many?"

"Two hundred million."

"Phew. That's a relief. I thought you said two hundred *billion*."

"Looks like your sense of humor isn't on paid leave. What're you doing?"

A pause as dense as Emery's. "I'm not prepared to answer that at this point in time."

No idea what that sentence meant, nor was Rhyme inclined to find out.

"I have a question. What size shoe do you wear?"

"Is this like a dog whistle?"

"A what?"

"A question that's really about something else."

"When I ask a question, Pulaski, it's about the question. What size?"

57.

THERE SHE GOES, another part of history.

He was eighty-eight years old, Simon Harrow was. His head bald, his spine curved. But on the whole, pain free—just those humid days of summer and spring . . . The remedy to the condition? Don't leave the house on humid days of summer and spring.

Just sit on his balcony and gaze out over downtown Manhattan.

There she goes, being destroyed by the developers.

He was looking at a patchwork of construction near the Holland Tunnel, that artery that led from the city, under the broad and regal Hudson River into New Jersey's industrial heart.

His own turf was for the time being safe from the wrecking ball. The ancient apartment in SoHo was rent-controlled, much to the dismay of the landlord, who sent the superintendent of the red-brick complex around occasionally to "see how he was doing," meaning to find out if Harrow had conveniently died, allowing the man to elevate the rent to the stars.

Harrow, however, was determined to remain alive for his

children, grandchildren and great-grandchildren, his parrot, Rimbaud . . . and the landlord himself.

Love was the motive for the first categories. Spite for the last one.

His coffee, cooling, the *New York Times* sitting folded upon his lap, he scanned the construction site. Demolition was done and a new series of buildings was beginning to emerge, though the job was on hold temporarily, thanks to some crazy man attacking jobsites.

His opinion about the end of yet another neighborhood in Manhattan—in this case the southwestern edge of SoHo—was by no means negative. Some had called New York City a living, breathing creature, but Harrow didn't think of the place in such a limited way. He considered the five boroughs an evolutionary tree, many species appearing and adapting to the times, or, if not, vanishing.

Natural selection urban-style.

This was one neighborhood that had been transformed significantly. In the last quarter of the twentieth century, South of Houston had grown from sooty industrial to professional and chic and artsy.

Change . . .

One of the most significant had been what he was looking at now: the Holland Tunnel, which had required a massive redevelopment of the neighborhood to make way for the ventilation towers and approach routes.

His eyes rose to the entrance. His father had been a boy when the tunnel opened in the late 1920s, and Harrow Senior had grown fascinated with the project the way other boys then loved dirigibles and cowboys and the Dodgers. The man regaled his son with stories about the tunnel's creation. Shields, like massive tin cans, dug through the earth beneath the river from both sides of the adjoining states. Those moving from New Jersey east were faster, as they had to push through ground that was mostly mud, the consistency of toothpaste. The sandhogs—tunnel workers—from the New York side had to contend with rock. Because of concerns about water and mud seeping into the tunnels during construction, the working areas were kept under high pressure and the sandhogs had to go through decompression after their shifts like scuba divers so they didn't suffer from the bends.

While Harrow was not troubled about the concept of a city molting its old skin, he wasn't pleased that one of the buildings going up nearby would cut off his view of the Palisades.

On the other hand, it might be residential, and the thought of what he might catch a glimpse of around a swimming pool made up for the altered vista of nature.

"Let's hope for residential," he said, sipping more cool coffee.

Rimbaud, sitting on a nearby perch, did not weigh in, occupied, as he was, with feather preening.

Harrow now frowned, noticing two bright flashes appear from the jobsite. Two loud bangs followed seconds later.

Something had happened at the base of the cranes.

Lord, this was one of the attacks!

The huge thing was starting to tilt.

He removed his glasses and wiped the lenses and replaced them.

The sound of a Klaxon began to fill the air.

It leaned farther and farther . . .

Then, like cutting a marionette's strings, it collapsed fast. His apartment was about a half mile away and it took a second or two for the sound of the collision to reach him.

"Shit," Harrow gasped, grabbing his phone and dialing 911, even though he was sure dozens if not hundreds of calls were already being made.

A voice nearby startled him. "Shit!"

He glanced up. Rimbaud was looking over the cloud of dust in the distance. He squawked once more. "Shit. Uh-huh. Shit."

58.

JENNY HAD MADE a joke when Martine was born.

"You ever notice the smell? It's Eau d'Hospital."

And Ron Pulaski had inhaled and said, "Yeah. They all smell alike. Don't do a start-up that sells it. I'd think it'd be a limited market."

Pulaski was aware of the same scent now as he walked, head down, along the corridor of the general administration wing.

He was in East Side General Hospital illegally. At least where he presently was, in the guts of the place. He could, of course, spend as much time in the visitor area as he wished. But strolling through the security door with the expired NYPD ID card and a silver badge that was a souvenir Brad had bought in the gift shop of one of the big movie studios after a tour? Nope. Not good. He wasn't in uniform—that would be an offense too far, he judged— but was in a dark suit and white shirt. A tie that he wore maybe three times a year.

So, a silver-badge detective. Probably no one would know that was a contradiction.

He'd signed in, but the scrawl was illegible, as was the lettering in the *Print Your Name* block. He thought of Detective Ed Garner's trick, getting him to draw a sloppy diagram of where the accident took place and of Burdick's plan of using his past medical incident to sideline him.

It took a moment to let the anger dissipate.

A pleasant nod to some nurses, two round men in good moods. He passed a lunchroom, a copier room, several meeting rooms . . . and then he came to the site of his second impending crime: *Records*.

He stepped into the large room—easily fifty feet long, twenty wide—and saw that it was unoccupied. He sat down at a nearby workstation and clicked on the computer. Medical files were stored here digitally as well as the original hard copies, he learned. To find them you first typed in the patient's name and date of birth, then the date of their admission. This called up the digital file and also gave the location of the physical file itself.

A strident warning against violating patients' privacy rights under HIPAA appeared. But that went away by itself after two seconds.

Now for the hunt.

He'd expected layers of frustration and challenge.

A knotty gut, sweating brow and palms.

None of that.

No passwords were required and in less than a minute he found exactly what he needed.

Twenty minutes later, he strode from the hospital, a dozen sheets, folded letter size, sitting in the right breast pocket of his wedding-graduation-funeral suit jacket.

Feeling good about the operation.

Now for the other part of his mission: a trip to a junkyard in Queens.

He was thinking about the best way to get there when he became aware of a vehicle slowing beside him.

A glance to his right, at the beat-up white van.

His eyes took in the driver's window and he stopped fast, seeing two things simultaneously. One was the ski-masked driver.

The second was the muzzle of the weapon pointing his way just before it fired.

. . .

"There's an issue, Mr. President."

Secret Service agent Glenn Wilbur, a tall broad-shouldered man in an impeccable suit, was looking into the second bedroom of the suite.

William Boyd glanced up from his daughter's luggage, which he'd been helping her pack. There were only so many stuffed animals and Disney sweatshirts and pairs of Uggs that would fit in a single gym bag.

He nodded to the living room and joined the agent, out of earshot of his family. His wife was on the phone, lost in a conversation, probably about campaign plans for the forthcoming election. She was his de facto campaign manager and a damn good one. If he won in November, it would mostly be because of her.

"Go ahead."

"Those cranes?"

"The attacks, right."

"Another one just came down."

"Jesus. I'll draft a statement. Anyone hurt?"

"Four people in cars in serious condition. No one killed."

"You think this is a security issue. For us?"

"We've discussed it, the team. The chatter is your infrastructure bill's making you a lot of enemies. And the crane that just came down? It did block the Holland Tunnel."

"Our route to Newark?"

"Yessir. The George Washington Bridge's parking lot. Everybody's diverting to it now. We'll have to use Exit Plan B."

"Which is?"

"Scramble Marine One. There's a helipad near the U.N. We'll be there in a half hour."

"We're close to the Verrazzano. Why not move Air Force One to JFK?"

"It's jammed up too. And even if the crane's just a coincidence, we have to treat the highways to all the airports as compromised."

The president smiled. "Out of an abundance of caution."

One of Wilbur's favorite expressions.

The agent nodded. It was his version of a grin.

"We'll take surface streets to the helipad. And a decoy convoy'll go via the Queensboro to LaGuardia."

He placed a call and put the phone on speaker.

"Agent Murphy," the voice said.

"Dan. It's Wilbur. I'm here with the president."

"Hello, sir."

"Dan."

Wilbur said, "We're scrapping Exit A. We're going to B."

"U.N., helipad. Roger that. Any specific threat factors?"

"Not at this time. Get Marine One there stat. I'm running Sirdee now for the route. I'll text it to the drivers and the rest of the team."

A whole new world now, Boyd reflected. Sirdee—the Secure Route Determining algorithm—resided on a huge computer somewhere and at lightning speed considered hundreds of factors in finding what was the safest course for government officials to move from one point to another. In presenting the program to the government, the company that had developed it gave an example. Their software factored in all the known parameters for the presidential visit to Dallas on November 22, 1963, and concluded that the least secure route from Love Field to the Trade Mart—where

President John F. Kennedy was to speak—was through Dealey Plaza and past the Texas School Book Depository.

Murphy said, "I'll call NYPD." He paused. "One thing. We can get eyes along the surface route, but there's no time to clear underground all the way to the U.N."

Wilbur glanced at the president. "Or we can stay put, wait for them to clear the tunnel entrance. Seven, eight hours, I'd guess."

Boyd said, "I'd guess there're a hundred possible routes to the helipad. The odds that somebody'd know exactly where to place a device? That's not going to happen."

Wilbur said to the phone, "Get the motorcades downstairs, Dan."

Murphy said, "Making the call now." He disconnected.

Wilbur walked to the door and stepped outside, to tell the hallway agents the new plan.

"Daddy."

The president returned to the doorway where his daughter was holding in both arms a large rabbit with a blue gingham kerchief on its head. "Elisabetta won't fit."

Too bad there was no algorithm that could figure out the best way to pack a ten-year-old's gym bag.

Boyd walked over and took the toy from her. "It's all right, honey. I'll put her in one of mine."

59.

"IT'S DONE," SIMONE told him.

For these final stages of the project, they were not using any electronic communications devices at all. Only in-person conversations.

Charles Hale, in the driver's seat of his SUV, was looking out the windshield. This part of the city was deserted. *Three* cranes reigned over the neighborhood and everyone was staying inside. If they had to get to the grocery store, they jogged.

He heard the faint voice of the newscaster on the radio and turned the volume up.

> "... *The authorities are speculating it will take eight to ten hours to reopen the Holland Tunnel after an explosion brought down a crane at a construction site on Varick Street this afternoon. This is the third crane that's been destroyed in the past two days ... Police still have no leads in the investigation. Most jobsites in the area remained closed ...*"

Hale looked toward the woman beside him. She was in leather pants, black, a dark brown sweater and a jacket that matched the trousers. Today her hair—now dyed brunette—was in a double braid, the strands of which were joined at the end with a crimson ribbon.

"A question," Hale asked slowly.

Simone lifted an eyebrow.

"Is there anyone?"

He found himself surprised that he asked.

But not surprised that she was hesitating.

While the question could have a hundred contexts, she knew his meaning.

Simone said finally, "I'm not good at things like that. It ends. It always ends. For his sake, for mine." After a moment: "The same for you, I'm thinking."

"The same."

She said, "I was married. Briefly. My idea. I was young. Not a good decision."

He was thinking of her time in Africa.

Circumstances changed . . .

A shake of his head explained that he had never married.

She said, "There are lines we have to live within. People like us. This is awfully philosophical, isn't it?"

He gave another smile. "But true."

A siren sounded in the distance. It got closer. He wasn't troubled and it was clear she wasn't either. If anybody were to come for them, they wouldn't announce it.

The police car or ambulance sound Dopplered into the lower, departing tone and eventually faded.

He looked at his watch.

He needed to move on to the next step.

Time, counting down.

Always, always . . .

He asked, "Do you know Prague?"

"We did a job there, my team. I would have liked to stay for a while. But we needed to evac."

"In Old Town Square there's a medieval astronomical clock. The Orloj. Tourists come to see it. Lots of tourists. Big crowds on the weekends. Hard for surveillance to see anything. I'll be there next year. The first Saturday in May."

She reached for his hand. The grip, fingers entwined, was far more intimate than a kiss.

In the rearview mirror, he believed he saw someone glancing at the SUV, the pose reminding him of the man he'd seen in the monitor at the mouth of Hamilton Court last night. He was carrying something, a suitcase, Hale believed.

He turned to look directly.

But the figure was gone.

Now that he was turned fully around, he lifted his backpack from the floor. He reached inside.

He extracted a white box, six by six by two inches. It was closed and fixed with a rubber band. He handed this to her. She frowned, then opened the lid.

And lifted out the bone clock, the one he'd told her about, the one the Russian political prisoner had made.

"Ah." She studied it for a long moment. "I was going to bring something for you. A wheel, the kind I use in my steam engines. Our wheels are real wheels."

"Not gears pretending to be something else."

A glance into his eyes.

He showed her how to set the time and where the switch was that released the tiny weights. He moved it now.

She held the clock to her ear and seemed to find the ticking pleasant. As he always did.

She reboxed the gift, and slipped it into her own backpack, where he saw the grip of a large semiautomatic pistol. She climbed out of the car and bent down to speak to him through the open door. "You're doing it now?"

He nodded.

He hoped if she said anything it wouldn't be common, like good luck or take care.

It wasn't.

What she said was a single word: "Prague."

60.

Lincoln Rhyme had been thinking of his earlier concern, of not being able to grasp the Watchmaker's strategy to win their deadly chess game.

But what if that was not the proper question?

Perhaps the query should be: What is your *real* goal?

What if you have no interest in taking the king?

Maybe it's the queen you want. Or her knight? Or the king's bishop?

Or a lowly pawn, which might one day ascend to the role of matriarch of the board by traipsing doggedly and unnoticed all the way to the distant edge of the checkerboard world.

And even if it's then checkmate to you, and your king is snagged . . . You don't care. You've won after all.

Lon Sellitto took a call. His conversation was lengthy—and apparently alarming.

He disconnected. "Okay, Linc. Stuff's happening. That was the mayor's office. The counter's disappeared from that website,

13Chan. And Computer Crimes and the Bureau were monitoring chatter. 'Kommunalka' was the keyword. CC intercepted an email. Anonymous account in Philly to an anonymous account here, Manhattan. It says, 'It's time. Do the last one, and place packages where discussed on alternate routes. And keep up the façade of Kommunalka. There are people who are checking, they don't believe it. We can't let them find us. Remember: "Men make their own history."—Karl Marx.'

"That's why we couldn't find Kommunalka. It's a front for some other radical outfit. Group X."

Mel Cooper said, "And 'Do the last one.' Does that mean a crane?"

Sellitto: "So it was Group X that hired the Watchmaker, and . . ." His phone hummed and he took the call. This conversation was troubled too. "No shit. Send me details." He disconnected. "Another one, Linc. A crane."

"Where?"

"Downtown."

Mel Cooper had tuned in to the news on his phone. He called, "It was at a jobsite near the entrance to the Holland. Nobody dead. Injuries. Some serious."

"What did it hit?"

Cooper examined his screen. "Odd. No buildings anywhere near it. Landed on a street is all. The injuries were in cars and trucks."

Sellitto lifted the phone away from his ear and filled in with information that was likely not public. "This one was different. He used C4."

"Ah, now that's significant."

"Why?"

"Time."

"Huh?"

"Obvious," Rhyme muttered. "He can't know for certain exactly when the acid'd eat through the counterweights of the cranes. But for some reason he needed this one to drop at a particular time. Down. To. The. Minute." Frowning at the murder board, the map of the city. "The Holland's closed?"

"At least eight hours, they're talking maybe longer. The traffic's a—"

"Yes, yes, yes, I'm sure it's a fittingly clichéd adjective or participle about vehicular congestion. Why that time, why that location?"

Rhyme settled on one particular entry.

Senator Talese reported possibly being followed to meeting at Water Street Hotel.

- *Subject was white male, in jeans, sunglasses, cap, sweatshirt (possibly throwaways). Medium build.*
- *Turned when it appeared that Talese and bodyguard might have seen him. Unknown if another watcher took his place.*

"We got it wrong, I think," Rhyme said, angry.

"How's that?"

"If he used C4 on the crane, he could've placed a device in a drone and killed Talese that way. No, the drone was about *tracking* Talese, not killing him. And when the Watchmaker found out we'd made the drone and he couldn't use it anymore, he switched to human surveillance to follow the senator . . . Why? He knows where Talese lives, he knows where his office is . . ."

Silence.

"But he *wouldn't* know where the meeting was this afternoon. Who Talese was meeting with. *That's* what he wanted to find out. Call him. We need to know now."

Sellitto pulled his phone from his pocket, scrolled, then made a call.

The senator answered on the second ring.

"Detective, what's the news?" came the irritated voice out of the speaker.

"Senator, I need to know something," Rhyme said.

A pause.

Sellitto said, "You're on with Lincoln Rhyme."

"Oh." Irritation had given way to reserved admiration. That again . . .

"You were on your way to a meeting today and you noticed someone was following. What was the meeting about? Who was there?"

The hesitation ended with the cautious words "There's a national security component here."

"I don't need state secrets. I just need to know who was at the goddamn meeting."

An exhalation of surprise, probably at Rhyme's sharp tone. "I was just saying, Mr. Rhyme, that I can't."

"The perp isn't targeting you. He's after the person or persons you were going to meet. He was using you to find them."

"Oh, Jesus. I didn't know . . . I was meeting with the president."

"I assume of the United States."

"That's right."

Sellitto said, "Okay, it's all making sense. There's some radical outfit, in Philly, that made up the Kommunalka Project. Which wants the city to do something it can't—transfer that property because it's toxic.

"That gives them the excuse to sabotage the cranes. The first two were just for show. The last one's all that really mattered: blocking the Holland Tunnel. The president's got to use an alternative route the Secret Service doesn't have time to clear. And Hale's planted bombs along them. Fuck, maybe that's what Eddie Tarr's in town for!"

Mel Cooper said, "Boyd, you know how unpopular he is. There've been threats . . . Something about an infrastructure bill he's trying to push through Congress. The Secret Service's already stopped three or four plans to assassinate him."

Rhyme was hardly aware of the conversations unfolding as Sellitto called the Secret Service and Cooper got in touch with the Visitor Security Division of the NYPD, a name that sounded like a public relations office for touring Boy Scouts, but in fact coordinated protection for domestic and foreign officials.

Holding the phone away from his ear, Sellitto said to Rhyme, "A decoy motorcade's going to LaGuardia. The real one's going to the helipad by the U.N. Damn, that's why he had Gilligan steal the diagrams and maps from DSE—all the tunnels and foundations. He's going to plant under the route."

The criminalist's eyes were on the whiteboard on which were taped the very stolen documents Sellitto was talking about.

"Linc, you with me?" Sellitto was brandishing the phone like a pistol.

"Hm." Eyes on the charts.

The detective held up his phone. "Linc! The Secret Service knows you understand Hale. And you know the city . . . The motorcade's in motion. Where do you think it's safe for them to go?"

"Lon, please. If you don't mind? Could you move a little to the left? I can't see the board."

61.

THE CALLS HE was listening to on the police scanner were in short-hand, but there was no doubt about their meanings.

The translation was assisted by the urgency in the voices.

Priority Deliv . . . Traveler One . . . Need a corridor west from Avenue A, and Eight to special loc at Port Authority. CC sending texts. EOTD, for route. Clear intersections, sweep shooting sites. Report to unit commanders . . .

EOTD . . .

Encryption of the day.

Charles Hale wondered if the authorities thought the new route for the presidential motorcade would actually be safe.

Or were they jittery and nervous and sweaty, wondering if they'd been double-bluffed again?

After all, they were responsible for the life of the most powerful man in the world.

Dozens of voices called in, some zipping to other frequencies . . .

He was in the front seat of his SUV, which was parked in the shadow of a gloomy tenement that was only five stories high, but with its dark façade seemed much taller.

In front of him, the blue-and-white police car, which had been parked curbside, hit the light bar and strobed out of view silently. An unmarked black sedan too, U.S. government plates.

When they were gone, and he was sure there were no others in the vicinity, he eased the SUV forward and parked just past a manhole in the middle of the street. He hit the yellow flashing light on the dash and climbed out. He was in a Department of Public Works jumper, an orange safety vest and a hard hat, this one off-white.

With a hook he pulled the manhole cover off and muscled Simone's phony bread maker out through the back of the vehicle and onto the ground. He removed it from the carton. He tugged a length of cable from the winch mounted in the back of the SUV, hooked on the device and eased it into the passage below the street. Next, he lowered a hand truck and finally his backpack.

Down the rungs permanently cemented into the concrete wall. They were slick so he moved carefully. On the floor he slung the backpack over his shoulder and, with some effort, scooped up the device with the lip of the cart and began a short journey into the dim tunnel, the way illuminated by an LED lamp mounted on his hard hat. He moved surely along the route, which he'd memorized from the charts that Andy Gilligan had stolen. When he was near his destination, he needed more precise guidance and so he examined the geo-positioning locator on his phone and continued another ten feet until he was precisely where he needed to be.

From the backpack Hale took a pulley and affixed it to an overhead water pipe. He then hooked a length of nylon rope to the "bread-making" device and pulled it upward as high as it would go. He locked the pulley and tied the end of the rope to a pipe at floor level. He reached up and opened the small door on the bottom and pressed the Armed button and a small dot of light went from green to red.

He paused.

He believed he sensed a very unmechanical scent coming from the base of the device. Was it floral? Yes.

And with that understanding, he realized why it was familiar.

He'd smelled it last night. In bed.

Then he climbed to the street and looked around. No one. Echoes of sirens glanced off the half-dozen buildings here and elsewhere, coming from a hundred directions at once in this architecturally complex city.

The traffic cones went into the back of the SUV, and moments later, the yellow light extinguished, he was cruising along the cobblestoned streets.

One stop to make, and then: his final mission.

62.

"IT'S CLEAR."

Lon Sellitto was looking over the screen of the computer attached to the security device, which he'd announced was just like those "newfangled TSA ones" at the airport.

Rhyme took his word for it, not having flown in years.

No, no explosives, no radiation.

They were looking at a wrapped brown paper package, addressed to Rhyme, no return label. It had been dropped off moments ago. The courier had left it, rung the bell and continued down the street.

Rhyme asked, "X-ray?"

Sellitto examined the device's screen. "Some rectangular thing. And an envelope." His phone whirred and he glanced at the screen. "It's the uniform I sent after the delivery guy." He answered and spoke into the unit: "What'd you find? You're on speaker."

"Sure, Detective. He works for Same-Day, a commercial delivery service. Local. It's legit. I know it. My brother-in-law—"

"Yeah, okay. What's the story?"

"He was at Starbucks, Fifty-Seventh Street. This guy comes up with a package, that package you got, and he says he's in a bind. He was on his way to drop it off, but he just got a call, some injury in the family, and he's got to get to Jersey like now."

Rhyme called, "Okay, he spun a story, offered the kid money and he took it—more cash than he told you, of course."

"Two hundred."

"More likely five. What'd the guy look like?"

"White, fifties, medium build. Jogging outfit. Cap. Sunglasses. Clean-shaven."

"He have anything else with him?"

"Backpack. Also black. He gave the messenger the box and the money and left. The kid took the train uptown and dropped it off at Captain Rhyme's. Oh, the guy said something else. Just leave it and ring the bell. The person who lives there doesn't like strangers."

Rhyme gave a laugh.

After Sellitto disconnected the call, Rhyme said to him, "The box. Open it, but in there." He indicated the biotox examination chamber. "No poison darts, from the X-ray, but that doesn't mean there's no poison. Remember our botulinum theory—Watchmaker's wanting to sneak some inside. Highly unlikely, but let's be safe."

Sellitto was looking over the unit, about two feet tall. Plexiglas, triple seals and negative pressure, feeding into a closed filtration system. There were thick neoprene gloves built into the side. "I don't know how the damn thing works."

"How hard is it, Lon? Open the lid, put the package in, close the lid."

"Yeah, yeah, okay."

With his back to Rhyme, Sellitto placed the package into the unit. Rhyme motored close and watched him work the paper off and, with a razor knife, cut the tape. Slowly. Very slowly.

"Don't make me nervous, Linc."

"What'm I doing?"

"You're staring at me."

"Where else am I going to stare?"

"What's that poison again?"

"Botulinum," he answered cheerfully. "The most deadly tox on earth. Eight ounces could kill the population of the world."

"Funny, Linc. Hilarious." A pause. "You're not kidding, are you?"

Rhyme gazed down into the large container as the detective removed the contents.

The standard technique for determining the presence of deadly botulinum—the Lethal Mouse Assay, which pretty much said it all—had been replaced by more humane techniques. But in this case no analysis was necessary. The objects, poisoned or not, could remain inside.

Sellitto extracted them now. The envelope and the rectangular thing: a billfold, which he opened, pulling out several cards.

"Well." A whisper.

He displayed them to Rhyme.

The card on top was Ron Pulaski's driver's license.

63.

GETS CONFUSING.

A homophone is a word that is *pronounced* like another word but is spelled differently and has a different meaning: flour and flower.

A homograph, a close cousin, is a word that is *spelled* the same as another but has a different meaning and might or might not be pronounced differently: bass and bass.

Homonym, most textbooks preach, is the umbrella descriptor that embraces both, though some purists—newspaper editors and nineteen-year-old English majors passionate about the subject, for instance—will occasionally take exception.

Charles Vespasian Hale was in Central Park once more, reflecting on these grammatical novelties, as he gazed at Lincoln Rhyme's town house through his bird-watching binoculars.

He was thinking of the word: "watch."

Here was Hale now, an expert at *watches*, pretending to *watch* birds while actually *watching* the abode of the man he was about to kill, all the while the police, whose shift is called a *watch*, are *watching* for him.

Some homonyms derive from very different roots: bass the fish is from the Proto-Germanic *bars*, meaning "sharp," because of the creature's dorsal fin. Bass, the musical tone and instrument, come from Anglo-Norman *baas*, meaning "low."

"Watch" is the more common variety, with all modern meanings deriving from the same root: the Saxon, *waecce*. The noun means "wakefulness," the adjective "observant," both in the context of guard duty.

After he swapped vehicles once again, at a garage on West 46th Street, Hale had paid a thousand dollars to a deliveryman to take the package to Rhyme's, then had driven here. He cast his heavy Nikon binoculars about, as if in search of a bird that had zipped to an accommodating stop on a nearby branch, but Hale always returned focus to the blunt, brown structure, where so many of his plans had been destroyed.

By the grain of sand.

Through the unshaded windows he caught the occasional flash of motion.

The cause of the activity would be the package.

Now he looked around for threats.

None. He knew the town house was well guarded, by nondescript humans and very obvious security cameras. But here, at some distance, he was safe. However important Rhyme was, the NYPD could not deploy a regiment of officers, fanned out through the park, to guard him.

He scanned again and stopped, noting someone to the east.

Far across the park was a man looking in his direction.

And was it the stranger he believed he'd seen twice before—at Hamilton Court and, not long ago, behind the SUV where he'd sat with Simone?

Too far away to tell.

If so, what organization was he with, if any?

Clearly not NYPD or FBI. They would have moved in by now.

A foreign operative would want him back in the jurisdiction where charges had been filed against him, and there were a lot of those. But extradition would also involve local authorities.

More likely this person had rendition—kidnapping—in mind.

Then too there were the enemies who would dole out justice quickly and extrajudicially.

Or, forget justice, just call it what it was: revenge.

But maybe, nothing at all.

Just another birdwatcher . . .

And indeed when he looked once more, the person was gone.

He turned his binoculars away from where they were trained—on a small jittery bird of brown and black plumage—back to Rhyme's town house.

Now there was a flurry of motion as Lon Sellitto hurried out the door. He spoke briefly to the pair of uniformed officers outside, who nodded, and the round detective walked quickly to a car and sped away.

The present had been opened.

64.

HIS HEADACHE WAS BRUTAL.

As his vision returned, Ron Pulaski inhaled deeply, like that might make the pain recede.

Curiously, the effort worked, a bit.

Or maybe headaches from being knocked out with horse tranquilizer just naturally diminished upon waking.

He was looking around. Taking stock.

He was lying on an air mattress, in the corner of a windowless room—a basement, he guessed.

The stark lighting was from a single overhead bulb. The door was metal—and, surely, locked.

He struggled to rise, which sent a new pinwheel of agony through his head, and his vision began to crinkle to black once more. He lay back. Then rose and checked the door.

Locked tightly, yes.

Then back to bed.

Remembering the minutes leading up to the blackness.

The ski mask.

The muzzle of the animal control tranq gun, the projectile apparently containing enough drug to knock a fair-sized horse to the ground.

During a case he'd worked with Lincoln and Amelia a few years ago, Pulaski had learned that the drug in question—used by wife on husband—was a mixture of etorphine and acepromazine. The side effects upon waking had not been part of that investigation, but Pulaski could now attest to one: it left you feeling really shitty.

He slowly sat up then, in relative control once more, rose to his feet again. Woozy, but he'd stay awake.

And upright.

Looking around more carefully now. On the floor on the other side of the mattress sat the medical records he'd stolen from the hospital. His phone and wallet, though, were missing. The first because it was Kidnapping 101 to take the victim's means of communicating with the outside world. The second so that they could prove they'd got him.

And who was *they*?

Hale was behind it, but he probably wasn't the ski-masked tranq shooter.

And there would be another player too. Lincoln had told him on several occasions that Charles Hale never worked for himself only. He always had a client.

And that person or entity?

High up, pulling strings. But no point in guessing their identity.

Not enough facts.

Pulaski noted there was no bottled water, no food, no toilet. The stay was going to be short.

Released soon.

Or they had more permanent plans in mind.

No windows or other doors, much less secret panels.

In the center of the chamber was a cage housing the HVAC system. But it was secured to the floor with thick padlocks. Still, he made his way to it, and feeling dizzy once more, he sat on the mesh, lowering his head.

Then he studied the cage.

No way to open it.

But wait. It wasn't HVAC at all. It was some kind of improvised device. He noted a sealed quart jar made of some kind of thick plastic. Inside was a liquid, reaching nearly to the top.

Pulaski sighed and scanned the label on the jar.

HF

Hydrofluoric acid.

Pulaski squinted and studied the assembly. Attached to the jar was a metal box about two by two by three inches. A short antenna protruded. Upon receiving a signal, the explosive charge in the box would detonate and shatter or melt the plastic, sending the corrosive liquid flowing into the room.

He recalled Lincoln Rhyme describing what the acid and the gas it created did to the human body.

He thought it wise to find a better place to sit and returned to the mattress.

Though he supposed the distance made no difference. Nowhere in the cell would be safe when the jar blew open.

Ron Pulaski lay back on the mattress and turned his thoughts to his family: Jenny and his children: Brad, Martine and, of course, Claire.

65.

LINCOLN RHYME WAS now alone.

Sellitto had left.

Sachs was downtown. And Thom was out as well.

Just before he'd left, the aide had poured a healthy dose of twelve-year-old single malt into a crystal glass. Rhyme's right hand now gripped the Waterford. While it wasn't a social sin to drink scotch out of a plastic tumbler through a straw, as he'd had to do for years, the beverage seemed to taste better in a glass. No double-blind study for this, but Rhyme was convinced.

He sipped and turned his attention back to the letter that had been in the package. Sellitto had taken a picture through the Plexiglas of the biotox container and the image now sat on Rhyme's tablet.

My dear Lincoln.

As you can tell, I have your associate Ron Pulaski. It will be impossible to find him, even with someone like you analyzing the evidence.

You must have figured out by now what my plan is. I could not get an IED into your apartment, nor shoot you with a sniper's rifle. I wouldn't want to anyway. That would be an inelegant solution to the situation. And, if you know anything about me, you know that I count the concept of grace as a fundamental one.

So I have arranged for an assistant to finish our work. And who? None other but you yourself. You'll die by your own hand, or young Pulaski will by mine.

And his death will be anything but pleasant. HF acid, as we've learned over the past few days, is the great white shark of substances. I can time-release it into the room where I've kept him. A death painful and prolonged.

Send everyone out of the apartment. Come up with excuses, though a good one would be to try to find poor Ron. Send them to, say, Jersey.

When you're alone, log on to the website below. It's proxied—a bastardized verb you would not accept, I'm sure—and untraceable.

Log on from the tablet attached to your chair.

And don't waste time.

The clock, if you will, is running.

Rhyme typed in the URL and almost instantly he heard the man's voice, in real time.

"Lincoln."

The screen was black.

Rhyme said, "It's not working. I can't see you."

"No. You won't. My camera's off. But you're visible to me. Now, go to the second bookcase from the back of the parlor. With the old books in it. The antiques about criminal investigation."

Rhyme frowned. "How did you . . . Ah, Andy Gilligan told you about it. My Judas." He motored to the oak stand. Three or four dozen volumes. One was not as ancient as the others. *Crime in Old New York*. It had been central to the first case he and Sachs had worked, tracking down a serial kidnapper nicknamed the Bone Collector.

"And?" Rhyme asked.

"There's a reproduction of a book dating to the mid-sixteen hundreds."

Even the facsimile was two hundred years old.

"Quite a title," Hale said. "Andy told me."

Looking at it, Rhyme recited, *"The Triumphs of Gods Revenge against the crying and execrable sinne of (willfull and premeditated) murther."*

A subhead added another ten lines or so to the jacket.

Rhyme said, "It's the first known true crime book."

The killer mused, "Crime . . . Always an obsession—the inequity, the cruelty we humans visit on one another. Look at the popularity of the TV shows and podcasts."

"I don't watch, I don't listen."

"I know you don't. I picked that book because it wasn't likely you'd be flipping through it to answer a thorny present-day forensics question."

"Ah, but never dismiss the old techniques out of hand. They can occasionally be helpful. We never want technology to substitute for sense, as I think you'd appreciate. The past should serve the present."

"Let's move along, Lincoln. There's something behind the book."

Rhyme lifted the volume off the shelf and clumsily set it aside. He reached in and extracted what had been hidden behind it, a roll of dark blue cloth. He set it on the chair's tray and unfurled it. He looked down at the two hypodermics.

"What's the drug?"

"Fentanyl. Now, that EKG in the corner? Hook yourself up to it."

Rhyme stared at the needles for a long moment. "No."

A pause.

The criminalist continued. "There's something I have to do first."

"The longer you wait—"

Firmly: "There's something I'm going to do first . . . The birds."

"The . . . ?"

"Peregrine falcons. They nest on my window ledge. Upstairs."

"I never figured you for someone who had pets, Lincoln."

A hollow laugh. "Pets? Hardly. They choose to live here. I don't know why. Fatter pigeons in this part of the park maybe? More stupid squirrels? But here they've settled and I've enjoyed watching them nest, propagate and hunt. I'm going upstairs."

Hale was apparently debating. "All right . . . Here's what you'll do. You have a pulse oximeter on the chair. Put it on one of your fingers and turn it so I can see its screen."

Rhyme did. "Clear enough?"

"Your oxygen levels are good, Lincoln. And your pulse lower than most people's under these circumstances."

"Pulse rates increase when adrenaline spills into the bloodstream because of the fight-or-flight response. I can't do either. So why get riled up?"

"All right, go upstairs, but keep the signal active. One phone call from me and Pulaski is dead."

A chuckle. "You've won, Charles. There're no tricks I can pull. I just want to see the birds one last time."

Rhyme guided the chair into the small elevator and pressed the button to take him to the second floor. He wheeled out of the cage and turned to the left into the hallway and then to the main bedroom, which faced Central Park West. The glass was bullet-proof and the view of the greenery and distant battlement of posh buildings on the East Side were distorted.

He looked down to the nest.

The birds—a couple and two fledglings—turned their heads his way. The faces, by nature, radiated hostile suspicion, whatever was truly in their hearts. Of the quartet, the youngsters were by far the more aggressive. They would spar for sparring's sake. Their parents took prey—at two hundred miles an hour—not for the joy of killing; for them the process was merely shopping for dinner.

He gazed at them for a full minute, then said, "All right. I'm ready." Glancing down at the hypos. "Two. In case I dropped one, I assume. Fentanyl . . ." He added sardonically, "Such a lovely concoction of phenethyl, piperidinyl, phenylpropanamide. You know you can change the potency by moving the methyl group into the three-position of the ring. I assume this is the strongest. Now, your word about Ron?"

"My word."

Rhyme sighed, looked at the birds one more time and slipped the needle into the vein on the back of his left hand. He slowly pressed the plunger.

By the time the last of the liquid was in the blood vessel, his head was lolling.

The heart rate on the sensor began a countdown.

In ten seconds, the small screen read *o*.

And there it remained.

66.

AS WITH SO many human constructs meant to interpret indifferent nature, time knows no natural intervals. We've decided on hours and minutes and seconds.

So while it could be said that Lincoln Rhyme died at 10:14:53 post meridiem on Tuesday, April 16, the most accurate way to put it is the truism: he lived the length of time from his birth to his death.

Requiescat in pace, Lincoln.

Hale put the tablet into his backpack and, still crouching in the bushes, pulled out his phone and read the message he'd received a few moments earlier. It was from the pilot, reporting that the plane was in Teterboro, the private airport in New Jersey, and ready to go at any time. The drive there would take forty minutes.

This portion of his mission was completed, yes, but he decided he'd been inaccurate to think of Rhyme's death as the finale. It was the penultimate mission—next to last.

Clocks are not moral or amoral. They count second by second, marking moments of joy and sorrow and pain and pleasure and cruelty, but they remain utterly indifferent to what occurs at any particular click.

This was the template too for Charles Vespasian Hale, who with no affect whatsoever carried out his jobs in the most logical way possible, regardless of the consequence to anyone.

And so it was with no regret—or joy—that he dialed the number that detonated the charge on the acid jar in the warehouse basement where Ron Pulaski was held. He'd kept him alive until now in case Rhyme had wanted proof that he was all right.

Lincoln Rhyme had died thinking that he had saved the life of the young man. That would have brought him some peace.

But Hale could not afford another grain of sand in the works of his life.

Pulaski was heir to Rhyme's skill and had that grit that would motivate him to do whatever it took to find Hale and either bring him back to New York for trial or—he believed the officer capable of it—kill him on the spot.

He had to go.

And Amelia Sachs?

She was less of a threat. Justice was within her, like a vein of a diamond. But revenge was not. She wouldn't choose to forgo her job of stopping evil in the city for the lengthy and possibly futile mission of pursuing her husband's killer.

Hale had been dramatic with Rhyme in describing the effects of HF gas on Ron Pulaski. There was no time-release mechanism on the device. All the acid in the jar would flood the room at once. A painful death, yes, but brief. He'd be dead by now.

Hale looked around him and, seeing no threats, lifted his backpack to his shoulder.

With a fleeting thought of Simone, he began the hike back to the SUV—and from there, to his new life.

67.

HER WORLD WAS ABUZZ.

A barred owl!

Rare in Central Park, and Carol would not miss it for the world. It was nighttime, yes, but serious birdwatchers took to the forest and field at all hours, especially in hopes of catching a glimpse of the stunning creature, which was as tall as the great horned— seventeen to twenty-five inches—and had the distinction of being the only owl on earth with brown eyes.

Like other birdwatchers presently in Central Park, she would be patient and dogged and happily ignore the pain of "bird neck," from staring straight up into the trees.

She was walking quickly, camera bouncing on her chest, night-vision binoculars in hand. You never strung two accessories around you. The tap and clank would scare off your subject. And always, rubber-soled shoes, quiet as spilling flour.

Then she slowed. Not because of the owl, or any other bird. She had noted a person not far ahead, walking her way. He was passing through a cone of overhead light.

Was it . . . ?

Yes, it was him! David. The fellow birdwatcher from the other day. The unmarried man, with a job.

He wore tan overalls—which gave a hint as to his profession—and had a backpack over his shoulder.

She'd been back to this area several times in hopes of seeing him again.

Couldn't wait to tell him about the barred owl—that would be a surefire catch—and maybe together they could stalk it.

Then, she might ask, Coffee?

Alcohol was never suggested by a woman first, but if *he* did . . .

Ah, the complex choreography of the mating game.

A bird flashed by—not a brown streak, so it wasn't the owl in question. She ignored it and slowed, fixing a smile on her face, standing a bit taller.

He walked closer yet, head down, examining a phone.

When he was about twenty-five, thirty feet away, she called out a bright "David!" Wondering if he'd remember her name. Of course she'd identify herself. She hated it when people assumed you knew who they were.

He stopped.

And looked up. He was frowning.

Damn, she sensed she hadn't handled it right. She'd been too far away when she called out. She should've waited.

But then Carol noted he was looking not at her but over her shoulder.

She turned and gasped.

A tall redheaded woman in jacket and jeans and bulletproof vest was trotting forward, leading a dozen other officers, some in full battle gear. She held a large black pistol. Others slipped from the bushes beside and behind David.

Who, she now guessed, might not be a David after all.

He shook his head and lifted his hands above his head.

Carol had had potential romances fail for any number of reasons.

None of them involved arrests.

"You, keep moving," the redhead said to her sternly.

"Well, no need to be huffy," Carol replied, but strode quickly away.

When she was some distance from the officers, she glanced back and watched David being handcuffed. His eyes were up, in the air, and she wondered if, whatever had landed him in hot water, he was in fact a birdwatcher and had spotted something important.

But, no, he was staring at the town house directly across Central Park West. She wondered what took the man's attention so completely.

She noticed the nest of peregrines on a ledge. But it couldn't be that; the birds were impressive but common.

Ah, then she saw he was looking *above* the nest, where a dark-haired man was sitting in the window.

After a moment, the occupant smoothly backed away and vanished, as if floating.

But then, ghostly men in windows and criminal romantic partners vanished from her thoughts, as a bird—then a half dozen, then scores—zipped into view.

They were male robins, which clustered on branches to sleep, while the females and young stayed on the ground.

Hardly a rare sighting, but the gathering—eerie in its reminiscence of the Hitchcock movie *The Birds*—was worth recording.

Carefully, so as not to scare them away, she lifted the camera, turned on the night-vision mode and pressed the button to add the stilling dormitory to her collection.

68.

RHYME EYED THE WATCHMAKER as Sachs led him into the parlor and seated him in one of the wicker chairs.

The tan jumpsuit the man wore was not a garment that looked natural on him, but Rhyme knew it would be a costume in today's drama.

He looked very different from the last time they'd seen each other. The cosmetic surgeon had given him ten years, and someone—or maybe he himself—had plucked out easily half his hair.

His wrists were cuffed and on his left was a large silver-colored watch, its dark face sporting a dozen small windows.

Complications . . .

Sachs wanded the watch with the nitrate detector.

"Clear."

His two phones were also clean, but—just to be safe—were sitting in the biohazard box at the moment.

Hale said, "Ron Pulaski."

"He's safe. Disappointed you lied, Charles."

Was there a fraction of relief in his eyes that the young officer had survived after all? Rhyme believed so.

Sachs announced, "I'm going to walk the grid in the warehouse—as soon as Fire finishes removing the HF." She glanced at Hale. "Might lead us in the direction of Woman X."

This *definitely* brought a reaction, a troubled frown. For an instant. Then, like mist under bright sun, it was gone.

After she left, Rhyme said to Sellitto, "Leave us alone, would you?"

"Linc . . ."

"I've got the panic button."

The detective nodded. "All right, but the uniforms stay outside."

"Fine."

Sellitto took a last glance at the Watchmaker, poured a cardboard cup of coffee from Thom's urn and walked outside.

Rhyme wheeled closer.

The man's frowning silence asked the obvious question. How?

"We got intel from England that they'd intercepted traffic about an attempt to kill me. Someone in the UK, communicating with someone here about the job.

"I asked a student of mine—really quite the brilliant mind—to pretend to be the killer. What would be the best way to do it? He decided the assassin would get to me through a weakness. Something vitally important to me. Something I couldn't be without. And that would make me careless. He posited evidence. And had the idea that the killer would plant botulinum in something Amelia collected at a crime scene."

Hale nodded and, despite the circumstances, seemed impressed. "Clever boy, your student. A not-unreasonable tactic. But botulinum? It's the devil to handle. Even worse than acid."

Rhyme continued, "And I decided sabotaging evidence was too obvious. But his premise was solid. Get to me through something vitally important. I have a reputation for being a curmudgeon, dyspeptic, rude. 'Asshole' is used on occasion too. But I actually *do* care for people. Well, some people. Ron is one of them. Amelia. Mel Cooper. Lon. A few others. People I would sacrifice myself for.

"I assumed you'd take Sellitto, Amelia or Ron, and probably Ron. He'd be easier to grab than my wife. She carries a switchblade, you know. And she's the best shot in the department. I had NYPD Tech Services hide a tracker in their shoes. We got to Ron ten minutes after he woke up in your cell.

"As for your visit here, the park." Rhyme nodded out the window. "You tried to kill the first crane operator because of what he'd seen in your SUV. Binoculars. And that book? With the gaudy jacket? We found it, finally. *Birds of New York.*"

"How did you figure out the hypodermics?"

"My hand's too unsteady for a firearm. Can hardly hang myself, now, can I? Poison would be perfect. How would you get it to me? Well, Andy Gilligan was working for you. He could've hidden something inside. He was interested in the old books, so that's where we searched first. We found the needles. Swapped the fentanyl out for distilled water and rigged a pulse oximeter that could be controlled remotely so it would count down to zero."

Hale's eyes radiated his dismay. "The falcons . . . That's why the falcons. I was going to have you hook up the full EKG down here." He nodded to the box. "But you'd planned on that. You went upstairs so the only vital sign indicator was the pulsimeter. *Tu es egregie excogitator.*"

"I accept the compliment. And mine to you." Rhyme shook his head with genuine admiration. "*All* the complications in your plot— to keep us misdirected. Impressive, Charles. First, the affordable housing demand. Kommunalka?"

"Did you like that, Lincoln? I pictured a bunch of bearded radicals living in a frame house in Astoria, taking turns reading *Das Kapital* to each other late into the night."

"When that turned out to be a sham, we decided it was all about real estate manipulation."

"What?" He seemed confused.

"Someone hiring you to sabotage the cranes to crash the real estate market. You were in the pay of a robber baron—if they still have those—who was going to scoop up property for a song."

Now a laugh from the man's lips. "Never even considered it."

"Really?"

"*You* get credit for that one, Lincoln. No, I wanted to lead you right to the assassination plot. A mysterious cell in Philadelphia, resentful of the president's infrastructure bill. The cranes tumbling down, the last one blocking the Holland Tunnel. The president has to get out of town via some alternative route and, bang."

"And so we'd think of that, you intentionally flew the drone in front of the Domain Awareness camera. The drones led us to Senator Talese. And Talese led us to the president. I assume it was Gilligan who gave you the details of his trip to New York and the meeting with the senator."

"Andy was a wealth of information."

"A good plan. It kept us from looking at other places, like, say, Emery Digital Solutions. So you could plant your device there."

"No," came the dismayed whisper. So emotionless otherwise, Hale didn't seem the sort of man who would ever give a response like this. What Rhyme saw actually chilled him.

Until this moment, the man would have the hope that his primary mission was still on track. Now he knew the plans were shattered.

The man's head dipped.

Rhyme said, "I kept wondering about Gilligan's death. Why would you kill him? And was there anything odd about the murder? One thing stood out. His computer—well, a computer *you* bought and wrote his name on. We wanted to get inside it, and who should appear to help us but Al Levine, NYPD Computer

Crimes investigator. As if we, or somebody on the team, contacted him. But nobody did. He initiated it. That is to say, *you* did.

"We found silicone—a main ingredient in plastic surgery wound healing—and a hair, one of yours, that had been plucked out. You made yourself older and balder. So Amelia wouldn't recognize you at Emery Digital. You needed her because you could masquerade as a cop all you wanted, but only a real officer could get a warrant to get inside Emery.

"And what was the purpose of the whole thing? To get inside the company and geotag the set of servers you were interested in. Then, this afternoon, you dressed up like a repairman." Rhyme nodded to the overalls. "Went underground and planted the device directly underneath them."

Rhyme now frowned. "But that's as far as I got. What I couldn't figure out—and still can't—is why. What was this all about, Charles?"

Endgame . . .

The Watchmaker gave a mournful smile. "Very simple, Lincoln. I was going to travel into the future."

69.

RHYME SAID, "I know that Emery does security for lots of government facilities, including the National Institute of Standards and Technology. You mean you were going to change the atomic clock?"

Hale tilted his head at what was apparently a curious comment. "There's no single atomic clock. There are nineteen of them around the world. If one were hacked, the others would override any deviation instantly."

The man's eyes took in the evidence boards. He nodded to them. "When I make a timepiece, I do the same thing. Plot it out on a board. At the end of the designing, when I'm ready to start, it's completely covered—notes, diagrams, flowcharts." He fell silent. Then he whispered, "The future . . ." He turned back to Rhyme. "My profession isn't as lucrative as you might think, Lincoln. Big fees, but big costs. I have retirement planned in a distant location . . . Where it's expensive to maintain anonymity."

Bribing officials can add up, Rhyme supposed.

"Do you know what NTP is?"

"No."

"Network Time Protocol. It sends the atomic time to networks that adjust clocks in computers, phones, GPS systems, scientific instruments, avionics . . . Anything that depends on accurate time. When your computer, your phone, your tablet, your car, the TV all show that it's 11:34 a.m., you have NTP to thank.

"Now, let's say you want to log on to a secure website—a bank, your brokerage account, an election committee, the U.S. Army, a porn site. You click on the uniform resource locator—the URL. Your browser needs to check the security certificate of the website to make sure it's legitimate. I won't bore you with HTTP versus HTTPS and secure sockets layers. All you need to know is that if the certificate's valid, you can log on and send and receive all the sensitive information you want—banking account information, passwords, socials, naughty pix, anything—and be sure it's safe.

"But certificates have an expiration date. After that, the data that users send are there for the taking, unencrypted. Emery handles NTP traffic security for hundreds of networks around the world."

"So your virus infects the networks and moves the time forward, past the security certificate's expiration date."

"Exactly. I log on, steal what I want, reset the clock and back out. It's weeks or months before anybody notices. If ever."

Rhyme found himself viewing what Hale had done with a grudging admiration.

"It's imperfect, but I figured that I could get into maybe fifty of every thousand networks I attacked. I'd be going after hedge funds and investment banks. Million-dollar transfers to my offshore accounts . . . Or that's what would have happened . . . Except for you."

"You didn't upload it?"

"No. I scheduled that for later, when the networks'd be clogged with traffic about President Boyd."

"So that's why the fake assassination."

"It tied up communications and police, and pulled the NYPD and FBI guards off Emery. An assassination is all hands on board."

Rhyme was looking at photos of the device that Hale had hoisted to the ceiling under the cybersecurity company. "But how would it work? Aren't the servers at Emery Digital shielded or something?"

"From cellular and radio intrusion, yes. But not from induction."

"Electromagnetic force." Rhyme knew about this from a prior case in which someone used the New York power grid as a weapon. "Nikola Tesla designed a system to transmit power over the grid wirelessly. Never got into widespread use, but we charge our phones on those pads."

A nod. "Well, power's electricity. So is *data*. That's what the device does. Electromagnetic transmission of the viruses to infect the time protocols."

Silence between the men now.

After a moment Rhyme offered, "I'm skeptical."

Hale turned from a photograph he'd been looking at. A picture of Rhyme and Sachs in Lake Como, where they'd not only gotten married but stopped a killer in the same several days. His brows rose. "Skeptical?"

"This plan—the cranes, the housing activists, the assassination—so you can line your pockets? It doesn't seem like you. I can't imagine you without a client."

"It was time for me to get off the merry-go-round." Then in a whisper: "Everything comes to an end, now, doesn't it? Don't you feel that way too?"

"What can you tell me about the woman you were working with? The one who kidnapped Ron?"

"Not a single thing, Lincoln, not a thing."

Rhyme knew that the evidence might give them leads, but Hale would remain completely uncooperative regarding his colleague.

Hale frowned as he saw something on the mantel.

"May I?"

Rhyme nodded.

Hale walked to the fireplace and studied a gold pocket watch, made by Breguet, a famed craftsman who'd lived many years ago. The face was white, the numbers in roman numerals. Some small dials showed phases of the moon and a perpetual calendar. Rhyme knew it also had a parachute inside, an anti-shock mechanism revolutionary for the time.

It had been a gift from the Watchmaker years ago and had been accompanied by a note of warning.

"You've kept it wound."

"What good is a watch that doesn't run? An object of beauty, maybe." Rhyme shrugged. "But beauty is overrated."

"Indeed." The Watchmaker put the Breguet back on the ledge.

Rhyme was looking out the window once more, gazing toward a spot about three hundred yards into Central Park. A faint glint in the distance, which then vanished.

Hale asked, "You've seen him too?"

"Twice. Surveillance tapes. Near the cranes."

Nodding, Hale said, "I don't know who he is. Do you have any idea?"

"Andy Gilligan's brother."

"Ah, Mick. That explains how he knew about the trailer on Hamilton Court—I saw him there last night. Andy would have told him."

"He's connected—organized crime." Rhyme added, "I saw him with a guitar case."

"So that's what he was carrying." A faint smile crossed Hale's face. "And I suspect he's not a student of Segovia or Jeff Beck."

"Do you see him now?" Rhyme asked.

Hale squinted. "No. Andy told me they used to hunt."

Rhyme said, "There's a back entrance here, it leads onto a

cul-de-sac. They can bring the detention center transport van around."

After a lengthy moment during which the only sounds were the occasional snapping of an old, settling structure and the shushing of traffic, Hale said, "Even without reading Einstein, we know how time expands and contracts. Fast when you're making babies, slow when you're having them. Do you know what time does when you're in a twelve-by-twelve cell, Lincoln? It turns on you. Your best friend becomes a python. That's not for me."

"I've adapted." Rhyme nodded to his wheelchair.

"We share quite a bit, Lincoln. But I have no interest in adaptation."

Rhyme noticed Hale's eyes had slipped to the evidence bag containing his burner phones.

"You want to make a call?" He was thinking of Woman X.

Hale debated, but whether it was from the slim chance that someone might trace it or for some other reason, he shook his head. "No. I think not." He sounded wistful.

Hale looked at the monitor depicting the street in front of the town house. Two police cruisers waited there, each with officers inside. No one was on the sidewalk.

His eyes met Rhyme's.

The criminalist nodded.

Hale walked into the lobby, disappearing from Rhyme's view. A moment later there was a click of the door latch. A patch of illumination grew into a trapezoid on the marble of the hallway as the door hinge squeaked softly. The man's stark, elongated shadow ran from the door to the security scanner.

There was silence.

Then Rhyme blinked at two sounds, a second apart.

The first was the thud of a bullet striking the Watchmaker's chest. The second was the resounding boom of a rifle shot from Central Park.

Hale was flung backward into the hallway, both he and the floor spattered with blood.

Rhyme heard shouts from outside as officers leapt from the cars and crouched on the side closest to the town house, scanning for a target, though Rhyme knew that the shooter was speeding away.

Almost immediately came the distant bleat of sirens, growing closer.

Rhyme concentrated on the man who lay on his back. Moving slowly, trying to draw his legs up, gripping air with long fingers as if reaching for a safety rope.

Or for a set of watchmaking tools.

Would he turn his head so that they might share a last gaze? Rhyme wondered.

He did not.

70.

"**TELL ME, CAPTAIN RHYME.** The details."

Detective Lawrence Hylton and his Caribbean-inflected voice were back again—the officer who glanced off all things Internal Affairs. The time was 9 a.m., the morning after Hale had died.

"The deceased and I have a history. I thought I could get him to tell me about what he was doing here, why he was behind the cranes collapsing, the assassination plot, the sabotage of the cybersecurity company. Who his accomplice was. We had a conversation. I think he looked at the monitor and thought he could make it past the officers outside. He got to the hall and opened the door, and he was shot before I could hit the panic button."

He nodded his head toward the control pad of his chair.

"Sometimes signals from my brain are a bit delayed." Rhyme rarely played this card. He decided this situation, though, warranted doing so, even though his words were not in the least true. "Where was the shooter?"

"We aren't sure, but we think that high-rise—Seventy-Second

Street. The middle of the park. Two hundred fifty, three hundred yards. Small caliber. Two twenty-three probably."

An assault rifle. The weapons had short barrels, but shot flat and fast, and with a good scope they were—obviously—accurate enough to kill at a distance. They also fit quite well into a guitar case.

"Who else was in the town house?"

Rhyme was hardly in the mood for any debriefing. But under the circumstances he decided to stay blandly cooperative.

"No one. I was alone."

"When did your wife, Detective Sachs, leave?"

"About forty minutes before the incident. The exact time'll be on the security cam time stamp. Lon Sellitto left then too. Amelia has alibi witnesses at the Ron Pulaski crime scene. And Lon went to One PP. If you were suggesting they might have been the shooter."

"I wasn't." The reply was flat. Hylton looked over his notebook. "And your assistant . . ."

Rhyme found himself oddly affected by what had just happened. Not rattled, but . . . *hollow*. That was the word. He corrected stiffly, "Not my 'assistant.' 'Caregiver.' Or 'aide.' An assistant has a different connotation—an easier job, all around."

"Your caregiver then. How did he happen not to be here?"

"Because he *happened* to be shopping."

"Ah. But by leaving you alone here, isn't that . . . Well, I mean, isn't it a risk?"

"Quads rarely self-immolate. Or starve to death over the course of an hour or two."

"Captain." Hylton spoke with labored patience.

"Thom Reston has many, many skills. Sniping is not among them."

"You can appreciate how odd this is."

"I made an error in judgment, trusting Hale. I thought he would be more cooperative if he were not chained to a radiator."

The officer said pointedly, "And just coincidentally a person was laying in wait to shoot him."

Rhyme chose not to say what came into his mind: A person *lies* in wait. A chicken *lays*, whether it's waiting for anything or not.

"The suspect was in custody. He was caught. He was going to spend the rest of his days in a twelve-by-twelve room. Do you really think there's an NYPD officer who would commit murder two just to shorten the judicial process?"

Hylton didn't respond. He looked to his notes for guidance. They apparently offered none. "Who do you think? If you had to guess."

"I don't need to guess at all. I know who the shooter was. Andy Gilligan's brother."

"I'll send a team to his house."

"Yes, you'll need to go through the motions."

"So he's gone, you think?"

"Gone."

Hylton closed his notebook. "I also need to get a statement from Patrolman Pulaski. Where is he now?"

Rhyme looked at the time on a nearby monitor. "Engaged at the moment. But I'm sure he'll call you when he's free."

71.

THE BURN RECOVERY was coming along fine.

Dr. Amit Bakshi paused and looked over the electronic patient records of Aaron Stahl, the student whose SUV the NYPD police officer had run into, resulting in a conflagration that apparently made quite the scene in Lower Manhattan.

An ER doc with twelve years of experience in the city, Bakshi had treated many people for auto accidents. In New York City, the injuries tended to be less severe, since one couldn't drive that fast—as opposed to New Castle, Pennsylvania, where he'd started practicing medicine, and State Route 17, with that curve.

Dead Man's Zone.

In New York, cars rarely exploded in flames, but the EMTs who brought him in had explained that the incident was a fluke occurrence, as the NYPD officer's car just happened to shove Aaron's SUV into some construction supplies, some bars or tubing, which ripped open the gas tank. Modern-day safety precautions by automakers, only got you so far when jagged metal was involved.

"Hey, Doctor."

"Hello, sir," Bakshi replied. He believed that being slightly formal bestowed comfort in his patients. Even with a nineteen-year-old.

He offered a nod and smile to Aaron's older sister, Natalia, who sat bedside.

The woman, late twenties, he guessed, nodded in return, with a reserved smile, and continued to text. Much signage here was devoted to forbidding the use of cell phones. Not a soul paid attention.

Bakshi had tried to deduce the nature of the family situation, but had been unsuccessful. Neither parent had come to visit. Perhaps these two were orphans.

Bakshi turned his attention to his patient to ask the basic questions that had to be asked, and to check vitals—and the informative less-than-vitals; like espionage, medicine was first and foremost about intelligence.

He examined the wound.

The young man was improving well.

"It's looking good. You can go home tomorrow."

Aaron winced. "The pain. Man, it's really bad still."

Comments like this always raised a red flag with Bakshi, as it did with all doctors, who might be in a position to prescribe pain meds. Of course, the drugs existed for a vital reason. But the border between relief and abuse was often thin as fishing line. Aaron had answered on the admission sheet that he had three glasses of wine a week and did not do recreational drugs.

The template response of ten million patients.

You could cut and paste it.

"It's just, it's not only the burn. My neck too the crash."

Aaron's ortho scans had come back negative, but pain was a creature unto itself. Both cunning and a master of disguise. It appeared, it vanished, it attacked, it retreated, then circled in from the rear.

"I'll give you four days' worth. Then check in with your regular GP."

"Great. Thanks." The gratitude seemed delivered with an edge of grudge.

Natalia was saying, "Tomorrow? Not today?" She hadn't lifted her head as she texted and Bakshi realized she was responding to his comment from a moment ago.

She continued, "I'd like to get him out of here as soon as—"

The sentence had ended abruptly and with a gasp.

"No one move," came a man's stern voice from the door.

Bakshi spun around.

"Shit," Aaron was saying.

"No!" A dismayed whisper from his sister.

Into the room was walking a trim blond man who, with an exceedingly grim face, was gazing from patient to sister and back.

"It's him, that Pulaski! He's the one who hit Aaron!"

"Sir—" Bakshi shut up when he saw the gun in the man's hand.

Pulaski said, "Could you give us a minute?"

"I . . . I . . ."

Natalia said, "He can't be here! He's not supposed to be here! Call security!"

Bakshi gripped the chart tablet and looked back at the nurses' station. It was empty.

"Help!" Natalia cried.

"Shhh," Pulaski said, wincing at her mini scream.

Pulaski glanced at Bakshi, who said in a whisper, "Can I leave?"

"I just asked you to, didn't I?" Pulaski now sounded almost amused.

The doctor backed slowly into the hallway and, when he figured it would be safe, ran silently to the nearest station and grabbed a phone from its cradle.

72.

"RON," CAME THE VOICE from the doorway. A tall, uniformed PD officer walked into the room. Her brown hair was gathered into a businesslike bun.

"Hey . . ."

The officer, Sheri Sloane, turned her long, dark-complected face to Aaron and looked him up and down, then took in the woman.

Aaron snapped, "The hell is going on?"

Natalia said, "You're suspended! He told us . . ." Her voice faded with the lapse. "We heard you were suspended."

Pulaski noted how she'd begun the sentence.

Sloane tugged on blue latex gloves and approached. "Could you stand please?"

"I—"

Pulaski snapped, "Stand."

Anger filling her face, the woman did as told. Sloane frisked her carefully. Then the policewoman went through her purse.

"Clean."

Her role and Pulaski's reversed. She drew her weapon and

Pulaski holstered his. They had worked together in the past and had the choreography down.

Pulaski pulled on gloves of his own and tugged the patient's bedclothes up, searching closely. His backpack as well. He too was unarmed.

The woman laughed in astonishment. "You're trying to intimidate us! Scare us out of suing you! When we get you in court, you're going to be so fucked . . ."

Pulaski frowned—an exaggerated expression. "Court? You think that's really a wise move?"

"You can't talk to us that way," Aaron said, sounding like a petulant schoolboy—though in actuality he was a student only in the sense that he hadn't graduated from high school.

"Shhhhh." Pulaski waved a palm like pushing away campfire smoke. "Now, let's get the technical stuff out of the way. Natalia Baskov and Aaron Stahl, you're under arrest for conspiracy to commit fraud, for subverting police procedure, obstruction of justice—always a good one."

"The kitchen sink," Sloane said. "One of my favorites."

"There'll be other charges too, but that's enough for us to get started."

Aaron muttered, "This is such bullshit."

Baskov—not a sister, not a relative at all, but the daughter of a Brooklyn mob capo. Aaron was a numbers runner for her father and all-around punk.

The officer ran through the Miranda warning and when they acknowledged understanding it, he said, "Do you wish to waive the right to remain silent? But before you answer that let me just tell you what we've found. Might be helpful."

Aaron began to bluster again. Baskov said, "Shut up." And turned back to Pulaski. "Go ahead."

"First, I've been reinstated as an officer. Just so you understand.

Now, I've also been authorized by the New York County District Attorney to discuss your assisting us in an investigation in exchange for possibly—and I said *possibly*—coming to some agreement about charging. I need you to listen. Are you going to listen?"

Aaron tried: "What the—?"

Baskov said, "We're going to listen."

"There were a few things that made me curious about the accident and I thought I'd check them out. First, I went to the city hospital records room and got your blood workup from the accident." He was looking at a suddenly less defiant and considerably more concerned Aaron.

These papers were what he'd had with him when Charles Hale's assistant, Woman X, tranqued him and hauled him off to the acid room. (Lyle Spencer's news that Burdick was probably planning to use a fellow cop's own medical chart about an old injury against him might have inspired someone else to slip into the hospital and steal and destroy those records. Which, of course, Pulaski would never do. "Borrowing" Aaron Stahl's file, though, while a little borderline, was really just part of his investigation.)

He continued, "Aaron, your blood work showed the presence of triamcinolone and lidocaine. Injectable painkillers. Which the responding medical technicians did *not* give you. You shot yourself up with them *before* the crash so that it didn't hurt too much. Because you were paid to drive in front of me and take the hit. I suspect you didn't expect to catch fire, but"—he shrugged—"every job has its downside, right? And also on your chart, Narcan, administered probably two days ago. You've got an opioid problem, Aaron. Which means you have a dealer—and therefore access to fentanyl. Somebody in the crowd helping me after the accident managed to get some on my skin. That's why I tested positive. Hell, you might even've paid off an EMT. I don't know."

Pulaski wondered if Aaron had intentionally passed an arm

through the unexpected flames at the crash, just so he could hit the doctors up for more drugs.

If true, nothing but sad.

"And after that I went to look at your burned-out SUV, the junkyard where they towed it in Queens. And guess what I found inside? A wad of plastic that had been an Opticom."

"Shit," muttered Baskov.

Opticoms are remote controls carried by many first responders to change traffic lights, so, say, a fire truck can turn all the reds it's approaching to green.

"You used it to switch the lights when I was in the intersection. Nobody was paying attention until the collision, so everybody saw my light was red, yours was green. Oh, and another thing that didn't get burned up completely? The crash helmet you wore. And one final thing we've got. The main witness who gave a statement that I ran the light? Theresa Lemerov? She isn't exactly what you'd call objective. A cop friend of mine in Brooklyn followed her. She was in your brother's house all day, and—"

"Wait," Aaron barked.

Pulaski lifted an eyebrow.

"My brother?"

"Evan Stahl. Theresa, the main witness, knew your family, and that—"

"My brother." His face was red with anger. "Did your friend say she spent the night?"

"What?"

"Did Theresa spend the night with my brother?"

Baskov: "Oh, Jesus, Aaron. Let it go."

Aaron muttered, "That bitch! She said she'd never have anything to do with him again. I take a fall, nearly get burnt alive, and the first thing she does is run to Evan. Oh, and that prick—"

Baskov said, "Would you just be quiet?"

Amen to that.

"So, where was I? Right. I knew Burdick was setting me up—but I thought it was just to get me fired because I dissed him in front of some reporters. But it was bigger than that. It was about me hunting for Eddie Tarr."

When Baskov blinked, his theory became proof.

"Tarr needed me off his trail for a murder I was investigating—just until he could finish a job here. He paid Burdick to get me out of the picture. First, Burdick tried to get me suspended at a crime scene and when that didn't work, he hired your father." A glance at Baskov. "He set up the crash.

"So here's the thing. I want Burdick. A solid case. Gold. I've got a circumstantial one. I want witnesses.

"If I was to give you a statement . . ."

"Hey, I know shit too!" Aaron's defiance had become desperation.

Being the daughter of a capo, she needed only one look to silence him. She said, "And emails, dates and places."

Pulaski said, "This's making my heart sing."

She shrugged. "What do I get?"

"We," Aaron blurted.

"The DA can guarantee the state won't go for anything more than four years, medium sec."

"Can I get it in writing?"

"No. And the offer's starting to melt."

"Okay, okay."

"Me too!" Aaron said desperately.

Because he'd ruined Pulaski's very comfortable car, he said, "I don't know we'll need you. I'll have to think about it."

Baskov said, "Well, it's pretty much like you said. Burdick had a partner in the department. Somebody named Gilligan. A detective."

Ah, interesting. He nodded for her to go on.

"But you got one thing wrong. Yeah, Burdick came to my dad

and paid him to get you off Tarr's ass. Only, the money—and the idea for the crash—came from somebody else. His name was Hale. Charles Hale, I think."

Jesus.

So, the device that took down the last crane was one of Tarr's IEDs.

Pulaski's homicide murder case, seemingly unrelated, brought them full circle back to the Watchmaker.

There was noise from the hallway; uniformed officers had arrived to take Baskov to Central Booking and Aaron Stahl to the detention wing of Bellevue city hospital.

After they'd carted away the prisoners, Pulaski called Lon Sellitto to tell him how it had gone. When he disconnected he and Sloane walked down the corridor toward the exit. She asked, "How'd you put it all together, Ron?"

He told her about the hit job of a report Burdick had submitted to the Officer Involved Accident board. And Lyle Spencer's comment about how much effort had gone into sidelining Pulaski.

"Then I was thinking about the call I got just before the intersection? From a tech in Crime Scene? It was a problem, chain of custody, the evidence from my scene. I don't make mistakes involving chain of custody. Never. I talked to the clerk today. Burdick'd forced her to make the call just so he could claim I was distracted."

Sloane said, "You've got Burdick. But the question is, you think you can turn him? To give up Tarr."

Pulaski considered this for a moment. "Depends," he answered.

"On what?"

"On just how much of a weasel he really is."

• • •

"Good evening, I'm Amber Andrews, here with breaking news. Agents with the FBI and Bureau of Alcohol, Tobacco, Firearms and Explosives

today raided the hangar at a small airport in Bergen County, New Jersey, arresting a man on the FBI's Most Wanted list. Eddie Kevin Tarr, forty-three, has been considered one of the most dangerous bomb makers in the world and has sold an unknown number of improvised explosive devices, or IEDs, to terrorists and organized criminals over the past decade. Tarr is allegedly responsible for the bomb that brought down the tower crane in Lower Manhattan yesterday, resulting in the closing of the Holland Tunnel for nearly sixteen hours."

III

OBIT

73.

"I THINK WE'VE got some pix," Pulaski said. "Her."

Rhyme understood: Ron meant the Watchmaker's associate. Woman X.

The two men and Amelia Sachs were in the parlor. Pulaski had been ardently tracking the woman, who'd been fast with the tranquilizer gun and had either constructed or commissioned Hale's magic induction device.

"I want her. Nothing personal." He'd said this offhandedly.

Which made it *somewhat* personal in Rhyme's mind, but no matter. Apparently, the young officer had had some success.

"I was scrubbing through video around Hamilton Court and found a half-second clip of the two of them together. Hale and the woman. I pulled a capture. It wasn't great, but I enhanced it with Stable Diffusion. You know it?"

"No."

"It's an AI—artificial intelligence text-to-image art generator. I loaded in the capture and kept making modifications—like witness artists do. Then I sent the JPG to Domain Awareness to start matching. I just got a call from them. They had some hits." He sat at the keyboard and typed. Seconds later they were on a video call—like Zoom, but with higher security—to the control room of the Domain Awareness operation.

Officer Bobby Hancock was a burly man with a beard not forbidden by, but uncharacteristic in, the NYPD.

"Ron."

"Bobby. Go ahead."

"Is that Lincoln Rhyme?"

The criminalist offered an impatient punctuation-free: "Yes it is go ahead Officer."

"Sure. From the image Ron gave us we did a citywide profile and found the subject. That Stable Diffusion thing? We talked to the brass and're going to be opening an AI-generative operation. Really smart."

Rhyme and Sachs shared a glance. He again felt a bit of pride for his protégé. He could see Sachs did too.

"Twice we placed her in the company of Hale. And we had a solo of her, West Side—Midtown. Here they are."

The images came onto the screen. Not high-def, but clear enough. She was in her early thirties, Rhyme guessed. Pretty in a wholesome, not runway model way. Slim, maybe athletic, but her clothes—jeans and a sport team sweatshirt—were concealing. Her blond hair was in a complicated braid.

In the first two, she was walking down the sidewalk beside Hale. In one they were looking around suspiciously. In the other, they were regarding each other.

In the third image she was on the sidewalk in a part of town featuring old brownstones, not unlike Rhyme's.

"Those're from videos," Rhyme said. "Any others worth looking at?"

"Nope. Just more of the same, walking. One, two seconds each."

Woman X wasn't holding anything, say, a coffee cup that—by

heavy-duty policework—they might've found and lifted prints from.

"Thanks, Bobby."

"Sure."

Pulaski said, "The one where she was by herself. I've been looking at images of neighborhoods. That could be a block in the West Thirties. Bad fire a couple of days ago. Arson. A pro job. Termite and napalm. Maybe a coincidence. But insurance scams don't use accelerants like that. The army uses accelerants like that. I've sent a team to canvass."

"And be sure—"

Pulaski finished the sentence. "That they know about acid IEDs."

Sachs studied one of the pictures for a long moment.

From her eyes, he could tell she was onto something.

"What, Sachs?"

"Her face. The second shot, looking at him."

"Hm."

Pulaski frowned. "What do you see?"

Neither answered. She asked, "How do we handle it?"

The answer struck him almost immediately. "Thom! Thom!"

The aide appeared. "I have a pot on the stove."

"Well, unstove it. We need some more help."

"Yes?" he muttered.

Rhyme said, "You have the way with words."

The man grimaced at the flagrant buttering up.

"It's true," Rhyme protested, seeing the expression.

"What do you need?"

"Simple. I want you to write an obituary."

74.

NEW YORK CITY is home to a number of neighborhoods in which celebrities and the powerful reside.

But no place has as many per square foot as these four hundred acres.

Woodlawn Cemetery in the Bronx, just south of Westchester County, is home to Miles Davis, Duke Ellington, Otto Preminger, Mark Twain, F. W. Woolworth, and Celia Cruz, the Queen of Salsa, and scores more of the famous.

The infamous too. Ellsworth "Bumpy" Johnson, the legendary gangland figure of Harlem, is interred here.

As is someone with an equally disturbing history, a recent addition: Charles Vespasian Hale, whose gravesite Amelia Sachs, Ron Pulaski and Lyle Spencer were now observing from a gardening shed near North Border Avenue, running roughly parallel to East 233rd Street.

Like most of the cemetery, this portion resembled a Long Island estate rather than an ominous gargoyle-filled setting for a Stephen King novel.

His gravesite had been chosen—by Lincoln Rhyme—because it was near a cluster of dense bushes, which were now providing cover for a half-dozen Emergency Service Unit officers in full military gear and camo.

In responding to his request—bordering on demand—the brass made clear they couldn't commit to a large number of officers, and they couldn't commit for very long. But Rhyme and Pulaski had made the point that Woman X would surely be leaving town soon, if she hadn't already left, and so the troop commitment wouldn't last longer than one day.

And what were the odds that she'd show up?

More than negligible, Rhyme and Sachs believed.

This was because of the second CCTV picture of Hale and Woman X, the one revealing a particular look on her face. It was the way he and Sachs occasionally regarded each other—and the way they'd seen Pulaski and his wife, Jenny, do the same.

There was no doubt that Hale and this woman were lovers.

So Rhyme had decided to lure her here via the obituary, which Thom had done a masterful job penning. It described how the man responsible for the crane collapses had been a career criminal and offered some facts about his early life. Much was speculation, but a paid obit did not need to adhere to the standard of true journalism. In fact, there was only one detail that mattered: his interment in Woodlawn.

By the time the piece hit the internet, an hour ago, Sachs and the others were already in place.

Would she indeed come to pay her last respects?

It was a sentimental gesture toward a man who was indisputably unsentimental.

Yet that look on her face—and the one suggested by his, though muted by the glasses—was undeniable.

In any event, they had no other options in their hunt for her. So here the trio waited in a hot shed, amid bags of fertilizer, which, Sachs reflected, maybe stank fiercely, but would provide good protection against bullets, should a firefight break out.

The day was suitably ominous, dark, and the sky was about to revisit an earlier rain.

Good for the operation. Few visitors were present.

Unlike some of the multimillion-dollar temples here, which were the resting place of multimillion-dollar corpses, Hale's grave was simple. A plaque, flat on the ground, for a tombstone. Of necessity it had been engraved quickly. Name and date. Thom had suggested putting a clock face on it. Rhyme had said, "No."

Another hour passed. Sachs radioed for the third time, "Stay alert."

The more likely danger in stakeouts is not gunplay but falling asleep and letting your subject waltz off to freedom.

She was scanning once more when she was startled by a series of shots and a ragged cry. They were coming from just outside the cemetery. "Help! Help me! Ambulance!" A man's voice.

"Bullshit," Pulaski said. "It's her. A diversion."

Sachs grabbed the radio and nearly shouted, "No one move! Stay in position!"

Damn. Too late. One of the ESU officers had risen and stepped from the brush. She dropped to cover quickly.

Instinct—and who could blame her? But the woman had, perhaps, given away the whole game.

"Ron, call the local house. They've probably got somebody on the way, but make sure they check it out. And have the respondings call us with what they find."

As he made the call, Sachs lifted a pair of powerful Nikon binoculars and scanned the opposite side of the cemetery, looking for lens flare, in case Woman X was using her own pair to surveil them.

Nothing.

But of course Sachs had been careful to make sure her binocu-lars were shaded; why wouldn't X do the same?

Into the radio: "Detective Five Eight Eight Five to ESU team leader. You see *anybody* near the gravesite?"

"Negative, Detective," the captain radioed back. "There was a groundskeeper and an elderly couple. Nowhere near the grave. And they took off when they heard the shots."

"K."

Pulaski said, "Not a soul in sight. And this is probably the only stakeout in history where *soul* makes sense."

She gave a faint smile and continued to scan. "Okay, Charles . . . Talk to me." A whisper. Maybe the others heard, maybe not. "What's your girlfriend up to?"

A call from the local precinct on her mobile. "Yes?"

"Five Eight Eight Five?" A man's voice, Bronx-inflected.

"Go ahead."

"Just heard from respondings. We've got him, Detective. Get this. Somebody, a woman, paid this homeless guy ten K, yeah, that's right, *ten*, to fire a gun into the dirt outside the cemetery and scream for help. We found him a couple blocks away. He was just sitting on the curb drinking a malt. No resistance. Seemed pretty fucking happy."

"He told you about her?"

"Yeah. He didn't want us to think he'd used the piece to hurt anybody. He just needed the money. Handed the weapon over. It's cold. No number on it."

She sighed. "Hair in braids? Blond? Thirties?"

"That's right. Except it was brown. Her hair."

So Miss Clairol had paid a visit.

"And what was she wearing?"

"Something dark. That's all he remembered."

"The money?"

"Said he gave it to a church."

"Yeah, right. We'll never see it." Sachs continued to scan the grounds. No sign of human movement.

The officer continued, "He's got a couple priors. Drugs. Drunk and disorderly. Even if he gets time, which I doubt, he'll do six months. Not enough leverage to give up the money."

And even if they found it—unlikely—what would it show? Woman X wasn't going to give anything away by touching the bills.

She disconnected, sighed.

Spencer asked, "Did she think we'd all go running to the gunshots and leave the grave unattended?"

"It was never about her getting to the grave. She ran the scam just to see if we were on stakeout."

"Flush us."

"Yep. She took off the minute the officer broke cover. Hell. My fault. I should've told everybody to expect something like that."

Nodding at the officers, Spencer said, "Instinct. I almost went too."

"Yeah."

The ESU commander called in. "She's gone, right?"

Probably, she thought. What she said was: "Maybe."

A pause. It was *her* operation. He needed her okay to leave.

"Stay in position."

Another pause, this one more irritated, if science can radiate that trait. "Roger, Five Eight Eight Five."

Two hours later, she got the inevitable call. "ESU to Five Eight Eight Five."

"Go ahead."

"Detective, we've gotta stand down. Sorry, but my people need to get back to watch."

"Understood."

The woman was surely long gone. Now that she knew there'd

been surveillance once, she'd assume there would always be eyes on the grave, maybe a camera, maybe plain-clothed.

The ESU team emerged from the trees and joined Sachs, Spencer and Pulaski outside the shed. They discussed who'd write the report up—ESU glancing at her in a way that said "Your op, you do the paperwork." She agreed. They started back to where their cars and an unmarked van were parked, in the shadows of a narrow street across 233rd. On instinct, Sachs stopped abruptly. Pulaski looked her way as she turned back.

"No," she whispered, nearly a gasp.

She, Pulaski and Spencer jogged back to the grave. There, on the plaque that was Hale's tombstone, was a folded piece of paper, weighed down by a red-painted ring about five inches across.

They scanned about them.

"The shots . . ." Sachs muttered.

Pulaski nodded. "It *was* a diversion."

It sure was. But not to shift attention away from the grave while Woman X slipped up to it. No, the purpose of the assault was just what they had believed: that it was a trick to flush them—to find out what the officers on surveillance duty were wearing.

So she could dress in similar gear. She must've had a wardrobe in her car or van. It was just the foresight Hale himself would have.

She'd strolled right up behind the officer, invisible, because she too was in a full ESU tactical outfit.

Which Sachs now found behind a tree about forty feet from the grave.

Woman X had been among them the whole time, since delivering the gun and cash to the homeless guy.

Sachs grabbed her radio.

"Detective Five Eight Eight Five to Central. K."

"Go ahead, Five Eight Eight Five. K."

"We're at the operation at Woodlawn, North Border Avenue

near the lake. Suspect was here ten minutes ago. But has left. I need citywide on a fugitive. White female, thirties, brown hair braided. Medium build. Possibly dark clothing. Probably armed. I'm uploading a Domain Awareness picture now." She lowered the phone and typed, sending the picture to Central's secure server.

"Got it, Detective." A pause. Woman X resembled about a hundred thousand residents of New York City. "Further to?"

She'd want vehicle, scars, footwear, other distinguishings, direction of travel, known locations.

Of which Sachs had none.

"Negative."

"Roger, Five Eight Eight Five."

They signed off.

She returned to Pulaski, who was looking down at the note, which he held in gloved hands.

"It's a poem."

Sachs couldn't help but give a brief laugh. Well, this was a first. After reading the words, she called Rhyme.

"I heard, Sachs. She gamed us." He sounded amused, as if part of him had believed all along that anyone who'd been close to Hale was easily smart enough to elude an on-the-fly police trap. "What'd she leave?"

"A poem."

"Hm. Read it."

Sachs pulled on her own gloves and took the sheet.

Season

For C.V.H.

Somewhere in the autumn apple's cells
A change occurs:
The curious investiture of ripeness.

So love, a type of season too,
Completes the heart
And moves us closer to fruition.

Unless . . .

A crow or sudden frost
Or spill of blood on parlor wall
Cuts short the time required for those ends,

And leaves behind the unfulfilled
To dwell on ways to make amends.

Rhyme grunted. Poetry, even less than prose fiction, did not figure in his world. "And it means what, do you think?"

Sachs chuckled. "It's a love poem, Rhyme."

"Hm. How?"

"It says that love changes us. Makes us whole, like a season ripens fruit. But that's only part of the message."

"What's the rest?"

"A threat. Making amends. She's saying she'll be coming for us. Ah, and there's something else?"

Rhyme said, "I caught it. The 'blood on parlor wall.' She knows how and where he died. She was in the park when it happened. Watching us."

They had lost one enemy, and gained another.

"Handwriting?"

"No, computer. Generic paper."

"Untraceable, naturally. And the hunk of metal?"

"A wheel." She picked up a dark-red-painted metal disk about five inches across. Spokes radiated from hub to ring. "Part of a clock, I'd guess."

"Show me."

Sachs turned on her video camera and hit the live stream app. She held up the wheel.

"It's not from a clock. We ran a case a year ago. The Brooklyn Museum of Industry."

"Remember. Vaguely."

"It's a miniature wheel from a steam engine. A toy maybe or a hobbyist's." After a brief pause: "I wonder if it's sentimental, or practical."

"How do you mean, Rhyme?"

"Heartfelt emotion was no part of Hale's makeup. I have a feeling Woman X is the same way. I think she left the wheel for a reason. To lead us somewhere. Or lead us *away* from somewhere."

"If that's true, then she's as good at engineering plans as he was."

She heard a faint laugh from the other end of the line. "How long did it take us to find Hale's real name?"

"Years. We knew him as, what? Richard Logan, Gerald Duncan, finally Hale."

"But we *always* knew him as the Watchmaker . . . Woman X needs a nickname too."

"Fine with me. Can't think of any at the moment."

After a brief silence Rhyme said, "Maybe here's one. Just thinking about her plots, all the planning. How does 'the Engineer' sound?"

"I like it. But you know what I'd like more?"

"Which is?"

"To see her in detention."

"That day will come, Sachs. That day will come."

She hoped so.

Though she could not push from her mind the last stanza of the poem.

And leaves behind the unfulfilled

To dwell on ways to make amends.

They disconnected.

Ron Pulaski had been on his phone, and he now disconnected. "I just called for a CS bus. I'll get started on the spiral."

"The what?"

"Oh, I'm searching in spirals now. Not grids."

Interesting idea. She'd watch him and maybe try it herself on her next scene.

The ESU team leader approached. The compact, crew-cut army vet was grimacing. "Sorry, Detective. No sign of her on the streets. And I checked the cemetery office. The CCTV was running when we got here, but somehow it got fried ten minutes ago. All the data's wiped."

No surprise there.

"Just no clue where she's gone."

Pulaski gave a fast laugh. "Oh, we've got plenty of clues. Where the homeless guy was when the two of them talked, the gun, the poem. The approaches to and from the grave. The grave itself. The wheel. Surveillance footage outside the cemetery."

"Still doesn't seem like much," the ESU man said.

"It doesn't need to be. It just needs to point us *somewhere*." Pulaski pulled on booties over his shoes and new latex gloves. "And we'll go from there."

75.

"LINCOLN. THE NEWS."

Thom's voice was calling from the kitchen, where he was fixing dinner. Rhyme didn't know what was on the menu, but it smelled good. He usually thought of food as fuel—his reverence was reserved for beverages—but occasionally he enjoyed a fine meal. And his caregiver was just the man for creating one.

Rhyme called in response: "Why?"

"I heard his name mentioned."

"Eight million people in the city, Thom. Can we narrow, some?"

"Just put it on."

"News," Rhyme murmured, clicking the remote, "is apprentice history . . ." The screen came to life. "It's an ad! Cosmetics, long hair and slow motion. Useless. No shampoo will give anyone that hair who didn't have that hair before the shampoo."

"Well," Thom offered, sighing, "either wait without complaining or change the channel."

He changed the channel.

A blond anchorwoman, her highly made-up face as serious as

could be, was saying ". . . *has denied the allegations. But supporters and donors are already distancing themselves from the representative.*"

A picture appeared, a postage-sized one in the lower right-hand corner of the cluttered screen, the man Lyle Spencer had spoken to about the Kommunalka Project.

Representative Stephen Cody.

The crawl read:

U.S. representative's emails show sympathy for presidential assassins.

Her low voice gave the details:

"*Among the emails discovered are those in which Representative Cody is alleged to have said it was, quote, 'a bummer the attempt didn't work. Boyd's still got a year to screw up the country.' In another he allegedly wrote, quote, 'Doesn't anybody see that infrastructure plan of his is going to . . .' I'm deleting the word he used. '. . . the middle class?' And, quote: 'How hard was it to kill an old man? Where's Oswald when we need him?'*

"*Oswald of course is a reference to Lee Harvey Oswald, the man who assassinated President John F. Kennedy in 1963.*

"*Whether the assassination plot was real or not is being investigated by federal and city authorities.*

"*Cody has denied writing the emails and calls them part of a conspiracy to damage his campaign. WLAN News has not independently confirmed the authenticity of the emails, although an aide, speaking off the record, has said that they originated on Cody's secure server, which only he had access to.*

"*Cody had been considered the front-runner in the upcoming contest against Marie Leppert, Manhattan businesswoman and former federal prosecutor, running for public office for the first time.*

"Fifteen years ago, Cody was convicted of trespass and vandalism during environmental protests in Pennsylvania."

Several other politicians chimed in with opinions, among them Senator Edward Talese of New York.

Thom stepped into the doorway. "How's that for a twist?"

He handed a glass of wine to his boss, who thanked him with a nod. A cabernet. Some people could tell where the grapes came from, the nature of the earth in which the vines had grown, the year it had been bottled. Rhyme could tell two things only: it contained alcohol and had a not-unpleasant taste.

His eyes returned to the TV.

An image came on the screen of the representative scurrying through a sea of reporters from a black sedan into his Manhattan town house, head down. Their voices swelled and rattled as their questions ricocheted around the front yard. The one question that was discernible through the TV was: "Representative, you support green reform, but you're riding in a limo. Could you comment on that?"

A criticism that seemed a bit milquetoast, considering the man had apparently just nodded favorably to the violent overthrow of the government.

As Thom disappeared into the kitchen, Rhyme motored into the front hallway. It had been released as a crime scene and the floor and walls had been scrubbed clean of the Watchmaker's blood.

Here he brought the wheelchair to a stop more or less on the spot where the bullet had landed. His eyes dropped to the marble.

Ten minutes later, he heard Thom's voice. "Who's here?"

"How's that?" Rhyme called absently.

"I heard you talking to someone."

"Hardly."

Rhyme returned to the parlor, set the wine on a side table and said to his phone, "Command. Call Sachs."

76.

RHYME AND LON SELLITTO were in his town house, listening over the speaker.

Amelia Sachs was at the garage on West 46th Street where, two days ago, Charles Hale had swapped one SUV out for another before driving to the park to send Rhyme to sleep forever.

She reported: "No cameras. That's curious. Nearly all garages in the city have them. Hale must've searched for a while to find this one."

Rhyme said, "And since he was planning on leaving right after he killed me, he wouldn't care if he was recorded only picking up a new car. But he *would* care if he was meeting somebody secretly. Somebody who'd be here after he was gone."

"Exactly, Rhyme. No cameras in the garage, *but* . . . I found one in a retail store across the street. I did a timeline. A limo entered the garage fifteen minutes before Hale got there and left three minutes after he did in his new SUV. I ran the limo's tag. And you're not going to believe who it's registered to."

• • •

"I make it one security," the ESU officer's voice came through the Motorola earpiece. He had the richest baritone Sachs had ever heard and if he decided to get out of policing, he'd have a future as a radio announcer or a narrator of audiobooks.

"Roger. I have eyes on two. ESU Team Two?"

"No one else I can see. Only the subject and the guard, who's armed. Saw a piece on his right-side belt. Large. Maybe a forty-five."

Sachs was in a store once again, this time electronics, not buttons. It was located in downtown Manhattan, not far from Wall Street. Under cover of the window merchandise, she was eyeing the two individuals who were walking along the street. The bodyguard was six three or so and of Lyle Spencer's side-of-beef build. His head was shaved, common among ex-military or ex-police security specialists.

She radioed, "Five Eight Eight Five to ESU Three. What do you see?"

The woman, Laticia Krueger, a sniper, was atop First Federal Bank, a five-story structure whose roof featured both a good view of the street and a perfect nest for a shooter and her spotter.

"Just the two, Detective. Subject and guard."

"K. ESU, all units. I'm going to make the call."

In total there were eight Emergency Service officers nearby.

Would they be needed?

Time to see.

She pulled out a mobile and placed a speed-dial call.

As she watched the pair approach, the security guard frowned and fished his own cell from his pocket. He glanced at the number and answered.

Sachs heard "Yo, Barney. We're on Rector. We'll be at the car in—"

"This is Detective Amelia Sachs, NYPD. I have Barney's phone. Your associate's in custody. Do not give a reaction to this call."

"What—?"

"I said, no reaction."

He fell silent.

"There's a team about to move in and arrest your boss. We know you're armed. You're surrounded by a half-dozen tactical officers and a sniper has you in her sights. No, don't look around. Just keep walking like nothing's going on. Say, 'That's right,' if you understand."

"That's right."

"Now, you're going to remove your weapon from the holster, thumb and index only, and drop it behind the standpipe you're coming up to. Keep walking another twenty feet. Then you'll stop and lie down face-first on the sidewalk. Do you understand?"

"Look, I—"

"Say, 'Sure thing' if you understand."

A pause. "Sure thing."

"Is your boss armed? And if you lie, it'll be obstruction of justice."

"No."

"Do you have a second weapon?"

"No."

"Any other associates in the area?"

"No."

"You're doing fine. You're a great actor. Netflix quality. All right, almost there."

Sachs stepped away from the window, then pushed outside. "Now," she said into the phone and disconnected.

The guard tossed the gun exactly as directed and continued along the sidewalk. It appeared that he was counting the steps. When he hit twenty, he went down. Harder than he needed to. He winced.

Into the Motorola, Sachs said, "ESU, move in, move in, move in!"

The guard's employer noted he'd lagged behind and turned to see him on the ground and stepped forward, alarmed, probably concerned he'd had a heart attack.

But then, with the officers moving in, it was clear what was going on. And concern morphed to disgust.

Sachs was about to call, "Raise your hands!"

But there was no need. Marie Leppert, the former federal prosecutor that she was, did so of her own accord.

77.

NORMALLY, A PRISONER went to Central Booking.

In this case, however, because Lincoln Rhyme was involved, the prisoner had made a detour.

At the takedown, Sachs had apprised Marie Leppert of her rights and arrested her for homicide, reckless endangerment, terrorism and that wonderful catchall charge "conspiracy," a spawn of the Racketeer Influenced and Corrupt Organizations statute. Under RICO—hated by the mob and white-collar wrongdoers alike—Leppert and Charles Vespasian Hale actually counted as an organization.

Go figure . . .

Now, fully enwrapped in Fourth and Fifth Amendment protective armor, Leppert sat across from Lincoln Rhyme in the same chair that Hale had perched in not long before.

Sachs and Lon Sellitto were present too.

In a whiny voice like that of an accused child, Leppert said, "It's not my fault."

Rhyme cocked his head. "No?"

"I swear . . . Everything that happened, all the *bad* things. That was Hale. Not me."

Sachs asked, "Where did you meet him? It was Texas, right?" She had largely recovered from the acid fumes, though her voice was still low and formidable.

Rhyme asked, "His Mexican projects?" Hale had business dealings down there years ago, perhaps thinking it would be a place to retire.

The candidate said, "That's right. I did research into the cartels and local politicians in the north, Chihuahua mostly. Some people I talked to told me—almost reverently—about this American. He was like a consultant. He helped politicians get elected."

Credible so far. Hale was more than a killer. Rhyme could see him doing oppo political work—though his schemes would probably involve far more than negative advertising and PR campaigns.

But was she feigning ignorance of this side of his "consultancy"?

Rhyme didn't know. And his human polygraph, Lyle Spencer, wasn't present.

She continued, "Who was he? I remember wondering." Now her face grew earnest. "I saw prosecuting only as a stepping stone. I wanted to be in office. I left Justice and tried running for a seat in Houston. That didn't work, not in a good old boy network like that. A New England girl didn't stand a chance." She offered a knowing glance to Sachs.

No sympathy was returned. His wife was not a woman to let any network of good—or bad—old boys divert her from whatever she set her sights on. Nor play any games to get there.

"I came back home here, worked on Wall Street for a few years and got donors for a PAC. I decided I wanted Cody's seat. But as soon as I jumped into the campaign, I could see it wasn't going to work out."

Her thin lips grew thinner.

Rhyme finished, "So you pulled in favors in Texas and got a message to this . . . *consultant*. Hale."

"I didn't think I'd ever hear from him, but he contacted me right away."

The woman leaned forward and Rhyme detected floral perfume or shampoo. The species of vegetation eluded him. "All I did was ask him to move the electoral needle in my favor. Oppo tactics, or whatever. Like candidates do all the time. He agreed and he got to work. He wanted to know about Cody's background. When he learned he'd been a radical activist, and had actually done time in prison, he said he'd use that. And he went off on his own. Sabotaging cranes, the assassination plot? He never told me any of that. I swear to God."

"You didn't think it was a little suspicious that he wanted payment in untraceable diamonds?"

In Hale's backpack was an envelope containing what was probably a half-million dollars' worth of gems—this would be the purpose for the meeting in the garage just before Hale embarked on his birdwatching visit to Central Park to kill Rhyme.

"Well . . ." She was thinking quickly. "I thought it was a tax thing. But that was his business."

Sellitto asked, "Were you going to deduct it as a business expense?"

"Uhm. Yes. Of course I was."

Rhyme had learned over the years that some suspects—often former law enforcers and attorneys—invariably think they can talk their way out of trouble. Had he been her lawyer, he would have said: Shut up. Now.

He asked, "So you knew nothing about the illegal sides of his plan?"

"No!"

Sachs added, "None of them?"

"No, no, no! The cranes, the assassination thing? Hacking into the security company and uploading the forged emails? That was all his idea!"

And with that:

Gotcha.

The choreography of the interview, carefully worked out by Rhyme and Sachs ahead of time, had had the desired effect. The trap snapped shut.

It was not public knowledge how the emails got into Cody's account. There'd been no press report about Woman X's induction hacking device or Emery Digital.

Their eyes met. She said, "I want my lawyer."

Sachs rose and, tucking the notebook into the same rear pocket that contained her switchblade, said, "You'll get that chance. Downtown."

Leppert turned back to Rhyme. In a whisper: "How? How did you find out?"

"Oh, I had an informer."

"Who?" Leppert asked bitterly.

But Lincoln Ryme did not answer.

• • •

Now, the day after Leppert's arrest, it was at last time for Thom's dinner.

The scent was arresting.

Rhyme detected mild fish, mushrooms more pungent than generic fungi, garlic, dry white wine. Vermouth, he decided. Fresh bread too.

Sachs was setting the table, and Lincoln Rhyme was once again in the hallway where Charles Hale had died.

An old Glenmorangie whisky was in hand.

He was thinking of the other day, his exchange with Thom, after he'd been in the hallway—parked on the spot where the Watchmaker had died.

"Who's here?"

"How's that?"

"I heard you talking to someone."

"Hardly . . ."

Ah, but that was not exactly the truth.

He recalled now his comment to Marie Leppert: that it was an informer that led to her.

And it was.

Charles Vespasian Hale himself.

Though more accurately: his ghost.

That was whom Rhyme had been talking to here in the hallway.

Charles, if anyone were to ask, I will deny to the hilt that I'm speaking with a person no longer of this earth. But I have to say that something is troubling me. You dismissed my comment that I was skeptical that you did this for yourself, claiming that, no, you had no client.

You pitched a good case for your self-interest—tweaking the NTP servers and collecting enough money to give yourself an unlimited bankroll for your life in Venezuela or wherever you would make your own personal Leisure World.

But on reflection I now believe I was right. A timepiece exists for a purpose: it serves its owner. For you, the same.

You are, if you'll forgive me, on the clock for someone.

But for whom?

Let's run through it all: I tip to the fact that the assassination plot's fake and your whole point is to plant the infamous device underneath Emery Digital. I confront you with it. And what do you do? Why, you improvise, of course, and spin the tale of hacking the network time protocols. But, when you look at it, wasn't that an awful lot of work just to make some money? Don't you have Romanian or Chinese connections happy to crack into a hedge fund or bank directly? A weekend's work, and suddenly you're a hundred million richer.

So take NTP out of the equation. You obviously breached Emery for a purpose. What was it?

Could Woman X's device possibly be used to doctor someone's email account? Maybe someone whose messages have made the news in a big way lately—because they spoke favorably about that most horrific of crimes: presidential assassination.

Representative Stephen Cody's?

A man whom my expert interrogator, Lyle Spencer, had vetted and to whom he'd given a clean bill of health.

And if so, who would gain from the forgery?

For one, the candidate who was behind Cody in the polls: Marie Leppert, former prosecutor in Texas, near Mexico, where you had a base of operation.

That's what this was about all along: discrediting Cody, just long enough for him to lose the election. The Kommunalka, its secret radical parent cell, the assassination . . . All complications.

You're not responding, Charles, hm? Hardly expect you to. Though I believe your eyes, those intense blue eyes that I am picturing now, are telling me that I'm spot-on.

Well, there's a way to find out for certain.

And so their "conversation" over, Rhyme had then motored into the parlor, instructing his phone: "Call Sachs."

While Rhyme had called Emery Digital and learned that, yes, Emery did handle both the .com and .gov email accounts of Stephen Cody, Amelia had gone to the garage where Hale had swapped SUVs one final time and learned of his meeting with Marie Leppert.

"*Quod erat demonstrandum*, Charles. I've proved my case."

Now, tonight, en route to the dining room, Rhyme paused. His eyes went to the pocket watch on the mantel. The Breguet.

And he gave a sudden laugh of understanding. Hale needed

some way to execute his sham assassination attempt by diverting the president. But he could have picked any number of ways—a series of bombs, ending with a small one in the Holland Tunnel. That would've done the trick.

But he'd decided to sabotage cranes.

Why?

Drama, certainly. A tumbling tower crane got the city's attention.

But there was another reason, Rhyme believed, and it was the source of his brief laugh.

Because cranes resemble the hands of timepieces.

Hands . . .

And was there yet one additional meaning as well? I'll forego the poker metaphor and pick this one: Was Hale saying that his complex plot here—his last, as it turned out—was, of all his schemes through the years, his finest sleight of *hand*?

A play on words for anyone who might get it, though Rhyme had a feeling it was meant exclusively for him.

"Dinner," his aide called.

Noting that no one was watching, Lincoln Rhyme now lifted his glass toward the watch and sipped.

He then moved from the parlor into the dining room, where Thom was placing the first course on the table, and Amelia Sachs was lighting candles.

ACKNOWLEDGMENTS

Novels are not one-person endeavors. Creating them and getting them into the hands and hearts of readers is a team effort, and I am beyond lucky to have the best team in the world! My thanks to the following (in no particular order because I was too lazy to alphabetize and didn't trust ChatGPT with the task): Sophie Baker, Felicity Blunt, Emilie Chambeyron, Berit Böhm, Dominika Bojanowska, Penelope Burns, Annie Chen, Sophie Churcher, Francesca Cinelli, Isabel Coburn, Lizz Burrell, Tal Goretsky, Luisa Collichio, Jane Davis, Alice Gomer, Liz Dawson, Julie Reece Deaver, Marco Fiocca, Aranya Jain, Jenna Dolan, Mira Droumeva, Jodi Fabbri, Cathy Gleason, Alice Gomer, Laura Daley, Ivan Held, Ashley Hewlett, Sally Kim, Hamish Macaskill, Julia Wisdom, Cristina Marino, Ashley McClay, Shina Patel, Bethan Moore, Seba Pezzani, Rosie Pierce, Claire Ward, Sophie Waeland, Kimberley Young, Harriet Williams, Abbie Salter, Roberto Santachiara, Deborah Schneider, Sarah Shea, Mark Tavani, Madelyn Warcholik, Claire Ward, Alexis Welby and, of course, everyone in the hardworking Production, Managing Editorial, and Sales departments! You're the best!